# ALL HIS ANGELS ARE STARVING

# ALL HIS ANGELS ARE STARVING

TESS C. FOXES

**Podium**

Podium

# All His Angels Are Starving

—from the lamentations of Rafa'el, the Scribe

# CHAPTER ONE

# TARNISHED ANGEL

*What delusion am I convincing myself of right now so that I can pretend I'm okay?* Jenny Huang picked at the thoughts fussing about in her head while she stared out the large windows of her first-period English classroom. It had stormed all morning, and the rain showed no signs of letting up. The sky, the road, and even the people rushing up and down the busy Manhattan streets all seemed drab and gray and dull beyond belief.

Mrs. Rivera droned on about *The Scarlet Letter*. The lesson involved something about symbolism and the priest who'd committed a major sin, but the words went in one of Jenny's ears and out the other.

All she could think about was how graduation was only a few weeks away. Then she'd be out of here. No more pointless schoolwork. No more dealing with her controlling mom. No more being surrounded by people she wanted to get away from.

She liked her stepfather or stepbrother okay but not enough to welcome them into her life. They had a polite rapport going on, the kind of amicable peace you have with strangers. In Jenny's mind, they were too close to her mother. They were her *mother's* people. With them in the house, there was even less space for her, and all of it felt suffocating.

She'd escape all of it and begin life anew. She imagined finally being able to breathe, to be herself, and to figure out what being herself even meant. She wanted to have a wild amount of sex, try falling in love, and just . . . *be*.

Most importantly, she wouldn't have to be her mom's daughter anymore.

Jenny had had yet another argument with her that morning. It was always over some dumb, stupid thing that didn't matter, but there was always something. "Who left the hallway light on? Electricity costs money." "Who left their shoes in the wrong place?" "Stop taking so long in the shower; you're wasting water." "Don't eat too much, you'll ruin your figure." "You're too thin. What will people say?" "When are you going to grow up?"

It went on and on and on, and this morning, it had been about not taking out the trash. Even though it was her stepbrother Oliver's turn. What was even the point of having a younger sibling and divvying up chores if Jenny still got screamed at when he didn't do them?

She sighed and tried to pay attention to Mrs. Rivera. But try as she might, the only thought in her head was freedom. She'd gotten several fully funded offers from prestigious universities across the country, but the one she'd chosen, the one she'd bought sweaters and T-shirts from, the one farthest away from New York and her family, was Stanford.

It wasn't a coincidence that as soon as her mom had read the acceptance letter, the conflicts at home had become unbearable. It meant that she couldn't keep trying to control Jenny. No more micromanaging things like when to eat, when to shower, her homework, exams, grades.

That was one thing about *The Scarlet Letter* that interested Jenny. In the story, Hester Prynne was marked as an outcast and an adulterer for choosing love. The woman just wanted to be free, and her society would not accept it. They cast Hester out and shunned her for it. That was how Jenny felt.

She just wanted to breathe. Have her own space and not feel bitter and alone and compressed and hurt all the time.

"Please turn to chapter twelve," said Mrs. Rivera, flipping the pages of her book and stepping in Jenny's direction.

First-period English should be illegal. Jenny wanted to climb back into bed, curl up under a thick blanket, and read the book on her own. Wasn't that more important than sitting in class and dissecting a bunch of old words?

"Jenny?" prompted Mrs. Rivera. She stopped in front of her desk and looked down at her expectantly through thick horn-rimmed glasses. She was an elderly Hispanic woman, stern but kind in her own way, and she'd often keep Jenny after class to talk.

But that also meant Jenny was always the first one called upon when it came to reading in class. She groaned and sat up straight.

"Would you please read for us, dear?"

"Sure," said Jenny, sucking in a deep breath. Then she licked her lips. All of a sudden, her mouth felt dry. Why did this still give her anxiety even though she'd done it a hundred times?

She cleared her throat and read out loud, trying to keep her voice from trembling. After two pages, Mrs. Rivera moved on to Harry Kim, who sat behind Jenny.

She let out a long breath, feeling hot under her red Stanford sweater. The rain wasn't even chilly; she'd only worn the sweater to spite her mom. Now she was regretting it because all she had on underneath was a thin tank top, and Mrs. Rivera would never let her sit there so exposed.

As Harry Kim read in that deepening voice he had, Jenny's thoughts shifted to prom. Nobody had asked her out yet. She glanced over at Susan Brown, whom Jenny considered her closest friend. Susan always reminded Jenny of old movies; talking with her and being around made Jenny's heart *ache*, and the closest word she could come up with to describe the feeling was nostalgia.

Susan had dyed her hair blue for the New Year and wore it tied up in a messy bun. At least, she called it messy. Jenny thought it was graceful and could never get her own long dark hair to do the same. She'd considered asking Susan to do it for her, but that thought made her blush, and she couldn't go through with it.

As Mrs. Rivera called upon the next person to read, Jenny wondered if anyone was going to ask her out. Or if she should ask someone out. Several boys in her grade seemed friendly and cute.

Again, she glanced toward her right, but this time, she met Susan's eyes. Susan's lips curled up slightly, and heat rose to Jenny's face as she pretended to adjust her grip on the book and turn the page. She tried to follow the words, but all Jenny could think about was how warm it would feel to press her cheek against Susan's.

Mrs. Rivera worked her way up the aisle and called on Susan next. Jenny shut her eyes and listened intently to Susan's soft, gentle voice. She had the perfect reading voice, giving each character a slightly different pitch and always emphasizing exactly the words that needed weight to give the story its proper momentum.

It was something Jenny always looked forward to when they gamed together. Shooting other people, hearing Susan laugh, talking about random bullshit. Susan always took charge, shot calling and helping everyone. Friends or strangers, it didn't matter. She was always so sweet, even if she was having a bad day, and Jenny loved talking to her. Chatting about nothing till four in the morning, just keeping each other company when they couldn't sleep.

A part of Jenny wanted to ask her to prom. As friends, maybe. Susan's boyfriend had dumped her recently. He'd decided to go with Leslie Garcia—who was a teen model—and broken Susan's heart.

Then again, Jenny couldn't even bring herself to look up from the book and glance at Susan again. Besides, what if she said no and things got too weird, and they never spoke again?

"Jenny," called Mrs. Rivera.

She perked up, her heart racing wildly all of a sudden. Would she have to read again? That wasn't fair. And she had absolutely no idea where she would have to pick up from. But all Mrs. Rivera said was, "Please sit up," before making her way to the front of the room.

Susan smiled sympathetically as Jenny shook her head, embarrassed.

The teacher cleared her throat, then asked everyone to put everything away and take out a sheet of paper. A few students groaned.

"Yes," she said. "It's time for a short pop essay."

"This blows," whispered Susan as she put her books neatly into her cute leather bag.

Jenny picked up the JanSport she'd had since middle school. "Still better than us acting out the scenes."

"Oh God," Susan replied with a snort, setting off a flurry of butterflies in Jenny's belly.

Mrs. Rivera wrote a quote on the chalkboard as Susan turned slightly in her chair to face Jenny, looking like she was about to say something.

Jenny's head spun. Was this a good time to ask Susan to prom? Would it be weird? *Hey, do you wanna go to prom together? Like, just to hang out? We could kiss if you want to.* But before either of them could say anything, she felt a trembling underneath her feet, as though the floor had started shivering and couldn't stop.

"Do you feel that?" asked Susan, her brows furrowed in confusion.

Mrs. Rivera dropped her chalk, then, all at once, the tables, chairs, and lights shook violently. Susan dashed out of her seat and caught Mrs. Rivera, who'd lost her balance. Books tumbled off the shelves in the back as someone shouted, "Earthquake!"

"Underneath your desks, everyone!" came Mrs. Rivera's voice from the front.

Jenny dropped to her knees as Susan helped Mrs. Rivera under the teacher's desk. The lights flickered out, and suddenly, everything was dark. Glass shattered and rained down around Jenny, who squeezed her bag tight, shut her eyes, and prayed.

Then, as abruptly as it had begun, it was over. A heavy silence filled the classroom, as though the whole world had decided to hold its breath. A ghostly white glow emanated from the windows now that the lights were off.

"Is it over?" asked a girl.

"There could be aftershocks."

"Whatchu know about earthquakes?"

"Earth science, bitch."

"Everyone, stay where you are," ordered Mrs. Rivera sternly. "Is anyone hurt?"

Jenny looked at all the glittering bits of glass around her. She guessed one of the lights had gotten loose and collapsed on top of her desk. She turned and glanced at Harry, whose face had turned red. Everyone seemed alright.

She wanted to call out and ask if Susan was alright. She didn't want to think about what might've happened to Mrs. Rivera if Susan hadn't acted so quickly and selflessly.

"Is anyone getting reception?" came Susan's voice from the front of the room, and Jenny felt some of her tension ease.

There was a flurry of motion as people reached for their bags. Jenny grabbed her own phone and powered it on. No signal. Not even the school Wi-Fi.

Nobody else seemed to have any connection either, and everyone started murmuring with worry. Jenny pushed broken glass away with her bag, trying to clear out a space so she could get out.

At least it wasn't pitch darkness, she thought. Even with it storming and gloomy outside, there was enough light to see . . .

*Wait.* She held her breath and focused. Other than the hushed voices of her classmates, it was quiet. Unbearably quiet. She turned slowly, grabbing the legs of her table to maneuver herself, and looked up at the windows.

There was no rain. The sky was gone. The storm, Manhattan, all of it. There was only a blank, pale emptiness outside. It wasn't darkness nor light but something in between that Jenny couldn't describe. A renewed sense of dread clogged her throat.

Someone screamed.

"What happened?"

"Look out the windows. It's . . ."

"Maybe it's cause of the blackout?"

"Dumbass, how does that make sense?"

"Yeah, but—"

"Quiet!" Mrs. Rivera shouted as she stood up in front of the classroom.

Everyone stopped, waiting for her to say something. Something to explain why there was nothing but a void outside. But she said nothing. She walked over to the windows and gasped.

Someone whimpered. Other people threw out theories:

"It must be some strange weather thing, like a really dense fog caused by the earthquake."

"What if we're all dead?"

Jenny started shaking. For a second, she thought it was an aftershock, but then she realized it was just her.

Was her mom okay? Her stepdad? Oliver? Oliver was two floors below her, right? In his freshman math class? Jenny prayed silently that he'd gotten under his desk or somewhere safe and that nothing had happened to him. He was just a kid. He must be terrified.

Suddenly, the fight from this morning felt stupid and far away. Jenny rubbed the letters that spelled Stanford on her sweater. They had earthquakes in California, right? Was this a sign she shouldn't go?

A sharp pain pierced the left side of her forehead, right above her eye. Pressing her palm against it, she cried out as everyone else did the same.

Pain blossomed through Jenny's head, spreading throughout her skull. Words appeared. A series of messages.

**Welcome to the Veil.**
**The Survival Challenge is in effect.**
**The victor shall be rewarded.**
**Human population remaining: 851**

"What?" whispered Jenny. The pain faded away, but the words . . . they showed up the way notifications did on her phone, but instead of on a screen, they were inside her head, as though her mind was a pool of liquid and the messages emerged one by one as fully formed thoughts.

*Except they weren't her thoughts.*

Was everyone else getting this too? Survival challenge? Human population? And why was it only less than nine hundred? Was that the number of people in the building?

She had a feeling some other message was about to emerge. It felt odd, like trying very hard to remember something that was just on the tip of her tongue. But before it could show, Mrs. Rivera cried out as a shadow stretched across the room.

Jenny looked up to see her teacher stumbling backward on her desk, her frail arms reaching behind her, trying to find support. Following her gaze, Jenny felt her heart thud to a stop when she saw what had frightened Mrs. Rivera.

Something was *climbing* up the outside of the windows, its thin figure illuminated by the pale glow of the void. With long blonde hair, translucent skin, and big eyes that were just the white part . . . it looked human, but a dizzying uneasiness told Jenny it wasn't.

Another message appeared.

**Tarnished Angel (Level 2)**

*Angel?* Tarnished? But if it was an angel, where were its wings? Its halo? Why did it look like a naked woman, emaciated and so skinny that Jenny couldn't help but think of the pictures she'd seen of famine victims in her world history class. She could see almost all of its bones. Its ribs stuck out painfully, and its face was just skin stretched over a skull.

Yet, it had an eerie, unsettling beauty, like a fragile glass sculpture. It stopped climbing once its entire body was in view, resting its bony feet on the windowsill. Then it opened its mouth, and what looked like blood gushed down its chin.

Before anyone could react, the angel let out a nightmarish scream, raising a fist and smashing it through the window.

# CHAPTER TWO

# FIRST BLOOD

The tarnished angel dropped to the floor in front of Jenny's table in a shower of glass. Little cuts bled all over its pale body. With a disgusting retching sound, it vomited more blood.

Jenny's mind went blank as she stared in horror. An angel? Like from the Bible? How was *this* an angel? She heard screams and shouts, followed by the clangs of knocked-over chairs and tables. That seemed to draw the creature's attention because it turned its head and locked those empty eyes on Jenny.

She backed away slowly. Jagged glass cut into her jeans, and she winced in pain. Something clanged, and she realized the table behind her had fallen over, blocking her exit.

The angel crawled forward, glass crunching underneath its exposed palms and legs. It didn't seem to mind. Its bones moved underneath its pasty skin, blood continuing to flow from its mouth. Jenny whimpered when its blonde head bumped her table, holding her bag in front of her like a shield.

Something struck the angel in the face with a heavy *thunk*. Hissing, it turned away from Jenny, letting her see what had hit it. A heavy-duty stapler lay splayed open on the floor.

"Get out of there, Jenny!" Susan's voice cut through the dread pounding in Jenny's head. She stood next to the chalkboard, now holding up the large hole puncher.

Mrs. Rivera was still leaning against her desk, staring at the angel and muttering in Spanish. After a moment, she stepped toward it, seeming transfixed.

Jenny pushed the table out of her way and got to her feet. Everyone else had run out through the door, and there was a rush of footsteps and screaming up and down the halls. Were there more out there?

The angel, still on all fours, fixed its blank stare on Mrs. Rivera. It was on its toes now instead of its knees. Jenny thought it almost looked like a cat ready to pounce.

"*Dios mío*," whispered Mrs. Rivera, spreading her arms as though she were welcoming the angel with a hug.

It leaped off the floor, baring its teeth. They collapsed together, and Mrs. Rivera screamed over and over as the angel wriggled on top of her, snarling and chewing. It pinned her arms down then sank its teeth into her neck. She went silent and stared blankly at the ceiling, muttering faintly about the Lord as blood pooled around her, the angel biting and hissing and slurping all the while.

Jenny couldn't make a sound. She clutched her bag, shaking, taking a step backward toward the door. She couldn't take her eyes off the angel chewing its way through Mrs. Rivera's neck. Its blonde hair and pale skin were now stained with blood.

Finally forcing her eyes away, she glanced over at Susan, who seemed petrified.

"Susan," whispered Jenny. But she'd either been too quiet or Susan was too terrified to hear her. Jenny took another step back, and her boot connected with a chair, knocking it over.

The clatter made her heart leap into her throat. The angel's head tilted toward her.

### Tarnished Angel (Level 3)

The new message didn't help. *Wasn't it just at level two?*

It bared its teeth, glistening red with bits and strands of meat hanging from its mouth. It crawled off Mrs. Rivera's body, shoulder blades rippling as it lurched forward.

*Jesus fucking Christ,* thought Jenny. Fear filled her head with so much pressure she thought her head would cave in. She couldn't bring her legs to move. She couldn't take a single step or look away from the white blankness of the angel's eyes.

Then, just when she thought it would leap onto her too, the angel paused. Raising its head, it sniffed the air before turning to face Susan, who hadn't budged at all.

*Run,* Jenny tried to say. Her tongue moved, but no sound escaped her throat. She didn't want the angel to come after her again. She could barely inhale. Her legs were shaking so badly, and she couldn't help but feel the tiniest bit relieved that the angel had turned away. She couldn't stop picturing it tearing her apart and chewing through her stomach, making her watch until she died.

It leaped onto Mrs. Rivera's desk, still hunched over, still sniffing. Susan still hadn't moved, and Jenny's heart was about to burst out of her chest. She wanted to shout, scream, whisper, *anything,* but she couldn't bring herself to make a sound.

Susan let out something halfway between a whimper and a cry for help. The angel hissed. It looked like it would leap, and that was when Jenny's feet suddenly felt free and weightless. She rushed toward the desk and swung her book bag as hard as she could.

For the first time, she was grateful she had to lug heavy hardcover textbooks around. The bag struck the angel on its side with a satisfying *thud*, knocking it off the desk. It landed on Mrs. Rivera's body with a screech, scrambling to regain balance, but its hands and feet kept slipping on the blood.

Jenny swung her bag again, this time raising it over her head—holding it up by one arm strap—then bringing it down on the angel's blonde head. Her bag tore open upon impact, and all her books and notes went sprawling across the floor as the angel crumpled beside Mrs. Rivera.

She shook, holding what was left of her bag, while the angel twitched face down in a pool of blood.

"Is it dead?" whispered Susan.

The creature hissed and then rolled away around Mrs. Rivera's desk.

"No!" shouted Jenny. "Susan, it's—!"

But Susan didn't even get a chance to scream as it leaped onto her. The hole puncher went flying out of her hands, and Jenny could hear the angel's teeth gnashing over and over.

Grabbing a chair, she rushed around the desk, bracing herself for the worst. But Susan had her hands on the angel's tiny torso, keeping its teeth away from her neck and face.

Thrusting with the chair, legs facing outward, Jenny pushed the angel off Susan. It screeched and howled, scratching at the chair, the chalkboard, and the floor, its legs kicking hard. The look in its eyes was empty and desperate.

With a shout, Jenny struck the angel again.

Susan got to her feet, breathing hard. The angel was on all fours again, its blond hair covering its bloodied face. Jenny thrust once more, feeling like she was keeping back a violent rabid dog or something, until the angel grabbed one of the chair's legs and yanked.

The momentum pulled Jenny forward. She hadn't let go in time and went tripping over the chair.

She heard Susan cry out, but Jenny thrust her forearm against the angel's neck and chin as she crashed on top of it. It gnashed its jaws over and over, the sound of its clacking teeth making Jenny sick. It scratched and pulled at her sweater and hair. The thick stench of blood clogged her nose.

There was a nasty purple bruise on its forehead from where she'd struck it with her bag before, and that gave her hope. If it could get hurt, then it could *die*.

It grabbed Jenny's face, who couldn't help but scream, and rolled the two of them over. Jenny's head struck the floor hard as it scrambled on top of her and tried to pin down her arms just as it had done to Mrs. Rivera's, but it couldn't get a grip as Jenny struggled.

Blood and drool rained on Jenny's face as she reached for something—*anything*—before her fingers closed around something cold and metallic and heavy.

*The hole puncher!*

She swung it hard, making contact with the side of the angel's head. With a cry, it went limp and fell to the side. But Jenny didn't stop. She swung the hole puncher over and over, using both hands as she sat up. So many times that she lost count. Until its face was a mess of red mush. She couldn't tell if the angel was screaming or if she was.

She didn't stop until she felt a hand on her shoulder.

"I think it's dead now," Susan whispered, her voice quiet and small.

The hole puncher dropped from Jenny's hands; it was covered in blood and bits of flesh. What remained of the angel's face was a gruesome mess. She'd completely caved in its nose, broken through its skull, and knocked teeth into its throat.

A slew of messages blossomed in her thoughts.

**You've defeated Tarnished Angel (Level 3)!**
**Experience has been awarded.**
**+10 Energy**

**First Blood Bonus!**
**Congratulations on your first kill.**
**A great amount of Experience and Energy has been awarded.**
**+100 Energy**

**Leveled Up!**
**Jenny Huang, Level 1 → Level 2**
**+2 Stat Points**

Jenny hardly registered the messages. They felt very much like video game notifications. Experience? Energy? Stat points? It was difficult to focus on that when she'd just killed something.

She stared at the dead angel. It lay there with one arm across its torso, the other limp on the ground. It looked sickly and drab, its skin no longer translucent. Whatever Jenny had thought made it look ethereal before was gone. Strands of blonde hair floated in the pool of blood around its ruined head.

Feeling like she was going to be sick, she couldn't shake the feeling that she'd just smashed in the face of a woman who'd been starved nearly to death. The angel's body looked exactly like the bodies of Holocaust survivors. Its stomach was completely sunken in. It had no flesh on its limbs, just bones and skin.

How was this an angel? The angels Jenny had learned about in Sunday school were nothing like this. She'd always imagined them as towering masculine figures of light with wings that stretched across the sky.

Susan knelt down beside her, and Jenny realized what had distracted the angel before. Susan had wet herself.

"Are you okay?" she whispered, her voice shaking. Her face was covered in droplets of blood.

Jenny shook her head. She shut her eyes and sat back. It was quiet in the room now. The hallway outside seemed to have quieted down, too. But something nagged at her thoughts. "Why do we have stat points?" she asked, partly to herself.

"What?" asked Susan.

"These messages," said Jenny. "In my head. Do you have them too?"

"Yeah," she replied. "It said something like welcome, and human population . . ."

They both went silent as a new message appeared. Jenny figured Susan had gotten it too.

### Human population remaining: 784

Susan started to sob. Jenny pulled her into an embrace, stroking her blue hair with bloodied hands. Whatever this survival challenge was, it had only been a few minutes, and almost a hundred people were dead. She wrapped her arms tightly around Susan and tried not to cry.

With the adrenaline fading, another thought burst through her head. But this wasn't a notification.

*Oliver!*

He was there somewhere in the school. What if his class had gotten attacked too?

Jenny swallowed hard, trying to listen carefully. But other than Susan's muffled sobs, she couldn't hear anything else.

She took a deep, shuddering breath. Susan's warmth brought her some comfort despite the fact that they were covered in blood and filth.

They were monsters. These angel things. They had levels like in games. She had levels too. She'd even gotten a bonus for killing one of them, which had gotten her enough experience to level up.

*How do I use it?* Jenny gritted her teeth. When Susan had mentioned the human population, they'd both thought about that and received an update. So then . . .

She focused hard on Stats.

**Jenny Huang**
**Human (Level 2)**
**Age: 6,801 days**
**Stats:**
**Power: 3**
**Durability: 5**
**Stamina: 3**
**Agility: 3**
**Stat Points Available: 2**
**Energy Available: 110**

It worked! There it was. In her mind, a chart depicting her name and age and everything else. She wondered how best to apply her two points, but then, the energy available caught her attention. The system seemed to respond to thought, so she focused on the question: *What are these points for?*

**Starting stats are based on your current physical prowess.**
**+2 Stat Points are awarded per level. They may be assigned as desired.**
**Every kill harvests Energy. Energy can be used to craft tools, equipment,**
**and weapons. Your capability and capacity to craft are highly**
**dependent on your imagination. The Guidance System will apply**
**a cost to your wishes.**

*A weapon* . . . The first thought to pop into her head was a gun. An assault rifle. She preferred snipers in games, but if her aim was terrible in real life, an assault rifle would give her a better chance.

**An Assault Rifle will cost 300 Energy. Additional Energy**
**will be required for ammunition.**
**Insufficient Energy.**

*Shit.* That wasn't going to work. How about a knife, then? Maybe a sword? No. A knife would be too small, and she'd always thought swords were dumb. She needed something practical. Something familiar.

Jenny remembered how last summer, when her stepfather, Henry, had whisked the family away to his cabin upstate by the Hudson River, she'd caught him and her mom "making love" by accident one morning when she couldn't sleep. She'd then spent the rest of that day out back near the woods, chopping firewood until her arms felt like falling off and her thoughts were mush. But she'd had a knack for hitting the wood just right.

**A Hatchet will cost 75 Energy.**
**Sufficient Energy.**

*Okay*, she thought. *Now what?*

Focusing on the weapon, a warm golden light enveloped her right hand. She whispered Susan's name, who got off Jenny and stared as it took shape, the light turning liquid and glistening before solidifying into a long dark wooden handle and the familiar flat metal head of a hatchet.

Its edge glinted briefly, and without even touching it, Jenny knew it was sharper than the one she'd used before. The handle felt good in her hand. The hatchet had a satisfying weight.

**Hatchet (Tier 1)**

**Energy remaining: 35**

# CHAPTER THREE

# HATCHET

Jenny stared in disbelief at the hatchet in her hand. It felt real. It existed. And it only existed because *she* had thought it into being. It had cost energy, and she had a sneaking suspicion that the only way to get more was through killing, but it was still satisfying to have created something with her mind.

"How did you do that?" asked Susan. She touched the flat side of the metal with her fingertip.

"That system thing," replied Jenny, "inside our head. I killed that . . . thing, and it gave me energy that I used to make this."

Susan's eyes went wide. She stared at Jenny, their faces very close. Then she gasped. "It says you're level two!"

"Oh, yeah." Pulling up her stats again, Jenny focused and figured the best place for her two stat points was power. As soon as the numbers shifted, she felt the slightest change in her arms and legs, and she climbed to her feet. Her head spun and, as Susan watched, she twirled the hatchet and moved her arm.

The weapon felt light in her hand. She pictured splitting an angel's head open like wood. Gruesome, but at least she wasn't defenseless. And she could keep getting stronger by killing them?

Jenny quickly explained to Susan what she'd figured out about the system. How getting the first kill would give her a lot of energy to use.

This felt like a survival game. *The Survival Challenge is in effect.* Jenny shuddered. She didn't look at the angel or Mrs. Rivera's body. Their English classroom was a mess from the earthquake and the mad rush to escape, but if there were more angels out there, then there was no point in staying here.

She thought of Oliver. He was just a little kid. An idiot, sure, who followed her around everywhere and seemed to always want attention, but he was just a kid. All the freshmen were. Hell, she was a senior, but she was just a kid, too.

"I have to go find my brother," she said.

Susan used the desk to pull herself up. Her legs were still shaking, and Jenny tried not to look at the wet stain on her tights. They were both covered in much worse now.

What would be waiting for them out there? The thought of seeing another angel made Jenny want to throw up.

"Survival challenge," spoke Susan quietly. "Does that mean we have to either fight or die?"

Jenny didn't know what to say. "It kind of feels like a battle royale game. Except with zombie angels."

Susan wiped her eyes, smearing blood over her cheeks. "Yeah," she murmured. Then she took a deep breath and walked over to the angel, picking up the bloodied hole puncher Jenny had used to kill it. "I guess we don't have a choice."

"I watch your back and you watch mine?" asked Jenny. It was something they'd say to each other when gaming online.

Susan nodded. "Let's do this." There was a determined look on her face, even though she was trembling.

Making her way to the door, Jenny looked out the glass window. The hall was dim, lit only by the same sickly white glow of the void. There was nobody out there, nothing stirring, and Jenny turned the knob slowly. She stuck her head outside.

Their classroom was at the end of the hall, farthest from the stairwell. Bodies lined the floor; bloody streaks covered the walls. Jenny swallowed the bile that rose to her throat. She spotted another angel down the hall beside the blue double doors that separated the English Department from the rest of the building. It was hunched over someone.

She shut the door and pressed her forehead against it. There was no time to think. No time to process. Those creatures were out there, and Oliver, if he was still alive, was in danger. He was still her primary goal, and if she wanted to get stronger, she'd have to fight those creatures regardless.

The shocked look on Oliver's face from this morning when Jenny had blamed him for not taking out the trash was fresh in her mind. Her heart constricted with guilt and terror.

"What's out there?" whispered Susan, who'd come up behind her.

"There's another one down the hall," said Jenny, not opening her eyes. "And there are . . . bodies."

The hole puncher rattled in Susan's hands. She'd almost dropped it. She didn't say anything.

A part of Jenny hoped that if they waited just a bit, the angel would move on. But that was delaying the inevitable. There had to be lots of those creatures if so many people were already dead. How many people were left?

**Human population remaining: 765**

"Fuck," whispered Jenny. She'd just wanted to graduate, move out of here, and begin her life somewhere far away.

She pulled the door open and stepped into the hallway before she could chicken out.

Susan followed closely, the two of them taking light, careful steps and trying not to look at the students lying still on the floor.

They could see the angel up ahead. There wasn't a message relaying its name and level; Jenny assumed they had to get closer for that. Suddenly, Susan grabbed Jenny's arm, letting out a small cry and pointing.

It was Harry Kim, the boy who'd sat behind Jenny in English all year. Now he was lying on his side with chunks missing from his face and arm. His eyes were wide open.

"Don't look," whispered Jenny, squeezing Susan's hand. They moved closer to the angel, and the message appeared.

**Tarnished Angel (Level 3)**

This one looked male, just as emaciated as the one they'd already fought, but it had brown hair and wider shoulders. It was chewing on a girl with her neck in its mouth, her body raised off the floor, hanging limp. A loud sucking noise filled the hall, and Susan cried out before clapping her hand over her mouth.

The angel turned, blood dripping off its face as it opened its mouth and let the girl's body fall to the floor. It blinked, cocking its head.

With a screech, the angel barreled toward them, galloping on all fours.

It was terrifying to watch something almost human move like that, but Jenny pushed Susan to the side and held up her hatchet with both hands. She was going to swing it like a bat.

The angel leaped as soon as it was close enough. Jenny shut her eyes and swung.

The impact was nothing like chopping wood. It felt more like cutting through a peanut butter and jelly sandwich, the hatchet slicing through the angel with ease. It collapsed to the floor, howling.

Jenny watched it wriggling, its side cut open. Guts and dark blood leaked from the gash, and she stepped away, wanting to retch.

Hissing madly, the angel crawled toward Susan, who'd dropped to her knees, shaking like mad. Jenny was about to attack again when Susan raised the hole puncher over her head, holding it with both hands. When the angel reached for her legs, she slammed her weapon down. It connected with the angel's skull with a resounding crack.

**You've defeated Tarnished Angel (Level 3)!**
**Experience has been awarded.**
**+10 Energy**

The messages appeared in Jenny's head even though Susan had been the one to finish it off, so they must have shared experience, though it seemed like she got the same amount of energy for the kill.

Now that the blood wasn't pounding in her ears, Jenny could hear faint screaming. Was it from the floors below, or just beyond the double doors?

The angel lay lifeless and still. Susan leaned back and rested her head on the wall. "I got the bonus. I leveled up."

"You can get a weapon now," said Jenny. Her hatchet was covered in blood and slime. She wiped it on her sweater, then shivered in disgust. "Maybe something sharp. I already tried making a gun, but we need more energy for that."

"A knife?" asked Susan. "Or should I get something like yours?"

"What are you familiar with?"

"Okay," said Susan. "I think I've got it." She shut her eyes, and her brows furrowed in concentration.

Jenny kept glancing down the hall. She half expected another angel or something to burst out of a classroom, but it was unsettlingly quiet.

A moment later, the same golden light as before appeared in Susan's hands. Strands of light coiled and formed what looked like a stick. Jenny thought for a second she'd chosen a hatchet as well, but no sharp metal face appeared. Instead, it looked like a black baton.

"What is that?" Jenny asked, stepping over the angel to get a closer look.

"A cattle prod," replied Susan in a low voice as she inspected it. "It cost eighty-five, but it looks exactly like the one my granddad had on his farm." She stood up and tried it out. There was an electric crackling noise, and she switched it off, looking perplexed. "It's not supposed to make a sound."

She jabbed the air again. And again, it made that sharp static cracking as it moved through the air.

"I've never seen one before," Jenny admitted, wondering how effective it would be against an angel. They'd probably find out soon enough.

"My parents would take me every summer," Susan said, switching it off and holding it. "I'd sneak out to the barn and fight . . . bad guys with this."

"Bad guys?" Jenny pictured a younger Susan swinging the prod through the air and keeping her family safe from invisible enemies. How did she manage to be so cute even in the depths of hell?

Susan was blushing. "I'd never use it on a cow . . ." She clicked it on then off. "It's crazy how it smells the same when you butcher an animal." She motioned toward the angel on the floor.

Its guts had leaked out with so much blood that some of it had reached Jenny's boots. Looking at all of it made her feel even sicker, and the stench of decay and insides wasn't helping.

"Seven hundred and two," whispered Susan.

Jenny didn't have to ask to know what that number meant. It hadn't been that long since this survival challenge had started. Dread wrapped its cold, sharp claws around her chest and squeezed. Feeling like she had to say something, she grabbed Susan's hand. "Thank you for not leaving me in that room."

Susan blinked, her eyes watery. "If I'd left, I'd probably be—"

"Doesn't matter," Jenny cut her off firmly. "If you'd left, we'd both be dead right now. But since we're together . . . I don't know. I feel like . . ." She took a deep breath. Prom felt so silly and stupid and far away. "I feel like we can do this."

"Me too," said Susan. She tried to smile, but it looked more like a grimace.

"Let's just pretend it's a new game we're trying out," continued Jenny. "A horror game, and we only have one life. But we're a duo."

Susan shut her eyes and nodded. "I hate horror."

"Same," said Jenny.

"Okay. Where's your brother?"

"His geometry class was downstairs." Jenny swallowed hard. "He might still be in his room, or . . ."

"We'll find him," declared Susan. Then she straightened her back and took a deep breath. It was something she always did when she wanted to focus. "Alright. I'll stop whining. Let's go find your brother and anyone else we can help."

Holding her cattle prod like a sword, she marched over to the double doors and looked through the little circular glass window each door had.

Jenny wondered if Susan was also thinking about their other friends. Their teachers. Their classmates. She tried not to think about Harry or the girl whose neck that angel had been sucking on. She hoped there were others who'd figured out how to use the system. Maybe if they could find a group, they could fight back. But what had the system said? *The victor shall be rewarded.*

Did that mean there would only be one winner? Would this survival challenge last until only one human was left?

Jenny squeezed her hatchet. She wanted to pray, but she didn't even know what to pray to anymore. It looked like she'd managed to give Susan some courage. Now, if only she could give herself some, too.

# CHAPTER FOUR

# HIDING IN A BATHROOM

Jenny looked back at the gloomy English wing hallway. The bodies on the floor. The bloody smears along the walls. It was quiet, but it was that thick pregnant sort of quiet right before something horrible happened in a movie.

She guessed that more angels had come in through the windows of the other classrooms, and while she and Susan had fought the one in their room, the others hadn't been so lucky. Most people must have run for the stairwells, the way they'd practiced for fire drills. But after the earthquake, and with these angel things . . . it must have been a blind panic.

Where would they even run to? The first floor? Could anyone even exit the building? They clearly weren't in Manhattan anymore. Jenny couldn't help looking at the girl on the floor.

Her head was at an awkward angle, with a few glistening strands of muscle still attaching it to her body. Her eyes stared blankly, her mouth parted in lifeless shock. She must have been a freshman. Maybe a sophomore. Jenny pictured the younger girl tripping in the mad rush to escape, screaming as an angel grabbed her leg while all her friends and classmates and teachers kept running.

"I don't see any more out there," said Susan, who was peering through the double doors.

Jenny took a breath, then together, they pushed through the doors and left the English wing behind them. Slowly, they stepped into the main area, where every wing of the floor met, leading to the central stairwell. Down the hall across from where they stood, a light flickered in the biology wing.

"Let's not take these stairs," whispered Jenny. She barely dared to breathe; those things seemed to be attracted to sound. Maybe their empty eyes couldn't see clearly?

Susan agreed. "Let's cut through here," she said, pointing to the Foreign Language Department. It was a narrow hallway that led away from the central stairwell to a smaller one.

They turned the corner slowly, trying not to look at the bodies that were thankfully face down on the floor. Susan stepped in some blood.

The foreign languages hallway was clear, but Jenny still held her breath as they walked toward the stairwell at the end. As they passed, something rattled one of the classroom doors hard. Jenny whirled around, ready to attack. "Someone's in there," she whispered, holding her hatchet with both hands.

Susan clicked her cattle prod on. Its static sound was almost comforting.

Jenny inched forward slowly, trying to get a look through the little classroom window. It was dark inside with most of the shades drawn, but she recognized it was the French class that Susan had taken last year.

A shadow moved through the gloom, rushing toward the door. Jenny stepped back just in time as the glass window shattered and an angel's head burst through, screeching and hissing, its cries echoing throughout the hall.

**Tarnished Angel (Level 4)**

Susan reacted first, thrusting her prod against its face. The prongs made contact with its nose, and it stopped screeching, violently jerking with its head stuck through the door. Jenny took the opportunity to bury her hatchet in its forehead.

**You've defeated Tarnished Angel (Level 4)!**
**Experience has been awarded.**
**+10 Energy**

**Leveled Up!**
**Jenny Huang, Level 2 → Level 3**
**+2 Stat Points**

Breathing hard, Jenny stepped back, wanting to study the angel. What was the difference now that it was level four? But they heard shuffling and hissing echoing down the hall from the direction of the Biology Department, and it was getting louder.

She glanced at Susan, whose eyes went wide. Then Jenny spotted the boy's bathroom. They'd never make it to the stairwell, but maybe they could hide. Grabbing Susan's arm, she pulled her inside, carefully shutting the door so it wouldn't make a sound. There was no knob, no lock. It was a push-to-open door.

The stench of the bathroom was thick and miasmic, and she clenched her teeth to keep from gagging. At Susan's gasp, Jenny turned around, keeping her back pressed to the door, and saw what was causing the smell.

On the floor beside the urinals was another blonde angel glistening in the dim white glow coming in through a small window near the ceiling. It wasn't moving. Neither were the three boys lying beside it, bloodied and torn up.

Gripping her hatchet tight as she heard shuffling in the hall, Jenny ground her heels against the floor, wondering how long she'd be able to hold them off if they pushed. She applied the two stat points she'd received for leveling up to power, hoping it would help keep the door shut.

One of the boys on the floor coughed, and Susan dropped down with an alarmed look on her face. She quickly pressed her hand over the boy's mouth, trying to stifle his coughing.

Jenny could almost feel one of the angels outside the door, breathing down her back. She bit her lip to stop it from trembling. She didn't want to die in a boy's bathroom, though it seemed like they hadn't heard the coughing.

Susan struggled with the boy on the floor as blood gushed from his neck. His arms moved feebly, trying to resist Susan's hand clamped over his mouth. His eyes were wide, and Jenny recognized him as Mark, the boy in her gym class last year who'd been nice to her when she had nothing to do during free-play time. He'd shown her how to shoot a basketball.

He was a junior now, and they didn't have any classes together this year, but they'd still say hi when they passed each other in the hall.

"Please," whispered Susan, bringing her face close to his. "They're right outside." She looked up at Jenny with a desperate expression on her face. Mark either couldn't hear her or he was beyond understanding. He kept trying to pull her hand off his face.

*We have to kill him.* The thought made Jenny's stomach lurch. He was clearly suffering, and if he exposed them, they'd all die.

She remembered what the guidance system had said. Equipment, tools, and weapons. Could she summon something to heal Mark?

She looked at the angel lying dead on the floor with its head in a urinal. She didn't recognize the two other boys beside it. They must have fought the angel together with their bare hands, but since they'd killed it, did that mean Mark had his First Blood bonus? If so, that meant he had points he could use, if only they could get him to calm down so they could explain.

She had to use her imagination, right? She had to imagine what she wanted, and the system would apply a cost. *Alright.*

She shut her eyes, tried not to think about the angels scurrying up and down the hall outside, and pictured a potion. Something like the ones she'd pick up in games to restore her health. She pictured a glass vial of red liquid. Red signified health, that much she was certain of.

## A Minor Potion of Recovery will cost 100 Energy.
## Insufficient Energy.

*Fuck*, she thought. She was forty-five short. She knew Susan wouldn't have any to spare after making her cattle prod. But Mark might. Now, how was she supposed to explain that to him while still holding the door?

She thought about the other angel she'd fought, the one in the French classroom. Angels didn't seem to understand how doors worked. It couldn't turn the handle, and it had attacked the door mindlessly. So maybe if she tiptoed, she could get to Susan and Mark and explain how he could craft a potion to save his life.

If they were quiet enough, the angels wouldn't hear them and try to get in. It was risky, but they could manage it. And if it worked, they'd have three people instead of two to fight them.

Just as Jenny worked up the courage to step away from the door, a loud crash made her freeze. A deafening hissing filled her ears, and Jenny realized there were way more creatures than she'd initially thought. But there was another crash, followed by a shrill scream that made her blood run cold.

She glanced at Susan, who looked just as terrified as Jenny felt. The walls shook. Violent sounds and hissing and screeching came from outside. Dust drifted down like snow on Susan's blue hair. Something slammed against the wall just beside the door, and Jenny shut her eyes, bracing herself for the worst if whatever commotion was happening outside forced its way into the bathroom.

It sounded like a fight. Something else was fighting these angels. Throwing them around. Cutting them down. Was it another student? Maybe one of the teachers?

Hope made her heart pound hard against her chest. Maybe someone else had figured out how to make use of this system thing and leveled up enough to fight these creatures head-on. She felt dizzy with relief. Were they saved?

Praying, she listened as best she could, trying to figure out what was going on.

She heard a pitiful mewling, followed by a thick snap. Then there was silence. No hissing or footsteps or anything, and Jenny couldn't take it anymore.

"I'm going to check what that was," she mouthed slowly to Susan, who shook her head no, looking frightened. Jenny bit her lip but turned anyway to pull on the door slightly, just a sliver.

Cool air from the hall tickled her nose. In the pasty white gloom, she saw what had caused the commotion. Her heart sank.

Several angels lay strewn about on the floor. None of them were moving. And on all fours was something bigger than the angels she'd seen before. Its back was broad, more defined, and wasn't just exposed skin. Instead, it was green and glossy, like an insect's exoskeleton. And it held one of the angels like a rag doll while it chewed on its face.

### Wretched Angel (Level 12)

It turned its head as it snapped off the thinner angel's skull. The wretched angel's face was covered in that same green scalelike thing. It had long dark hair that bounced while it chewed, and while it was still slim, it wasn't as ragged and bony as the other angels.

It dropped the now headless angel corpse and moved to another. Its movements were strange, even though it was on all fours like the other angels had been. It favored one arm over the other, and as it moved, Jenny saw a nasty gash across one of its green shoulders. It was hurt from the fight.

The wretched angel . . . Was that some sort of evolution, then? Did it level up as well? From killing people? Killing other angels?

Jenny realized with a chill that the angels were in the system too. They were partaking in the survival challenge. She nearly dropped the hatchet. Her palms were sweating. The angels were also getting stronger.

She realized it was only a matter of time before it noticed her or ventured into the bathroom, and if they wanted to get to the stairwell, to get to Oliver, they'd have to fight it—or something like it—at some point.

And she didn't want to fight it in the bathroom where there'd be no space to swing her hatchet.

She took a deep, shaking breath while she listened to it eating the other angels. Sweat ran down her back as she bit her lip. There was one thing she knew for certain: If she wanted to live, she'd have to get much, much stronger.

This was so unfair. All she'd wanted was to get on with her life. Graduate. Get away from her family. Get away from her mom.

Her mom's voice filled her head, screaming at her to find Oliver.

She wondered what her mom would do in this situation. How would she handle all this carnage and death? Jenny just wanted to sob and scream and pull her hair out. She wanted to break all the mirrors in the bathroom and smash everything she possibly could. But what good would that do now?

It was oddly familiar to how she felt at home. Fighting with her mom, slamming the door, sobbing into her pillow, wishing she wasn't here.

But she *was* here. Stuck in this nightmare. And she was at least getting stronger. She'd killed a bunch of them already. This wasn't like home. She wasn't powerless. She wasn't just going to hide in her room and cry and play video games until she passed out.

She shut her eyes and sucked in a breath, making her decision.

Clutching her hatchet, feeling the tiniest bit comforted by having it in her hands, she looked back at Susan, who had Mark's head on her lap trying to console him, still pressing her palm down on his lips as he struggled.

Without a word, Jenny stepped out into the hall. She didn't want to see Susan's reaction. She didn't want to second-guess her decision to fight this thing. At the very least, she resolved to lead it away from the bathroom so Susan and Mark could figure out a way to get out.

# CHAPTER FIVE

# FIGHT OR DIE FIGHTING

Jenny licked her lips, not taking her eyes off the wretched angel. It had noticed her as soon as she'd stepped out of the bathroom, but it hadn't attacked. Instead, it seemed to be observing her with those vacant white eyes. Its green face glistened like an insect's shell, and she heard it swallow a chunk of angel flesh, a wet, *disgusting* sound that made her grimace.

The creature dropped down on all fours, favoring its uninjured right arm. It still looked oddly human, just like the other angels had. Its long dark hair fell across its face, and Jenny brushed her own back.

The green skin didn't cover everything; its breasts and belly and inner thighs were still pale and bare, but it was looking less like a skeleton with skin. She got the feeling that it wasn't fully transformed yet, and she didn't want to know what a completed transformation would look like.

The angel opened its mouth, revealing glistening, bloodstained teeth.

Unlike the tarnished angels, it didn't hiss. It hadn't even charged her mindlessly. She'd braced herself for that, ready to rush into the stairwell to lead it away. Instead, it seemed wary of her hatchet and was sizing her up. It had intelligence, she realized. Could these creatures think?

Jenny stepped over a corpse. There were slash marks across its face and body that looked very much like claw marks. She glanced at the wretched angel's hands and saw long green fingernails. So, it wouldn't just grab her—it would scratch and tear and rip her open. But its green covering gave Jenny an idea.

She adjusted her grip on the hatchet, painfully aware of how quiet the hallway was and the stench of blood in her nose. *Armor,* she thought. Just like with the healing potion, she could imagine herself some protection.

Without looking away from the angel's blank stare, Jenny pictured what she wanted. Something lightweight that wouldn't slow her down. Something to keep those nails from ripping through her. Something to stop those teeth from sinking into her flesh.

**A Light Armor will cost 30 Energy for upper body equipment, and 25 Energy for lower body equipment. Sufficient Energy.**

*Fuck yes!* She had just enough.

**Energy remaining: 0**

Golden light encircled her, and she saw the wretched angel's eyes widening as it took a step back.

The light felt like a weighted blanket, comforting and warm. Her Stanford hoodie melted away, and she shuddered as her jeans did the same. For a moment, she was bare and trembling as the angel watched. It seemed afraid of the light, hesitating like a wild animal startled by fire.

She shuddered as the light turned liquid and pressed against her body. It felt cool and warm at the same time, oddly soothing as it solidified. The red fabric of her hoodie became layers and layers of what looked like fish scales, dark red and glistening. It was like she was wearing a long sleeve made out of some metallic fabric that also covered her hands like fingerless gloves.

Her grip on the hatchet felt studier; she wouldn't have to worry about it slipping because of sweaty palms. Her dark jeans had changed as well: dark blue scales that ran down her legs. The armor hugged her body without feeling constraining.

A wild thrill filled Jenny's chest as she stared the angel down. It was so much stronger than her, if levels meant what she thought they did. Green and monstrous and a cannibalistic nightmare. And she was just a tiny high school senior . . . So why was she giddy?

There was something freeing about choosing to fight, she realized. It was fight or die, and she was betting her entire life on this. No holding back. No respawning. A fight to the death. Or was she so beyond terrified that she was delirious?

"Alright," she said, sucking in a deep breath and preparing herself. "C'mon, then, you stupid fuckface. Eat my ass."

The hallway was dim and gloomy again. The angel bared its teeth and placed one hand in front of the other, its green skin glistening like a roach's shell. She got the feeling it was studying her change, calculating.

She stepped forward, holding her hatchet with both hands, mindful of the bodies on the floor; she didn't want to trip and give it an opportunity. The angel screamed, the same warbled scream she'd heard earlier from the bathroom, and then charged. Its gait awkward and clumsy, it knocked the other angels' bodies aside and rushed towards her, a look of pure malice on its face.

It closed the distance so quickly, Jenny barely had a chance to react, sidestepping and swinging as the angel swiped with its good arm. She struck nothing but air, the angel's attack bouncing off her armor in a flurry of sparks as it went flying by.

Jenny stumbled back. The impact of its nails against her armor hurt, and she knew she'd definitely be lying on the floor with her chest split open if it weren't for its protection. She tried to steady her breath, adjusting her grip on the hatchet. One clean hit. If she could just chop off an arm, or better yet, bury her hatchet in its neck, then it would be enough.

The wretched angel circled around her, limping in a strangely chimplike way, its green skin glistening; its face distorted in rage. With a snarl, it lunged, the movement so sudden and quick, it was in her face in seconds, throwing all of its weight against her.

Crying out, she landed on her back but managed to bring one knee up, driving it into the creature's exposed belly. It growled and slobbered, but it couldn't reach her face with its teeth. Saliva and blood and chunks of flesh rained down on her face as she struggled to keep it away with her leg while it grabbed her hair and yanked so hard she swore it would rip her scalp off.

Screaming, Jenny raised her left arm out of reflex, trying to push the angel off, but it took the opportunity to bite down on her forearm instead. The armor crackled as its teeth sunk in, its eyes—empty and ferocious and bulging—staring right into her own as pain shot through her arm.

Her vision blurry from the pain, she swung the hatchet with her other arm. There wasn't enough space to get proper momentum, but the edge sliced into the exposed flesh of its belly.

The angel released her and shrieked, a loud, throaty screech that echoed all over and made her head spin.

"Get off," she screamed, kicking it with all her might. Her boot struck where she'd cut the creature, and it scrambled away, clutching itself.

Blood splattered the floor with its every step, and it clambered over another angel's corpse, snarling.

Climbing to her feet, breathless and sweaty, Jenny looked at the teeth marks in her arm. Some of the red scales were cracked, and it felt wet beneath the armor, where the angel's teeth had punctured her skin. Her head felt like it was on fire from where it had pulled her hair, and tears ran down her cheeks, but she couldn't help but feel triumphant.

She wiped the blood and sweat off her face with the back of her hand, ignoring the sharp pain in her arm. Her heart raced, and everything ached, but she felt alive. So much more alive than ever before. This rush was like nothing she'd felt before. Sure, she'd pop off in games and go on a kill streak while everyone cheered her on, and that would feel exciting and awesome—but *this* . . . this was exhilarating beyond belief.

The angel seemed hurt pretty bad now. She was glad she'd put her points into power before, but maybe next time, she'd try agility or stamina. Her lungs burned, and the only thing keeping her going was adrenaline. She was too slow. If the angel hadn't already been injured, she had the feeling it would've been much faster, and she'd never have kept up.

If one of its claws had found her face, it would've gouged out an eye or ripped out her nose.

Blood dripped off the sharp edge of her hatchet as something wet dribbled down her forehead and onto her eye. Blood or angel spittle or sweat, it stung. Out of reflex, she raised a hand to wipe her brow, and that's when the wretched angel charged again.

This time, it didn't scream. Blood spilling from its belly, it rushed forward with a surprising burst of speed on its hands and feet. Jenny swung hard in a desperate bid to decapitate the creature, but it dropped low to the ground, dodging the hatchet, then leaped from underneath her, ramming its shoulder into Jenny's torso with enough force to push all the air out of her lungs and knock her off her feet.

The hatchet skidded away as the back of her head struck the floor with a loud crack. Pain—blood red and hot—burst through her thoughts and clouded her vision. It hurt to breathe, but she sucked in several shallow breaths, wondering if this was how she died. She should've just run and let it chase her down the stairwell or something. Anything.

Groaning, she reached for her hatchet, but the dark hallway seemed to be spinning uncontrollably.

She blinked as she felt a weight on top of her. The angel's lips curled into a sinister grin, its green face hovering over hers. It raised an arm, and she clenched her jaws, unable to even raise her arm to fight back.

But instead of slashing her across the face, it froze. Its entire body trembled violently, its green skin shimmering uncontrollably as it let out a distorted wail. Jenny heard the crackling of Susan's cattle prod and then saw her blue hair.

The angel whirled around and struck Susan, knocking her against the wall before it lunged and grabbed her leg, pulling so hard that her head struck the wall as she collapsed to the floor.

Susan cried out, kicking and trying to scramble out of its grip, but the angel bit down on her leg, its teeth sinking into the round flesh of her calf. Susan screamed.

The sound was so shrill and loud and heartbreaking that Jenny felt goose bumps. Forcing herself up, she reached blindly and desperately for her hatchet until her fingers curled around its handle, and then she crawled as quickly as she could over to the angel.

Suddenly, it wasn't a rush anymore. There was no excitement—only the cold, hard feeling that she wanted the creature *dead*.

With a shout, she swung the hatchet with every ounce of strength she had left.

The sharp edge connected with the angel's lower back, slicing into its green covering with a *crack*. The angel stopped tearing into Susan's leg and let go. What sounded like a wail came from its bloodied lips as its face hit the floor.

Huffing, Jenny wrenched the hatchet out of its back, blood spurting out of the gash. The angel's entire body convulsed, and she realized she'd cut through its spine.

The angel crawled forward, pulling itself with its arms and even using its chin, still trying to get to Susan. Its legs didn't move. It wailed. The sound was gut-wrenching, like watching baby animals crying for their mothers, but Jenny only paused for a second.

She struck again, aiming for the back of its neck. This time, the edge sliced all the way through and clanged against the hallway floor so hard that the vibrations ran up her arms.

**You've defeated Wretched Angel (Level 12)!**
**Experience has been awarded.**
**+50 Energy**

**Leveled Up!**
**Jenny Huang, Level 3 → Level 7**
**+8 Stat Points**

**Hatchet Upgrade!**
**Tier 1 → Tier 2**

# CHAPTER SIX

# HOW DOES A BUILDING GO MISSING?

Rain and wind battered her as soon as Nancy Huang Spencer took the stairwell out of the underground subway station. She struggled with her umbrella; the wind threatened to steal her away, and a part of her almost wished it would.

Her pink rain boots splashed through the puddles. She crossed several streets, then turned the corner and finally arrived at the upscale restaurant where she worked. It was just off Times Square, and even with the unrelenting rain, countless people bustled up and down the busy city blocks.

Nancy stepped inside, smiled at the morning concierge, waved to the kitchen staff, then rushed into the women's changing room to change and apply her makeup, and convince herself not to cry.

Dressed in the white shirt, black pants, and black apron of her uniform, she tied her hair back into a neat ponytail. Like her daughter, Nancy also had long dark hair. She was slender and pale, and she'd often get hit on by men mistaking her for a student. Even with the ring on her finger, guys couldn't seem to leave her alone, and a part of her still loved every bit of the attention.

That was how she'd ended up pregnant during her second semester of college by her classical history professor. He had been married with children and tenured, and she hadn't wanted him to get into any trouble, so she hadn't told him.

Her parents, furious, had demanded to know who the father was, but Nancy had kept quiet. Her friends, everyone she knew, had begged her to get an abortion, that this would ruin her life. She was only eighteen and being stupid and she couldn't even admit who the father was.

But Nancy had held firm. She couldn't explain why, but she had known she *had* to have this child. It wasn't rational. She knew it wasn't reasonable. It wasn't about pro-life or pro-choice like so many people had argued with her. It wasn't even about her Catholic upbringing. The whole thing sucked—being pregnant and the disapproval and bitter disappointment from her family. But she didn't care.

She'd just wanted her baby more than anything. She'd dropped out of school and raised Jenny as best she could. Her parents had let her live with them till Jenny was three, and then Nancy and her baby had been out on their own. She'd done her best, hadn't she? She'd found work. She'd stopped sleeping around and smoking weed; she'd sacrificed everything she could for Jenny.

She still woke up in cold sweats wondering if she had enough in her account to see herself and Jenny through the week. If she could keep the electricity on in their one-bedroom run-down apartment. If she'd have to tell Jenny that she was trying yet another diet and that's why mommy wouldn't be eating tonight; tap water would be plenty. It was strained, and maybe Nancy had screamed too often and lost her temper a lot, but it was the best she could do.

Nancy had tried talking to Henry about how she felt. She'd known him for four years now, and they were finally a family, but he'd taken Jenny's side. He wanted her to do what was best for her, and while Nancy admired that . . . she didn't want to let her daughter go.

"Fuck," she whispered when she'd finished tucking in her shirt. She had to pee.

She got into a stall, undid her pants, and sat down, wishing she could call Henry, if only just to hear his deep, comforting voice. And then she could pretend that she was at home, safe in his big, strong arms, kissing and touching one another till nothing else mattered . . .

But intimacy felt impossible these days. Ever since Jenny had announced her decision to go to Stanford and begun flaunting that dumb sweater all the time, it was one argument after another.

She couldn't even remember the fight from this morning; it all blurred together. It was always something dumb—she knew it was dumb. But she couldn't help herself. It felt like the only way to get Jenny's attention these days. The girl seemed to be constantly pushing away, and Nancy knew the things she said to her daughter didn't help at all. "How could you be so selfish?" "Why do you want to leave us?" "Are you punishing me?" It made her sound like her mother, and she didn't speak to her mother.

"Stupid, stupid," she said to herself as she flushed. Ever since Henry and Oliver had moved in, Jenny had drifted further and further away. Oliver would follow Jenny around, begging to play games and watch movies, but she would just distance herself. She was irritable all the time, she had stopped going to church, and now this Stanford thing was too much.

Why couldn't she understand that all Nancy wanted was for her not to suffer like she had? Not to make the same dumb mistakes.

She took a deep breath and straightened her shoulders, smoothing down her apron.

"Okay, Nancy," she said to herself, eyes shut. "Big smile. Everything will be okay." Tonight, she'd sit with Jenny and talk and figure it all out. And if Nancy had to move to California and take care of Jenny, then so be it.

As she pushed open the stall door, the lights flickered. The floor lurched violently, and she fell back onto the toilet seat, the door slamming shut as its metal parts rattled. She slid to the floor and brought her knees to her chest, hands over her head, trying to make herself as small as possible while everything shook. The water in the toilet sloshed, and the lid dropped with a loud bang. *An earthquake? Here?*

As suddenly as it had begun, it was over. Nancy hesitantly lowered her hands. Other than the lights flickering, the rest of the bathroom looked fine. She got to her feet and stepped back into the changing room. Two other women were there, both of them looking as shocked as she felt but otherwise okay.

The taste of iron was in her mouth; she'd bitten her tongue, but it wasn't too bad. Just a surprising shock. She sighed with relief, hoping the high school where Jenny and Oliver went was okay.

Pulling up her daughter's name, she pressed call. It went to voicemail. "Okay," she told herself, pacing the room. It might've disrupted a cell tower or something. Or maybe everyone was dialing loved ones and emergency lines. There could be partial blackouts.

The other two women were saying something, both of them looking at their screens, but Nancy couldn't think straight. Her heart was racing much harder than it had when she'd been stuck in the bathroom during the earthquake. Thoughts kept nagging and tugging, and she felt like she was choking.

She called Oliver and got the same result. She texted both of them. Then called Jenny again. Nothing worked.

Finally, nearing the point of hysterics, she called Henry. He picked up.

"Oh my God, Nancy," he said, breathing hard. In the background, there was incessant honking and shouting and the drumming of the rain. He must still be on his way to work. "Are you alright? I've been calling and calling, and nothing would connect."

"Yes," she replied, hugging herself with one arm and still pacing. She was vaguely aware of one of her coworkers sobbing. "I'm safe. Nothing happened here. But I can't reach the kids."

Henry was silent.

"Henry? The kids, Henry. Do you think you can drive by the school?"

"Nancy," he said, but then his voice broke. "Something's happened here. I'm stuck in traffic. I don't think I can get out anytime soon."

"Are you hurt?" she asked, wishing she'd asked him that sooner. She was struggling against the urge to chew off her fingernails. "Henry, are you hurt? Is it bad out there?"

"No," he replied. He took a loud breath. She heard him moving around. "I'm in the car. I'm fine. But listen. A building here just . . . It's gone. There's just a big, ugly hole in the ground now, and people are freaking out. *I'm* freaking out."

"What?"

Had something hit him on the head? What was he talking about?

He continued. "It was a hotel. The whole building . . . just gone. And look at the skyline. Nancy, this—"

The line went dead.

"Hello?" she whispered. She looked up as one of her coworkers rushed out of the changing room, the other one still sitting on a bench holding her phone. "The Empire State Building," she said. "It's gone."

Nancy rushed over to look at the phone. There was an ugly hole in the ground with exposed metal beams where the Empire State Building once stood, a massive crowd of people forming around it.

How could places just disappear? Dread and worry twisted into one sharp pain that throbbed from the center of her chest and radiated up to her head. She texted Jenny again. Then Oliver. The messages wouldn't even send.

"Please," she whispered over and over as she looked through the news websites. Article after article popped up, and she read every headline quickly before swiping for the next.

***Global Earthquake Shakes Every Corner of the Planet.***
***Scientists Baffled.***
***Buildings Vanish in Freak Earthquake.***
***Hundreds of Thousands Presumed Missing.***
***Millions Without Energy.***

Hospitals, holy sites, schools, hotels, museums, warehouses . . . She was tapping furiously at this point. St. Peter's Basilica, Oxford University, Masjid al-Haram, the Space Needle in Seattle; the lists just kept coming, each one longer than the last. She finally got to a webpage for New York.

Not daring to breathe, she scrolled through the list. Every few seconds, the page updated and she lost her place, having to start again. An elementary school. A library. A hotel. A college building. A restaurant.

She dropped the phone when she read *Manhattan High School for the Sciences.*

She rushed out of the changing room. In the main dining area, chairs were knocked over. Coworkers and the customers from the morning rush were huddled and taking pictures and consoling each other. Nancy felt like she was seeing them through a thick layer of plastic that cut her off from the rest of the world. Someone tried to speak to her, but she didn't even recognize them. She marched out the front door and stepped into the pouring rain.

Traffic was completely clogged. She looked down the street, seeing nothing but taxis and large SUVs and even a mail truck. Everyone was honking. The rain was relentless, somehow worse than before, and she knew there would be no way to get a cab in this.

Her feet moved on their own. She'd forgotten her boots and her coat; she was still in her restaurant uniform, running in black sandals. People were rushing back and forth; she weaved between them, her apron flapping, her arms pumping.

She slipped at an intersection when the strap of one of her sandals broke, and she broke the fall with her hands. Someone tried to help her up, but she pushed them away. Her pants were torn at the knees. Her palms were bleeding. Nancy yanked off her sandals and kept running.

The rain soaked her completely. Her ponytail whipped her cheeks as it flopped every which way. The pavement was unforgiving to the soles of her feet, but at least she didn't have to stop at any lights.

It couldn't be true. It was impossible. It must be a hoax. They must be lying. *Buildings don't just go missing.*

It could be a sinkhole. Maybe that was it. Maybe Jenny and the others were buried, and first responders were digging them out right now.

*Please, God,* she begged with every bit of her soul. *Please. Please just let them be okay.*

By the time she got near the school, some nineteen long city blocks later, Nancy was bleeding profusely from her hands and knees and feet. She was drenched in cold rainwater and sweat. Her lungs were on the verge of collapsing. Every step she took burned, and she was sure there was a pebble or piece of asphalt lodged in her heel.

She couldn't see the school. It simply wasn't there. The surrounding buildings seemed just fine, but the school, her children's school, was gone.

She pushed through the crowd of other parents wailing and shouting. She ducked under umbrellas and squeezed and squirmed her way to the front. She only stopped when she got to the blue barricades the police had set up. A cop shouted at her, something about staying back, the site was dangerous, but all she could hear was her own heart pounding.

She rubbed the rain from her eyes and blinked at the jagged hole in the ground. It was brown earth, with the rain collecting in a dark pool. As though some enormous entity had reached out and scooped the building up in an unruly fist.

She dropped to her knees, balling up her apron with both hands. She squeezed the cloth tight, unable to take her eyes off the gaping hole in the ground. She'd stopped crying. Stopped gasping for air. Stopped rambling. All she could do was stare.

# CHAPTER SEVEN

# Minor Healing Salve

Sinking to her knees, Jenny dropped to all fours, breathing hard. Her sweat-soaked hair stuck to her face. She felt like puking. Next to her lay the wretched angel's corpse, its head now separated from its green body by her hatchet. She felt so gross and tired and empty; all she wanted was a hot bath and to pretend this was all a nightmare.

But beneath the gritty exhaustion, she felt something else, a pulsing. She'd *killed* this creature that seemed so powerful and monstrous. She now had a strength she'd never had before, and she wanted to kill more of these nightmarish things.

Susan's sobbing cut through her thoughts, and Jenny turned to face her. She wiped the sweat off her brow, trying not to think about the blood running down her arm beneath her armor. It was nothing compared to Susan's leg.

The angel had bitten off the fleshy bit of her calf. Exposed muscle twitched, and blood spurted from several places where Jenny swore the strands of flesh were actually exposed blood vessels. She thought she could see the white of Susan's bones.

Susan squeezed her thigh with both hands, the back of her head against the wall, her eyes shut tight. Jenny wanted to comfort her, but she was afraid of causing more pain.

*What do I do? What do I do?* Jenny's thoughts spiraled as she kept picturing the worst. "Susan," she whispered, her heart breaking each time Susan sobbed.

"It's okay," Susan said through clenched teeth. "It doesn't hurt too much."

Jenny shut her eyes tight, trying not to cry. Trying to remember the medical things she'd seen in war movies. Apply pressure to stop the blood flow. Wrap it tight with something. Cauterize it?

*Energy,* she thought. *Okay. I got fifty from that damn angel. That feels too low. Why didn't that big-ass thing give more?* She grimaced, glancing at the wound again. It was all red and ugly and angry.

Jenny didn't know what to say. She wanted to slap Susan for rushing into the fight, but that felt hypocritical. Then she realized Susan had leveled up as well because she'd attacked the wretched angel.

### Human (Level 5)

Which meant she had gotten energy too.

"Susan," Jenny whispered urgently. "How much energy do you have?" She was going to tell her about the healing potion she'd imagined earlier for Mark.

But Susan wasn't responding anymore. Her face had gone pale, sickly and ghostly, almost like one of the angels. She was shaking violently.

*Fuck, there is no time. Potion. C'mon.* Jenny concentrated so hard that her head hurt.

### A Minor Potion of Recovery will cost 100 Energy.
### Insufficient energy.

*No, fuck that. Give me half. Give me half the potion. Not the whole vial. Just something,* she pleaded with the system, her nails digging into the bit of her armor that covered her palms, begging with everything she had.

Finally, it said:

### Sufficient Energy.

She almost collapsed with relief when golden light appeared in her hand. It was the vial with the stopper, red liquid glistening inside. Like something she might've stolen from the chemistry lab rooms. It wasn't completely full, but it had cost her all her energy, and if it could take *some* of the pain from Susan, then it would be enough for now.

How did this work, anyway? Should she bring it to Susan's mouth?

Something nudged her thoughts, giving her the impression she'd have to pour it over the wound for direct application. Biting her lip, Jenny prayed this would work. And if it didn't . . . She didn't want to think about that.

Pulling the stopper out with her teeth, she poured the red liquid onto the shredded flesh of Susan's leg. It splattered then shone with a warm red glow before seeping into the wound.

A moment later, Susan stopped trembling and opened her eyes, wide. She stared at Jenny then pulled at the torn cloth of her leggings.

The chunk of her leg was still missing. It was still bleeding, but it didn't seem so fresh and raw anymore. Some of the flesh had turned a soft shade of pink, looking like new skin. She let out a shuddering sigh. "Jesus fucking Christ," she whispered, then looked up at Jenny and nodded weakly. "Nice outfit."

Jenny sobbed, muttering a thank you to . . . she wasn't sure what. God? The system? The universe? She squeezed Susan's hand. She tried not to think about Mark suffering in the bathroom. Or the headless angel beside them. She tried not to think about how many more angels might be on their way. She was just happy Susan was okay.

"Please don't do that again," said Susan.

"Do what?"

Golden light folded around Susan's hand. Jenny watched as a little circular container appeared, and Susan popped the lid off to reveal a pink cream. As she scooped it out with her fingers and applied it to her leg, the same red glow from before appeared, but this time, there was a faint fizzing. She sighed, shut her eyes, and said nothing for a while. Then she closed the container and thrust it into her pocket.

"Don't rush off like an idiot," she finally spoke. "Please. I thought we were in this together?"

Jenny bit her lip and nodded. She knew it had been dumb. But . . . she wasn't going to mention that a part of her had found the whole thing *exhilarating*. "I'm sorry," she said instead.

"I suppose you thought you were being the hero."

Jenny shook her head, but she couldn't find the words to disagree with. She felt like crying. But not just crying—she felt like sobbing till she collapsed. Gut-wrenching, ugly screaming. Relief and heartbreak and fear and the unrelenting desire to get stronger struggled inside her.

"The boy died," continued Susan softly.

Jenny nodded, more sadness clogging her throat. "Did you . . . ?"

"Yeah," said Susan softly. "I made a minor healing salve for him, too, and I kept putting more and more on him, but I think I was too late."

They didn't say anything for a while. Jenny listened intently for any sign of other angels that might attack them, then pulled her hatchet out of the floor, trying to ignore the angel's wet hair floating in blood.

Susan mentioned doing her stats, and Jenny listened to her talk about stamina and agility. Jenny had eight points available, so she applied four to power. Immediately, she felt a shift in her muscles, much more apparent when applying four points. The remainder she put into stamina and agility, remembering how her fight with the wretched angel had gone.

Her breathing felt less strained as soon as she'd applied the points, and she wondered how agility would manifest. She figured she could skip durability for now, since she had her armor.

**Jenny Huang**
**Human (Level 7)**
**Age: 6,801 days**
**Stats:**
**Power: 11**
**Durability: 5**
**Stamina: 5**
**Agility: 5**
**Stat Points Available: 0**
**Energy Available: 0**

Satisfied with her new stats, she pushed that thought away. But she had zero energy. What if she needed to replace the armor? She glanced at the crack on her forearm. She needed headgear too. She supposed she'd just have to kill more angels.

Once again, that curious bit of excitement flared up inside her. *Kill. Kill. Kill.*

She looked at Susan, who was brushing blue hair to the side of her head as her brows furrowed in concentration. "I went for durability," she informed. "I think I'm fucked in the speed department for now." She pointed to her leg.

"Makes sense," said Jenny as she wiped the blood off her hatchet. She noticed the wooden handle seemed slightly darker, as though the wood it was made from had changed. It felt sturdier and thicker without having changed in size at all. The metal part seemed sharper somehow, and it, too, seemed bigger.

That's when she realized it *was* bigger. The sharp edge was now curved slightly, giving it more surface area. She swung it and heard the wind whooshing as she cut through the air. She could swing harder. Move quicker. And the more angels she killed, the stronger she'd get.

This really was just like a game. Except instead of fighting goblins or wolves or some cute little slimes, they had to fight angels. She'd have to fight her way to Oliver. And she had to get stronger to protect him and Susan until this whole nightmare was over. Was Oliver even still alive? How many people were left now?

**Human population remaining: 302**

Her eyes went wide. It'd dropped by *that* much? How?!

Susan got to her feet, cattle prod in hand. "It looks like my cattle prod is stronger," she noted. It looked the same as she held it out to inspect it, but then she continued. "It says I can shoot electricity now."

Aiming it down the hall, a bolt of blue lightning burst from the top and stretched all the way to the door, illuminating the gloomy hall with its blue glow. It made a soft cracking sound, like distant thunder.

"Holy shit," whispered Susan. She switched it off and stared at her weapon in awe. "Did you get something too?"

That was when Jenny noticed the thought that had been nudging her gently this whole time but she'd been too preoccupied with Susan's wound, her own growing bloodlust, and worrying about Oliver to pay it any attention. It finally came through.

### Hatchet (Tier 2)
### Your Hatchet can now be retrieved on command.

She read it out loud, unsure what it meant.

Susan scratched her chin, still leaning on the wall. "Try putting it down then having it go back to your hand? Sounds like you can recall it."

Jenny passed Susan her hatchet then took a few steps back, stepping over a corpse. Holding out her hand, she concentrated on it coming back to her. It felt silly, more like a magic trick than an actual ability, but she gasped when she felt a slight pull. It felt magnetic.

With a soft burst of golden light, the hatchet flew out of Susan's hand and straight into Jenny's, positioning itself perfectly in place so that she could wrap her fingers around the handle.

"That might come in handy." Jenny admired her upgraded weapon. Both their upgrades felt very useful, but they didn't have time to keep trying things out. "We should keep going," she said. "Downstairs. I don't know . . . I . . ." The words fluttered out all awkward. She bit her lip.

Susan nodded then stepped away from the wall. She limped slightly, but there was a determined look on her face. Golden light encapsulated her torso. For a second, she was naked, and Jenny looked away. Then, blue armor with matching scales to Jenny's appeared on Susan's body. On her head was a pink bicycle helmet.

"Safety first," she said, fastening the straps in place under her chin. "I didn't have enough for something cooler."

For the first time since their nightmare began, Jenny wanted to laugh; the pink helmet looked so innocent and out of place. She just wanted to hug her.

Before she could say anything, one of the doors of the central stairwell burst open. A large figure stumbled into the hall, accompanied by hissing and screeching.

# CHAPTER EIGHT

# STAY HYDRATED

The figure stumbled into the hallway, illuminated from behind by the large windows of the stairwell. Susan counted four . . . No, five angels clinging to the man who'd burst through the door. It was Mr. Kim, one of the assistant principals. He was Harry Kim's father.

Harry, who was lying just outside their English classroom, dead.

Mr. Kim, roaring and swinging a hammer at the angels, stumbled into the hall.

Susan squinted, seeing that he was now a level four. Which meant he'd killed a bunch of these angels just to get here. His eyes widened when he saw them, but his dark suit and pants were torn in several places, and Susan could spot the blood and missing flesh.

He tripped and landed with a resounding thud, grunting and crawling forward as all the angels pounced. The sound of fabric tearing filled the hall as they ripped through his clothes, his white shirt stained in many places with blood.

Susan swallowed hard, wanting to rush in and help. She glanced at Jenny, who looked just about ready to jump into the fray. And before Susan could say anything, that was exactly what Jenny did.

She watched as Jenny flung her hatchet at the angel about to bite into Mr. Kim's back. The weapon spun through the air before its sharp edge sliced cleanly through the angel's forehead and skull. It landed flat on Mr. Kim's back, its brain matter spilling like runny eggs.

There was a flash of golden light, and then Jenny was standing over Mr. Kim, swinging her hatchet and screaming and cutting down the angels one after the other. Two more fell to the floor and didn't move again, their chests and faces split open and gushing. But there were still two left standing. One of them knocked into Jenny head-on, and she stumbled back, tripping over Mr. Kim's arm.

Susan flicked her cattle prod almost without thinking, as though it was already second nature. A slight movement of her wrist, and a blue bolt of electricity burst from the tip and crackled toward the angels.

For an instant, lightning connected Susan to the two angels. It skewered them both through the chest, and they shook and sizzled and screamed before collapsing, burnt to a crisp.

**You've defeated Tarnished Angel (Level 4)!**
**Experience has been awarded.**
**+10 Energy**

**You've defeated Tarnished Angel (Level 3)!**
**Experience has been awarded.**
**+10 Energy**

**Leveled Up!**
**Susan Brown, Level 5 → Level 6**
**+2 Stat Points**

She hadn't meant to put so much into the attack, and the drain on her stamina left her feeling breathless and weak, but she'd managed to save Jenny. She leaned against the wall, breathing hard, while Jenny helped Mr. Kim.

The cattle prod felt right in her hands. It made her feel the slightest bit safer, and the added power she had from leveling up was proving effective. This new lightning ability felt so intuitive, almost like she was zapping someone with a wand. It was perfect, especially now that she couldn't move as easily with her injured leg.

Just this morning, Susan's biggest concern had been getting home to game with Jenny. Her parents had been gone for a week now, and wouldn't be home for another few days, which meant Susan could be as loud as she wanted to on the mic. She didn't have to worry about them listening and then shaming her for playing children's games when she could've been studying. Or applying to some internship. Or some other bullshit overachiever thing they wanted her to do.

She'd gotten into a great university here in New York, received a generous scholarship, and had already applied for work-study programs. Hadn't she done enough?

On top of that, her boyfriend, Kevin Ponce, had dumped her a few weeks before prom just because he'd found out some other girl liked him. Did he want an upgrade? Was she not good enough? Was any of it even real?

*Everyone always leaves.* That was what Susan lived by, so she'd decided Kevin's bullshit wasn't her problem. She just wanted a quiet life, and she just wanted to game with Jenny. Jenny, who might be the only exception to *everybody always leaves.*

Gaming with Jenny was the only time Susan felt like she had meaningful control of her life. Susan usually played an offensive support role, being able to call out where her team needed to be, when to push, and when to fall back. She loved that. Giving commands. Being firm. And Jenny was usually playing point, doing the most damage. She was the only person Susan trusted in every single match.

Where Jenny was quiet and focused, Susan was more outgoing and confident, and that made them an unstoppable duo. So why the hell had Jenny left her in that bathroom to fight that big-ass angel by herself?

Now Susan had a chunk of her leg missing. It throbbed with every beat of her heart, but she stifled the searing pain because she didn't want Jenny to see it. Jenny was already dumb enough; Susan didn't want to risk her making even more dumb decisions trying to make up for her shortcomings.

She'd copied Jenny's armor and added the pink helmet, something she thought might make Jenny smile a bit, but also because she hadn't had enough energy for the blue metal helmet she'd initially pictured. It would've been sleek as hell. But she figured if this kind of helmet was enough to save someone's life in a bike accident, then it would do just fine if an angel hit her or knocked her head against a wall again.

"Susan?" came Jenny's hushed voice.

She inhaled deeply, applying her two new stat points to stamina so she could recover quicker from the exhaustion.

**Susan Brown**
**Human (Level 6)**
**Age: 6,870 days**
**Stats:**
**Power: 5**
**Durability: 8**
**Stamina: 6**
**Agility: 4**
**Stat Points Available: 0**
**Energy Available: 35**

Renewed strength flowed into her muscles. Trying to ignore the searing pain in her leg, and trying not to limp, she walked over to where Mr. Kim was lying face down on the floor. She wished she had something stronger than a minor healing salve; it felt like her wound would burst open with each step, and every one of those felt *wrong* now that a chunk of muscle was missing.

"He's not responding," said Jenny in a hushed voice. She nudged his arm gently.

He was lying still, his head to one side, his hammer on the floor beside him. Blood oozed from the scratches on his neck and back, and there were several injuries that reminded Susan of the horrifying mess that wretched angel had made of her leg.

He must have fought and struggled all the way up here from the main offices just to find Harry.

"My son . . ." he said, his voice raspy and painful to listen to. More blood gushed from his neck. He coughed violently. Jenny squeezed his hand and looked up at Susan.

Grabbing the healing salve out of her pocket, Susan's heart ached as she tried to find the words to tell him that Harry was dead. Jenny wasn't saying anything either. Her usual resting bitch face was gone; she looked like she was about to cry. Susan knew they were both picturing the same thing: Harry's body.

Jenny was terrible with stuff like this, so Susan knelt, scooped up some of the salve, and pressed it to Mr. Kim's neck. She could feel his pulse; his heart was racing like mad. His blood rushed down her fingers, and the salve turned into a slimy wet mess as she applied it. She didn't think it would work, but if it could help even a little bit, how was she not supposed to try?

"Mr. Kim . . ." she started, then she had to swallow a sob. "I'm sorry, but Harry was in our class when . . ."

At the sound of his son's name, Mr. Kim let out a groan. He moved like he might try to get up, but he couldn't lift himself off the floor. Jenny tried to help, but the man collapsed, weeping. Snot ran down his lips. "My beautiful boy . . . What will I tell his mother? What will I do?"

The salve glowed warmly, but it didn't matter. She tried to scoop up more, but Mr. Kim let out one final shuddering breath and then went still. Susan pressed her fingers to his neck again. His pulse was gone. His hammer evaporated into golden sparks that drifted away and fizzled out of existence.

She twisted the lid of her healing salve back into place, her shaking fingers covered in Mr. Kim's blood. She looked at Jenny, who was gripping her hatchet so hard it looked like her knuckles would burst out of her hands. Susan couldn't help but imagine Jenny in Mr. Kim's situation, searching for Oliver, desperately hoping he was still alive. What if Jenny found Oliver's corpse?

Susan didn't want to think about all her friends and classmates and teachers . . . but the notification triggered, and the thought burst into her head the same way electricity shot out of her prod.

**Human population remaining: 294**

That couldn't be right. *No*, she thought. *No!* She wanted to scream. She wanted to go home. She wanted to hug her parents and hold them tight and never let go. She wanted a hot shower and a hot meal. She wanted to hear her parents bother her about her grades and her papers and her exams. She just wanted to be home, where her parents would take care of everything, and she could just shut her eyes and sleep.

Jenny was the first to move, kicking one of the angels so hard that the fleshy *thud* and the crack of its neck made Susan wince. Then Jenny walked over to the large stairwell, the door held open by Mr. Kim's feet.

Susan tried to say something, but she couldn't get a word out. She cleared her throat.

"I thought we were going down that one?" She pointed over her shoulder at the smaller stairwell they'd tried to get to before that wretched angel had shown up.

Jenny shook her head. "If Mr. Kim managed to get up here, then I think we should be fine going down. That way, we might hear more of what's happening on the lower floors." She paused and readjusted her grip on the hatchet. "And if we run into trouble, we can just come back here. I think that big green one killed the others on this floor, and the rest of them chased people down."

Sniffling, Susan shut Mr. Kim's eyes. It was something she'd only seen in movies before, and she hadn't realized she'd been staring at his unseeing eyes till Jenny stopped talking.

She took a deep breath, then wiped the blood off her hands and followed Jenny through the doorway into the school's main stairwell. She thought it would be smarter to stick to their original plan of using the smaller, more secluded path, but she trusted Jenny.

She just wanted to get out of this alive. With Jenny. With Oliver, if he was all right. And with whomever else they could find. She'd given up hope of saving any specific friends.

Their names and faces filled her head, but she pushed them away. How many of them were dead now, like Harry? She'd seen Mrs. Rivera get eaten alive. She'd pissed herself. And she couldn't get the horrible image of that green wretched angel chewing through her leg out of her mind. How many other kids had seen the same thing but weren't lucky enough to survive?

A part of her was glad she was with Jenny. Not just because they'd saved each other's lives but because Jenny was her closest friend. They'd stay up till sunrise sometimes just chatting about movies and books and songs and games, and what they wanted to do, the places they wanted to go. It was Jenny she texted at 4:00 a.m. when a nightmare woke her up. It was Jenny who always responded nearly right away.

And now that they were *inside* a nightmare, Jenny was pushing forward. Like the edge of that hatchet, Jenny seemed fiercer and more decisive. In games, Jenny was never one to make callouts, to hang back and figure out the best way to push. She seemed to instinctively know when to attack and when not to.

Even while they were playing with other people, Jenny seemed to dance around whomever she was with. She had her personal style and made it work no matter who they were with. And Susan loved that. It let Susan's support shine, and she just trusted Jenny to always be there. She felt like Jenny's style brought out the best in her.

That was what seemed to be happening now. *It's just like gaming,* Susan thought to herself. *Just like a video game. We're duoing. The mission is to save Oliver.* It was stupid. It felt stupid. But it helped. This was the only way she could make sense of any of it.

Jenny led the way down the wide stairs, clutching the handrail on the right, beside the wall. Susan followed slowly, wincing with every step but biting her lip to keep quiet.

After killing those two angels, she had enough energy to make armor for her legs now. Or maybe bandages or something. But she didn't want to use any energy yet. Her healing salve was almost out, and a part of her regretted trying to help Mr. Kim, but she knew she would've regretted it more if she hadn't tried. She'd just hold on to her remaining energy until she could get more.

And she had to be careful with her cattle prod now. The lightning seemed to draw from her stamina, not some battery or anything. *She* was the battery. She was sweating, exhausted, and feeling gross already, so she had to be careful with when and how she used it next.

Then she remembered something. Something she'd always remind Jenny of in between matches. *Hydrate.* Could she use the system to make water?

Like with the healing salve, she pictured a bottle of water, and the thought came to her.

**Water will cost 1 Energy.**
**Sufficient Energy.**

Exhaling a sigh of relief, she let the golden light fill her hand, drawing Jenny's attention as it lit up the stairwell slightly. Susan offered the bottle to Jenny first, but she shook her head and pushed it gently back, so Susan unscrewed the cap, realizing how unfathomably thirsty she was, and drank half of it in several greedy gulps.

Water ran down her chin. She was breathing hard, loving how cool and refreshing it felt. The burning in her leg eased just a bit, and her throat didn't feel as ragged. She sighed, wishing this tiny moment of relief would last, but it was already fading away.

At least water wouldn't cost them much. Staying hydrated was going to be vital with all this actual fighting and surviving they had to do.

Jenny made her own bottle as they stood in the shadow of the stairwell, a few steps away from the large window that showed nothing but the pale mist of the void outside. The quiet was thick and stifling, broken every so often by the echoes of distant screaming.

# CHAPTER NINE

# DOWN THE STAIRWELL

The water had helped immensely. Jenny had been seething with rage after watching Mr. Kim die, and the terror that tugged on her every thought only made it worse. She kept picturing herself finding Oliver's body, torn open and disfigured. She kept picturing everyone who'd struggled against the angels, dying gruesomely because these skinny creatures were what? Hungry?

**Human population remaining: 191**

It had dropped so much now. She wasn't sure if Oliver was even . . .

There wasn't any point in even entertaining that thought right now.

They'd been on the third floor. Oliver's math class was on the first. She wondered if he'd gotten out with his classmates, if he'd rushed to the lobby and tried to get out, or if he'd found another place to hide, but that didn't matter. She still had to check his classroom, if only to be sure his corpse wasn't there.

She could hear Susan's sharp intake of breath with every step. The wound must still hurt. And of course it did. A part of her leg had been torn out by teeth, and it had only healed slightly. They needed to get her to a hospital with painkillers and doctors and something to cleanse the wound.

What kind of bacteria lived in those angels' mouths? They reeked and had emaciated bodies . . . Were hospitals even around anymore? Had they been torn away from home, or had the rest of the planet become that strange emptiness outside?

Jenny clutched her hatchet tight. *Let's just worry about one thing at a time.*

She went slightly ahead down the next set of stairs to scope out the second-floor landing and nearly tripped. Someone was lying on the bottom steps. A boy, his arm reaching for the top of the stairwell, his shirt torn open with blood flowing down to form a puddle at the base of the stairs.

The rest of the second-floor landing looked similar. Jenny swallowed hard, trying to keep from throwing up, and felt Susan come to a stop behind her. On the floor were the bodies of her classmates and teachers, bloody smears and hand-prints everywhere.

She recognized most of them. She didn't know them all by name, but they were faces she would pass in the halls. People she'd see sitting by their lockers or eating lunch in the cafeteria or just laughing and hanging out and doing dumb things. She forced herself to look at every single body in turn to make sure they weren't Oliver. And with each mangled body, each blank face, Jenny felt more and more rage twisting into a burning hot ball of flame in her head.

There were several angel corpses as well. Their gaunt faces stared blankly, their naked, uncomfortably thin bodies glistening in the pale glow of the Veil. Wounds exposed their insides, and Jenny took some pleasure in knowing they'd suffered too.

"We should keep going," whispered Susan.

Jenny stepped carefully over the boy on the steps. She turned to help Susan avoid slipping on the blood, but hissing made her freeze. Susan's eyes went wide. They heard shouting next—human shouting, followed by the unmistakable pitter-pattering of countless angels. It almost sounded like the rain from earlier in the morning. An angelic stampede?

Jenny looked over her shoulder, barely daring to breathe, as she saw several hunched-over angels rushing by in the second-floor hallway.

They brushed past the doors, stumbled over bodies, and slid with the blood, but they seemed to be zeroing in on the shouting like a pack of carnivorous beasts. They weren't coming out into the stairwell, and Jenny and Susan went unnoticed as they rushed by.

She could see their bones rippling beneath their skin, all of them moving on all fours. She even saw the distinct coloring of wretched angels. One of them was green, another was yellow with black stripes, and a third one was red. Dark red, like Jenny's armor.

She'd already killed one of them, but that had been dumb luck. And even with the level up she'd gotten from the angels attacking Mr. Kim and the two points she'd put into power, it wasn't enough. They would snap her like a twig and suck her guts out before she could take just one of them down.

Jenny hadn't moved, her hand still reaching for Susan's arm. She wanted to fight. She wanted to butcher as many of them as she could. But she wouldn't leave Susan here. And she wouldn't draw their attention to Susan. There was no way they could survive *three* wretched angels, never mind the dozens of tarnished ones.

And Susan had been right earlier. Why did Jenny keep imagining herself as some sort of hero? What would she do? Jump into that throbbing mass of angels, swing her hatchet, and kill as many of them as she could before they overwhelmed her? Why did she want to martyr herself so badly? It was such a violently frightening urge to fight; the same thing she'd felt when she'd faced the green wretched angel. *Kill. Kill. Kill.*

She exhaled a shuddering breath as the halls turned quiet again. If they ever got out of this, she was going to make some therapist either extremely upset or very, very happy.

They could still hear the muffled hissing and shouting moving away from them toward the honors science wing of the second floor. It was strange, almost like déjà vu, to think about how her locker was in that hallway. What if she'd been there when this whole thing started?

She wondered about the shouts they'd heard. Definitely human. If wretched angels were heading there, too . . . whoever was fighting didn't stand much of a chance unless they were really strong. It was either Jenny and Susan tried to help them and they all died fighting, or they pushed onward. There was no way to help those people.

"Okay," whispered Jenny, looking back at Susan and her pink helmet. "I think they're gone now."

She helped Susan go over the body, then they turned to the next flight of stairs, moving slowly, making sure none of their steps made a sound. She'd grown accustomed to the stench of death and blood, but she could sense it was getting worse as they descended.

Jenny wished she was stronger. Wished she had more energy. She wanted to keep Susan safe, but fighting angels was the only way to get more strength, the only way to gain more energy. But that meant risking their lives, and while she was more than willing to risk her own, she didn't want to risk Susan's. It was a frustrating catch-22.

They moved around the bodies on this stairwell, necks torn open, blood dripping down the steps. There were guts and chunks of flesh and vomit all over. The stench was unbearable now, and even the air seemed thicker. The Veil, whatever it was, seemed to be more present the closer they got to the first floor. It was like walking through a clear mist that got denser with every step.

More screaming echoed all over. It set Jenny's teeth on edge. When they finally got to the first-floor landing, something large and glistening was waiting at the base of the steps. Jenny almost swung her hatchet, thinking it was one of the larger wretched angels with red skin, but it was her world history teacher.

He was flat on his back, his shirt torn open, and almost every bit of him was covered in blood. His golden compass rose pin glittered in the gloom, still attached to his tie. Several angels lay beside him, unmoving.

"Mr. Ahmadi . . ." Susan said. She'd been in his class last year, loved him, and insisted Jenny take his history class this year.

Mr. Ahmadi had been a large man. He loved his sweets, and every Friday, he treated his students to chocolates, candies, and pretzels. For Thanksgiving, he'd baked several large cheesecakes and shared them with each one of his classes. For Lunar New Year, he'd introduced them to his wife, who was from China, and made dumplings and sweet rice balls for everyone.

He was jolly and awesome, and on parent-teacher's evening, he spoke warmly about Jenny's grades in his class and her papers, and even said she'd make a fine historian if that was what she wanted to pursue.

Jenny looked at the angels. He must have strangled them to death. Knowing Mr. Ahmadi, he'd tried to hold off as many as he could while students tried to escape. She blinked away tears. She didn't want to cry. Not yet. Even though she wanted to sob and scream, she knew it wouldn't help. And Susan must be feeling the same way.

She knelt and shut his eyes, pushing his tongue back into his mouth. One of the angels had bitten off his ear and a part of his cheek. Susan nudged her gently, and Jenny finally managed to look away from Mr. Ahmadi. There were tears streaming down Susan's face, but her lips were pressed tight, and she didn't say a word.

The remaining flight of stairs would lead down to the basement. More blood and bodies. Something—or many somethings—was moving down there. After a quick glance at the first-floor hall to see if it was empty, Jenny pushed one of the doors open, Susan following close behind.

They were met with sounds of chewing, teeth gnashing, and the gross, wet sounds of swallowing. To their left was the lobby, and the sight of it made Jenny's stomach turn worse than anything yet.

Tarnished angels, dozens of them, on all fours. Feasting on the flesh of countless people like pale, glistening, hairless hyenas. She spotted the dark-blue uniform of the security guards. She saw teachers, some of the nurses, the lunch staff, and so many, many students, their clothes torn, their necks ripped open. *Some of them were still alive.*

They were begging for help, their voices nothing more than whispers and sobs. Some of them were praying. One teacher—Jenny didn't know him by name, but he was an art teacher—was on top of a pile of students, a bald angel picking through his chest with its fingers while the teacher murmured words in another language.

The glass doors of the main entrance were cracked and shattered, but it looked like nobody had managed to make it outside. Were they bolted shut somehow? Had no one at all managed to escape the building?

It was more than Jenny could take. She pictured the initial rush to get out, the panic, the fear . . . only to be trapped in the lobby. How many of them had tried to fight back, only to be swarmed? How many had been trampled to death?

A pressure built up in her stomach and rose so swiftly to her throat, she couldn't stop herself. She retched all the water she'd downed. What was left of her breakfast. Stomach acid. Blood.

Almost in unison, every single angel in the lobby turned their heads at the sound of her vomit splattering the floor, blood and viscera dripping from their mouths. All of them hissed.

Jenny stumbled back as the angels rushed at them, scrambling over the bodies, kicking up blood. They all looked to be tarnished angels, with levels ranging from five to nine.

Susan was screaming something in her ear, but Jenny couldn't hear a thing other than her beating heart. With a cry, she swung her hatchet at the first one that reached them. It was a brunette, its tits swinging, its eyes wide and white, and its face smeared with blood.

Jenny cut through its head, and before it could even hit the floor, she buried her hatchet in the next one's chest.

She didn't even bother pulling out the hatchet. Golden light flashed, and it was back in her hand, then she was swinging again.

# CHAPTER TEN

# AND INTO THE FRAY

**You've defeated Tarnished Angel (Level 6)!
Experience has been awarded.
+10 Energy**

**You've defeated Tarnished Angel (Level 7)!
Experience has been awarded.
+10 Energy**

Her rage had completely taken over, and she swung and swiped and butchered. Flashes of lightning streaked by her, and she knew Susan had her back. The angels screeched and hissed, but they kept tripping over the bodies on the floor. Wherever they placed their hands and feet, they skidded on blood and tumbled over one another. Jenny and Susan stepped back as they had to, both of them screaming and striking as best they could. At least they were all tarnished angels and easy enough to kill now that they'd leveled up and strengthened their stats.

**Leveled Up!
Jenny Huang, Level 8 → Level 9
+2 Stat Points**

**You've defeated Tarnished Angel (Level 9)!
Experience has been awarded.
+10 Energy**

**You've defeated Tarnished Angel (Level 7)!
Experience has been awarded.
+10 Energy**

**You've defeated Tarnished Angel (Level 7)!**
**Experience has been awarded.**
**+10 Energy**


**Leveled Up!**
**Jenny Huang, Level 9 → Level 10**
**+2 Stat Points**


**Ranking Bonus!**
**Stage I → Stage II**
**Congratulations on breaching the first threshold!**
**+30 Stat Points have been awarded.**
**+1 Energy Core has been awarded.**


Her head felt as though it would implode. The thoughts kept coming, and the strain on her muscles kept increasing. She was running on pure adrenaline, her stamina nearly out, and she couldn't even make sense of the ranking bonus message. What was an energy core?

She struck the next angel down, and it landed at her feet, blood gushing from its mouth and the huge gash she'd made in its neck.

**You've defeated Tarnished Angel (Level 8)!**
**Experience has been awarded.**
**+20 Energy**


More energy? They gave more energy now? Before she could process it, another angel grabbed her leg with both hands. With a scream, she swung her hatchet, separating its arms from its shoulders, and it landed on its face, teeth still gnashing. It wriggled toward her as she kicked off its arms, and she ended its life with another thwack, bringing down her hatchet just as she would on firewood.

**You've defeated Tarnished Angel (Level 9)!**
**Experience has been awarded.**
**+20 Energy**


They'd been forced back, down the hallway, away from the stairwell. Jenny was sweating all over underneath her armor. Her breathing was ragged, and there were only split seconds to catch her breath. How many angels had she killed already? How many were left?

She glanced at Susan, whose pink helmet had been knocked slightly. She was bleeding from several scratches on her face, but any angel that got near her fell to the floor after a jolt from her cattle prod. Every once in a while, a bolt of lightning erupted from it and pierced through any angels that seemed like they would crowd Jenny.

And more than once, if an angel got the best of Susan, Jenny would throw her hatchet at it, either killing it outright or cutting into its back and giving Susan an opening to finish it off. Golden light flashed each time Jenny recalled her hatchet.

**You've defeated Tarnished Angel (Level 8)!**
**Experience has been awarded.**
**+20 Energy**

**You've defeated Tarnished Angel (Level 8)!**
**Experience has been awarded.**
**+20 Energy**

That same wild thrill from earlier filled her chest. Was this a second wind? What runners felt when they reached the point of exhaustion but managed to push through? A burst of inner strength . . .

Maybe it was because she'd ranked up. She felt a wave of strength even as her lungs burned with every shallow breath. She felt like she could do this forever. She wanted to kill every single one of these creepy fuckers.

**Bloodlust Ecstasy Bonus!**

A thought emerged in her head, but she couldn't quite focus on it. It came and went, and she had to push an angel back with her hatchet's handle, its teeth having been inches from her face.

**You've defeated Tarnished Angel (Level 7)!**
**Experience has been awarded.**
**+20 Energy**

**You've defeated Tarnished Angel (Level 9)!**
**Experience has been awarded.**
**+20 Energy**

**Leveled Up!**
**Jenny Huang, Level 10 → Level 11**
**+3 Stat Points**

They were nearly at the double doors that would let them into the math wing, where Oliver's class had been. The school library was down that way, too. If they could just get through the doors, it would slow down the angels enough. Maybe they could even get into a classroom and bolt the door. If they could just get a chance to rest and use their stat points.

But before she could yell at Susan, a scream—shrill and loud beyond anything else in the hallway—echoed all over.

Her blood ran cold. She recognized it.

Then there was another. This one was higher pitched and sounded like a group of women screaming at the top of their lungs.

The tarnished angels stopped attacking. Only about a dozen were left now, with many of them dead on the floor. Jenny and Susan stepped back, shaking and trying to steady their breathing as they saw the two figures standing in the lobby. Two wretched angels. They must have come from one of the other halls.

Sweat ran down the side of Jenny's face. She felt cold. She felt like she might throw up again.

The first one was massive, bigger than the one she'd killed earlier. It had a glistening black covering with what looked like tendrils coming off its back. It had muscle, that much was obvious, looking about as big as the senior boys who'd spent all their free time in the weight training room. And it was male, judging by the thing swinging between its legs as it moved on all fours.

**Wretched Angel (Level 26)**

The other one was thinner, covered in light blue and with two antennae sticking out of its head like an insect. Its limbs were long and thin, and it had flowing golden hair. While the bigger male angel was covered completely in that black shine, this one was female, and its front was pale and uncovered.

**Wretched Angel (Level 21)**

Jenny had the odd impression that the two were a couple. And somewhere in the back of her mind, she wondered if these angels had some form of society. If they mated. If they felt love.

Sweat drenched her back, her sides, everything. Her hair was stuck to her face. She was breathing hard, and could see that Susan didn't have much left in her either. She was barely able to stand. Both their armors were worse for wear, with scales missing, scratched up, and dented in other places.

Was this it, then? Was this as far as they went?

The tarnished angels backed away. They'd stopped attacking as soon as the bigger angels had announced their presence with their screaming, so there was clearly a hierarchy. Some distant memory from when she'd studied pack animals came to mind.

She swallowed and adjusted her grip. There was a tremor in her arms and legs that bothered her, so she pulled up her stats, wanting to use up the bonus she'd gotten when she hit level ten. Maybe if she could strengthen herself and boost her stamina and agility, then . . .

She never got the chance.

The female angel dashed forward and was in front of them before they could blink. Susan cried out as it swung her long blue arm and hit her in the face, knocking her back and against a wall while it skidded to a stop a few feet away.

Jenny barely had time to turn before the angel's face was right beside her leg, its teeth sinking into her thigh. Her armor crackled and gave way, and Jenny screamed as it bit straight through and into her leg. She wanted to swing her hatchet; she could bury the edge in the angel's blonde-haired head. But motion in the corner of her eye drew her attention.

The other angel. The large, muscular male was rushing for Susan, galloping on all fours.

"No!" cried Jenny, forcing a step forward, turning her body even with the first angel grabbing her waist as it bit her again.

She flung her hatchet.

It struck the black covering of the angel, clanging as though she'd hit metal, but her hatchet's edge cut through, and the wretched angel howled in pain.

Tendrils wriggling like mad, it turned to face Jenny. She could see straight into its white eyes, and she recognized the look, even though it wasn't human: That was fury. That was complete and utter fury; a look she'd seen on her mother's face one night when Jenny had gotten caught with her stash of weed.

Blood rushed down one of her legs. She felt the hallway spinning as she fell to the floor. The one chewing on her leg had stopped, instead scratching and pulling at her armor where it was broken. As though Jenny were a fruit and the angel was trying to get to her flesh. The creature stared with unblinking white eyes, a fierce scowl on its face as blood and drool ran down its chin.

The bigger one lumbered toward her on all fours, limping slightly with her hatchet sticking out of a shoulder blade.

Jenny covered her face with her arms, trying to turn away, trying to summon her hatchet. And before she knew it, she was struggling with both of them. It was all a blur of black metallic skin, tendrils, the blonde hair of the other angel. Blood. And teeth. She recalled her hatchet with a burst of golden light. She kicked the black one in the balls, and it howled.

But before she could attack with her weapon, the blonde knocked it out of her hand, and Jenny's fingers slid into its mouth.

There was a *crunch*, and she screamed again. Nails clawed her face, and she thought this was it. This was how she died. She screamed again and again till her throat broke, still trying to push them off. Trying and failing to recall her hatchet as one angel chewed on her hand and the other grabbed her by the hair.

Just as the male was about to bite through her exposed neck, a burst of light filled the hall.

Several lights. They cut through the gloom of the Veil, and both angels hissed painfully, scrambling back to cover their eyes, leaving Jenny coughing and limp on the floor.

*Am I dead?*

*Is that . . . holy light?*

*It's so bright . . .*

The last thing she remembered was a figure bending over in front of her. They were just a mass of brown and black, a silhouette in all the light. Was it another angel? A person? Jesus?

"Susan . . ." she tried to say. *Don't touch her. Don't you dare touch her.* But she couldn't speak. She was barely holding on to consciousness. She felt hands go underneath her, and her body came off the ground. Her head lolled back. Everything went black.

# CHAPTER ELEVEN

# ADRIFT

The sound of trees rustling in the wind filled Jenny's ears. It was comforting, soothing . . . so nostalgic and warm that she wanted to cry. Her eyes were shut, and she was drifting. Floating.

*Wait. I don't know how to swim.*

With a shudder, she sucked in a breath and opened her eyes to see a sky full of countless stars. Billions upon billions of them. She'd only ever seen three or four at most growing up in the city. Was this what it was like in the countryside? Away from light pollution? Except they weren't just distant dots of light; she could see each one as though they were right in front of her face.

*Holy shit, stars are beautiful.* Burning balls of flame, and there were so many colors and sizes, each one distinct and unique. They had dark and light patches, and their surfaces seemed to be shifting, as though they were all oceans of energy, with waves and tides and movement. And they had *sound.* She could *hear* the stars. It wasn't trees rustling in the wind she'd heard before; it was the sound of stars.

Everything blurred in and out of focus, and Jenny realized the stars themselves were moving across the night sky. Everything hung in a strange balance. Everything was floating. Just as she was. Tears filled her eyes. There was a beauty to the universe she'd never even fathomed before, a cosmic balance that kept everything in an inexplicable harmony.

And there were so many different kinds of stars.

Gigantic red ones that burned ferociously. Bright yellow ones that filled her with a sense of home. And blue ones . . . These ones seemed to draw her in, as though she could leap out of the water and dive into thrumming blue stars with a splash. They reminded her of Susan.

*Susan. Is she alright? Is she dead too?*

Her thoughts were mush. Her mind felt inside out. She only remembered glimpses of what had happened before she'd passed out. There'd been angels, and blood, and her fingers . . .

Jenny raised her left hand. It was a mangled mess. The only thing she recognized was her thumb. There was no pain, but the odd sensation of trying to move fingers she no longer had made her uneasy.

And as if that wasn't enough, she saw her pale skin in immense detail, just as she could the stars. She could see the little pores, the tiny, nearly invisible hairs. Her bones and the fluid between them. She could hear blood moving through veins, sounding like water in the pipes of her home. She could see individual tiny cells, expanding and retracting and wriggling.

Water trailed down her bare arm. Her armor was gone, and she was drifting completely naked. She raised her other hand, and through this one's fingers, she looked at the stars again, focusing in on an enormous blue one. It felt like it was just out of reach, like she could grab it and squeeze it in her hand and never let go.

*What would it be like to bite into a star?*

*Am I dead?*

*Why am I so hungry?*

The wind picked up, sending chills up and down her body. She was naked and wet and trembling; she wrapped her arms around herself.

*How do I get out of here if I can't swim? And why is the afterlife so cold?*

As if the water sensed her thoughts, it parted slightly. The waves moved gently away from her legs so that her feet lowered. She felt like she was on a reclining chair, except it was made of water, and it was freezing. Her toes touched sand, and she was standing now, the water coming up to her navel. *At least I won't drown.*

Jenny's teeth chattered. Her body trembled. The water was dark and featureless except for the ripples and little waves from her movements. Even though the night sky was full to bursting with stars, the water reflected nothing. She felt like a pale ghost standing in liquid darkness.

In the distance, she could see trees. She was standing in a lake surrounded on all sides by forest. Just as it had been with the stars, she could *see* every individual leaf. She could see the veins on the leaves and holes from insect bites. She could see the scars on the tree bark, the branches that twisted this way and that. Bugs crawled up the roots, rested on the leaves, and hid inside little holes. She could see their reflective exoskeletons, count the many legs, and even their tiny compound eyes.

She didn't recognize any of their species. As curious as she was, the sensory overload was getting to her. She saw too much, could hear too much, and it was so cold now that her body was going numb.

"Hello?" she called out, but her voice was barely a raspy whisper. She tried again, this time shouting at the top of her lungs, but instead of *hello*, her voice morphed into a desperate scream.

As soon as she ran out of breath, the stars blinked. Every single one of them went dark in unison then came back before going dark again. Jenny stumbled back, splashing through the water, feeling sand kicking up with her every step as she turned, staring at the night.

With each blink, the stars moved closer and closer to the center of the sky above her head. They knocked into one another, each collision like balls of liquid fire crashing together. Jenny clapped her hands over her ears. It felt like she was in a movie theater watching footage of the atomic bomb, except the speakers were right next to her ears with the volume set way beyond the max.

She watched as the stars coalesced. They turned into one big wriggling mass, burning white and yellow with flashes of blue and red. The colors churned into one another as the coagulating mass shrunk, glowing brighter and brighter before finally settling into a silver hue. Almost like moonlight, it was the only source of light left in the sky.

It blinked again, and this time, Jenny wasn't sure if that thing had blinked, or if she had. Then it poured like a silver waterfall from the sky and into the dark water where she stood. It didn't disturb the waves. There was no sound, no splashing or splattering; it was graceful and eloquent, and once the big orb of light in the sky had fully drained, the only light left was the shimmering spread of silver in the water.

Jenny didn't know what to make of it. *Is this what it's like to trip on acid? I should've experimented with more than weed.*

She stepped back slowly, watching the silver light spread as the waves began to churn. The light shook and bounced as the water foamed and frothed. There was nothing like this in the Bible. Or the Quran. Or in any of the other scriptures she'd studied. Was this from Hindu mythology, then? Egyptian? One of the Native American beliefs?

From the foaming waters, a figure emerged: a woman dressed in a long flowing gown of silver light. She had no face, no hair. No discernible features other than a humanoid shape. She was the same silver as the light, and she took a step forward, revealing a slender leg. She walked on the surface of the water.

Jenny took another step back. Almost like a reflex, she tried to summon her hatchet, but there was no response. Then, before she could even cry out, the silver figure stood right in front of her.

She stared up at it. It wasn't a woman anymore. Now, it was a man with wider shoulders and a muscular form. It still wore the same gown, and it sat down, cross-legged, turning into a thin little boy. Then a girl. Then once more into a woman. With each transition, the silver of its body melted and wiggled and shifted like gelatinous metal.

It sat on the water's surface, its hands resting on its thighs. Since it had no facial features, Jenny couldn't tell if it was staring or not.

**Welcome, Jenny Huang.**

Jenny's eyes went wide. She knew it was talking to her, but it wasn't speaking. It didn't have lips. And the words appeared in her mind like the notifications from the system thing did.

Suddenly, her memories became clear, rising up quickly and painfully. The angels she'd fought and killed flashed through her head. Their bony bodies, their blank eyes, the blood . . . She saw Susan too, clearly this time. Her blue hair, the matching armor, the pink helmet. Then she remembered the two wretched angels . . . her fingers chewed off. Teeth pressed against her throat.

*That bright light that drove the angels away.*

"What are you?" whispered Jenny, stepping back through the water. "Where am I?"

The figure shifted again, turning into a hunched-over elderly man.

**You are in the seventh world.**
**Unnamed. Unexplored. Unbecoming.**

"What?" she asked, blinking at the silver figure. What was it even talking about? "Am I dead?"

**Death is the third world.**
**This is not Death.**

It shifted again, this time into a short curvy woman. A slit appeared horizontally across the bottom of its face. It turned into lips. It smiled.

**Why do you not fear?**
**I only sense confusion.**

"I've had enough of fear," said Jenny, bitterly. Compared to the angels, this was far less frightening. She clutched her injured hand. *If I'm not dead, and this is some weird, fucked-up dream, then I have to wake up. Right now.* She squeezed as hard as she could, crushing what was left of her fingers, but it didn't hurt at all. She only felt cold.

**I assure you this is not a dream.**

Jenny clenched her teeth. "You can read my thoughts?"

**I am already a part of your thoughts.**

"So, you're the guidance system, then? That thing in my head? What are you?"

**I have been known by many names.**
**Chaos. Entropy. Eve.**

This time, the thought message came with imagery: a whirling mass of stars and planets, everything rushing in elliptical patterns, colliding, separating, condensing to form new stars and new planets and all their many features. Oceans and landmasses, forests and mountains, and underground caverns. Civilizations rose and fell, countless creatures struggling and fighting and dying in the seas, on the lands, and even in the skies.

Storms filled her vision before giving way to the emptiness of space. Then she saw a luscious garden. A male form strolled through it till he reached a female form. They were both naked, and when their bodies touched, the vision turned into blinding light before fading into darkness.

**I am still forming.**
**Naming. Exploring. Becoming.**

Jenny thought her mind would explode. She shut her eyes and squeezed her injured hand, dropping to her knees with a splash. Only her head was above the water.

She had so many questions. What were these numbered worlds? Why did it call itself Eve? What did any of this mean?

**I am of imagination.**
**The source and the manifestation.**

Jenny inhaled loudly through her nose, trying to make sense of it. "So, what is all this? Why am I here? Why are you talking to me? I'm nothing special."

*I just want to live my damn life. Is that too much to ask for?*

The dark water rose up all of a sudden, and Jenny found herself submerged completely, holding her breath and staring at the silver figure. It now had three heads, a woman's body, and the gown was gone. It shone so bright that Jenny had to squint, but it looked like each head had a face now. Three sets of large eyes stared back at her.

**All beings are special.**

CHAPTER TWELVE

# THE LIBRARY

The three-headed entity stretched out a hand and touched Jenny's cheek. She flinched, trying to retreat, but her feet kicked uselessly in the water, and she couldn't move away. It drifted closer in a flurry of bubbles and golden light. Its touch felt warm and soft, with a gentle electronic hum.

She didn't know which of its faces to look at. Each one was distinct. The central face was a woman's. The one on her left seemed manly, and the third one was an indiscriminate child's face. Its body remained female, so Jenny looked into the eyes of the woman's face. It seemed somehow familiar . . .

It looked like her mom! But no, not just her mom. She saw herself in it, too. And then Susan's nose and facial structure also appeared. *Its face is shifting.* There were so many faces. Some she recognized as women in her life, crushes and teachers and neighbors.

She glanced at the other two, turning her head and feeling its fingers still on her cheek. These faces were changing as well, but before she could study them closely, more thoughts pushed against her own.

**Such intense bloodlust . . .**

A shudder went through Jenny, and she closed her eyes, unable to maintain eye contact any longer. She sensed it pulling on her memories as though it had found a piece of string and would yank on it till all her life broke loose. It pushed inside her, reaching deep into the recesses of her mind with all her thoughts in disarray.

Then she felt its body press against her own, energy flowing between them. The water seemed to push her arms up till she was embracing the light, and the light embraced her. Chest against chest, she felt its lips against her own, and she wasn't sure which face she was kissing. She was too afraid to look.

She was melting in the same way all the stars had, and she was grateful for the warmth. The entity reached into her life and wrapped its hands around every nostalgic truth, every one of her deepest yearnings.

**I am evolving, changing, shifting alongside you, Jenny Huang. Becoming more and more ingrained with the fourth world. Catalyzing the forces that translate thought. Taking root in the material world.**

A warm vibration began in her navel. Between her thighs. Against her throat. It felt like she was touching herself. It felt like she was daydreaming. It felt like she was asleep and lost in some wonderful dream.

**The world of pleasure. The world that is yours.
You shall birth me into the fourth world.**

Jenny tried to open her eyes, but found she couldn't. Her body moved on its own, reacting to the touch and throbbing of the system, even as she felt its thoughts. It was shifting still, its slender arms and legs becoming thicker, rougher. It squeezed her tighter, and at first, it felt good. It felt *really* good.

Then she heard a *snap* and felt her ribs buckle. Her lungs burned like she'd inhaled fire. The warm vibration turned furious, as though she'd swallowed a molten stone and someone was trying to dig it out of her stomach with a knife.

She wanted to scream, but the thing was still kissing her. Its tongue found her teeth, and energy kept her from speaking. Was she even breathing now? She still clutched it tightly, even as it squeezed the life out of her. Her bones broke one by one.

**Such untapped capacity . . . Such brilliant creatures . . . Such yearning.**

Jenny struggled as much as she could, screaming silently, trying to make anything move. Her eyes, her toes, anything. Nothing responded. She couldn't even twitch. Her body was no longer hers to command.

**You have only skimmed the surface of your potential.
All that you imagine can be brought to existence.**

Visions filled her thoughts, but they were blurry, as though she were seeing them through a filthy window. She saw Manhattan, recognizing the buildings near her school. She floated high above it. An ugly crater was in the ground, with hundreds of people around it, and at its center, a dirty puddle that had formed in the rain. It seemed to be growing, churning up, as though something or many somethings were struggling underneath the murky surface.

Arms reached out, and Jenny saw the all too familiar bony bodies of the angels. They struggled over one another to crawl out of the water and get to the awaiting crowd.

### Everything and anything.

This time, she saw a golden orb of light. She saw herself, her naked form drifting in dark water with the golden light circling her over and over. Then she saw the shape holding her. The three-headed figure, except now it had large, luminous wings which unfurled till they filled her entire vision with golden light.

The pressure inside Jenny swelled to an unbearable degree. She felt like she'd burst right open, her heart and insides spilling from her chest. Every single one of her muscles strained, until finally, like a rubber band snapping after being stretched to the extreme, everything burst. Darkness engulfed her completely.

### And you, Jenny Huang, are mine.

Jenny opened her eyes and sat up. There was a flash of golden light, then her hatchet was back in her hand. The other hand hurt so much, but then again, everything did. Her ribs ached. Her face stung. Her leg felt like someone had tried to rip it off. She looked around her wildly; the only thought on her mind was Susan.

"Wait, wait!" came an alarmed voice.

Jenny blinked several times, ready to slay anything, but she realized it was a man she recognized standing beside her. Dr. Lee, the honors biology teacher. He hadn't taught her class, but he'd been her lab instructor when she had biology.

### Human (Level 4)

He was a square-faced man with large glasses and a head of dark hair that was usually kept neatly to one side. Now it was about as messy as his outfit, a lab coat covered in splatterings of blood and goggles hanging around his neck. He held up his hands, showing Jenny his palms. She'd been all but ready to bury the hatchet in his face.

She lowered the weapon and clutched her side with her injured hand, not daring to glance down at the bloodied remainder of her fingers. There was a lump in her throat, and she had to swallow several times before she could speak. "Where's Susan?"

Dr. Lee smiled slightly, lowering his arms. "Susan's alright. She's resting with Mrs. Monique. The poor girl sat by your side for nearly an hour before she passed out."

"Mrs. Monique?" repeated Jenny, taking in her surroundings. She was on a long wooden table, and there were bookshelves nearby, moved to barricade the windows.

They were in the school library. And that was when she noticed the light.

It wasn't like the gloomy glow of the void outside. Instead, it was bright and fierce, and it almost stung, but it was *light*, electric and familiar, coming from several corners of the room. Squinting, she realized there were several other people, some of them holding up their phones with the flashlights on while they whispered to each other. She couldn't see their levels, but they were covered in blood, and many of them looked injured.

Dr. Lee stepped closer and explained. They'd heard the screaming and fighting, and a group of them had ventured out with the phones to drive the angels away. Apparently, the creatures were remarkably sensitive to focused light.

Dr. Lee went off on a tangent about the evolutionary development of eyes, expounding on how the angels seemed to lack retinas, but they actually had very faint ones that resembled those of deep-sea creatures. He then shook his head, apologized for rambling, and described how he'd picked Jenny up while another student helped Susan. They'd brought them back to the library, where it was safe.

"Well," he said, shrugging. "Moderately safe. We're lucky Mrs. Monique keeps a collection of external battery packs fully charged for all her students." There was a note of dread in his voice, and she knew he was also wondering what would happen when the batteries ran out.

Mrs. Monique was the young librarian who'd just started at the school that year. She had instantly become everyone's favorite, not only because she was more helpful than the crotchety old librarian had been but also because she was so friendly and welcoming. Even the shiest students opened up to her, and she had turned the library into a warm sanctuary where students could relax and study in peace.

Dr. Lee looked like he was bursting with questions, like he just absolutely had to get to the bottom of this and make some grand discoveries, but Jenny's head was spinning, and she wondered how long she'd been out. The last thing she remembered was the blonde wretched angel chewing on her fingers, the black one with its teeth about to separate her throat from her neck . . .

She bit her lip when she glanced down at her hand. It was covered in cloth now, everything stained with blood.

"Hey," said Dr. Lee, waving his hand in front of her face. "Are you with us?"

She realized he'd been speaking. She sighed, her body trembling. Someone had ripped open what was left of her armor and treated the wounds, and she knew it had been Susan and her healing salves without even asking. She was sure the pain would've completely crushed her otherwise. But every breath she took *ached*. Her ribs were definitely broken. And she was in her tank top, feeling vulnerable and exposed.

Dr. Lee held something. A vial of dark red liquid, much darker than the one she'd made before.

## Major Potion of Recovery

She let go of the hatchet and accepted it. He was still talking, but she wasn't listening. That was the kind of teacher he'd been, even in just the labs, and it was habit by now to tune him out.

Something about the vial felt like Susan, and a part of her wondered if a person's essence was involved in the creation of these things.

The hatchet. The cattle prod. The armor.

Feeling as though she'd pass out again, she removed the stopper with her teeth then downed the entire thing.

The taste of strawberries surprised her. Sweetness bloomed in her mouth, its warmth going down her throat and filling her belly before expanding. She shut her eyes as what was left of the pain faded away. There were *cracks* and *pops* and *snaps* as her ribs adjusted, making her body twitch and convulse.

Her left leg jerked violently, and she balled her good hand into a fist, shaking. The pain in her injured hand faded away to a very dull aching. She left the wrapped clothes on, but she felt like new skin had covered the wounds. She didn't want to look at it, didn't know how to process that the fingers were just gone.

It must have only been a minute or two at most, but it felt as though hours had passed while the potion worked inside her. Finally, she felt the warmth fade away, felt that her body was healed. Her leg didn't hurt anymore, and her ribs felt like they were back in their proper places.

She took a deep breath.

Her stomach lurched, and she thought she might throw up again, but it was a dry heave. Dr. Lee rubbed her back.

She looked at the others in the library, every single face. There were ten other students in the library; one of them she knew by name. Leslie Garcia. None of them were Oliver, and the little bit of hope she'd had to find him here went out like a blown candle.

"I had a look at this after your friend ripped it open," said Dr. Lee, readjusting his glasses. He held up a piece of her armor. The maroon scales were scratched and chipped, but he seemed excited. "It's partially *organic*, but it's unlike anything I've ever seen before. The microscope Mrs. Monique has isn't as strong as the ones in my lab, but I can see *cells. Moving.* It's very much alive."

Jenny took the piece back from him.

*It's alive? I wonder if it shares DNA with me, since I was the one who made it.* But she didn't voice the thought. She didn't want to explain how she'd made it, and she didn't want him to ramble on about this. She had so many questions, and everything Dr. Lee was saying only drummed up more, but they would have to wait.

"Susan?" she asked softly, looking around.

Dr. Lee helped her off the table. After a few steps, she felt like she could walk on her own. She left the hatchet behind and made a bottle of water to drink. That seemed to fascinate Dr. Lee, but he didn't say anything as he led the way to the front desk.

Susan was asleep in the big leather chair, her pink helmet still on, a dark jacket draped over her. Her face was smudged with blood, and seeing her injured leg made Jenny's heart constrict.

She sat cross-legged on the floor beside the chair and placed her hand on Susan's knee. She took a deep breath, but when she exhaled, it threatened to come out as a wail, so she clenched her jaw and forced it down. It wasn't time to cry yet. Her thoughts were on Oliver. What were the chances he was still alive? And what about the whole survival challenge thing? There were about a dozen people in the library . . .

### Human population remaining: 74

She winced as the number appeared. Down to double digits. Were there other groups like this one out there? Other people who'd fought these creatures and grown strong enough to survive? Had anyone else seen that *thing* that she had?

Jenny knew it hadn't been some bizarre dream. She sensed that something had happened while she was out. Something had shifted inside her. That thing . . . that entity . . . whatever it was. She knew it hadn't all been a bizarre dream, and she had a feeling it would have answers.

*Are you there?* Jenny asked the darkness of her mind as she shut her eyes. She was vaguely aware of people moving around her. Someone touched her hand, but she ignored it. She sat motionless, her back straight, her hand still touching Susan.

**Yes, Jenny Huang.**
**I am here.**

*Is my brother still alive?*

# CHAPTER THIRTEEN

# QUESTIONS

*Is my brother still alive?*

Jenny pictured Oliver's face: his curly red hair, his pudgy dimpled cheeks, and his thick glasses. She couldn't imagine how he would've survived, soft as he was. Even though he was in the ninth grade, he was on the shorter side, and Jenny couldn't help but think of him as a baby who followed her around wanting to play games or talk about the latest movies. But if he was dead . . . if he'd died horribly here . . .

Jenny swallowed hard, waiting for the response. It seemed the thing was taking its time, as though it was searching or computing or . . . What if it was stalling? Or what if no time at all was passing, and she was just freaking out?

*C'mon . . . C'mon!* she urged. *Aren't you some kind of all-powerful spirit thing?* Finally, a thought surfaced in her head.

**Oliver Spencer remains an active participant in the Survival Challenge.**

She let out a long breath, feeling like a balloon deflating. Her shoulders relaxed, and she raised her face to the ceiling. The little idiot was still alive. He was still alive!

But that meant Oliver must be fighting, too. Had he figured out how to use the system?

She bit her lip, picturing him dealing with all this. He was just a kid, for God's sake.

Or maybe he was with another group like this one. Maybe he was safe. Only a few people in the library were higher than level one, but they'd at least fought off a few angels and survived. Other people had to have, too, even if the human population had dropped so much. But if people were alive, that meant they were either fighting or had found a safe place.

That's when she realized nobody else here had weapons.

Dr. Lee had studied her armor and found it to be biological, but surely he must have made some of his own? She felt her heart rate quicken. Why didn't they have anything here? What was going on?

No equipment or armor or anything. She looked around, trying to spot anything that might have been created like her hatchet or Susan's prod or Mr. Kim's hammer. There were a few bloodied textbooks scattered on the floor.

Had they really just survived using their bare hands and flashlights? Jenny stared at the others in disbelief. Maybe the system wasn't so intuitive, after all? She'd had to explain to Susan how to use it before, too. It must just seem like a fever dream to people.

She licked her lips. Had Oliver managed to figure it out? They'd heard shouting earlier, and those angels on the second floor had been chasing *someone.* Maybe a few someone's. Poor Mr. Lee had managed to create a hammer; other people must have, too. She concluded that most were too panicked to make sense of anything.

Someone came up and sat beside her. It was Mrs. Monique, the librarian, a dark-skinned woman with her hair braided to one side. There was an ugly gash on her face. Her right eye was covered by a piece of torn cloth taped to her forehead and cheek, but it was still bleeding. Blood ran down that side of her face. Her sweater was torn all over, the soft blue fabric covered in dark stains.

## Human (Level 3)

Mrs. Monique looked like she wanted to say a lot of things. She wasn't that much older than the seniors; she was sweet and caring, and always someone anyone could talk to when they needed a friendly ear. But now, she looked as though she'd crawled through hell.

She touched the remnants of Jenny's armor, what was left of the maroon scales that lined her torso and arms.

"Where did you two get this stuff?" she asked. Her voice was ragged, like she'd been screaming. It was no longer the soft, welcoming tone Jenny was accustomed to hearing every time she walked in during her free periods.

Jenny swallowed the lump in her throat. Her hand slid off Susan's knee, and she took Mrs. Monique's, giving it a squeeze.

"We made it," she replied, finally finding it in her to say something. An overwhelming wave of sadness washed over her, and a part of her knew it was stupid to relax after the system had told her Oliver was alive. But she couldn't help it; that immense relief had opened the floodgates to all her other feelings.

Beneath all of that, there was that throbbing, burning rage at how unfair all of this was. How unfair everything was. She wanted to *kill. Slaughter.*

She ground her teeth even as Mrs. Monique touched her injured hand with a delicate finger. She wanted to get away and question the thing in her head more. Wanted to know if it was in anyone else's head, too.

**I am not.**
**I have chosen you, Jenny Huang.**

The thought came, and she winced.

Mrs. Monique withdrew her hand quickly, apologizing as though she'd hurt Jenny.

But Jenny shook her head. She looked at the glistening blood on the librarian's cheek and pushed the creepy vibes aside. *What could help Mrs. Monique?* she wondered.

The thought nudged her.

**A Minor Potion of Recovery will cost 100 Energy.**
**Sufficient Energy.**

She'd still have 338 energy points remaining. How many angels had she and Susan killed near the lobby? And hadn't the energy received from the angels doubled at some point? Did that have to do with the energy core?

She sensed that the system or that entity was about to respond, the thought lingering at the forefront of her mind, but she needed to help Mrs. Monique first. She'd figure the rest out as soon as she could be alone.

Golden light solidified in Jenny's hand, turning into the familiar glass vial of red liquid as Mrs. Monique stared in awe. Jenny didn't say anything as she pressed it into the woman's hands.

Several of the students wandered over, as well as Dr. Lee, who squatted down and adjusted his glasses, staring hard at the vial.

"This looks like a lighter variant of the vial Mrs. Susan Brown left for you," he noted. When Mrs. Monique looked up at him with a questioning look, he motioned for her to drink it. "It'll heal you."

Mrs. Monique held her phone up to the vial and swirled the liquid. For a second, Jenny wondered if they had any access to the system at all. Couldn't they see what it was? But then one of the students, Leslie Garcia, read out what it was called. "A minor potion of recovery."

Understanding seemed to dawn on Dr. Lee's and Mrs. Monique's faces as if it had just registered for them, too.

As soon as Mrs. Monique pulled out the stopper and downed the vial, she seemed to relax. The jagged scratch marks on her face lightened to a dull pink, and she even peeled off the makeshift eye patch to reveal a gaping dark hole. It glistened with blood and what was left of her eyeball.

But as Jenny watched, even that healed over. The angry red of her socket softened, the blood flow ceasing. Mrs. Monique used her phone's front camera to inspect it, her working eye tearing up.

"Thank you," she whispered, sniffling. "The pain . . ." She wiped her nose, squeezing her one eye shut as she struggled with her words. "It's a lot better now." She took a deep breath to steady herself before reapplying her eye patch and securing the bloodied tape to her skin.

That was when Leslie dropped down and grabbed Jenny's hand. "How did you do that?" she asked, her nasal voice obnoxiously loud as she jutted her nose in Jenny's face.

## Human (Level 1)

Leslie Garcia was a short, brown-skinned junior whom Jenny knew from the physics class they'd both shared last year.

Leslie was ridiculously hot, with thick curls of blonde hair—which Susan swore was dyed—a high forehead, and sharp cheekbones. She was blessed by genetics with curves that made almost every guy in school fawn over her, and she flaunted it too, wearing revealing, tight clothes, and using her charm to finagle her way out of any trouble—or into any situation she wanted to be a part of.

She already had modeling contracts, and everyone knew she got some of the nerdier boys to do her homework for her. And she was dating Kevin, the school's rising football star who'd dumped Susan as soon as Leslie had shown interest in him.

Jenny had hated her instinctively.

She clenched her jaw, almost wanting to summon her hatchet, but she jerked her arm away from Leslie's grip. If she still had fingers on her other hand, she would've peeled Leslie's hand off.

Leslie scowled as though she'd been burned, but sat back on her legs and haughtily shook out her hair. She was wearing a black sweater, zipped up just enough to highlight her lack of a bra. The white T-shirt underneath didn't hide much, and her black leggings were torn strategically in several places to show skin. She wasn't covered in blood. In fact, looking at her, anyone would think it was just an ordinary day at school.

"Well, are you going to tell us or not?"

The girl got on Jenny's absolute last nerve, the sense of entitlement pissing her off like nothing else. Jenny squeezed her wrist, right below the injured hand, and explained as best she could about the guidance system.

*They have access to it, don't they?* Jenny thought when she'd finished explaining. She downed the rest of her water bottle.

**Yes. All participants have access to the guidance system.**

*Then how come they aren't using it?*

**A human's capacity to utilize the guidance system directly relates to their grasp of imagination. Utilization necessitates an open mind and an open heart.**

*But it looked like the others could see things once they were pointed out.*
Leslie was only level one, which meant she hadn't gotten her First Blood bonus yet and had no energy, but she still had seen what the minor potion was and announced its name. Then Dr. Lee and Mrs. Monique had been able to see it too, and they at least had energy they'd be able to use.

She got the sense it was like studying math. It seemed impossible at first, but once the solution was pointed out, the rest fit into place.

Dr. Lee had stayed uncharacteristically quiet while Jenny explained, and he was still quiet. He'd nodded and observed but was now staring intensely at Jenny. She didn't like the way he was looking at her.

**He has tapped into the guidance system.**
**He is beginning to understand. As are the rest of the humans in this room.**

Jenny blinked and looked away, seeing Mrs. Monique talking with Leslie and two other students. Dr. Lee seemed lost in thought.
*So, if you're in my head, how come you know what they're doing?*

**I am connected to the guidance system while it remains confined in the Veil.**

She didn't like the sound of that either. She remembered the three-headed thing she'd met in the water, in that other world, where it had taken her after she'd passed out. She remembered kissing it. Feeling it inside her. Inside her body, inside her thoughts.
*What do I call you? Chaos? Eve?*

**You may call me whatever you wish.**

Jenny remembered the vision of the naked woman strolling toward the naked man. They had to have been the first humans. Had that woman been this thing? Or had this thing become the first human woman?

*Alright then,* she thought. *I'm going to call you Eve.*

**Very well, Jenny Huang.**

*Can you talk like a normal person?*

**I do not talk. I do not speak. I simply am.**

*So that's a no.* Jenny sighed. Still, at least it now had a name. And whatever it was, Eve knew enough of the system to know what others were doing. To know that Oliver was still alive. Maybe it could explain the system to her. Maybe she could use it to figure out a way to end all this.

*How many people are left? Is Oliver still alive? Is he safe?*

**Human population remaining: 72**

**Oliver Spencer remains an active participant in the Survival Challenge. His current location is the western end on the second floor of this structure. There are several human participants with him.**

That was the floor with all those angels.

Her eyes went wide. And he was still alive? With other people?

Hope flared up like a drum inside her chest. But the way Eve talked about the survival challenge unnerved her. And what had that initial message said? *The victor shall be rewarded.*

*Victor . . .* singular.

She inhaled deeply through her nose and hesitated. What if the answer to that question was exactly what she thought it was? But before she could make up her mind to question Eve, she heard a cry from her side. Susan dropped down and wrapped her arms around Jenny so tight, she thought her ribs might break again.

# CHAPTER FOURTEEN

# MORE QUESTIONS

Jenny held Susan tight, even as the pink helmet nearly bashed her in the face. "It's alright," whispered Jenny. She rubbed Susan's back.

Susan pulled away, tears glistening down her cheeks as she scowled. "Alright? How is any of this alright?" She shut her eyes and took a breath. "When I saw them . . . those angels were going to . . ." She shuddered, seeming to choke on the words. "I couldn't do anything to help you. I felt so weak and useless and . . ."

**Human (Level 8)**

Jenny blinked at the thought. Susan hadn't leveled up as much as Jenny had. But, except for the chunk missing from her leg, she looked uninjured. She must've made her own potion or salve, then used up a lot of energy to make that major potion of recovery.

"We should've just gone the other way," Susan continued, wiping her cheeks. "The other stairwell."

"I know," said Jenny. She felt terrible. That stairwell would've taken them right in front of the library, where they would've noticed the lights and found everyone else without having to deal with the angels. Jenny had let the anger get to her head, and they both should've been very much dead by now.

It was exactly what she'd do while gaming. If someone from the other team was being toxic, Jenny would vow vengeance, killing everyone she could get her hands on, no questions asked. But unlike in a game, she wouldn't respawn here. And more importantly, neither would Susan.

"And Oliver . . ." Susan whispered. She bit her lip. "I don't know what we're going to do."

Jenny put her hand on Susan's shoulder. Her blue armor was still intact, except for a dent in the center and a bunch of chipped scales. Jenny didn't know how to tell her about Eve, or what she'd seen in that other world. "We'll figure it out."

Susan just shook her head and grabbed Jenny's other arm to look at the injured hand. She stared at the bloodied cloth wrapped around it, peeled some of it off to inspect the now healed wound, then lowered the hand gently. Her bottom lip wobbled. She opened her mouth to say something, but she didn't make a sound.

Jenny understood exactly how she was feeling. It felt like her chest might collapse with worry and heartache and anxiety. The internal screaming didn't help either. A part of her kept thinking she'd wake up any moment now from this horrible dream.

**Dreams belong to the sixth world. The world of shadows. The world of impossibilities.**

*Why does that sound ominous? Also, you keep talking about these* worlds. *Which one are we in right now?*

**We are in the absence between worlds. It has been known as the Abyss. The Veil. Purgatory.**

Jenny wasn't sure what to do with that information. There was so much to learn about these "worlds" and what they meant, but the most important thing right now was surviving.

*Can you fix Susan's leg? Can you fix my fingers?*

**A Minor Potion of Reconstruction will cost 1000 Energy. Insufficient Energy.**

*Great. So nothing I can do now.* Jenny was vaguely aware of Susan and Mrs. Monique talking, but Jenny couldn't concentrate on what they were saying. Her head swarmed with thoughts and doubts and horrible images, yet, beneath all that, thrummed the desire to kill.

She'd felt that burning anger roar ferociously to life back by the lobby. Now, it was like embers were nestled between her lungs, but every little worry stoked it and agitated it. She knew it would flare up again into a giant blaze. And just thinking about it quickened her breath.

If it weren't for those two wretched angels . . . She recalled their glistening hard skin, their teeth . . . Inside her head, she replayed the sight of the black angel ramming into Susan and knocking her away. Over and over.

Jenny bit the inside of her cheek. If only she'd been stronger.

**You are stronger, Jenny Huang.**

That thought rose up like a cool breeze. She shut her eyes as Eve reminded her of the available stat points from ranking up, the energy core, and the Bloodlust Ecstasy bonus.

Flashes of the fight flickered through each notification.

**You have breached the threshold. You are now Human (Stage II).**
**The Bloodlust Ecstasy Bonus increases experience gained in battle.**
**Energy Cores are awarded with each Stage. It doubles the Energy harvested.**

Leslie Garcia's nasal voice cut through Jenny's focus, and the thoughts drifted away. It seemed like Eve had more to say, and Jenny was bursting with questions, but Leslie squealed with excitement, and Jenny turned to see her doing a little dance.

The girl was fanning herself with her hands as golden light took shape in Dr. Lee's hands. The light extended upward, shining brightly before fading away to reveal what looked like a sword.

Jenny squinted.

**Katana (Tier 1)**

"It's just like the one I have at home," said Dr. Lee breathlessly, adjusting his glasses and studying the long metal blade closely. "It's exactly the same!" He turned it this way and that, the sword glinting as someone turned their flashlight on it. Leslie grabbed his elbow and murmured excitedly while pressing her chest against his arm.

Susan made a sound of disgust, and Mrs. Monique shook her head. But Dr. Lee seemed to like the attention from Leslie. He was showing off his blade and talking about how he'd had the handle custom made and shipped from Japan. Leslie hung on to every single word, keeping her fingers wrapped around his arm.

*Girl, get a hold of yourself!* Jenny couldn't look at them anymore. It seemed like exactly what Leslie would do: try to cozy up to the science teacher, who not only was the sole adult male in the room but now had a capable weapon. That was the same reason Leslie had gone after Susan's ex. Kevin had been on a hot streak in the school football games, rising as a star and becoming popular, and . . .

*None of this matters. This is all so stupid and pointless.*

Jenny stared at her injured hand, trying to wriggle fingers that were no longer there. All she had left were four stumps.

She had to go find Oliver. She had to kill more angels. And she had to get stronger.

Before time ran out.

The flashlights and phones were keeping them safe for now, but how long would the batteries last? Days? Even if they did, the angels would be getting stronger in the meantime. What if they evolved better eyes?

Leslie was still sucking up to Dr. Lee, who let her hold the katana, and she gave him a hug that lasted a little too long. The other students gathered around them, and he explained what he'd done. As though he'd discovered it himself and Jenny hadn't explained it a few moments ago.

Swallowing the desire to throw up again, Jenny stood and walked away, telling Susan, who was reluctant to let go of her arm, that she needed to think. Just then, golden light blossomed in Mrs. Monique's hand, so Susan gave Jenny's arm a squeeze then turned to see what Mrs. Monique was creating while Jenny hugged herself and walked by the library's entrance.

She was careful not to touch her injured hand. Though it no longer hurt, the difference in weight and feeling unnerved her. The entrance had been barricaded with several tables, and beyond the glass, Jenny could see the dark hallway. The tables obscured the view of the floor, but she imagined there were several bodies lying there. For a second, she pictured that blonde wretched angel staring at her through the glass.

Three students guarded the door, phones and flashlights at the ready. They were all covered in blood, sporting several injuries and torn clothes, but had no weapons. Two of them were level two. The third was a redheaded senior boy she recognized but didn't know by name; he was missing an ear, blood matting his hair on that side. He was level three.

He nodded, but she sped away to the other side of the library where she'd woken up, figuring Susan or one of the others would explain the system to them.

The table she'd woken up on was covered in dried blood. Her blood. Bits of armor lay strewn about her hatchet, and she picked up the pieces; it almost reminded her of finding seashell fragments on the beach. Rubbing the pieces between her fingers, the broken bits felt very different from the armor still left on her body. Now they were brittle and dried out, and they crumbled away.

Just as Dr. Lee had said, this stuff was organic. Was she a host for the armor, then? She looked down at the parts she still had on. Her left thigh and chest were exposed, as were bits of her sides and arms. She remembered that first wretched angel she'd fought in front of the boy's bathroom on the third floor. How it bit her arm and cracked the scales. Did wretched angels have armor too? That glistening hard layer on their skin? Was it all somehow similar?

Thinking about that made her head hurt. Jenny stared at a bookshelf; it was half empty, with most of the books scattered on the floor. Less light reached this corner, and she was grateful to be somewhat in the dark.

She took a deep breath, shut her eyes, then pulled up her stats.

**Jenny Huang**
**Human (Stage II - Level 11)**
**Age: 6,801 days**
**Stats:**
**Power: 13**
**Durability: 5**
**Stamina: 5**
**Agility: 5**
**Stat Points Available: 37**
**Energy Available: 338**

Right away, she used seven of her available points, applying them to power to bring that up to an even twenty. That made the numbers look nice and tidy, except now she almost regretted conjuring those water bottles earlier. They'd each cost one energy, and she'd have to make a few more to bring her available points to a multiple of five.

Maybe she could give a few out to the others to even out the number? Why hadn't she already? She should've at least made sure Susan had some. Before she could kick herself further for being shortsighted and selfish, a tremor ran through her body in the form of a violent shudder.

"Fuck," she gasped. Jolts raced up and down her spine before shooting into her limbs. The muscles of her arms and legs contracted and throbbed before finally relaxing. She felt like she'd just completed a full circuit of training in the school gym, except her gym teacher wasn't around to shout at her for slacking off. Mrs. Reid was probably dead.

*No point in thinking about that right now.* She still had thirty points left to use, and three remaining stats that she'd been neglecting.

She put five points into durability, bringing it up to ten. There wasn't a jolt of energy this time. Instead, it felt like someone had run a feather over her chest, trying to tickle her. Clawing off bits of her armor, she pulled on her undershirt to look. Nothing seemed different.

She poked herself then gasped again, softly this time. Her skin still felt soft, but it took considerably more force to press her fingernail into it. She barely felt it when she scratched herself. *Okay, that's kind of cool.* She felt like she could tank a punch. Like a movie star who could take a hit and not even flinch. *Though I'd probably need a lot more points to pull that off.*

She wondered about stamina and agility. If she got stuck facing down a bunch of angels, stamina would be crucial, but agility would be important too. Those wretched angels had closed the distance so quickly, they'd attacked before Jenny could make sense of what was happening. She needed to be quicker, and she needed to last longer. With twenty-five points left, what was the best way to split them?

*Eve. What should I do?*

**Trust your instincts.**

*Well, that's very helpful.* Jenny massaged the palm of her injured hand, looking over her stats again. *Wait,* she thought, unable to suppress her smile. *I'm being stupid.* She put five more points into durability, then split the remaining twenty evenly with stamina and agility.

**Jenny Huang**
**Human (Stage II - Level 11)**
**Age: 6,801 days**
**Stats:**
**Power: 20**
**Durability: 15**
**Stamina: 15**
**Agility: 15**
**Stat Points Available: 0**
**Energy Available: 338**

She'd applied them so quickly that they took effect all at once, that tingling sensation returning manyfold, like someone had lit a match inside her chest. The feeling surged through her as her body convulsed, shoulders twitching and legs jerking. It almost looked like she was doing some strange New Age dance. Either that or that she was having a mental breakdown.

"Gah!" she spat, bending over and hugging herself, making a mental note to apply stat points gradually in the future. She was drenched in sweat and breathing hard like she'd run a marathon.

Except, she felt like she could run another *ten* marathons. Her heart raced as she straightened up, marveling at the difference in her body. She felt lighter on her feet, as though she might jump straight through the ceiling at any given moment. Her tummy seemed flatter, so she pressed her hand against it and realized she had abs. *I have abs!*

She yanked her undershirt up and looked at them, turning so that they caught the light. Her abs were so well defined and flat and . . . She wanted to be excited. This was something she'd always wanted, to be like those models she saw online. But this didn't feel sexy—it was tactical. This was all for survival. This was all to reach Oliver and keep him and Susan safe. This was so she didn't die the next time she ran into a strong angel.

*Alright, Eve.*

*What the hell does "Human (Stage II)" mean?*

# CHAPTER FIFTEEN

# HUMAN (STAGE II)

*What the hell does "Human (Stage II)" mean?*

**Growth presents in stages. Thus far, you have experienced being an embryo, infant, child, and adolescent. These are known as natural stages. Insect inhabitants of your world undergo metamorphosis. Reptiles shed their skin. Plant life changes drastically from seed to sapling to flowering tree.**

Jenny saw a caterpillar construct a chrysalis, then day and night blurred by as the leaf it clung to trembled in the wind. Finally, it emerged, tearing apart its old life and spreading glistening wings. She saw tadpoles hatch and squirm away before growing legs and leaping out of a pond. She saw snakes wriggling out of their skins, growing larger and changing their colors.

Seeds sprouted in the darkness. Little green plants pushed to the surface then grew into towering trees reaching for the sun.

She saw herself as a baby, nursing from her mother. They lived in a fancy house—Jenny's grandparent's estate. Then they moved into a shoddy apartment with one room. Her childhood flashed by: Crying out of hunger. Getting slapped. Screamed at. Hiding under the bed to avoid her mother. Grades. Anxiety. Extra homework. Praying desperately to God for happiness.

Middle school and high school blurred into a terrible frenzy: getting bullied, guys hitting on her and making racist jokes, Becky Smith punching her in the face for not handing over her lunch money. She saw the blood she'd found between her legs one morning, how she didn't scream; she'd just done the laundry and found out later that an angel hadn't impregnated her while she slept.

She saw her first kiss, the first time she touched herself, and the first time she hugged Susan and was struck by a dizzying wave of want. She shuddered as Eve continued.

**The angels evolve as well. You have seen that firsthand.**

*Yeah*, she thought. *Don't need visuals for that. Am I going to get weird, scaly skin?* She pictured herself covered in an exoskeleton from head to toe, then she remembered that female wretched angels had no frontal coverage and got grossed out. She didn't want to think about their mating habits, though Dr. Lee would probably find it fascinating.

**The guidance system allows for growth beyond the natural stages. Preternatural stages present uniquely for each individual, evolving from some combination of your subconscious, imagination, and what the system deems fit.**
**A stage two human's body begins to transform. As your mental and physical prowess advance, you now have access to your first awakened skill.**

*My first skill?* She held her breath, studying her hatchet. Once this thing had become tier two, she'd been able to recall it at will. Would it be a skill like that? What would hers even be?

**Your love of history proves helpful.**

Before Jenny could ask what Eve meant, her mind flooded with more imagery: She saw broad-shouldered, muscular warriors towering over armies. One of them grabbed a bolt of lightning from the sky and hurled it with a thunderous roar. She saw a woman, draped in a beautiful shimmering gown, leaping from cloud to cloud and pulling a tidal wave behind her.

She saw another figure completely enshrouded in flames so that all she could see was a shadow of a silhouette. The flames rose up suddenly, blocking out the entire vision and leaving Jenny breathless and clutching her chest.

*The gods? The people of stories and legends? Eve? They're all real?*

**Yes.**

Excitement rushed through her. Her heart continued to pound, and she paced back and forth. Questions surfaced faster than she could even properly word them;

papers she'd written, all the books on mythology from around the world she'd devoured. But she shoved her overflowing thoughts down.

*Not yet. But I'm going to ask you a billion things when this is all over, okay?* She stopped pacing and, clutching her injured hand, she focused on Skills the way she'd focused on Stats.

### Ignite (Tier 1)
**Exhale a flame generated within. Draws on Stamina
and requires sufficient oxygen.**

*Holy . . .* Jenny kept that thought in focus, reading it over and over again. *Eve? I can breathe* fire?!

**Evidently.
However, I do not recommend activating the skill at this present location.**

Smoke rose from between her teeth as she willed herself to stop. Feeling sheepish, she grinned and wiped her mouth. Heat singed the back of her throat; it felt like inhaling too strongly from a vape pen.

She coughed once, trying to clear it, but that only led to a fit of coughing, and she needed a break to catch her breath. Blinking away tears, she made a mental note to be more careful with it.

The warmth in her chest faded, but she was too excited to stand still. She paced faster and faster, back and forth, in front of the table.

*I can breathe fucking fire. Like a dragon! What the actual fuck.*

**At level thirty, you will breach the next threshold and unlock more skills. They will be as much a surprise to you as they are to me.**

Somehow, she couldn't imagine Eve being surprised. Eve was just a voice in her head, the same way the system presented itself, but she couldn't help but picture the three-headed entity she'd met.

She glanced down at her ruined fingers. *I can breathe fire because of my temper, right? That's what the system sees in me?* Trying to use Ignite brought about that same furious feeling she'd had before. The unrelenting rage, the blinding desire to kill every single one of these angels. After all, that was why she had the Bloodlust Ecstasy bonus.

**It seems fire is your attribute, Jenny Huang. Fire is not solely anger and fury. Fire is also warmth. Safety. Life.**

But she wasn't convinced. *Why did you even choose me? Why do I have to "birth" you into my world? Can't you do it yourself?* Jenny pictured her belly swollen and purple and veiny, screaming as she pushed out a three-headed baby. She'd seen enough child-birthing videos to know she never wanted to do that in her life.

**All living beings have the potential for greatness. But not all beings can reach that potential.**

*But I'm not . . .* she started, then remembered what Eve had said before: All beings are special.

**You forced the guidance system to follow your will. You halved the potion of recovery when Susan Brown was injured and you lacked sufficient energy. You halved a construct beyond your understanding. You bent reality where others would have faltered. Where many have failed. You are more powerful than you allow yourself to accept.**
**The capacity for greatness is inherent to all beings. For great benignity or great malevolence. Yet, countless billions choose not to act. It is difficult, and increasingly so, for one to express their will and push the boundaries of comfort. Quick gratification has disfigured the paths of accomplishment.**
**What you do is what you are. And what you are is what you seek.**
**Choice was my gift to all living-kind.**

Jenny covered her face with her good hand. For some reason, she wanted to cry. She wanted to sob and wretch and scream her lungs out. All her life, she'd done what she was told, what was expected of her. Never once had anyone pushed her to be herself.

*So I can actually become anything? Like those old gods? Is that why you showed them to me? Were those gods a part of this?*

**All that you imagine can be brought to existence.**
**The ones you know as gods and legends were former victors of the Survival Challenge.**

Jenny's thoughts swam with everything Eve had explained. Her rational brain screamed that none of this could be real. It was more like something she'd fantasize about while trying to fall asleep, giving herself powers and ravaging the world and flying.

*Wait. Can one of these skills let me fly?*

**That remains to be seen.**

Jenny rubbed her throat, wishing she could test Ignite out already. She heard footsteps approaching.

"You look different." Susan limped toward her. She'd taken off her helmet and was holding it by the straps, her cattle prod in her other hand. She set both things down on the table, briefly touched Jenny's hatchet, then turned.

"What do you mean?" asked Jenny.

Already out of breath, Susan pulled herself onto the table and sat with her feet dangling. Her sneakers were stained dark brown with blood. Her tights were torn in several places, especially so around the chunk of missing flesh where her calf should've been. She eyed Jenny up and down.

"I've never seen you stand so straight. You're usually more like this." She pulled her shoulders forward and arched her back slightly, sticking out her bottom lip.

Jenny couldn't suppress the chuckle; she shook her head. She'd always been teased about slouching and poor posture—by her mom, by her teachers, and even by Susan. It was something she did out of habit, but now, she wondered if it was because she'd always tried to make herself smaller. To hide. To not be noticed.

"But also your face," Susan continued. She stared intently at Jenny. "Your cheeks, your eyes . . . I don't know. You look, like, more intense. Like you've seen some shit."

"I think we've both seen enough shit," replied Jenny, stepping closer to Susan. She looked ragged. Her blue hair had come slightly loose and poked out every which way. The usual glow of her skin was now lifeless and pasty. Even her lips looked less plump, though Jenny still wanted to kiss her for all she was worth.

"You look bigger, too. Not like . . . You know what I mean." Susan touched Jenny's arm. "Like you have more muscle."

Susan's touch might as well have been the shock of her cattle prod. In the midst of all this hell, Susan's touch felt like . . . Jenny didn't know how to explain it. It was warm and safe and the only thing she wanted.

"I got a bunch of stat points." Jenny explained everything she'd learned about the second stage. She explained evolving and how she'd used her points, but left out that Eve was inside her head, showing her things, wanting to be birthed.

Susan listened, wide eyed. Her fingers slid down Jenny's arm, over the armor, until she found her hand and held it.

After explaining, Jenny fell quiet. She licked her lips, happy to be holding Susan's hand like this, to be so close to her, listening to her breathing.

The first words out of Susan's mouth were, "So you can breathe fire now?"

"Yeah," she replied with a half smile. Discussing this out loud was surreal, not at all like talking to Eve.

The excitement faded quickly from Susan's face. "You're planning on going alone, aren't you?" She let go of Jenny's hand, a hurt look on her face.

For a second, Jenny thought Susan would cry, and her heart dropped. How do you tell your best friend you have to leave them behind? She knew they were both thinking about Susan's injured leg. That it would slow them down. It would get them killed. But she'd be safe here with the others and the lights.

Susan grabbed her knees, her knuckles whitening as she squeezed, her entire body trembling. She struggled to say something, but all she managed was a sob. Tears flowed freely down her cheeks. "I'm sorry," she managed to choke out.

"No," whispered Jenny. There were so many things she wanted to say, but her heart tightened and the flurry of emotion threatened to buckle her. She wrapped her arms tight around Susan; so tight that Susan's armor dug into Jenny's chest, and if it weren't for her increased durability, it would've hurt. She wished it hurt.

Susan squeezed her back with her legs and arms. They held each other, Jenny stroking Susan's hair as she sobbed.

"It's going to be alright," whispered Jenny. She blinked away tears and pressed her cheek to Susan's blue hair. "We're going to figure this shit out. It's just another game we're gonna get so good at that nobody's gonna wanna queue up against us."

That made Susan laugh, but it was the weak sort of laugh someone did when they were falling apart. After that, they didn't say anything for a while. Jenny focused on the heat of Susan's body, the faint scent of strawberries in her hair. She thought about prom again, about her dumb crush, and how far away and childish all that seemed. With the energy core, she promised herself she'd gather enough for a minor potion of reconstruction for Susan's leg.

"You'll need new armor," said Susan finally. She wiped her eyes then touched the bits of ruined scales still stuck to Jenny's ribs. "And what about your hand?"

"I've got some ideas," she replied. She shut her eyes. She'd need something more substantial than light armor this time. While it'd worked against that first wretched angel by the boy's bathroom, the other two they'd fought near the lobby had made short work of it.

**Energy remaining: 338**

Then again, she now had enough energy to create that assault rifle she'd first thought of.

**An Assault Rifle will cost 300 Energy. Additional Energy
will be required for ammunition.
Sufficient Energy.**

She almost went through with it, picturing herself gunning angels down and clearing out the halls, but she hesitated. Her armor was falling apart, and she wouldn't have enough energy for both a gun *and* new armor. On top of that, bullets would cost even more energy.

Though she supposed with the rifle, she might not need armor. And wouldn't she be able to kill angels fast enough to replenish her energy?

Jenny inhaled deeply through her nose as Susan gently grabbed her injured hand. She removed the makeshift bandages.

Which led to another thought. Jenny wasn't sure if she could use the gun one-handed. She might be able to prop it on that arm, but what if she was overrun? What if the wretched angels rushed her before she could even fire a shot? What if there were stronger things out there?

The more she thought about it, the less tempting a gun seemed. Her hatchet had served her well, plus its tier two ability let her use it like a ranged weapon. What would happen at tier three?

Besides, she could breathe fire. Just thinking about that shot a jolt of curious excitement up her spine. She concluded that armor was the way to go for now. The energy core she'd received would help her get more energy soon enough. But what kind of armor should she make?

**Allow me.**

Hearing Susan gasp, she opened her eyes as golden light enveloped her. It shone brightly, strands twisting in a vortex around her torso and arms. Her old armor crumbled away. For a moment, she stood between Susan's legs in her underwear, and she felt heat rise to her face as she glanced to the side.

Then the golden strands settled over her skin in repeated layers. The light took shape, coiling around her arms, chest, and even neck. Red scales blossomed up and down her armor, forming a second layer of protection. Each scale reminded her of a flower petal, and she knew without touching them that they were harder than the ones that had covered her light armor.

**Medium Armor**

She shuddered as the light faded. The new armor felt snug, the scales over her legs a darker shade than the bright red covering her torso and arms.

**Energy remaining: 168**

"That," said Susan, reaching out to stroke Jenny's chest where the armor protruded slightly with a thicker layer of scales, "looks kinda sick."

Before Jenny could check herself out fully, golden light shone again. This time, it coagulated around her left wrist—her injured hand. The light stretched and formed a bracelet that hugged the red scales of her armor. From the bracelet, the light seemed to unfurl into a large disc.

## Shield (Tier 1)

It was a round metal circle, dark red to match her armor, and roughly the length of her arm. The shield could cover her upper body completely. Moving her arm around, she held it over their heads like an umbrella. Did it feel so light because she'd increased her power stat?

More importantly, did she now have to lug this thing around?

As if in response to her question, it shimmered. In the blink of an eye, the metal turned into golden strands of light then vanished into the bracelet. It shone brightly for a moment before fading away.

Looking at the stumps of her fingers, Jenny realized the shield was perfect.

# CHAPTER SIXTEEN

# I'LL BE RIGHT BACK

Jenny waited by the entrance of the library with Susan. Her hatchet rested on the floor, and she had her shield retracted.

Two students worked on removing the tables and chairs barricading the glass doors. They moved quietly and slowly so as not to make any loud noises and alert any angels that might be nearby. Three others stood with their phones and flashlights at the ready.

Jenny's new armor glinted in the lights, the vibrant red scales shining. It was a much brighter red than the old armor had been, but noticeably heavier, though her increased stats enabled her to carry the weight without issue.

She thanked Eve, though the sensation of another entity working her imagination was bizarre. It was strangely intimate, like having someone else's fingers in her mouth, except that finger could stir her thoughts and poke her from the inside. She wondered if there was a motive behind Eve's assistance.

Did Eve just want to keep her alive? That image of her swollen belly rippling as she screamed her head off came to mind. Was she just a vessel for Eve's birth? And why hadn't it helped when she'd asked for advice applying her stat points?

**Stats are a representation of life force. Your choosing of them is inherent to free will. That cannot be interfered with.**
**With equipment and creation, I am happy to assist. But it is your intention, your spirit, that makes the ultimate decisions.**

*So, in a fight, you're pretty much useless.* Jenny squared her shoulders, trying not to focus on how alone she'd be out there.

Susan had explained to the others what Jenny's plan was: move quickly, find Oliver and whomever he was with, and bring them back here. Dr. Lee had questioned how Jenny knew Oliver was alive, and she'd explained it away as something that cost energy. He hadn't looked convinced but didn't press it.

Mrs. Monique wished Jenny luck, trying to smile, but it came out more like a grimace. She'd made herself a long wooden spear with a sharp golden tip. Dark chain mail covered her torso and arms. The students who had enough energy had copied her armor, holding knives, swords, and spears.

None of them wanted to go with Jenny. She'd had little hope of any volunteers, but she figured this was for the best. The more people who remained here, the safer the library would be. Susan would be safe. Besides, it also meant she could go all out. Nobody to worry about. Nobody to slow her down. *And no witnesses*, she thought with grim amusement. Nobody else would find out she could breathe fire. Nobody else would know about her Bloodlust Ecstasy bonus.

As terrified as she was about facing the angels again, Jenny couldn't wait to see exactly what she was capable of now.

*Oh wow*, she thought. *Is this what self-confidence feels like? Like, I know I might fail and get torn apart, but also, I feel like I can do this. I've never really felt this way before.*

Eve didn't respond. Jenny rubbed her injured hand, thinking about what Susan had said earlier. That she'd changed. That she was changing. Was she changing for the better? On one hand, more confidence had to be a good thing. But on the other . . . she trembled with fury and bloodlust.

Leslie hovered nearby while Dr. Lee inspected Jenny's new protection, annoyed that he was so focused on Jenny. He held up a piece of her old armor, comparing the scales, then adjusted his glasses. "I wish I could borrow some of your new scales to analyze them. And why specifically scales? It looks reptilian."

Before Jenny could respond, he voiced another question. This one was a request. He wanted to bring in a few specimens; at least that's what he called them. They both knew he meant the angel corpses. He wanted to study them, explaining he had enough energy to make rudimentary autopsy instruments and proposing that cutting one open might lead to vital discoveries.

Everyone stared at him like he was mad. Even Leslie seemed unnerved. Jenny didn't care. She'd already cut a bunch of them down and agreed with the science teacher.

After a heavy pause, Mrs. Monique sighed and nodded. "The more we know, the better. We know about their sensitive eyes, but they might have more weaknesses."

Jenny didn't want to touch those angels any more than she had to, but if there was something more to those creatures, then she wanted to know. Though she had a sneaking suspicion that Eve could answer those questions easily, instinct told her to keep that a secret. Or maybe it was Eve manipulating her subconscious.

The barricade was nearly cleared. Only one table remained, then the doors would open, and Jenny would be out there again.

"Please be careful," whispered Susan. Her voice was quiet and small, not at all like the confident shot caller she was in video games. She seemed tired and hurt and . . . Jenny couldn't bear to see her like this.

"I'll be right back," Jenny replied, speaking softly and squeezing Susan's hand.

"Yeah, but I won't be there to watch your back. What if something happens? What if you get hurt? And none of these guys wanna go with you." She let out a frustrated sigh and screwed up her face. Jenny couldn't tell if she was about to cry or curse someone out, but then she rushed toward the librarian's desk.

Susan rummaged around for something as Mrs. Monique went over to help, then returned with her pink helmet, a flashlight, and a roll of duct tape. Yanking out a strip of tape, she used her teeth to tear it, then, as Mrs. Monique held everything in place, Susan secured the flashlight to the top of the helmet. She added a few more strips, and once she was satisfied it would hold, she brought it back to Jenny.

"You're taking this," she said firmly, setting it on Jenny's head. She brushed away loose strands of hair before pushing the helmet down. "Just click the button up top." She did it a few times as the light clicked on and off.

Jenny just looked into Susan's eyes, at the determined look on her face as she snapped the straps together under Jenny's chin.

"Okay," exhaled Susan. Her bottom lip quivered. Their noses nearly touched, and Jenny could feel the warmth radiating off her.

"Thank you," said Jenny. She shut her eyes. She thought about leaning forward and kissing Susan, pressing her lips to hers. *Just do it. Do it. You might never get the chance again.*

Somehow, this was more terrifying than having a wretched angel's teeth against her throat.

"If you're not back in an hour, I'll . . ." Susan placed her palm against Jenny's cheek. "I'm gonna come looking for you." Then she wrapped her arms around Jenny, their armor clinking, and they held each other tight.

*Eve. Please tell me if anything happens to her.*

**I will alert you of any changes in Susan Brown's status.**

Jenny swallowed the lump in her throat and asked the question she'd been dreading. *This stupid survival challenge. I need to know.*

**The Challenge ends when one human participant remains.**

She didn't think or say anything after that. She let go of Susan, who wiped away her tears and picked up Jenny's hatchet for her.

The tables now cleared, the metallic stench of blood rushed into the library. Mrs. Monique stood at the entrance, holding her phone's flashlight and carrying her spear. Dr. Lee joined her with Leslie a few paces behind him. She shook so hard that the light from her phone bounced all over the place.

Jenny's newfound confidence was fading. If only one person could emerge from this, she knew she'd slit her own throat in a heartbeat if it meant either Susan or Oliver would be the victor. But how could she choose between them? And what about everyone else?

On top of that, would Eve let her? Could Eve stop her?

And Eve already knew her thoughts. This was something to figure out later.

Taking a deep breath, she brought forth her shield, which erupted from the bracelet around her left arm in a flash of golden light before forming its circular shape. Dr. Lee shot her a curious glance, but it was too late for any more questions.

"If there's a fight, make sure they don't scare the angels away with the light once they're all safely inside," Jenny whispered to Susan, who shook her head in disbelief, but before she could respond, Jenny tapped her pink helmet with her hatchet. "Trust me."

She then stepped into the hall, trying to appear brave and confident so Susan wouldn't worry, knowing fully well that was all Susan would do until she got back. And she firmly intended on making it back.

In the hall, the unmistakable sounds of chewing and retching echoed from wall to wall. The lobby was up the hall to her left. A few feet away, to her right, was the metal door leading to the stairwell they'd initially planned on taking down from the third floor. If they'd taken it, they would've come right upon the library, seen the lights, and been safe.

If they'd taken it, Jenny never would've reached the second stage or interacted with Eve.

Something hissed nearby. The flashlights moved, illuminating the dozen or so bodies that lined the hall. One of them was moving.

### Tarnished Angel (Level 9)

It was one of the angels she'd struck down earlier, a gray-haired female with dark skin. Jenny had cut off its arm at the shoulder then buried her hatchet in its hip. Its legs weren't working, and it dragged itself forward, smeared blood marking its path like the trail of a snail. Had it come all this way seeking revenge? This one was close to level ten, too. Then it would become a wretched angel.

Dr. Lee whispered excitedly about grabbing that one, but Jenny wasn't listening. She squatted down beside it, keeping her shield between them, and stared into the angel's empty eyes.

*Kill it,* was her first impulse. She wanted revenge. Wanted to smash its head in, even though the sight of it was gut wrenching. The tarnished angels looked too much like famine victims; she'd seen enough footage and photographs in her history classes: the bones jutting out of stretched skin, the cheeks so sunken that she could see the shape of its skull. Blood spurted out from between its teeth as it hissed again.

*Eve. Can angels feel pain?*

**All beings experience suffering.**

Jenny thought about the two wretched angels. The ones that seemed like a couple.

*Do they love?*

**All beings experience suffering.**

The angel retched and dribbled, smashing its hand against Jenny's shield. Burning hot rage filled her chest so suddenly that she couldn't stop herself. She lifted her shield then brought it down hard on the angel's fingers, cutting right through and making a loud clang against the floor.

Dr. Lee shouted behind her, but it was too late. The angel let out a hideous wail of pain that filled the hallway, crying at the top of its lungs, and then there was more hissing. Too much hissing for one creature.

Several angels appeared at the end of the hall, scurrying toward Jenny on all fours. All the lights flicked in that direction right away, and the angels screeched in agony as they scrambled to cover their faces and fell forward, tripping over one another in a flurry of bony limbs.

Jenny licked her lips. She'd done something stupid again, but now, it was time to fight. She waved with her hatchet for the others to grab the angel and get back in the library.

"Reckless," whispered Dr. Lee through his teeth as he grabbed the struggling creature by its hair. It smacked his arm and leg, but without any fingers, all it did was spray blood everywhere. He dragged it back through the glass doors.

Mrs. Monique hesitated, her light still shining at the angels covering their faces and screeching. The others were already inside, and as soon as she left, the direct light would be gone too, and the angels would attack.

"It's alright," said Jenny. She glanced over at Susan, who was gripping her cattle prod, looking as though she'd rush out and join the fight. Jenny shook her head. "It'll be alright."

It was Leslie who finally grabbed Mrs. Monique's hand and urged her back inside. The door shut with a clang, and she heard them dragging tables over. There was no need to be quiet and careful now. The angels were already here.

With the light gone, the creatures regrouped.

Jenny bent her knees slightly, trying for a better stance. She'd never studied martial arts, even though she'd wanted to, but she'd seen enough movies to know to lower her center of gravity. The library was to her left, the angels straight ahead, and if she had to, she could retreat up the stairwell behind. She also had the flashlight on her helmet.

Her heart wasn't pounding this time. Instead, it was slow and even. She knew she could do this. Her body knew she could do this. They were just tarnished angels, and she was so much stronger now.

With a wild cry, she stomped forward on her right foot and hurled her hatchet with as much force as she could muster. The air rippled as the hatchet spun down the hall, a dark blur. The first angel didn't even stand a chance.

Its head erupted in a cloud of blood and bone as the hatchet cut right through. Before its body hit the floor, the weapon struck the next angel on the forehead, the sharp edge right between its eyes, handle sticking straight up into the air. This angel's head snapped back as its body continued moving forward, propelled by its arms.

For a moment, it was horizontal midair. Then, it landed on its back, twitched twice, and died, blood spurting out like a geyser from the wound.

**You've defeated Tarnished Angel (Level 8)!**
**Experience has been awarded.**
**+20 Energy**

**You've defeated Tarnished Angel (Level 9)!**
**Experience has been awarded.**
**+20 Energy**

"Jesus Christ," she whispered. Golden light flashed, and her hatchet returned to her hand, blood dripping off its metal face. The other angels clambered over the dead, completely unfazed, hissing and screeching and coming for her.

# CHAPTER SEVENTEEN

# SAC

Five angels scrambled down the hallway, each one hissing and desperately trying to be the first to bite into her. A few tripped over the two she'd just killed. Only a few hours ago, she would've been terrified, frozen to the spot while awaiting her certain demise. Now, excitement coursed through her.

After all, she could throw her hatchet with enough force to burst heads open. She was much stronger now. But that throw took a significant amount of stamina, and her arm throbbed from the effort, so she decided it might be best to reign it back. These were only tarnished angels, and she didn't want to tire herself out before she even got to Oliver.

Throwing her hatchet again, this time with less force, Jenny caught an angel on the shoulder. The force of the blow sent it spinning backward, its long red hair flicking through the air. She recalled her weapon and raised her shield to block the first angel to reach her, a brown-skinned male. It was already missing an eye, and blood covered that side of its face.

It thumped hard against the shield, but Jenny held her ground as it tried to break through; her increased power made this almost too easy. She thrust forward, taking a step and knocking the one-eyed angel away. It toppled over the one behind it, and Jenny didn't give them a chance to recover.

She swung her hatchet once, then again backhanded, swiftly cutting through their throats before striking another one with her shield, slamming it back against a wall.

She heard the two on the floor screaming, gurgling, and as the notifications of their deaths appeared in her head, she swung around and lodged her weapon into the chest of one more.

**You've defeated Tarnished Angel (Level 7)!**
**Experience has been awarded.**
**+20 Energy**

**You've defeated Tarnished Angel (Level 6)!**
**Experience has been awarded.**
**+20 Energy**

She let go of her hatchet, and that angel sank to its knees, clutching the handle and trying to yank it out with its skinny arms. Light flashed, the weapon returned to her hand, and blood spurted out of the creature's chest. It wheezed, staring at Jenny with lifeless eyes, making a feeble attempt to grab her leg.

Jenny kicked it hard in the face. Its teeth gave way to her boot, its nose crumpled, and its head struck the wall, the back of its skull bursting open and splattering everything with blood.

**You've defeated Tarnished Angel (Level 8)!**
**Experience has been awarded.**
**+20 Energy**

Two angels remained—the pale, redheaded female angel she'd struck on the shoulder before, and the one she'd slammed with her shield. This one was male, writhing on the floor but not moving much more.

The female was clutching its arm. Only a few tendons of muscle held it to its shoulder, and as the angel tried to move, its arm bent disgustingly, like a loose tooth that was nearly ready to fall off, hanging on by the tiniest bit of flesh. The angel couldn't figure out how to balance without its second arm to lean on, and it hissed furiously at Jenny. Its long red hair covered its face. It was almost beautiful. Almost.

Jenny brought her hatchet down on its head, spraying everything around them with blood as the angel convulsed violently before going limp.

**You've defeated Tarnished Angel (Level 7)!**
**Experience has been awarded.**
**+20 Energy**

Jenny raised her hatchet, still buried in the angel's head so that it rose to its knees, blood streaming down its red hair. Even dead, it seemed to be glaring at her. Shoving the body away with her shield, she pulled her hatchet out of its skull, splattering herself with even more blood.

The shield was proving to be more than useful. None of the angels had even landed a scratch on her, and on top of that, she could use it offensively. That and her increased power more than made up for her missing fingers. She couldn't swing with both arms anymore, but she could still do lethal damage.

The final angel had been the one she'd struck away with the shield, and now it lay on the ground, its head bent at an angle. It looked like its neck was broken. The angel blinked and bared its teeth, but no sound came from its throat. Its fingers twitched, its legs jerked, and she saw the rise and fall of its thin chest, but the creature was definitely paralyzed.

Jenny wiped her brow with the back of her hand, listening for any more. There was nothing else. It was just her and the paralyzed angel. She took several deep breaths, nearly gagging at the stench of blood and death, then squatted down beside it. She studied it like how she imagined Dr. Lee would.

Light skinned with long brown hair, it had shriveled male genitalia. Its legs were so thin they almost looked like chicken feet. Skin wrapped around bone. How could they even balance like that? Was that why they moved on all fours?

Besides the emaciated form, they looked astonishingly human up close: The feet with five toes each, the skin with little hairs on the arms and legs. This one even had curly chest hair and pubes. It even had a belly button—an innie. If it weren't for the empty eyes, and if it gained some weight, nobody would ever know it wasn't human. At least until it started hissing like a snake and tried to eat people.

Its hand jerked suddenly, and she flinched, but the angel couldn't raise its arm. Exhaling, Jenny set her hatchet down slowly, then pressed her fingers to its neck. Blood gushed out of its mouth and ran down her hand, but she felt a heartbeat.

Angels had hearts. This one was beating like mad, each pulse pounding hard as its teeth opened and closed slowly. She wondered if it could think. If it was afraid. If it knew she was about to kill it.

**Their minds have not fully formed. They are only driven by base desires.**

She'd figured as much.

Golden light blossomed in her hand. She slit its throat the way she'd seen a butcher kill a chicken once, the sharp edge slowly moving across its throat. The angel shuddered, staring up at her, as blood streamed from the cut she'd made. Its shoulders twitched, then it lay still. The eyes remained lifeless and unchanged; she didn't bother closing them.

**You've defeated Tarnished Angel (Level 7)!**
**Experience has been awarded.**
**+20 Energy**

**Leveled Up!**
**Jenny Huang, Level 11 →Level 12**
**+3 Stat Points**

Jenny shuddered as she relaxed beside the dead angel. She wiped her hatchet on its sunken belly, then thought about how this was the first time she'd seen a guy naked up close.

*Actually, does this really count?*

A part of her wished those two wretched angels would've been around. She still wanted vengeance, but she'd cooled considerably after fighting these tarnished angels and working off her nervous energy. At least now none of these would turn into wretched ones and wreak more havoc.

She looked around at the mess she'd made. The first angel whose head had burst open—her hatchet had blown right through its face, and chunks of skull and brain matter littered the floor. The others, she'd slashed to death. Blood pooled all over, and she stepped through the puddles, walking back toward the library.

She didn't want to see the sight of the lobby again, and she didn't want to take the main stairwell to the second floor, just in case the wretched angels were near there. But also because of what she'd seen on the way down from the third floor—that stampede of angels. She was stronger now, and she'd just slaughtered a group of them, but she didn't want to face that many head-on.

The quicker she got to Oliver, the better, so she planned on taking the back stairwell and sneaking upstairs.

At the library's entrance, the glass doors glistened with light. Susan must have kept the others from interfering, and Jenny was grateful. She'd gotten to test out her new strength, *and* she'd leveled up. Quickly, she assigned her three new stat points to power.

**Jenny Huang**
**Human (Stage II - Level 12)**
**Age: 6,801 days**
**Stats:**
**Power: 23**
**Durability: 15**
**Stamina: 15**
**Agility: 15**
**Stat Points Available: 0**
**Energy Available: 248**

They'd barricaded the doors again, though she imagined Susan was on the other side, listening carefully. Jenny let her hatchet drop to the floor, and she pressed her hand against the glass. It was cold to the touch. She was sweating hard underneath the armor, and she wished she could see Susan's face.

A part of her wanted to knock on the glass and beg them to open the doors again so she could get inside and hold Susan. And they could just hold each other until this whole stupid thing ended however it did.

*Have faith, right?* That's what she'd asked of Susan. Then Jenny had to do the same. Have faith in Susan's faith. *Concentrate on what you gotta do right now*, she told herself. *Find Oliver. Drag his ass back here. Do that, then figure out what's next.*

She turned away quickly, adjusting the pink helmet on her head. Somehow, it felt like Susan was still with her, watching her back and protecting her. It brought her some comfort. Golden light flashed, and her hatchet returned to her hand. At the door of the stairwell, she grabbed the metal handle and pulled slowly, in case anything was lurking inside.

Without any windows, this stairwell was dark and grim. The only light came from the hallway, and once she'd stepped inside and shut the door behind her, pitch blackness threatened to swallow her completely.

At least with the door shut, nothing would sneak up behind her. Tucking her hatchet under her left armpit, she turned the flashlight on. Taping it to the helmet had been a genius move on Susan's part, and once again, she felt like her best friend was right here with her.

A beam of yellow light illuminated the steps she had to take. There weren't any leading down to the basement, so the only way to go was up. Unlike the main stairwell, this one was narrow, with only enough room for two people side by side.

She climbed each step slowly, holding her breath, her light bouncing this way and that. When she turned to take the next flight of stairs to the second floor, she heard it. Slurping. Like someone finishing a bowl of ramen. She couldn't see it from the bottom step, but she knew it had to be an angel. Could it see her light from there?

Jenny clenched her jaw, wondering what to do. If it attacked, there wasn't enough space to properly swing; she'd have to bash it with her shield. The slurping stopped; something shuffled around. She heard a low moan, then retching sounds. Something wet splattered the floor.

*What the fuck is it doing?*

Then there was a strained, raspy voice, so quiet she wouldn't have heard it if she'd been breathing. It said, "Please . . . Please, just let me go."

Her eyes went wide. Her heart pounded so hard she thought it would break against her ribs as she climbed the steps without thinking, her light hitting the creature at the same time she saw it.

**Wretched Angel (Level 19)**

It was a pale female with long dark hair; skinny, but not as skinny as the tarnished angels. Instead, it looked almost like Jenny.

Screeching in pain, it raised a clawed hand to cover its face. It didn't run away or attack, however, instead turning so that its back faced Jenny. The angel's skin was covered in a glossy white layer that reflected rainbows with her flashlight. She could see its spine sticking out of its back; could see its hips and the curve of its ass as it hugged something. Something big and pinkish white and lumpy. It looked like a giant sac, and the creature was shielding the wriggling thing with its body.

Before Jenny could get a better look, she spotted the boy lying on the floor beside the angel. There were several other bodies, but his was the only one moving, breathing. He was large, with a round torso and a pudgy face. His glasses were askew, his T-shirt torn open, with blood flowing from his neck.

## Human (Level 1)

He was barely breathing, but each breath sounded painful, and his eyes were shut. His body limp, he was still whispering for help and weeping. A glistening trail of blood came from the steps leading to the third floor. The angel had dragged him and the others down here. But why? And what was it protecting?

*Eve?*

But before the response came, there was a screech from above. Looking up, her light flashed over another angel. This one clung to another big pinkish-white sac stuck to the ceiling.

## Wretched Angel (Level 22)

It was covered in a glossy purple layer and was cowering away from the light, covering its eyes with one large hand. Definitely male—it was massive, with broad, muscular shoulders. It had to be over six feet tall, much larger than any of the other wretched angels she'd run into.

And that sac it clung to. There were four more just like it spread over the ceiling, each one wriggling as though they were alive.

Hissing distracted her. Before she could glance down, the female rushed her, a flash of its pale face and its red teeth all Jenny saw as she brought up her shield.

The angel crashed right into it with enough force to send them both tumbling down the stairs she'd just climbed, her light bouncing all over the place.

# CHAPTER EIGHTEEN

# SAVAGE THROW

If it hadn't been for Susan's pink helmet, Jenny was sure she'd be dead. Or at the very least unconscious, which in this case might as well mean dead.

The angel's attack had knocked Jenny down the small flight of stairs. She'd hit the bottom steps before her head bounced off the floor, and though her helmet had absorbed most of the impact, her insides felt jostled, as though her brain had gotten knocked loose inside her skull.

She saw stars every time she blinked, but that could've just been the glare of the flashlight, which shone on the underside of the stairwell above them.

Jenny lay on her back, the wretched angel wriggling on top of her. The shield covered her face and torso as the angel struck it repeatedly. Over and over, its claws raked the smooth surface, making high-pitched, jagged sounds like nails against a chalkboard, which Jenny felt in her teeth. She thought her ears would start bleeding; it felt like knives puncturing her eardrums.

Grunting, she shoved the creature off with her shield. It backed away unsteadily on its legs, a furious expression on its face. Jenny had exposed her chest to knock it off, but before the angel could get the chance to attack again, she lifted her head off the floor. The light of her flashlight fell directly on the angel's face.

Its eyes went wide, the white glossiness of its eyeball glistening before the wretched angel wailed and covered its face with both hands. Instead of normal fingers, each one looked like long, slender bones ending in razor-sharp tips. Rainbows bounced off its pale skin covering, but dark red blood spurted from its face.

In its rush to cover its eyes, the angel had scratched its forehead and cheeks. It kept scratching as if it were trying to claw its eyes out. Screeching, it fell back onto the steps, turning over and trying to get back to the top, away from the light.

Jenny stared at its pale ass as the angel scrambled and slipped on the steps. Its spine jutted out from underneath its skin, and she could see its shoulder blades rippling. For a second, she almost thought she was looking at a person. Some deep-rooted instinct wanted to help the creature, help it to its feet and up the stairs, as though it were an old lady that had fallen over on the stairs and needed help.

Unlike with the other wretched angels, Jenny couldn't immediately tell what was skin and what was that exoskeleton-like layer of armor they had. It and its coverings were pale; except, the covering reflected direct light in little scattering rainbows.

The angel just seemed like an average-size human; it reminded her too much of herself. Pale with waist-length dark hair; skinny with long limbs. They were even about the same height, and Susan would point out that Jenny was usually hunched over the same way the angel was.

*If I were an angel, this is what I'd look like.*

She shuddered, thinking about earlier, when the two wretched angels had attacked her and Susan on the first floor. They'd looked like a couple, and she'd been right. The angels *were* mating. Or doing whatever it is they did, because she was certain those sacs carried their babies.

*Dr. Lee would love to get his hands on one*, she thought. Angel biology, mating habits, and birth. She could already picture the reports, the experiments, and the published journals.

But she'd counted almost five sacs earlier: one on the floor beside the boy, and the others clinging to the ceiling with the male angel. How many children would they have? Would they produce more tarnished angels?

Somehow, that seemed wrong, as she hadn't seen a single angel that resembled a child yet. Every single one seemed like a fully grown human. What if the creatures in the sacs looked like human babies?

She'd have to kill them, she realized with a shudder. It felt wrong, vile . . . like finding a nest of bird eggs in a tree, only to knock the branches loose and send them hurtling to their demise. Maybe if she just killed the two wretched angels, then the sacs would die on their own. Killing the adults didn't seem nearly as gruesome as hacking through babies.

**Once the fetuses are blooded, they will emerge within hours.**

*Blooded? Are they vampires? Fuck.* Jenny slammed the shield into the floor, cracking it beneath her. She used that to pull herself up into a sitting position. She wasn't hurt; at least, she didn't think she was. Stuff ached, but nothing was broken or bleeding. The moment of rest seemed to have cleared her head, and she sucked in several deep breaths as the female angel reached the top step. She heard blood splashing as it crawled across the floor.

Jenny got to her feet and recalled her hatchet, preparing to kill the wretched angel that looked eerily like her. Those claws were dangerous, but its attacks hadn't felt strong. She was confident she could beat it. *How much experience would I get? Maybe I'll even level up again.* A fresh wave of bloodlust went through her. Jenny squeezed her hatchet's handle.

Just as she was about to climb the stairs, a blur of purple shimmered into the beam of her flashlight. The other angel, the male, rushed down the stairs. Where had it been this whole time?

Her increased agility enabled her to see its movements. It was like a freight truck barreling down a freeway. Sounded like one, too, as each one of its heavy steps made the stairwell shake. She leaped to the side and raised her shield defensively.

The angel's purple hand struck it hard, forcing her to stumble backward as the creature crashed into the wall. She saw its bulging muscles, its purple coverings glistening in the flashlight. This creature was *strong*—but maybe a little *too* strong.

The angel's left side was completely lodged in the wall, with only its head, right arm, and right leg loose. Screaming, it struck the wall over and over with its free arm, each loud thump making everything shake. Its purple head turned every which way as it struggled to break out while dust rained down on its short dark hair.

There was no way in hell Jenny would let this chance slip by; the angel was much too high-level for a proper fight. She aimed the light onto its face, making it hiss as it covered its eyes with a big hand, then stepped forward quickly, keeping her shield up in case it swung blindly.

It was gigantic up close, definitely over six feet tall. Its free arm and leg were thick and muscular, and it almost looked like a professional bodyguard or bouncer. Maybe a wrestler. Its leg was as thick as her entire body. She knew that if it grabbed her, it could probably tear her to pieces without much effort, even with her increased durability.

She felt tiny compared to it, but if she could land a hit on its stomach and cut through anything vital, that would weaken it severely. She remembered the first wretched angel she'd fought. Its arm injury had slowed it down enough for her to fight without the level difference overwhelming her. If she could just incapacitate this purple one, she'd stand a much better chance of getting to the third floor alive. She didn't want to end up as food for angel babies.

Jenny swung as hard as she could, hyperfocusing on its exposed navel where the covering didn't seem as thick. But just before impact, the angel's leg shot up.

Her hatchet sunk into the side of its thigh, its purple covering crackling like aluminum foil. Her edge cut straight through and struck bone so hard that her entire arm vibrated, feeling as though it might snap off her shoulder.

A howl of pain erupted from the angel's lips, who lashed out, trying to hit her. She ducked low and to the left, dodging its fingers by mere inches. She tried to yank the hatchet out, but it wouldn't budge at all. For a moment, panic rushed through her head, then with an impact that sounded like thunder, the creature banged on the wall with a mighty roar, and the entire wall cratered.

Dust and debris rained down from above as a massive fissure worked its way down to the floor and up the stairwell. It almost felt like another earthquake. This part of the building really might collapse, she realized, horrified at the thought of getting buried in the rubble with these angels trying to tear her apart.

Jenny kicked the creature's wounded leg and slid away from it. Just as she was about to recall the hatchet, the angel grabbed the handle and wrenched it out of its thigh. Blood sprayed the wall and floor, but it didn't seem to care. It glowered at her, its brows furrowed in rage, then hurled the hatchet straight at her.

Golden light flashed right as the weapon's edge sunk into her helmet, immediately spinning safely into her open hand. Jenny gasped in relief, breathing hard. The wretched angel raged against the wall, thrashing its arm and clawing at the crater, from where it ripped off chunks and hurled them over her head.

Shaking with adrenaline, Jenny licked the sweat above her lips. She should've been terrified. Her body ached, her helmet was partially cut, and she desperately needed water. But she felt a strange sense of giddiness. The creature had nearly killed her with her own hatchet, yet she didn't even feel shocked. No terror. No desire to run away. It was the same sensation as before; the confidence of betting her entire life on this fight.

The angel's throw reminded her of what she'd done in the hallway in front of the library—launching her hatchet with enough force to burst a tarnished angel's head open. How much damage would that attack do against a wretched angel as strong as this one? She couldn't wait to find out.

The adrenaline rush was stronger than any high she'd ever felt before, and she stood, trembling with anticipation.

**Skill Acquired!**
**Savage Throw (Tier 1)**
**Throw an object with increased power and speed to deal heavy damage.**
**Draws heavily on Stamina.**

The notification blossomed in her head like a flower. Her flashlight had the angel screeching and struggling relentlessly, and Jenny's lips stretched into a smile, not needing Eve's explanation. She'd *felt* the change inside her, the way she'd manifested the ability into existence. And it felt . . . *good*. Like she'd discovered something marvelous and beautiful. It was visceral proof of her growth.

She raised her arm, ready to stomp forward and throw, using her hips and legs to drive the motion. She imagined the hatchet bursting the wretched angel's purple head open, splattering the ruined wall with its blood. She could almost taste the notification of its death.

Instead, something slammed into her from behind. The female angel had thrown its weight against Jenny's lower back, forcing her to tumble forward within reach of the male.

Eyes wide, Jenny raised her shield, the edge knocking away the wretched angel's purple arm just before its fingers reached her face. The impact sent her hurling backward, toppling over the angel pushing her.

This time, she didn't land on her back. Instead, Jenny flexed her core, rolled off the female angel, and landed on her feet.

*Whoa.* Before she could celebrate the crazy gymnastics move, the female whirled around, screeching like mad on all fours. Its dark hair streamed down the side of its head, drenched in sweat and blood. Its face made Jenny's stomach twist.

Blood ran down its pale cheeks like ruined mascara; the female had clawed its eyes out, the only thing staring back at Jenny the dark, gaping voids of its empty sockets. Its lips curled back, exposing its stained teeth and retreated gums as it hissed.

The light no longer affected the creature, and it sniffed the air once before pouncing.

# CHAPTER NINETEEN

# ALL BEINGS EXPERIENCE SUFFERING

Jenny couldn't help but scream. It was a guttural response, a deeply rooted, instinctive response to something that seemed straight out of her worst nightmares. She could see into the creature's head. Her light shone on the exposed flesh and what Jenny swore were the glistening gooey remnants of its eyes.

She swatted the angel with her shield, stumbling away till the back of her feet found the steps, then threw her hatchet, aiming for the angel's head. The edge struck a pale shoulder, and the female dropped, hissing in pain as it tried to claw the hatchet out.

Jenny didn't care. She turned and ran up the steps as fast as she could. The male wretched angel was almost out of the wall, and the female had become even more horrifying. This was too much. She was going to grab the boy and get to the third floor, then figure something else out.

At the top of the steps, she saw the sac was no longer on the floor. That must've been why the male hadn't joined the fight earlier; it had secured the sac to the ceiling with the others. They looked like giant grapes, each one a blob of pinkish-whitish flesh that reminded her of raw chicken breast. They glistened in the light, blood dripping steadily from the newest one. The drops hit the puddle of blood beside the boy.

*Blooded* was what Eve had said. She shivered in disgust.

The boy on the floor was unconscious but still breathing. His neck injury didn't look too good. A part of her wanted to throw him to the angels; something to distract them while she escaped. The thought made her shake.

She glanced over her shoulder to where the female had managed to rip the hatchet out. It sniffed the air, turning, trying to find Jenny.

Meanwhile, the male wrenched its arm out of the wall. With a roar, it dropped to one knee, and Jenny winced at the sound. She'd nearly cut through the large creature's leg; there was no way it could support any of its weight. Both angels were hurt, but she knew they could rip her to pieces if she gave them the chance.

Light filled her hand, and the hatchet flew back to her. The male touched the female's face, and the angels seemed to shush one another.

*Are they . . . talking?*

Her flashlight shone on the male's face. Its eyes were shut, its chin pressed to the female's forehead. Then it blinked, its brows furrowing, its nostrils flaring as it hissed, squeezing its eyes shut. It pushed the female aside and then clambered forward, using its arms to pull itself up the stairs. The injured leg dragged and bounced on each step, leaving behind a trail of blood, but that didn't seem to slow it down at all.

Jenny glanced quickly at the stairs to the third floor. Her hopes of escaping evaporated.

It was barricaded with mangled bodies—students and teachers and naked tarnished angels piled on top of each other. *Did they stock up on food?* She'd never climb over all the bodies before the wretched angel reached her.

Crying out in desperation, she struck the angel in the face with her shield just as it was about to grab her. She struck it again—a punching motion—the shield clanging hard against the angel's cheekbone. She knocked its arm away then kicked it in the chin. She'd aimed for the throat, but her kick still launched the wretched angel a foot off the stairwell, flipping it onto its back.

It crashed on top of the female, and they both tumbled back down the steps. She knew a kick wouldn't be enough for something so high-leveled, but a part of her wished she'd broken its neck. It could've just done her a favor and died.

She grabbed one of the bodies blocking the doorway to the second floor. It was a girl, probably a freshman or a sophomore, with braided hair and a once-cute pink cardigan. She was lying on her back, her eyes open and bulging, her exposed chest a mess of blood and flesh.

Jenny didn't recognize her.

"I'm sorry," she whispered, before dragging the body with one hand, holding on to the girl's ankle. The body slid easily with all the blood slickening the floor, and Jenny used the momentum to swing it around and lob it at the two wretched angels.

The body landed on the male just as it was about to get up. The female angel screeched and savaged the girl with its claws while Jenny turned away, feeling sick to her stomach. Only one more body blocked the doorway now. It was the boy, who was still alive. She couldn't just throw him to the angels.

But what would be waiting for them on the second floor? What if there were more wretched angels? Maybe she could use the boy as bait.

*Fuck.* Her heart pounded. Indecision made her dizzy. She just had to get out of this stairwell, she told herself. The metallic stench of blood clogged her nose and lungs, burning at the back of her throat . . .

Her eyes went wide. *Burning . . .*

She'd forgotten her new skill in the frenzy. She had no idea how it actually worked, but it was worth a shot. Would she just cough up a fireball?

What if she only managed smoke?

"Fuck it," she whispered. The male roared behind her as it climbed up the stairs again, making everything shake. Jenny turned to face it, wiping the sweat off her brow.

This time, the female angel was on top of the male's broad back. Blood streamed in ribbons down one of its pale arms, and its empty sockets seemed to be staring right at Jenny.

She clenched her teeth, trying to use Ignite, but the angels were getting too close. "Fuck it!" she shouted, stomping forward on her left foot and launching her hatchet straight at the female's head with as much desperate strength as she could muster. *Savage Throw.*

The air rippled. Wind teased her sweaty face. The hatchet spun toward the female's bloodied face. And then the male jumped, its purple covering shining. The other angel fell off its back, and the hatchet hit the male right in the chest.

It gasped, choking on its breath as it grabbed the weapon's handle. The sharp edge was buried deep, and the angel's purple covering was cracked. The creature's face writhed in agony, eyes shut tight, then it fell forward, landing face down with a heavy thud. Jenny winced as the edge of her hatchet burst out of the angel's back.

A high-pitched wail erupted from the other creature, so shrill and gut-wrenching that Jenny slammed her palms against her ears, nearly hitting herself with the shield. Every bone in her body seemed to rattle from the wailing.

Before she knew what was happening, the female wretched angel was in her face.

Its pale claws brushed her helmet, tearing the flashlight loose, and light spun in every direction as it clattered away. Then the angel's elbow connected with Jenny's lips, and she tripped over the boy.

The creature sniffed once before reaching blindly till it found Jenny's arms. Breathing heavily, its chest heaving, the angel pinned her down. The look on its face, even without eyes, was one Jenny knew well: agony. The female was consumed by fury or pain, or some bitter painful mixture, and Jenny couldn't help but feel responsible. Like she'd done something unforgivable.

Tears slid down the sides of her head as she stared into the nightmarish sockets. Her lips were bleeding. Her teeth ached. But she felt she deserved worse.

*Why aren't you attacking?* Jenny looked past the angel's horrible face at the sacs on the ceiling. A drop of blood fell, sparkling in the light from wherever the flashlight had fallen, and splashed onto the angel's dark hair.

The creature brought its face next to Jenny's and sniffed twice. She could smell the rot of its breath, could see the blackened state of its gums. Blood squirted out of its eye sockets and splattered Jenny's face. An involuntary whimper slipped through her lips.

*Fuck you*, she thought. She was shaking with fear and anger and hurt. Then she realized the angel was trembling too. Was it trying to cry? Could they even cry?

It had her completely pinned down. She could move her hands, but her arms were stuck to the floor in the angel's fierce grip. Its knees dug into Jenny's sides, keeping her legs locked. She strained, trying to break out of its hold, but she still didn't have enough power.

It was going to feed her to one of its babies, wasn't it? That's why it was keeping her alive even though she'd killed its mate?

The angel's face was so close to her own, she couldn't help but sob. This creature had clawed its eyes out to protect its young. Was it driven by love? Jenny thought about Susan. About Oliver.

This time, it wasn't anger that flared up in her chest. It wasn't bloodlust. It was just fear. She didn't want to die. She wanted to keep her promise to Susan. She wanted to survive this bullshit.

*Ignite!*

The thought enveloped her mind. Warmth rose like a storm cloud from the back of her throat. The muscles of her throat convulsed painfully, like she'd swallowed steaming-hot ramen too quickly, and then, she screamed right in the angel's face.

Fire burst out of her mouth.

Once, she'd gone to use the bathroom during calculus and ran into some girls she'd shared joints with before. They'd been having fun with a spray can of Febreze and a lighter, making a makeshift flamethrower and setting napkins on fire in the sink. She'd thought it was cool as fuck. Stupid, but cool. The fire had looked so pretty flickering in the bathroom mirrors.

That was how her fire streamed out. As though someone had squeezed her throat and forced out blue-and-orange flames, lighting up the entire stairwell. Waves of heat made the air tremble as her eyes stung and watered. She couldn't even see the angel's face anymore, just a shifting dark silhouette in the fire. And all the while, Jenny was screaming.

As soon as she stopped, she gasped up one final puff of flame and then saw what she'd done. The female angel's entire head was scorched. Its once pale covering was now gray and falling apart like charcoal, exposing twisted, burnt flesh. All that was left of its hair were short, burnt strands, with smoke drifting off its head. It let out a wheeze. The blood on its face had boiled away, and its sockets were dry and empty. The creature was still alive.

A sulfuric stench threatened to suffocate her, and fire still flickered overhead. Jenny stared in horror at the sacs on the ceiling, all of them wriggling, all of them burning. She could hear faint cries and wails, and so could the angel.

It raised its ruined head, its entire body shaking as it lifted its arms. The angel was on its knees, as though it were praying. One of the burning sacs dropped from the ceiling and burst to Jenny's left. It was like watching a jar of strawberry jam hit the floor. Gooey, wet stuff splattered her face and armor, and the angel crawled off Jenny to sort through the ruined sac. Chunks of it were on fire, burning steadily all around.

Jenny's throat hurt. Her lungs ached, and she rapidly sucked in air, hyperventilating as she watched the angel bring something small and lumpy out of the sac. She could see little limbs struggling, and that was more than Jenny could bear. Pain and heartbreak and a retching sensation bubbled up in her throat.

Another scream burst from her lips. *Ignite! Ignite! Ignite!*

Fire billowed out of her mouth as Jenny got on all fours. She scorched the wretched angel even as it raised an arm in defense and held the baby to its chest. Jenny didn't care. White-hot rage clouded her vision, and she turned her head this way and that, screaming and scorching everything around her as she stood to her feet. Jenny paused only to inhale, her shoulders heaving, and then roared more flame into existence.

The other sacs fell into the blaze, bursting open, as Jenny, the angel, and the little creatures in the ruined sacs all screamed in agony.

**You've defeated Wretched Angel (Level 19)!**
**Experience has been awarded.**
**+100 Energy**

**You've defeated Fetal Angel (Level 0)!**
**Experience has been awarded.**
**+2 Energy**

**Leveled Up!**
**Jenny Huang, Level 12 → Level 14**
**+6 Stat Points**

When she couldn't scream anymore, Jenny stopped, her shoulders shaking. She was breathing hard, drenched in sweat. Ashes floated all around her. Little flames flickered, and countless shadows danced across the walls.

**You've defeated Fetal Angel (Level 0)!**
**Experience has been awarded.**
**+2 Energy**

She received several notifications about the fetal angels, and she pushed those thoughts away. All that was left of the wretched angel was blackened bones, burnt to a crisp. Several sets of smaller bones littered the floor around it, as well as another full skeleton that Jenny at first thought was the male wretched angel.

**You've defeated Human (Level 1)!**
**Experience has been awarded.**
**+200 Energy**

"No," she whispered, dropping to her knees beside the bones. She glanced over her shoulder. The purple wretched angel lay where it had fallen near the stairwell, with the edge of her hatchet still sticking out of its back.

This skeleton could only be the boy. The boy she'd tried to save.

"No," she said again, her bottom lip wobbling. Her throat constricted. She couldn't breathe. She touched his rib cage, and it crumbled away, his grinning skull staring back at her.

Jenny jumped to her feet and backed away. She bit her lip, tears streaming down her cheeks. She squeezed her shield with her other hand so that the edge cut into her palm.

*What have I done? What the fuck did I do? Eve? I messed up. I messed up.* A sob escaped her. *Eve, I can't breathe. I can't . . . No. It was an accident.*

*It was an accident!*

*He was going to die anyway. There was no way to save him. I had to . . . There wasn't . . .*

She turned away from the charred bones, then she heard a groan. The male wretched angel. She'd never gotten a notification of its death. She looked down at its purple, muscular form. What was going through its head? It made that shushing sound again. Was it trying to speak? Was it mourning its mate and children?

*It's their fault. It was their fault the boy died.*

The creature had to be near death. It wriggled, and blood gushed from its back. It was struggling toward the dead.

She remembered asking Eve if angels loved.

*All beings experience suffering.*

Jenny wiped away her tears. It was unfair. It was so unfair. If the angels just wanted to have children, couldn't they do it without killing her schoolmates? Without putting everyone through this hell?

Golden light flashed, and the hatchet appeared in her trembling hand. Blood dripped down from its edge. Clenching her jaws, she glared at the creature as it lifted its head.

Its purple covering shone brightly as flames flickered behind her. Its eyes were wide, all white and empty, but it seemed to be accusing her of what she'd done. She raised her hatchet and brought it down on its head with a *crack*.

# CHAPTER TWENTY

# THE ANGEL ON THE TABLE

In front of the barricade, Susan sat on the floor with her knees up, hugging her legs as she stared at the tables. They were stacked to completely block the view of the hallway, the top tables leaning against the glass doors with their legs facing inward. She suspected it was so nobody would have to see anything out there; most of the students were freaked out because of the angel Dr. Lee had dragged inside.

Susan couldn't look away from the tables. She was trying to see through their dark wooden forms—with gum stuck to their undersides—though she knew Jenny wasn't in the hall anymore.

Everyone had listened to Jenny's fight with bated breath; the screaming and hissing, Jenny's cries of rage. The scuffle had seemed to last an eternity, and then it was over as soon as it had begun. The hallway had fallen silent, and all Susan could hear was her heart pounding. She'd even tried to climb on top of a table, but her leg hurt too much, and Mrs. Monique had to help her get down.

Not knowing if Jenny was alive was eating her up inside, though she'd promised she wouldn't let anyone interfere. She knew she had to have faith, but it was much easier said than done.

*Stupid, stupid leg.* Her fingernails dug into her palms. She wanted to bang her head against something. Wanted to cut her leg off. It wasn't the pain that bothered her so much; it was the fact that a small part of her was thankful she didn't have to go back out there.

What slithered up and down her esophagus was a familiar feeling of disgust and self-loathing. A feeling she'd only ever told one person about. Jenny, who'd understood and tried her best to comfort Susan. She felt as though her soul was so misshapen and ugly that it couldn't properly fit inside her body, and when she felt useless and stupid, that feeling threatened to burst out of its hiding place beneath her skin. Then everyone would see how awful she truly was.

She glared at the torn, ruined flesh of her calf, hot tears streaming down her cheeks. She cursed the injury. Cursed herself. If only she'd been quicker. If only she hadn't gotten bitten. She should be out there with her best friend, fighting beside her and . . . *I'd only get in the way.*

*What if Jenny's already dead?*

She grabbed her cattle prod, flicked it on, and nearly shoved it into the wound. She stopped just before making contact, holding the prod as though it were a knife. It shook, crackling softly with electricity; she could almost feel the sting. She let it clatter to the floor and buried her face in her hands.

Somewhere in the back of her mind, there was a nudge. The "human population remaining" notification. But she bit the inside of her cheek hard and kept it out of her head. She didn't want to see that count dropping further, didn't want to wonder which number might be Jenny.

Another scream erupted from the other end of the library. During Jenny's fight, Dr. Lee had dragged the tarnished angel by the hair, sliding its bleeding body across the floor to the table where Jenny had slept. She wondered what he was doing to it. She wanted to feel pity for it—after all, it was still a living thing, not one of the dead frogs she'd dissected in biology labs—but every time it screamed or cried out or made that snakelike hissing noise, Susan's head lurched with fear.

She wanted to kill it. To put it out of its misery. Or to spare herself its haunting cries.

"Hey." Leslie tapped Susan on the shoulder. "We could use your help."

Susan sniffed, hating that Leslie could see her so upset. "With what?"

"We need another pair of arms," she said. "The angel keeps moving." Leslie had her dark sweater wrapped around her waist. Her brown arms and forehead glistened with sweat, and her T-shirt's neckline was ruined, as though she'd been chewing on it. Her cheeks were flushed. She'd tied her blonde hair back into a ponytail with a band, and without its usual bounce and curls, she looked slightly deflated. Her face appeared smaller, her eyes less vibrant.

She held out a hand to help Susan up, but she ignored it and painfully got to her feet, putting most of her weight on her uninjured leg. Leslie harrumphed and turned away. "Wait," said Susan, trying to ignore the pain shooting up her leg. "Any idea what happened to Kevin?"

Curling her lips downward, Leslie shrugged. "We were hanging out when everything started shaking. You know that stairwell beside the gym that nobody goes to?"

Susan nodded, trying not to think about her ex kissing Leslie or their bodies pressed together.

"Yeah," Leslie continued. "We were just having fun, and then one of those . . . those *things* came at us." She motioned toward the other side of the library with her head. "Kevin told me to run, and I did." She spoke so nonchalantly that Susan was taken aback.

"You just left him?"

Leslie shrugged again. "What did you want me to do? I just ran upstairs, and it was crowded and disgusting, like holy fuck. Everyone was pushing and screaming. Then Dr. Lee saved me and brought me to the library." Her frown turned into a smile as she placed a hand on her chest and sighed. "He promised to keep me safe."

Susan had already stopped listening. She squeezed her cattle prod, wanting to stick it into Leslie's model-perfect neck. She couldn't help picturing Kevin pressing his lips against Leslie's throat while whispering all those things he'd once said to Susan.

But the anger faded away; she only felt heartbroken, a dull aching in her chest. She felt empty and unwanted. Kevin had dumped her for a girl who didn't even seem to care that he'd most likely died.

"Well, are you going to help or what?" Leslie waved her fingers in front of Susan's face. "Do you need a moment?"

Susan was too sad to be irritated. She'd already mourned Kevin after the breakup, and now, she didn't know how to process mourning him again. There was sadness for what once was, for what could've been, and what could now never be.

She limped behind Leslie. They followed the trail of blood, Susan watching the girl's sweater bouncing around her hips, thinking about how jealous she'd been not too long ago. Wishing she was hotter. Fitter. With bigger boobs. Thinking that somehow she might win Kevin back. Maybe if she talked more like Leslie, with that whining, bitchy attitude . . .

Her thoughts shifted to Jenny. Jenny, who was always down for a phone call, who'd drop pretty much everything and anything if Susan texted her. Even when she felt ugly and wanted to hide from everyone and everything, even Kevin, Susan knew talking to Jenny would pull her out of the hole. Jenny was always there to listen, to hug, to game with, to complain with.

And Susan felt ridden with guilt, feeling like Jenny always had to save her. And now that she wasn't there but out fighting and trying to find her brother . . . there were too many things bubbling in her thoughts. Anxiety and heartbreak and horror, and she just wanted to see Jenny's face and hear her voice.

"I'm sorry," she whispered. She wasn't sure who she was apologizing to. Jenny? Kevin? Maybe even herself. Maybe even Leslie.

"What's that?" Leslie asked without turning her head.

Susan didn't bother answering. At the table, two students stood ten feet away from the angel, holding up phones and flashlights to provide light for Dr. Lee while he stood over it, his lab coat buttoned and green goggles strapped to his face.

Mrs. Monique was on the other side of the table, her metallic armor shining in the light as she firmly held the angel's right shoulder and elbow. The creature wriggled and hissed and screamed, and Susan saw it was missing fingers on that arm. The other was missing from the shoulder, cut away by what Susan suspected had been Jenny's hatchet. She could see the white of its bones sticking out of red, pulsing flesh.

## Tarnished Angel (Level 9)

The angel was dark-skinned, with gray hair draped over the front of the table. It was female, as skinny and emaciated as the other tarnished angels with a flat chest and sunken navel. Its eyes were white and wide open. Saliva and blood dribbled down its chin and cheeks as it hissed and kept trying to bite Mrs. Monique.

A nasty gash glistened on its hip; its bone seemed broken. Its legs hardly moved. Every so often, they jerked and twitched slightly, but Susan didn't think it could run away or chase anyone. They just had to keep away from its teeth.

Dr. Lee had his phone out, recording the female angel and dictating observations. Susan couldn't hear what he was saying. It wasn't just because he spoke too quickly, because Leslie was talking to her as well, and Mrs. Monique was muttering something. Susan just couldn't pay attention. A ringing sound filled her ears.

Her heart pounded, each thud echoing through her head as she stared at the struggling, suffering angel. She had to remind herself to breathe, to not stare into its eyes. She was trembling, feeling dizzy, her chest tight; it was just like before, when she froze up seeing the angel kill Mrs. Rivera.

Then Leslie was forcing Susan forward. Dr. Lee shouted what he needed her to do, and Susan moved on autopilot. Her job was to hold down the angel's head, something Leslie had refused to do. But Susan was beyond the point of caring. She was just relieved to be useful.

With her thumbs on the angel's forehead and her fingers in its gray hair, she squeezed and held it in place as best she could; its scalp was slick with sweat and blood. Leslie took the phone from the doctor and continued recording.

First, Dr. Lee grabbed the angel by the cheeks, pushing his fingers in deep, forcing its jaws open. It tried to bite him—Susan could see its jaws moving—but with its cheeks and Dr. Lee's fingers in the way, it was harmless.

He pulled out what looked like scissors, except they didn't end in sharp points. She recognized them as a tool a dentist would use. The system gave them a name, so she assumed it was something Dr. Lee had created.

## Forceps (Tier 1)

Did they count as a weapon? She wanted to study that further, figure out how the system discerned tools and weapons and armor, but it was difficult to concentrate on anything with the angel's head squirming between her hands. Blood dripped from one of its earholes onto the table, and a rotten stench wafted up from its throat.

Hunching over the angel, Dr. Lee gently lowered the tip of the forceps into its forced-open mouth. The angel's pink and narrow tongue darted out. It was covered in a layer of white bumps, and Dr. Lee didn't seem to mind as it licked his fingers.

The forceps clinked softly against a tooth. He repositioned himself, then, with a grunt and a sudden jerk, he wrenched a tooth out. Blood spurted onto its chest and his lab coat as the angel screamed hideously. Susan shut her eyes, still holding its head tight. She didn't want to throw up all over it.

Dr. Lee held the forceps up to the light, turning the glistening tooth as he inspected its roots. "Remarkable," he whispered. "The incisors are exactly the same. Exactly the same. Covered in plaque, but with proper care . . ." He trailed off, mumbling to himself as Leslie recorded him and the tooth.

Susan caught herself gently rubbing the angel's forehead with her thumbs. She stared down into its eyes; the creature seemed to be glaring right back at her, but since it had no irises, she couldn't tell which way it was really looking. It wasn't wriggling or making any noise. Susan would've thought it was dead from shock, but its bony chest was rising and falling, and its rotten breath felt warm on her face.

"Think we can hurry this up?" asked Mrs. Monique in a strained voice. She'd been quiet this entire time, just going along with Dr. Lee's instructions. Susan hated seeing her like this: Missing an eye, covered in dried blood, and wearing metal armor. Her spear was leaning against a bookshelf behind her. She seemed so subdued and withdrawn, no longer the bubbly, warm librarian that everyone loved so much.

Dr. Lee nodded, apologized, then placed the tooth into a little baggie. He readjusted his goggles before bringing out a pocketknife. "It's not a scalpel," he said with a small smile, "but it'll do." There was no system message for this one. It must've been something he always carried.

He motioned for Leslie to stand right next to him. She seemed hesitant, so he pressed his palm against the angel's chin, forcing its bleeding mouth shut. "Keep her steady," he whispered. Then he called over one of the students holding up a flashlight, a redheaded boy named Alan whom Susan knew vaguely from psychology class.

### Human (Level 3)

"Shine the light directly into her eyes," said Dr. Lee. "I want to see the exact reaction. After that, we'll be cutting into her abdominal cavity." He sounded nearly giddy with excitement, and somehow, Susan found his intense stare, the hint of a smile on his lips, and sharp focus creepier than the vacant eyes of the angel.

She knew there was something wrong with this. They should just kill the creature and get it over with. But she also remembered Dr. Lee's lectures on how medical advances had been made through torture and autopsy and careful study. But did he have to be so thrilled? If Jenny were here, what would she do?

Even Leslie seemed unnerved. She nervously looked from Susan to Mrs. Monique, chewing on her T-shirt, her eyes wide with fright.

Alan positioned himself right behind Dr. Lee, shining the flashlight over the doctor's shoulder. He was tall, freckled, and had thin strands of hair on his chin. He was missing an ear, and dried blood stuck to that side of his face. He was shaking so much that the light did too, all over the angel's face.

It shut its eyes tight, exhaling through its teeth, making a sound like static from a radio.

"Careful now," said Dr. Lee softly, pressing the tip of his blade into the space between its left eyeball and cheekbone. The point drew blood; the angel strained in Susan's hands, and Dr. Lee shushed it gently, as though he were quieting a baby.

Alan's hand shook even more violently, and Susan looked up to see his face flushed red and sweaty. He clearly didn't want to be here, didn't want to be this close to an angel, and definitely didn't want to see Dr. Lee cutting into it. He'd been the only student with energy who hadn't made a weapon or armor or anything.

She wanted to comfort him somehow, but she felt queasy herself. She couldn't even look at what Dr. Lee was doing as he murmured more observations for the recording; she just held its head as firmly as she could, bracing her weight on her good leg, her arms shaking as the angel struggled to break free.

Leslie was recording with her eyes shut, the phone angled slightly away from the angel's face. Dr. Lee barked something about holding the light steady, and Susan glanced down to see the angel's eyeball slipping out of its eyelids, forced by Dr. Lee's fingers. It squished out like a grape squeezing out of its skin.

That seemed to be all Alan could take. The flashlight slipped from his fingers, and it struck Dr. Lee's wrist, who cried out as his hand jerked and the eyeball burst free.

A shrill scream came from Leslie, who threw the phone away in a panic. It caught Susan on the nose, and she stumbled back, pain blossoming across her face as blood ran down her lips. She'd let go of the angel's head.

Mrs. Monique swore as the angel jerked violently, its eye still connected by wirelike strands of flesh. It bit the shocked Dr. Lee on his forearm, and he punched it in the face over and over, even hitting the swinging eyeball so that it gushed liquid.

There was so much screaming from the angel, from Dr. Lee, and from Leslie, that Susan couldn't tell what was happening. Blood gushed from her nose onto her hands. Alan had fainted and lay on the floor beside the table. Mrs. Monique was the only one trying to restrain the angel, grabbing it by the throat, but it jerked its head and tore off a chunk of Dr. Lee's arm, who roared with pain and swung blindly.

His elbow hit Mrs. Monique, and the angel wriggled out of her grip and slid off the table, landing on top of Alan. Susan reached for her cattle prod, yanking it out of her back pocket, but it was too late. The angel's teeth were deep in Alan's neck, and golden light enveloped the creature.

Something bright blue and gelatinous burst out of the angel's spine. Dr. Lee backed away, clutching his bleeding arm, his goggles knocked loose. The angel writhed, its flesh expanding, muscles growing, as an orange, jellylike substance, slid all over its body, covering its shoulders and legs and arms.

The golden light vanished as steam rose from the angel's body. It was covered in that glistening orange material, and it no longer seemed skinny and fragile, though it was still missing an arm. Its wounds were healed. The orange covering clinked like heavy armor against the floor as the angel crawled off Alan. It glowered at Susan and hissed, blood dripping from its empty socket and down its shiny orange cheek.

**Wretched Angel (Level 10)**

With a furious scream, the angel launched itself off the floor and onto Susan.

# CHAPTER TWENTY-ONE

# REJUVENATION

**You've defeated Wretched Angel (Level 22)!**
**Experience has been awarded.**
**+100 Energy**

**Leveled Up!**
**Jenny Huang, Level 14 → 16**
**+6 Stat Points**

The notifications filled her mind, lingering while she stared with wide eyes at the wretched angel's cracked-open head. The thoughts faded away till the only thing left was a blunt emptiness. Her hatchet dropped, clattering to the floor. The sound startled her; it seemed much too loud in the now quiet stairwell.

"Fuck," she whispered. It was too hot. Too damn hot under her armor and the helmet and everything. She tugged on the strap beneath her chin, feeling like she was suffocating. A trembling began in her core before spreading through her chest and into her arms and legs. After a struggle, she unlatched the strap and wrenched the helmet off. Her hair was drenched with sweat.

The stairwell seemed to close in on her, pressing from every side. Her heart raced so quickly she thought it would burst. She was too aware of the blood pulsing through her body, could feel it in the fingertips of her right hand. She felt it in her neck. Felt it in her navel and her toes.

In her head, she kept replaying images of the angels, the fight, the empty eye sockets, and the blood running down its cheeks as it attacked her. She pictured the boy, lying on the floor beside the pile of dead people. He was just a pile of bones and ashes now. She'd killed him. She was a murderer. *I'm a murderer.*

It wasn't the same as killing angels. They wanted to eat her. They'd kill her without a second thought. But the boy had been alive. He was human. He just wanted help. He just wanted to get away. And she'd burnt him to a blackened skeleton. Had he felt any pain? Had he suffered? Had he been screaming in agony while she'd set everything on fire?

*Could I have saved him?*

**That participant was named Joshua Bennet.**
**His status was critical when you discovered him. The chances of fending off both wretched angels and healing him were extremely low. He would have perished within minutes regardless of your actions, given the circumstances.**

Eve's words didn't make her feel better in the slightest. She still blamed herself. She kept hearing his strained voice begging the angel to stop.

If that wasn't bad enough, she glanced down the stairs and saw the girl. She'd thrown her body onto the angels to distract them, and now it lay motionless underneath the ruined wall. Her pink sweater was shredded to bits. Jenny couldn't see where the girl's head was.

Was there any justifying her actions? *What delusion am I convincing myself of right now so that I can pretend I'm okay?* It was something she'd read once in a story or book, or maybe a poem. A line she thought about all the time, wondering how she was lying to herself so she could pretend to be normal. But that was much easier to do when thinking about fighting with her mom or her crush on Susan, or the stupid things she'd say or do.

What the hell was she supposed to do about this? *I'm a murderer.*

The female angel's skeleton lay face down on the floor. Between its ribs was another set of smaller bones—the baby it was trying to protect from the flames.

Jenny stared for a long time. The other sacs were burnt away, leaving behind smoke, ash, and a sulfuric odor that stung her nose. Her breaths came quick and sudden, her shoulders shaking. Panic climbed up her chest, burying its claws deep into her flesh before clogging her throat. She grabbed her injured hand and raised her shield so she could rest her forehead against the cold metal inside.

For a moment, she wasn't there. She hadn't done what she'd done. She was in a tiny little space that was just her own. Like she was under her blanket, safe from any monsters crawling underneath her bed. She inhaled deeply through her nose and held her breath. Tears threatened to overwhelm her, but she squeezed her eyes tight and tried to will them away.

*I can't unravel right now. Not yet.*

After several deep breaths, Jenny managed to focus inward, noticing how drained she felt. Ignite used up a lot of her stamina, and there was no way she'd survive another fight like this. She wondered if there was a potion for that. If she could restore health and heal wounds, then why couldn't she think of something to recover stamina?

**A Minor Potion of Rejuvenation will cost 100 Energy.**
**Sufficient Energy.**

*Makes sense to me,* she thought as light took shape in her hand. A vial of emerald-green liquid shimmered in her palm. She held it up and swirled it, wondering what it would taste like.

Then she yanked out the stopper with her teeth, tipped her head back, and downed the entire potion in one go. It tasted like strong coffee with no sugar or milk. The bitterness made her wince as she swallowed, but nearly instantly, her breathing slowed.

A little tremor went through her arms and legs. Her shoulders relaxed, and her head stopped spinning. She rubbed her eyes with the back of her hands, her shield retracted. For a long moment, she stood where she was, eyes shut tight, trying to figure out what to do next.

*Are they still okay?* She didn't have to clarify who she was talking about; Eve already knew.

**Susan Brown remains an active participant in the Survival Challenge. Her current location is the first floor, in the room designated as the library. There are several human participants with her.**
**Oliver Spencer remains an active participant in the Survival Challenge. His current location is the southwestern end of this floor. There are several human participants with him.**

**Human population remaining: 67**

She felt the tiniest bit of relief, but held the thoughts in her mind. So many, many people had died already. She remembered how quickly the number had dropped earlier, but now, it seemed to be slowing down. Before, in the library, the count had been seventy-two.

Were the remaining people fighting? Or were they hiding like the others in the library? And how many of that count were people being kept alive by the angels to feed their young? She shuddered, remembering how the boy had begged the angels to stop. She'd remember that for the rest of her life.

"I'm sorry," she said finally, forcing herself to look at Joshua's skull. "I'm sorry."

*I'm sorry I killed you.* But that part she couldn't say out loud.

Jenny glanced over at the female angel's skeleton. It had clawed its own eyes out to avoid the light, trying to protect its young. But it had been torturing Joshua. It was going to do the same to her. It wasn't fair. None of this was fair.

She raised her leg to stomp its skull to dust, shaking with anger. But she stopped.

"It's not fair," she whispered, exhaling and lowering her foot. She left its remains alone.

The game was to survive. That was how she'd rationalized this nightmare to Susan. A dumb survival game. But what was the point if she turned into a monster? Again, she wished Susan was here. She would know what to say.

Jenny had to be better, stronger. And not just physically. It wasn't enough to raise her stats; if she wanted to make it out of this hell alive and protect anyone, she had to master her mind, too. Accomplish something she'd always struggled with: self-control.

She sensed Eve was about to remind her of the survival challenge conditions, but she had another question for it. *Why isn't there a stat for improving the mind?*

**The human mind cannot be bound by the guidance system. That would betray free will.**

Again with the talking in riddles, but she didn't press the question. Her throat hurt much less. The potion of rejuvenation had helped tremendously.

She checked her body, noting that she hadn't been injured at all in the fight. Her armor was completely intact; none of the scales were cracked or missing.

Her helmet was scratched and dented in several places, however. She stared at the pink casing, realizing Susan had saved her life with this. That brought up a funny feeling, like butterflies in her stomach. Sighing, she touched her face and scalp, looking for scratches or bruises, but she was fine.

She'd fought two high-level wretched angels in a cramped stairwell and was virtually unscathed.

Was it a mixture of dumb luck and Ignite being much more effective than she thought it would be? The flames had been hot enough to burn flesh away . . . She shuddered, thinking about all that power inside her. The first time she'd used it, she'd only slightly scorched the angel's face and burned away its hair. But when she'd freaked out, it had gone out of control and burned several magnitudes hotter.

It was definitely connected to her state of mind and intention.

"Yeah," said Jenny. She couldn't keep letting her emotions get the best of her. Her lip wobbled, and she swallowed the impulse to start crying, walking over to where the flashlight had rolled to a stop beside the stairs leading to the third floor. She didn't look at the bodies piled on the steps.

The duct tape was still attached to the flashlight's body, looking like a set of gray wings. Jenny set the helmet back on her head, brushing the hairs away from her face and tucking them underneath the helmet as neatly as she could. It was frustrating trying to snap the latch back into place under her chin with one hand. She'd even tried to use her left one, only to feel the stubs of her missing fingers.

Once it clicked into place, she picked up the flashlight and placed it on top of the helmet. She smoothed down the tape on each side and prayed it would stick. Satisfied that it wouldn't roll off as soon as she moved, she clicked the light off, and the entire stairwell went dark. Then she turned it back on, not wanting to step on any of the bones by accident.

With that done, there was just one last thing left to do. Assign her new stat points.

**Jenny Huang**
**Human (Stage II - Level 16)**
**Age: 6,801 days**
**Stats:**
**Power: 23**
**Durability: 15**
**Stamina: 15**
**Agility: 15**
**Stat Points Available: 12**
**Energy Available: 558**

She thought it over for a moment, then applied two points into power, bringing that to a neat twenty-five. A slight shock went down her spine, but with a deep breath, the sensation faded.

She figured she could skip durability for now; her new armor had held up completely against these wretched angels. She'd need more stamina if she had to use Ignite again; she didn't want to be caught exhausted. Agility would also be necessary; they moved so quickly, she had to be faster as well.

Deciding that was the best course of action for now, she split the remaining ten points evenly between stamina and agility. The tingling sensation went through her muscles, and each limb twitched slightly before relaxing. She shook hard for a moment, then stamped her foot as though it had fallen asleep, and rolled her shoulders.

*Will I ever get used to that?*

But at least her stats still looked neat and orderly, and she had a good amount of energy now.

**Jenny Huang**
**Human (Stage II - Level 16)**
**Age: 6,801 days**
**Stats:**
**Power: 25**
**Durability: 15**
**Stamina: 20**
**Agility: 20**
**Stat Points Available: 0**
**Energy Available: 558**

Then she remembered how much energy the boy had given her, and panic rushed up to greet her thoughts again. *I'm a murderer . . .*

*Fuck.*

*Eve? Why do people give so much more energy than angels?*

**Life energy is released upon death. The amount correlates with the potential for life.**
**In their current state, the angels exist in a deteriorated form, ruled by base desires and instinct, and thus have decreased potential.**

*This has to do with free will, doesn't it?* Jenny knew there was so much more to this whole thing. The gods, the myths, the angels, the violence, life energy . . . A part of her wanted to hide somewhere and write all this down.

It was too much to think about. Her head ached trying to make sense of everything, so she thought about the only thing that mattered to her right now: finding Oliver and taking him back to the library, where Susan was.

"Okay," she whispered, trying to ready herself. Her shield extended from her arm, and with another flash of light, her hatchet returned to her hand. She then pushed the metal door open, its latch clicking, and stepped into the second-floor hallway.

She'd fully expected screaming. Hissing. A group of angels rushing at her.

To her surprise, the hallway was empty. There weren't any bodies on the floor. Her light shone on streaks of blood, as though someone or something had dragged everything away.

"What the fuck?" she exhaled, stepping slowly and cautiously into the hallway. The door closed gently behind her, and her heart pounded as she strained to listen, hoping to hear anything, any sign of danger or Oliver or people.

Thick globs of red glistened on the floor. Flesh. Torn clothes. Book bags ripped open with their contents spilling. She spotted a leg lying beside a classroom door.

# CHAPTER TWENTY-TWO

# INSIDE THE CLOSET

*What's going on?* She held her breath, shining the light on every chunk of flesh, every bloody smear on the wall and floors. The leg beside the classroom door was covered in a long sock that went up to the knee. On the foot was a leather shoe. The thigh was bare and led to the exposed red flesh, darkened around the edges.

*Eve?* thought Jenny, turning away and inspecting the rest of the hall. At the end was the central area where all the hallways connected, and then the entrance to the main stairwell. That was where she and Susan had seen dozens of angels rushing by. Yet now, there was nothing to be found.

**I am not attuned to the presence of angels.**

*Is there anything you can tell me?*

**There are human participants nearby. Oliver Spencer is among them.**

She pressed her lips tight, peering into a room. This door was wide open, held in place by a wooden doorstop. Nobody was inside. One of the windows was broken and stained with blood. The chairs and desks were knocked over, and there were several pools of blood, but each of them was smeared toward the door, as though the bodies had been dragged away. There were bloodied feet and handprints as well; those had to be the angels'.

Jenny walked slowly, taking each step with care so as not to make a sound. It was disturbingly quiet, and the air felt heavier, making it increasingly difficult to breathe. She squeezed her hatchet tight, ready to slice anything that jumped at her, keeping her shield in front of her defensively.

Everywhere she looked, there was blood. And all signs pointed to several bodies having been dragged out of classrooms and down the hallway. Some of the blood was dried and rust colored; some fresh and glistening by her flashlight.

The silence was freaking her out. Every one of her breaths felt too loud, like they might give her position away. She decided to check the chemistry wing first; that was the direction the angels had been heading before. Something must have happened.

Near the very last room of this hallway, she heard a noise. A faint cry.

Her heart thumped against her chest as Jenny stood beside the door. She recognized the place; it was the computer lab. Students could access the room during free periods or lunch to finish up work or print assignments. Was someone in there? Was it an angel?

What if it was Oliver?

The door to the computer lab didn't have a window to see inside, but after standing still for a minute or two, she didn't hear any hissing. No movement.

Then she heard the faint cry again. Sucking in a breath, she turned the handle as slowly as she could, pushed the door slightly, and shone her flashlight through the tiny opening. She raised her shield in front of her; if anything jumped out, she was going to knock it back and then sink her hatchet into its face.

Nothing hissed or screamed or rushed at her, so that was a good sign. But nothing moved either. There was no sound, no sign of life.

She pushed the door further open. It creaked.

Holding her breath, she looked up and down the hall, expecting the worst, but there was still only silence. The room was large, with several long white tables bolted to the floor. It was dark with the shades down, and the beam of light from her flashlight shone on rows of flat-screen monitors. Many of them were knocked over.

There was no sign of fighting in this room. No blood. No bodies. Jenny stepped inside and gently shut the door behind her. Could this be another safe area like the library? The door was thicker than normal classroom doors, and the windows were completely covered. Someone could turn the lock and hide in here for a while. Jenny walked past the tables, shining her light on the wooden doors of the closets that made up the far side of the room.

There didn't seem to be anyone in here; nothing that could've made the faint cry she'd heard.

*Maybe I'm just hearing shit now.* Then something grabbed her leg.

Swallowing a scream, Jenny stepped back and tried to wrench her foot free, ready to attack. A monitor rattled to the floor from the table beside her. The sound startled her, and she turned her head, shining a light on everything, trying to find what had grabbed her.

It was a thick computer cable; she'd stepped into a bunch accidentally. With a groan of embarrassment, she kicked it off before breathing a sigh of relief, trying to steady her nerves. She gave the room a cursory glance then turned to leave. That was when she heard the cry again.

It was much more audible this time, and accompanied by hammering, like someone was trying to break the door down. But the sound came from the other direction—the closets.

Worried it would attract angels, she rushed over. *Eve, is anyone nearby?*

Before Eve could respond, the closet rattled. Someone or something was inside, trying to get out.

Slowly, she stepped over a fallen monitor. Each storage closet had two doors. The one in the center, where the sounds came from, had something pulled through the handles. Shining her light on it, Jenny saw that it was a thick computer cord. Someone had looped it through the handles and then plugged it into itself, effectively locking anyone who was inside. Or anything . . .

"Hello?" whispered Jenny, her voice barely more than a croak. There was no response. She cleared her throat to try again, her head spinning with what-ifs. What if an angel was in there? What if she let it out and the screaming drew more attention to the computer lab? Someone had obviously shoved something into the closet and locked it for a reason.

She decided it was worth the risk. If it was a tarnished angel, she'd kill it and take the energy. If it was a person, then she'd help.

"Hello?" said Jenny, raising her voice and knocking lightly on the closet with her hatchet.

"I'm in here!" came a girl's voice from inside. She sounded faint and hoarse. The girl rattled the door again. "Oh, thank God. Please, just let me out!"

Jenny's eyes went wide. A girl? A human . . . She was sobbing inside the closet. *Who locked her in here?*

Holding her hatchet with her left armpit, Jenny tried to unplug the chord, but it was stuck tight, and she couldn't get a grip with one hand. This was stupid. Calling out for the girl to move back and cover her face, Jenny struck the cable with her hatchet, cutting right through and splintering the closet doors.

Using her hatchet, she pulled one of the doors open slowly. Her light shone inside, and Jenny saw a girl sitting on the floor with her legs folded beneath her. Her black hijab was pulled back and loose, and her denim shirt was wrinkled as though she'd been clawing at it.

## Human (Level 1)

Jenny's jaw dropped. "Miriam?"

Miriam's eyes were wide and red from crying, her mascara smeared across her cheeks. She blinked repeatedly and raised a slender arm to shield her face from the light.

Jenny knelt, retracting her shield and trying to keep the flashlight out of Miriam's eyes. "Were you in here this whole time?" She couldn't believe it. Had the angels not heard her? Or had they, but they just couldn't get into the room? What was she doing in here, anyway?

Nodding, Miriam sniffed. She slowly got to her feet, leaning against the side of the closet for support while Jenny held her arm. Her legs shook violently. "I got scared," she said, her voice raspy and strained. "We had earthquakes back home, and . . ." She bit her lip. "I panicked and ran in here . . . then I heard someone putting something through the handles. And they wouldn't open. I kept banging and trying to push it, but . . ."

"It's alright," whispered Jenny, helping Miriam out. Shutting the closet door behind her, Miriam leaned back against it, her eyes shut as she muttered something in Arabic.

Jenny knew her from Robotics and the Classical Movies club. Miriam Khalique was a junior, tall and fragile and ghostly pale. She was badly underweight and had nearly translucent skin because of some condition, which had the unfortunate side effect of making any hair on her body more pronounced. It didn't help that her hair naturally grew dark and thick, and some of the girls took it upon themselves to make Miriam's life even more miserable.

She had once come to school with the shadow of a mustache, and several mocking pictures and videos had gotten shared online. One of the photos had ended up on a "Vote for me for class president" poster, and someone had pasted it on nearly every locker in the school. Miriam had stayed home for two weeks after that.

She was a sickly girl who'd been locked in a closet during an earthquake, and now Jenny had to explain the actual situation to her. She didn't really know Miriam that well. They'd spoken a few times, and even worked together on a project for robotics once, but it was nothing more than the occasional small talk.

Jenny had always thought Miriam was exceptionally pretty, with pronounced cheekbones and piercing green eyes, but Miriam kept to herself mostly. She had a slight accent, as she'd grown up in the Middle East, but Jenny always got the sense that she preferred her own space and peace to spending time with other people; something Jenny could respect.

Someone had probably locked her in the closet as a cruel joke and then rushed off when the screaming started.

Once Miriam calmed down enough, she stared at Jenny.

"I thought you might've been a firefighter or something . . ." She blinked, looking at something on Jenny's face. "Is that . . . blood? And what are you wearing?"

Jenny touched her cheek, feeling the crust of dried blood. She nodded.

Miriam held up a hand to block the flashlight's beam as she got closer to look at the scaly armor. When she noticed the hatchet on the floor, her eyes went wide.

She opened her mouth to say something, perspiration glistening on her pale skin, then shook her head and simply said, "Nope."

She stumbled past Jenny, looking around the room and setting one of the monitors upright on a table. Pulling her bag out from underneath, she placed it on the chair with a heavy thud, then rummaged through it, muttering about her head and being dehydrated. She grabbed her phone and powered it on.

"That's not going to . . ." Jenny started.

Miriam dialed anyway, holding the phone up to her ear, her other hand on her hip. Her denim shirt was oversize and hung loose. She was wearing dark jeans that flared out at the bottom, and pink sneakers. When she spoke again, her words came like rapid fire.

"It's not working," she said, on the verge of tears. "Why's it not working? Aren't there first responders? Emergency services? I need to call my dad. How bad was the earthquake? We had a 7.1 once back home, but this didn't feel that strong. Was there structural damage? Am I hallucinating right now?"

Jenny rubbed her eye with her palm. Her head ached. She was *so close* to finding Oliver. Should she take Miriam back to the library first? But what if they ran into an angel? Or several?

*What should I do? Can I just leave her here and circle back?*

But what if Oliver and the others were hiding too? Jenny remembered the shouting and the stampede of angels . . . There'd definitely been fighting. But now, all the bodies were missing, the halls were empty. So what was even going on?

Jenny looked up to see Miriam with her hand on the doorknob. *Oh shit.*

"Wait!"

# CHAPTER TWENTY-THREE

# TOWARD THE CHEMISTRY WING

Jenny dashed forward, far more quickly than she'd anticipated or intended to, and pressed the flat of her palm against the door, forcing it shut.

It was a sudden, lightning-quick step that took her by surprise. One instant, she was by the closet. The next, she stood right in front of Miriam, whose hand was still on the doorknob and was staring at Jenny with a shocked look of disbelief.

Exhaling slowly and looking into Miriam's green eyes, Jenny shook her head. "Don't go out there yet."

Miriam rattled the doorknob and tried to pull it, but it didn't budge in the slightest. She blinked repeatedly, looking from Jenny's hand to her face, her lips parting, but sound failed to come out.

Jenny tried to find the words to explain things, but how did you tell someone that angels were eating people?

"Look," she said finally. She still couldn't believe Miriam had been trapped in a closet this entire time and avoided detection. Maybe all the fighting and killing had kept the angels too busy? She wished Susan were here; she'd know how to keep Miriam calm and explain everything. "Was there, like . . . a message in your head while you were in there?"

Miriam's brows furrowed like she was trying very hard to remember. "Yeah," she replied, pausing to nod. "There was . . . Something about a survival challenge?" She shook her head, her loose hijab fluttering. She seemed pained. "I don't know what that was. It was dark in there, and I was freaking out. I just need to . . . Why aren't we getting out of here?"

That was when Miriam noticed Jenny's left hand. She had tried to hide it from view, keeping her arm at her side, but Miriam let go of the doorknob and covered her mouth in horror. "Jenny!"

No use in hiding it now. Jenny raised her arm and revealed the little stubs. She could wriggle each one, the longest being her pinky. *Maybe I could use this to explain how dangerous it is out there.* "Miriam, this is going to sound stupid crazy, but . . ." She sighed, still struggling to find the words. She decided to be blunt. "An angel bit my fingers off."

Miriam's nose wrinkled in confusion. Slowly, she lowered her hand, tugging on her sleeves absentmindedly. She didn't say anything.

Jenny unveiled her shield next. It sprang out of her left arm and formed its now comforting circular shape. Miriam flinched.

"It's alright," reassured Jenny, trying to keep her tone relaxed and soothing. "This is my shield. It's saved my ass a few times already."

Miriam poked it with a fingernail. "It feels real."

Jenny then explained the rest of it as best she could. She quickly went over the messages in their heads, the guidance system, and the human population. She described the flesh-eating angels as extremely skinny creatures that looked like people. Miriam listened, nodding along, taking everything more calmly than Jenny thought she would. Maybe this wouldn't be so bad.

She explained about making weapons and equipment next. "It's like a game," said Jenny. She left out the part about the winning condition. Golden light filled her hand, and she revealed her hatchet. She was running out of patience; she wanted to get to Oliver already and get back to the library.

"There's a safe space," she continued after Miriam touched the weapon. "Mrs. Monique has the library secured. I'll take you there as soon as I find my brother." *Stepbrother,* went a thought in her head. But there was no point in clarifying that.

"Nope," Miriam said abruptly, her lips twisting in an ugly smile. She shook her head and repeated herself. "This is some sick joke. You guys are so fucked up, you know that? And I always thought you were cool, Jenny. But you're just like the rest of them." She sniffled, tears streaming down her face. "I don't know where you got all this stuff or if the earthquake even happened or—" She turned the doorknob suddenly, pulling the door open.

Jenny didn't bother stopping her this time. She'd have to set her hatchet down to grab the door, and she'd explained enough of what was out there. If Miriam didn't believe her, then there was only one way to prove it.

She followed her out of the room, all her senses on high alert. The halls were still empty and quiet.

Miriam was staring at the bloody streaks on the floor. When Jenny's light shone on the torn leg lying across the hall, Miriam made a sound halfway between a squeal and a whimper.

"C'mon," whispered Jenny, nudging the other girl lightly with her shield. She was done trying to explain. Miriam would just have to figure it out now.

But Miriam refused to move. She was frozen to the spot, holding her hands to her mouth, petrified.

Jenny glanced down the hallway before stepping in front of Miriam. "Look at me," she said roughly. "Look really hard. Does the system tell you anything?"

Miriam blinked and kept her eyes shut for a long second. "Human," she whispered. "Stage two? What does that mean?"

"Look at my shield. My hatchet. They have names too, right?"

"Mm-hmm," she hummed, nodding vigorously after glancing at both things.

"Okay then," said Jenny. "This is real. This is happening. Now, c'mon. I'll keep you safe."

Jenny kept thinking about the boy in the stairwell. Joshua. She'd failed to save him . . . *I'm a murderer.* But she shoved that thought down and focused instead on what she could do now, listing it off in her head. Keep Miriam safe. Find Oliver and whoever he was with. Get to the library. Get back to Susan. She led the way to the corner, her light shining on the doors of the main stairwell.

The windows on two of the doors were shattered. The loose glass was scattered across the floor, some of the shards stained red. Bloody handprints and smears glistened on the peeling blue paint. The stairwell was empty, and through the broken windows, Jenny could hear the distant, fading echoes of screaming.

She bit her bottom lip, wondering about the library, wondering who was screaming. There weren't that many people left, after all. She pushed one of the doors open slightly, glancing at the steps where she and Susan had seen several bodies on their way down to the first floor.

Every single body was missing. Bloody trails led to this floor, though some of them seemed to go down the steps toward the first. Nothing stirred, so Jenny turned away, swallowing the lump in her throat, not liking the eerie quiet one bit.

A long corridor led to the chemistry wing, lined on both sides with tan lockers that covered the walls. That was the direction the angels had stampeded toward earlier. That was where she suspected Oliver and his group might be, based on Eve's information.

She glanced back at Miriam, whose skin gleamed with sweat and had taken up a faint greenish hue. Miriam tugged nervously on the side of her hijab, the black cloth coming even looser and revealing her hair. She kept glancing behind.

Jenny felt sorry for the other girl. She was already prone to getting sick; this was definitely not good for her fragile constitution. "Here," whispered Jenny, bowing her head. "Take this."

With the sound of tearing tape, Miriam pulled the flashlight off the pink helmet. She nervously wrapped the tape all the way around its black handle, pointing the light at the floor while Jenny explained how the angels' eyes were underdeveloped. "They're sensitive, so shining light in their faces is going to freak them out."

Miriam nodded, holding the flashlight with both hands like a club, but she still looked frightened out of her mind. Her legs shook. Her teeth chattered, and the sound set Jenny on edge. The girl hadn't even seen an angel yet. Jenny was glad now that she'd refrained from describing the wretched variants and the one that had ripped its eyes out to avoid the light.

Sighing, Jenny undid the clasp under her chin. "You can have this too." Her heart squeezed painfully as she handed over Susan's helmet. *Why am I trying so hard to make her feel better?*

**It is counterproductive. The conditions for completing the Survival Challenge—**

Jenny cut off Eve's words. It was strange to abruptly stop a thought that wasn't hers, but it felt comforting knowing she still had power over her own mind. Eve couldn't just say or do what it wanted. And she didn't want to hear anything more about the survival challenge bullshit.

As Miriam set the pink helmet on her head, Jenny glanced down the hall. She stepped quickly, trying to keep silent as Miriam tiptoed behind her. The light shone all over the place. Dried blood covered the lockers. Some of them were open, revealing jackets and umbrellas and textbooks. The streaks of blood concerned her. She couldn't tell which way the bodies had been dragged. Were they headed toward more danger?

At the end of the corridor, the hallway split in two. To the right were the lecture rooms, with the teacher's lounge at the far end. To the left were double doors separating the labs and other classrooms. There was a girl's bathroom just past those doors, which were stained with blood. It looked like someone had tried to resist being dragged, their fingers clawing at the paint.

Miriam gasped and shone the flashlight through the little windows as Jenny raised her shield in alarm. She blocked the light, her heart racing. What if there were angels on the other side? What if they'd spotted the light? She was sure the labs were where the bodies had been dragged to; there had to be something on the other side. Panic flared up, making it harder to breathe.

*Eve? Where's Oliver? And the other humans? Are they hiding somewhere?*

But Eve's response never came. Instead, Jenny heard the now all too familiar roar of a wretched angel, a terrifyingly haunting sound that made her heart sink into her stomach. It was coming from beyond the doors; her guess had been right.

Miriam whispered something, but Jenny wasn't listening. She motioned down the other hall. "We'll hide in the teacher's lounge," she said frantically.

Stumbling, Miriam nearly tripped, but then started running down the hall. Everything shook, and Jenny knew the wretched angel would burst through the double doors any moment now. She could run past Miriam with ease, but she forced herself to hang back, to keep the other girl safe. The light bobbed up and down the hall, and they'd nearly made it to the end when another roar echoed from behind them.

Jenny stopped running. She whipped around to face it, and she gasped, surprised. It was the male wretched angel who had attacked Jenny and Susan on the first floor. Covered in shining black, it was the one who had nearly bitten through her throat.

The creature stood on its legs now. Its muscles bulged, and the tendrils coming off its back seemed to be longer. They fluttered up to the ceiling.

### Wretched Angel (Level 29)

"Get inside," she whispered to Miriam.

But the only response she got was a thud. Jenny glanced over her shoulder to see Miriam had passed out on the floor.

*Shit.*

For a dizzying moment, Jenny flashed back to the boy lying on the floor in the stairwell. She wished she could take her helmet back, but she figured it had kept Miriam's head safe during the fall. She clenched her jaws in frustration, wishing she could at least pick up the flashlight, but with only one set of fingers, she'd have to drop her hatchet first. It didn't help at all that the light shone the other way, illuminating the space behind her. That wasn't going to help at all against the angel.

*At least if anything tries to sneak up on us, the light will keep it away.*

Jenny sucked in a deep breath, eyeing the wretched angel. It seemed to be sizing her up too. Did it recognize her? Could it tell that she'd changed?

*I'm stronger now. This won't be like last time.*

But where was its mate? The blonde one covered in light blue with insectlike antennae. Wherever it was, Jenny knew she'd have to do something to hurt this angel before its mate showed up.

Taking a step forward, she held her shield defensively, squeezing her hatchet. She had to bring the fight to it; she couldn't risk letting it get too close to Miriam. The creature cocked its head before falling forward till it was on all fours, its tendrils whipping the air. Then the wretched angel roared again, shaking the entire floor.

"Oh, shut up," said Jenny through her teeth. She rolled her shoulders, preparing herself for the fight. She wasn't afraid. She wasn't even angry. She just didn't want someone else to die.

And she wanted to kill that dumb fucking wretched angel.

Willing her body forward, she tried to recreate that burst of speed from earlier, when she'd stopped Miriam from opening the door. But a sudden motion to her right caught her eye from one of the lecture rooms. Through the little window on the door, she saw the flicker of movement. A face. A boy she didn't recognize.

But that moment of hesitation was all the angel needed. A dark blur suddenly rose in front of her face, the wind blowing her hair back. The creature aimed for her head, swinging a large, muscular arm covered in black as its teeth flashed, spittle flying.

Jenny managed to knock its wrist away with her shield, feeling the impact in her bones. Then, with a scream, she swung her hatchet as hard as she could, aiming for its neck.

# CHAPTER TWENTY-FOUR

# REMATCH

The hatchet caught the wretched angel on its collarbone with a resounding clang, its black covering cracking upon impact, but that was as far as her weapon went.

Screeching, the angel leaped back before the edge of her hatchet could cut any deeper. There was no blood. The angel's tendrils swished madly over its head as it hissed, clutching its collarbone, a furious expression on its face.

*Fuck.* She hadn't expected that. She'd hoped to hit it hard enough to maybe chop off its head, or at least slow it down. Jenny shook out her arms and straightened her back. Just hitting it hurt like hell. Knocking its arm away with the shield had made her shoulder and elbow ache.

This one was definitely denser than the other high-leveled wretched angel in the stairwell. It was thicker and more muscular, and its covering felt harder, like she was trying to cut through a thick layer of metal. The purple male from the stairwell had been much easier to slice, except for its bones, but she'd assumed that was because her power just hadn't been high enough.

It was obvious now that raising her power wasn't the only thing that mattered. She'd need to increase her durability as well; otherwise, her body wouldn't withstand the blows. It wasn't just for defense.

Jenny licked the sweat above her lips, not taking her eyes off the wretched angel. She wanted to check the lecture hall, find out who was inside and if Oliver was with them, but that would have to wait.

The angel's tendrils whipped the air, then the creature hissed, launching itself forward on all fours. It was even faster now, and she recognized the attack. That was how it had knocked Susan away before; it was going to barrel into Jenny.

The creature slammed into her shield like a train ramming through a truck stalled on the tracks. The impact launched Jenny. The air rippled, and the next thing she knew, her back crunched against a wall.

Jenny sank to the floor, her head spinning with nausea, the metallic taste of blood in her mouth. She'd flown over Miriam and was right beside the teacher's lounge now. The flashlight pointed at her, blurring her vision with its bright light. Squinting, she could make out the blurry dark figure of the menacing angel.

She coughed up blood. A series of swear words filled her head, but the only thing she could spit out was more red liquid. Touching the back of her head, she felt it slick and wet. Her fingers came away glistening with blood, and she blinked several times, trying to clear the spots in her vision.

She slammed her shield against the floor, sputtering, struggling to climb to her feet. Where was the hatchet? This stupid light was hurting her eyes. A groan filled her throat as piercing pain shot down her spine and into her legs. What was the angel doing?

It seemed to be hesitating. Sniffing the air. Was it smelling the boy in the room?

No. It set its eyes on Miriam's limp form. It was going after the easy prey.

Jenny exhaled slowly, trying to ignore the gurgling sound in her lungs. She couldn't let the creature get to Miriam. Gritting her teeth, Jenny took a shaky step. Then another.

A minor potion of recovery flashed into existence in her hand, costing her a hundred energy. She bit the stopper and yanked it out, downing the red liquid while eyeing the wretched angel. It had paused when Jenny moved and cocked its head curiously when she created the potion.

*Stupid angel.* Steam rose from her body; more light flashed as she summoned her hatchet. Her healing became smooth, and the sharp, shooting pains lessened to a dull throb. Then she stomped forward, throwing her weapon with all her might. *Savage Throw.*

The hatchet spun through the air. The angel roared, trying to swipe it away, but the edge struck its face, snapping its head back. The handle jutted out upward, pointing at the ceiling, the hatchet now lodged in its jaw.

Blood gushed from its mouth as Jenny recalled her hatchet, seeing the damage: she'd cut right through its bottom jaw, splitting it in half. The angel grabbed its face, screaming.

Not wanting to waste the opportunity, Jenny dashed forward, leaping over Miriam. She slammed into the angel with her shield, wishing she could just repeat that burst of speed from earlier; she could've hit the creature just as hard as it had hit her. But it felt like the more she tried to force it, the less likely it was to manifest. How had she turned Savage Throw into a skill?

Frustrated, she struck the angel again with the shield, hitting it right on the split jaw. Stepping forward, something crunched beneath her boot as she swung with her hatchet, aiming again for its throat.

The angel spun away from her attack before swinging. Its muscles glistened. Its fingers closed right in front of her face as she flinched, splattering her with droplets of blood. It was trying to grab her.

But she'd gotten a close look at its ruined face. Her hatchet had gone through its lower jaw, splitting the bottom of its skull in half and cracking the black covering around its neck. It was missing teeth, and the tip of its tongue stuck out painfully from the bottom of its head, lodged between the two halves of its cracked jaw.

Jenny stumbled back and stepped to the side, dodging the angel's next attempt to smack her. It clasped its hands together and tried again, this time trying to smash her into the floor with an overhead attack, but she'd raised her shield, letting it absorb the blow. The vibrations rocked through every single bone, and she dropped to her knees.

"Fuck," she spat, pain ringing throughout her arm and shoulder.

From this position, the angel's legs were exposed. If she could cut one deeply enough, she'd slow the creature down. Before she could attack, however, it grabbed her shield, its massive fingers curling around the edges.

Her eyes went wide as it wrenched her off the floor. Her legs swung through the air, and she felt like a rag doll. Then her body crashed hard against the lockers, crumpling several of the rectangular metal faces before collapsing on the floor. Her armor clinked as she landed on her left side, pain staining her vision red.

The angel towered over her, muscles bulging, blood dripping from its ruined jaw. It tried to grab her again, reaching for her head with its oversized hand. Every muscle in her body screamed for air, but she held her breath, focusing as hard as she could on the angel's fingers nearing her face. She didn't want to mess up this next attack; she wanted revenge.

Golden light filled her palm, and she swung upward. Her hatchet sliced through its fingers, and with a screech of agony, the angel backed away, clutching its hand as blood spurted all over the place. Jenny sucked air into her burning lungs, and before the angel's severed fingers hit the floor, she was on her feet.

She bashed the creature with her shield, hitting it right on the injured hand. "How's that feel?" she hissed, striking it across the hip with her hatchet. The angel's face was twisted with rage. Her weapon bounced off its side, chipping away at the black covering. Before she could hit it again, it seized her arm.

All of a sudden, she was airborne. Her nose whizzed past the ceiling—for an intense fraction of a moment, she saw the dotted paint pattern on the tiles above— then she was hurtling down the hall. The angel had grabbed her by the arm, turned, and launched her over its own head.

The lockers and classroom doors blurred by, the floor rushing up to meet her face. She had just enough time to turn midair so that she landed on her shield.

Slamming into the floor, she bounced twice then skidded several feet, tearing up the tiles beneath her. She felt like a meteorite crashing into Earth, kicking up sparks and debris and dust.

When she finally came to a stop, there was a ringing in Jenny's head, like someone had smashed a gong and the sound was reverberating, bouncing from one ear to the other and back.

Grunting, painfully aware of the throbbing in her left side, she got to her feet and leaned against the wall for support. She'd landed near the double doors that led into the labs. One of them was knocked askew, hanging off a hinge, from when the wretched angel had burst through.

She tried to steady her breathing, keeping her focus on the angel. It was on all fours, picking something up off the floor. Its fingers and teeth.

Did it understand that loss? Was it hurting? Coming to the realization that it could never grab anything again with that hand, scratch itself, poke something, or hold someone's hand?

*That's right, you stupid piece of shit.* Jenny winced, rolling her shield arm and feeling something crack in her shoulder. *Your mate took my fingers. I took yours.*

She remembered reading somewhere that anyone could bite a finger off like a carrot. The human jaw was more than strong enough, and fingerbones were delicate. It was the brain that stopped people.

A bitter sense of satisfaction gave her strength. The dizzying feeling faded, and she didn't hurt anywhere except for the aching in her shoulder. She wouldn't need to use another potion.

She glanced down at her right arm, the one the angel had grabbed. A few of the scales were cracked, the armor dented inward around her forearm. The angel's grip was no joke, but at least now it could only grab her with one hand. Its other one was just as useless as her own.

*Maybe I should cut off its penis next*, she thought, watching it sniff one of the severed fingers. That would *really* send a message to its mate. If they did the deed the way she thought they did, at least.

Summoning her hatchet back to her hand, she was just about to throw it when she saw what the angel was doing. Jenny froze, recoiling in disgust.

The angel was eating its own fingers. It turned its head to look at her, one long black digit wriggling between its teeth; except that its bottom jaw was split, and each side moved independently, giving the creature an even more grotesque appearance as blood gushed between its chin. The crackle of its fingerbones made Jenny shudder.

Its tendrils fluttered over its back, and she focused on them instead of its ruined mouth and cannibalism. Her ears still rang from being thrown, and she tried not to think about what would've happened if the angel had smashed her against the ceiling instead of just flinging her. At best, her nose would've been punched inward. At worst, her head would've burst, her insides splattering the tiles like modern art.

Golden light shimmered and drew her attention. But Jenny wasn't making anything—it was the angel. The light danced around its injured hand, and her heart sank as she watched its fingers grow back, snapping and crackling and echoing down the hall. Long and black and sleek, covered in more armor than before, the new fingers grew into fully formed claws.

Then it grabbed its jaw with both hands. Jenny heard a disgusting *crunch*, and the light shimmered around its chin and neck. The angel dropped to all fours and hissed, its newly healed lips stretching into a wide grin as it bared its new fangs.

*That's not fair. What the fuck? Could they do that this entire time?*

**It appears this wretched angel has developed a skill.**

*What?* But before she could press Eve for more, she saw the angel sniffing the air. The creature turned away from Jenny, staring at Miriam.

"No, you fucking don't," whispered Jenny. Seeing the angel rush, an explosion of sudden movement, she threw her hatchet, trying to put every ounce of power into the attack.

*Savage Throw.*

The hatchet whistled through the air, the resulting wind blowing her hair back. But her stomach sank. She knew it wasn't going to land; she'd overthrown, misjudging the angel's speed.

It sailed right over the creature's shoulders, missing its head by inches before smashing into the other end of the hallway, right into the crater from when Jenny had crashed into that wall earlier.

The sound drew the wretched angel's attention for a split second. Its tendrils wriggled and snapped, then it continued stomping toward Miriam's body.

*No, no, no, no!* She blinked. She'd missed.

The world seemed to slow. Her hand shook as she tried to summon her hatchet again, but there was no time. The angel was almost upon Miriam, and she'd never be able to throw the weapon again before it grabbed her. And what if she missed again? Her head spun, picturing the worst. With Miriam's delicate composition, she wouldn't last a second.

Light flashed in her hand, twisting and flowing. Time thrummed to a standstill, and the space between every one of her heartbeats filled with a deafening silence. She had to rush forward, the same way she'd stopped Miriam from opening the door. That impulsive motion she'd done out of instinct. That same burst of speed. She had to do it. And she had to do it *now*.

**Skill Acquired!**
**Instant Acceleration (Tier 1)**

# CHAPTER TWENTY-FIVE

# FORTIFICATION

The hallway melted away; her peripheral vision blurred and faded till all that remained was the target. She threw all of her focus at the muscular black form of the angel, willing her body forward, propelling herself with nothing more than the desire to move at the speed of sound.

Rocketing toward the creature, Jenny's shield smashed into the wretched angel's back, the impact flashing like a bolt of lightning. Cracks spread through the angel's covering, and in that same instant, it slammed into the wall at the end of the hallway.

Her ears rang. Her cheeks stung from how her hair had whipped her face. She'd hit the angel with enough force to crumple the lockers to her right, as well as roll Miriam over.

The angel's head was buried in the ruined wall. Its body hung limp, knees on the floor, and if it weren't for the fluttering tendrils that rose from its spine, she would've thought it was dead.

A phlegmy cough erupted from her chest, and she struck a nearby locker with her hatchet as she doubled over and spat up blood. The impact had gone straight to her bones, and a lesson from physics teased her thoughts. Newton's third law: for every action, there is an equal and opposite reaction. She was surprised all the bones in her left arm weren't shattered.

"Is it dead?" came a small voice.

Jenny blinked away her tears to see Miriam cowering on the floor. She was on her stomach, frozen with fear, staring at the angel's large body. Its back covering was cracked, several chunks missing, revealing pale white skin that glistened wetly in the flashlight.

"Can you move?" whispered Jenny, scraping through her thoughts, trying to figure out what to do. Her body ached so much. The angel twitched, and loose debris rained down from the ceiling. "Miriam!" Jenny hissed with more urgency when the girl didn't respond.

Miriam looked back over her shoulder, tears running down her cheeks. She nodded slightly, the pink helmet rattling.

"Okay," said Jenny, shutting her eyes. Just taking a breath sent sharp, shooting pains from her ribs to her spine and down her legs. "Back there, in the AP Chem room. 223. I saw someone in there. Go." She heard Miriam's shuffling beside her, and she looked down to see the other girl on all fours, too terrified to even stand.

Miriam crawled to the classroom, sobbing. She knocked so lightly on the bottom of the door that Jenny almost didn't hear it. But whoever was inside must have, because the door opened quickly. There was a pause. Jenny spotted a shadow moving, then Miriam crawled inside, and the door shut firmly, leaving her alone in the hall with the wretched angel.

*Could've at least left me the helmet . . .*

With the angel struggling to get out of the wall, Jenny took a moment to steady her breathing, trying to will the aching and hurting away. Her heart was still racing, but a fresh wave of excitement sizzled inside her. Not only did she no longer have to worry about Miriam's immediate safety, but she'd done it! She'd created a new skill, the same way she'd made Savage Throw.

*Instant Acceleration . . .*

Using it was *draining,* to say the least. She could go fast—insanely fast—but only in a single direction. She realized she'd seen it before. In the stairwell, the male wretched angel had done something similar, rushing down the stairs to attack her. It hadn't been as quick as her skill, but it had still been fast enough to do serious damage. *Did I pick that up subconsciously?*

Jenny took a shaky step and winced as pain blossomed in her knee. Her leg nearly buckled. "Fuck," she spat, saliva running down her chin. Her eyes unfocused as her head throbbed.

The angel was stuck. This was the perfect opportunity to finish it off. Just one more blow to its back, maybe, where the covering was cracked and falling apart. But she could barely move. This was not good.

*I'm sorry, Susan . . .* Jenny had wanted to save as much energy as she could to heal Susan's leg, but it didn't seem like she had a choice now. Though it would be stupid to make two separate potions for healing and stamina. Why not make something to restore both?

On top of that, something to at least temporarily buff her durability. Her attacks were getting stronger with her increased power and new skills, but they'd be pointless if her body ended up falling apart.

Jenny tried picturing what she wanted, shaping it with her thoughts like a sculptor would caress a slab of marble. She shut her eyes tight, trying to ignore her body, but she heard the angel break free. It landed on the floor with a heavy thud, and her heart sank. She'd lost her opportunity.

Squeezing her hatchet, she focused on the potion she was trying to will into existence the same way she'd willed Instant Acceleration. Thinking without straining, trusting her instincts. Imagining it.

A round, spherical glass bottle, bigger than the vials. It had to be bigger because it had to do more. She pictured it full of glowing orange liquid; she pictured it fortifying her bones and muscles, restoring her strength.

It felt like running her hand through a beam of light that snuck through her bedroom window every morning when the sun was angled just right. Her fingers fluttered through specks of floating dust, never feeling anything but knowing the photons and microorganisms must be there.

Her breath caught in her throat. She felt a snag, as though her mind had come upon *something*, and that something pulled on her. Her hatchet fell from her hands.

**A Minor Potion of Fortification will cost 350 Energy.**
**Sufficient Energy.**

Warmth pulsed around her right hand. Opening her eyes, she found golden light forming a sphere on her palm.

**Minor Potion of Fortification**
**It will restore your Health and Stamina, as well as temporarily**
**boost your Stats.**

It was a large flask with a rounded bottom, a vibrant orange liquid sitting inside. The color reminded her of candy, of something intensely sweet and citrusy, but there were also streaks of silver that appeared when she swished the flask.

Pulling the stopper out with her teeth, she downed the potion, chugging its contents till every last drop was down her throat. The taste was shocking, like the first bite into a fresh, juicy peach: an earthy sweetness that bursts in your mouth and leaves you breathless.

A gasp escaped her lips, and she exhaled a thick cloud of steam. Strength surged through her limbs as she heard a few snaps, her ribs itching like mad for a few seconds before she was whole. More whole than she'd ever felt, even with the missing fingers.

**Jenny Huang**
**Human (Stage II - Level 16)**
**Age: 6,801 days**
**Stats:**

**Power: 25 (+16)**
**Durability: 15 (+16)**
**Stamina: 20 (+16)**
**Agility: 20 (+16)**
**Stat Points Available: 0**
**Energy Available: 108**

*Holy . . .* She'd created a remarkably powerful potion, but she didn't have time to celebrate. It was a temporary boost.

*How long will it last? Eve, can you keep track of that?*

**Given the parameters of your current form . . . the potion will remain in effect for ten minutes and seventeen seconds.**

Down the hall, the angel lay on its back, breathing loudly. Jenny could see the rise and fall of its large chest from here.

She coughed again, covering her lips with the back of her hand. The empty potion vial hit the floor and shattered into luminous dust before fading away. Then light flashed once more, her hatchet returning to her hand. Something throbbed in the back of her mind as she stepped forward. She felt strong, like she could cut down anyone and anything, and nothing was going to hold her back; nothing was going to stop her from killing this creature.

Reckless desire pulsed to the forefront of her thoughts. *Kill. Kill. Kill.* Her breathing steadied. Her vision cleared. Her heart slowed, each beat feeling stronger than the one before. Blood pulsed to her limbs and back.

But she heard another voice, too; one that spoke over the psychopathic murder spree she wanted to go on. It was Susan, telling her to be careful. *Don't rush.* Jenny exhaled, wishing again to be with her best friend. Or to at least have the pink helmet back.

Golden light danced around Jenny's head, and a metallic red helmet took shape, holding her hair in place, hugging her cheeks, and covering her nose. Without looking, she knew it was a Spartan helmet; something she'd drawn several times in her notes when she was bored in class. She planned on giving it to Susan later; she'd love it. But for now, it fueled her raging fighting spirit even more.

The wretched angel hissed and screeched. Its face was covered in dust, but she could see the cracks from where she stood. Its breathing seemed heavy and labored. *Maybe I hit something vital. Maybe I ruptured a lung.*

But the creature let out a furious roar, pushing itself off the floor and bouncing off the wall to stand. Its muscles bulged. Its chest was cracked, too, and the black covering glistened in the light as the wretched angel shielded its face with its large, clawed hand.

It seemed unsteady, and the light was affecting it now, too. Exhaling, Jenny bent her knees slightly, lowering her center of gravity as she concentrated. All her focus was on the angel. Her body trembled with the potion's boost, her muscles aching to be used.

But just before she moved, the angel tore at its chest, and she hesitated.

With its claws, it peeled off the black layer to reveal smooth pinkish-white skin underneath. It sounded like tape tearing.

*What the fuck is it doing?*

The creature, still covering its eyes with one hand, bit into what it had torn off. Its own flesh.

Jenny grimaced, realizing it was eating itself again to heal. *What kind of stupid ability is that?* She had to kill it before it got any stronger, and definitely before her potion ran out. She didn't have enough energy for another.

She launched herself forward. *Instant Acceleration.* Her feet barely touched the tiles as she flew, the hallway blurring again. The angel shone brightly, the flashlight guiding her to the target.

The shield struck its exposed chest, knocking the creature back into the wall with a thunderous crash. Bricks came loose and rained down, one rolling off the angel's head, and another striking Jenny on the shoulder.

The angel coughed up thick globs of blood right into Jenny's face. Some landed in her mouth, but she didn't flinch, even as the salty flavor washed over her tongue. She looked the wretched angel in its empty eyes, her shield having crushed its chest, hoping this time she got its lungs for good.

She planted the balls of her feet firmly onto the floor, trying to completely crush the angel against the wall. Its arms flailed limply as hushing sounds escaped through its teeth, stained red by the blood dribbling from the corners of its lips. The black covering of its face was completely ruined now, bits and pieces knocked free by the impact of her attack. She could see the pale skin. The outline of its skull.

It wheezed, and Jenny was ready to end this fight.

She inhaled deeply, ignoring the taste of its blood in her mouth. Heat swirled and climbed from her chest to her throat. *I hope you burn in hell,* she thought.

But before she could exhale the flames, the wretched angel twitched violently, the clawed arm shooting up and striking her on the shoulder, swatting her away with enough force to send her crashing through the wooden door of the teacher's lounge.

Her helmet sounded like a gong. The door burst off its hinges, and together, she and the door sailed across the room to crash into something large and dense.

A massive fissure raced up the wall to the ceiling, where the tiles came loose. Debris from the room above rained down on Jenny.

# CHAPTER TWENTY-SIX

# A Fight in the Teacher's Lounge

She was covered in dust and chunks of ceiling. Groaning, Jenny tried to get up. Her core strained, her teeth clenched, but she collapsed, breathless. Her head ached maddeningly.

Smoke rose from between her teeth. The wooden door of the teacher's lounge was folded beneath her; they both had crashed into the fridge, knocking it against the wall, which, upon impact, had cracked. The ceiling had caved in slightly, chairs and books and bits of plaster and wood raining down like an avalanche. She heard shuffling above, but couldn't see anything in the gaping darkness. She wished she had her flashlight. Her armor looked gray, caked with dust.

The door had cracked through the middle, splintered wood sticking out like a demonic smile. A shattered coffee pot lay on the floor near her leg, its dark contents pooling. She'd knocked over a large wooden table, breaking two of its legs. Mugs, papers, and a pair of cracked glasses were strewn all about between her and the exit.

She coughed up dust and more smoke, feeling around wildly with her right hand for her hatchet. She pricked her fingers on splinters and touched something cold and spongy before she remembered she could recall it.

Golden light flashed. With it back in her hand, she felt the tiniest bit of comfort. Jenny managed to pull herself to her feet, wood crackling against her armor. Her right shoulder ached fiercely with a throbbing pain, and the scales were shattered, exposing a layer of dark mesh.

The angel had hit her *hard*, but her armor and the minor potion of fortification had saved her.

She rolled her arm, wondering if it was dislocated and she just couldn't feel pain yet because of the potion. Something seemed to click in her shoulder—the same sensation as cracking her knuckles—but other than that, it seemed fine. She'd just have to be careful and not let the angel attack her there now that the armor was compromised.

Jenny groaned, shutting her eyes, trying to quell the wave of nausea. She exhaled forcefully through her nose, blowing out dust and snot, then stumbled out of the debris, wrenching her boot free, trying not to inhale any more of the dust.

Squinting, she realized the wretched angel hadn't followed her inside. Instead, it was on all fours, eating the bit of black covering it had torn off before, chewing loudly and wetly before slurping and swallowing. Its exposed chest was caved in, the semicircular shape clearly the work of Jenny's shield, and its breathing was raspy and labored.

It was eating itself out of desperation.

As the angel tore more of its cracked covering off, the substance turned gelatinous, and Jenny realized as soon as the angel started chewing that the stuff didn't remain solid. It slurped it up like ramen before munching.

*How much time do I have left before the potion wears off?*

**You have eight minutes and seventeen seconds.**

She limped forward, eyeing the rest of the room. There was a red leather couch beside her, torn up and with two corpses lying on top of it. One was naked and bony, with its head angled so that its empty eyes stared at Jenny. The other was a thin woman.

Though the skin of her face was still attached to her head, it was torn off enough that Jenny couldn't recognize the teacher. She noticed the pen sticking out of the angel's neck. They must have died together before the woman could use the system.

Jenny nearly slipped in the puddle of coffee but managed to catch herself. More debris rained down behind her, and then she heard hissing. Her blood ran cold. Something large plopped down from above, landing on the ruined door with a clatter. Without hesitating, and as soon as the thought registered in her head, Jenny slashed it across the face.

**Wretched Angel (Level 15)**

Her hatchet's edge cut clean through the center of its head, from one ear to the other. The angel, a male covered in dark green, made a low rasping sound, as though it were surprised. But its arms and chest and chin were already stained with blood; it had lived more than long enough. Jenny watched its body collapse, the top of its head slipping off like the lid of a clay pot.

**You've defeated Wretched Angel (Level 15)!**
**Experience has been awarded.**
**+100 Energy**

She waited to hear if any other angels were going to drop down. Straining her eyes at the dark hole in the ceiling, she could see what looked like a dangling arm. She couldn't tell what it belonged to, but it wasn't moving.

**You have six minutes and fifty-nine seconds.**

*Just tell me when I have three minutes left.* She took a shaky breath, glad that Eve was in her head keeping track of the timer. It almost felt like cheating, but she didn't care. It wanted something in return, and she didn't want to die.

The wretched angel in the hallway hissed loudly. Golden light filled its chest as it held its clawed hand against the exposed skin. Grabbing the ruined doorframe, it stood upright, saliva dripping from its jaws as it eyed Jenny. She could hear its horrid breathing, could see the cracks in its facial covering, light shining across its face.

She remembered how the first wretched angel she'd fought had shied away from the golden light. This one didn't seem to care at all. Or maybe it was immune to its own light?

And it could heal . . . after eating itself. She remembered the terrible way it had chewed its own fingers then healed its jaw and hand. Except that hand had regrown with dangerously large claws.

The angel growled and pressed those same claws to its face next, before more light illuminated the ruined teacher's lounge. Jenny could see its new chest; it was now covered in a thicker layer of that solid black material, with a spike jutting out of the center. She did *not* want to get impaled on that.

Why was this only getting more and more difficult to deal with? Why was this angel so much more adept than the others in the stairwell? They'd been high-level, too.

**Those particular wretched angels were drained from mating.**

*So I just got lucky? The angels were weak from . . . Ugh.* She kicked a book away in frustration, trying to think of some way out of this. The teacher's lounge was roomy, so at least she wasn't completely boxed in, but the only ways out were either through the angel or out a window—and something told her it wouldn't be fun to fall through the void outside.

Jenny sensed Eve was about to answer and explain more properties of the Veil, but that would have to wait. The angel lifted its new face, black covering slicked back with spikes protruding from the top and back of its head, almost like gelled hair.

*Why hasn't it leveled up? It's only getting scarier.* There was a ferocious look on the creature's face.

**Level thirty is a threshold level. It requires a great amount of—**

The angel rushed her with a roar. But she'd been ready. She knocked its large claws away with her shield, then whirled around that arm, keeping distance from the spike on its chest.

She kicked a mug so that it shattered against the wall. The sound made the angel twitch, its head turning in that direction, and Jenny seized the opportunity to slash its neck.

Her hatchet bounced harmlessly off the black covering as she stumbled back in shock. The angel's tendrils swished madly, and it glowered at her. Then, with a roar, it turned to slash her face.

She ducked, its claws whistling over her helmet, and she saw her chance. Using a burst of Instant Acceleration, she slammed into the creature from that position.

Another shock wave went through her body, but the impact launched the angel away. It crashed through the couch, tearing up a cloud of fluffy white material as the bodies on it went flying. Bookshelves collapsed on the other side of the room, and paintings clattered to the floor, their glass faces shattering, further confusing the wretched angel as it whirled around.

Jenny wasn't going to let up. She stomped forward on her left foot, a booming scream filling her throat as she flung her hatchet. The boost from the potion was palpable; the hatchet tore through the space between them before striking the angel with a thunderous crack, right below its new chest spike.

The angel roared in pain, thrashing against the broken shelves and debris. Jenny was breathing hard, drenched in sweat; she was running out of time. Her throw was stronger, but it wasn't enough to kill the creature, who clawed a sizeable chunk of wall off and hurled it at her.

Jenny almost tried to block it with her shield, then thought better of it and rolled out of the way. The chunk of wall crashed loudly behind her, but she kept her eyes on the wretched angel. Its breathing was just as labored as her own, but its chest was only dented slightly. There were no cracks; its new covering held strong.

She spat blood. The angel wasn't just healing itself through self-cannibalism— it was fortifying the same way her potion had.

It ripped the hatchet out, but Jenny was already rushing forward.

Summoning her weapon back with a flash of light, she leaped over the ruined couch and slashed the angel. Sparks glittered on its forehead as the hatchet bounced off, and the creature hissed, trying to grab her.

Blocking its claws with her shield, she stepped back, moved swiftly to the right, then landed another blow. This time, the edge bounced off its dark cheek.

The wretched angel's head snapped to the side. Then, slowly, it turned back to stare at her, showing its teeth as if it were grinning and mocking her.

Furious, Jenny swung again, this time aiming for its leg, which she knew hadn't been fortified yet. But the angel's claws shot up, grabbing her arm.

"No!" she shouted, trying to use Instant Acceleration to step back, but the angel held her firmly, glaring down at her. Her insides jolted in place, the failed attempt making her vision spin violently.

She thrust her shield into its chin, forcing its head upward, realizing she'd made a stupid mistake again by letting the angel goad her into attacking so blindly. Then, in the heat of the moment, an idea burst through her thoughts.

*Ignite.*

Fire erupted from her mouth, illuminating the room with a warm, orangey-red glow as the flames engulfed the angel's chest and arm. It howled in pain, releasing its grip as she tried scorching its face, but the creature slammed its knee into her tummy, driving all the air out of her lungs.

The fire flickered out into spittle. A choking gasp escaped her throat, then she was tumbling backward through the debris, coming to a stop after her helmet bounced off the floor.

She turned over and retched. Blood and water and stomach bile splattered the loose tiles and textbooks as pain coiled in her belly, but that only fueled her rage.

Not even wiping her mouth, she leaped back to her feet as Eve relayed how much time was left.

**You have three minutes remaining.**

She spat, trying to ignore the horrid taste of vomit and ash in her mouth. The wretched angel's shoulder was scorched, and it writhed in agony, its tendrils flickering in every direction. The black covering was melted and lopsided, and a sulfuric stench clogged her nose. She only wished she'd gotten the arm with the claws.

Jenny lunged again, knowing if she didn't finish this quickly, the potion's effect would wear off, and she'd definitively die.

The angel leaped as well, and they collided midair. Her shield took the brunt of its claws, clanging loudly. Its burned arm moved too slowly, and she swung her hatchet upward from below. The razor-sharp edge found the creature's armpit, where the black covering gave easily now that it was slightly melted. Screaming in the angel's face, Jenny followed through with the motion.

She cut through the flesh and bone connecting the angel's arm to its shoulder. Blood sprayed everything as the wretched angel lumbered backward, its eyes wide open in shock.

The arm hung off the shoulder, only a few remaining tendons keeping it attached. Blood rushed down its muscles and side.

Jenny could see the strands of exposed muscle, and if it weren't for the angel holding its arm with its claws, she knew the weight would've finished the job for her.

She hissed at the creature, mocking it just how it had mocked her. Raising her shield and bending her knees slightly, she decided to hit the angel again with Instant Acceleration. She'd follow it up with another burst of Ignite, then cut off its stupid head.

But just as soon as she stepped forward, as the room blurred, as time rippled, the wretched angel tore off its own limb and swung it back.

The glistening dark muscle of its arm made it look like a large club. She was moving too quickly. She couldn't adjust her direction or duck or dodge.

The arm connected with her shield, slamming it into her face.

Her nose caved. Her head snapped back. Her feet came off the ground. And once again, she was flying backward, her consciousness threatening to slip into an empty darkness. She was only vaguely aware of crashing into something; the sound never reached her ears. All she could hear was an intense ringing, drowning out even her heartbeat as she felt the sharp edges of her teeth tearing into the back of her throat.

She tried to open her mouth, but her jaw wouldn't work. Pain screamed from both sides of her face; blood gushed down from her shattered nose.

The wretched angel towered over her.

*C'mon . . . C'mon!* She tried to will her body up, to raise her shield, recall her hatchet. Her heart pounded furiously. But all she managed to do was raise one foot slightly off the floor.

The creature stared down at her, blood dripping in thick spurts from its shoulder. It was still holding its arm. As soon as it ate it, the angel would get even stronger. There was nothing more she could do.

*This is it,* she thought. *I lost . . . It's over.* She didn't look away from its empty eyes, daring it to finish her. She was going to watch. *If this is it . . . I'm sorry, Susan. Oliver. Eve . . .*

But the angel didn't hit her again. Instead, it put its severed arm between its teeth, holding it like a dog might hold a large stick, then leaned down and grabbed Jenny's leg with its claws. The armor crunched as the angel turned away, walking on two legs and hunched over as it dragged Jenny's limp body out of the teacher's lounge.


**You have one minute and forty-seven seconds remaining.**

# CHAPTER TWENTY-SEVEN

# BROKEN TEETH

Her helmet and armor and shield rattled against the floor as the wretched angel dragged Jenny out of the teacher's lounge, her eyes rolling toward the back of her head. She struggled to stay conscious, but her vision blurred and faded and came back. She couldn't swallow; her teeth were stuck in the back of her throat, each one piercing her in a different place, sending shooting pains into her ears from inside her mouth.

She was too terrified to swallow the pooling saliva and blood. It took tremendous effort to part her lips—her lower jaw felt bent out of shape, as if it hung at an angle, as if her skull had been reshaped by the impact—but she managed to open her mouth, and blood flowed out, leaving behind a slimy trail as the angel dragged her past the chem room where Miriam and the boy and possibly some others were hiding.

*Please save me,* she thought, wondering if any of them would even stand a chance against this angel. She spotted the light from the flashlight, and, for a moment, hope flickered through her head. It had rolled so far away from where Miriam had initially dropped it, but maybe this was a stroke of luck. Maybe the light would freak the angel out, giving her a chance to escape.

But the wretched angel just hissed before its foot came down on the flashlight with a decisive thud, extinguishing the brightness in an instant. All that remained was the deep, rolling gloom of the darkened hallway.

Jenny wasn't sure if she could've grabbed it, anyway. She blinked sadly at its crushed remains, thinking about how Susan had carefully taped it to the helmet. She was glad Susan wasn't here. Glad Susan wouldn't have to suffer this. She was safe in the library, and Jenny wouldn't get to keep her promise.

Her nose gurgled and whistled with every breath. She wanted to touch it, to make sure it was still on her face, but she couldn't move her arms. They trailed behind her, limp and lifeless as she struggled to stay conscious. Her eyelids felt heavier and heavier. At one point, her body bounced on the torn-up tiles from earlier in the fight, and a violent fit of coughing overtook her, shocking her fully awake.

The teeth cutting into her throat shot out of her mouth and scattered like little stones. There was still one left, stuck to the soft bit behind the roof of her mouth. She touched her gums with the tip of her tongue, finding a few jagged bits of teeth sticking out like shards of broken glass.

**You have sixty seconds remaining.**

The notification hovered in her mind for a moment before fading away. What did it matter now? All she was doing was counting down till the boosted durability wore off, and then, she'd be completely powerless.

She tried to use her shield as a brake, digging into the floor. The resistance only lasted a second before the angel yanked hard on her leg. She cried out as her entire body bounced again as though she were a rag doll. She tried kicking with her other leg, but it was futile. Its legs were too thickly covered, and she couldn't get any leverage. Her boot bounced off harmlessly.

They were nearly to the blue double doors. She glanced down the other hallway; the one she'd come through with Miriam. Nothing stirred. No bodies. No other angels. A part of her had hoped someone else would show up. Maybe the people who'd been fighting here before. But if the boy had been hiding back in that classroom, then there wasn't much hope.

*What am I supposed to do now?* Her face throbbed with pain. Jenny tried to summon her hatchet, but no warm light filled her hand. Nothing flashed. She couldn't activate it. She couldn't recall it. Her head was a vast, pulsing darkness where the only thoughts left were hurt and self-pity.

Maybe she could use Ignite somehow. The flames had melted and softened the angel's covering before . . . She looked at her raised leg, the angel's large claws crushing the scales of her armor and holding her firmly. Even if she managed to use the skill, she'd burn herself, and she didn't think she could hurt the creature enough for the sacrifice to be worth it.

Licking the jagged edges of her ruined teeth, Jenny had another idea. She inhaled slowly, tearing up at the pain, but she sucked in as much air as she could before exhaling, bracing herself. Then, she wriggled the tooth stuck to her throat free with her tongue and swallowed.

She had to swallow several times, scratching and cutting and tearing her insides before the tooth stopped resisting and went down.

"C'mon . . ." she thought miserably, her eyes shut as she concentrated, trying to will the skill into existence. She wanted to regrow her missing fingers and restore her bones and teeth the way the wretched angel had after eating itself. But would a tooth be enough?

She remembered not to force it, but to mold it carefully from her imagination, the same way she'd learned Instant Acceleration.

But a moment later, the angel slammed into the double doors with a grunt, turning its large body and dragging Jenny through. The door swung and bounced off her helmet, and her concentration faltered.

No new skill appeared in her head. She blinked several times, trying to keep the tears at bay as her head rang. It was warmer in this hall. Much warmer. Humid and thickened air threatened to suffocate her, as if her breathing wasn't enough of a struggle. The angel seemed to have an easier time dragging her now, too. Her body slid along the floor slick with blood.

There were piles of bodies against the walls and doors. She saw a girl lying on her side, staring blankly with her eyeballs bulging from their sockets. She had no lips. No cheeks. The rest of her body was a torn mess of intestines, and it was impossible to tell what she'd been wearing. The others looked similarly unrecognizable, faces and flesh torn apart, limbs missing.

Most of them were humans. Some of them were tarnished angels. A few of them were wretched angels, their colorful coverings sticking out brightly.

The stench clogged her nose. Even with the cartilage smushed inward and her nostrils bleeding profusely, she could still smell the unbearable miasma of rot and blood and exposed innards.

Jenny's right arm twitched, wanting to summon her hatchet again as her mind twisted with rage. But again, it didn't work. Even if she had managed it, as soon as the light flashed, the angel would notice and . . . If it attacked her again in this state, she knew she was done for.

Her shield bounced off the doorframe as the wretched angel dragged her into one of the labs. It dropped her foot unceremoniously at the front of the room, beside the whiteboard and the storage closets. The angel blocked her view of the tables, but a cold, bluish light emanated from something large behind it. The light shone vibrantly before fading then glowing again in a steady, almost calming rhythm. She looked up to see the creature finally eating its arm.

It chewed the exposed muscle first, its fingers dangling over Jenny's face. Its teeth ripped and tore, blood raining down. Looking past the sickening meal, she saw the sacs—too many to count, each one of them wriggling all over the ceiling, bunched together like glistening grapes.

As the angel snorted and slobbered, Jenny heard a gasp from her right. She turned her head, the movement making the room spin as though the entire building had decided to rotate suddenly. Her eyes seemed to move slower than her head as pain shot through her neck and shoulders, and she was still trying very hard not to swallow again. But finally, she saw who'd gasped.

A boy with a shock of red hair covered by a green military helmet. Glasses, one of the lenses cracked. Freckles. Leaning against the closet that housed all the beakers and test tubes. His leg was bent the wrong way, a glistening white bone sticking out of his thigh, and his arms were wrapped around a girl who wasn't moving, the two of them covered in dry blood. His eyes were wide, filling with tears as he whispered Jenny's name.

### Human (Stage II - Level 14)

Jenny's mouth opened and closed, spittle and blood gushing out every time she exhaled. She blinked slowly, trying to gather her thoughts as the wretched angel stomped away.

It was Oliver. He was alive. Hurt, but strong . . . He was a stage two human, just like she was. A strange sense of pride filled her chest, even though she'd never let herself grow close to him, never accepted him as her younger sibling.

Throughout this entire ordeal, she'd only thought of him as her responsibility. Her duty. Had to save him for her parents' sake. But seeing him now . . . seeing that he'd struggled and fought and survived so far . . . Tears rolled down the side of her face. It felt cheap to finally feel something familial for him. And all it took was a hellish nightmare . . . She almost wanted to laugh.

Almost.

Oliver wore dark-green armor. It looked similar to the wretched angel's covering, except he wore it like a jacket. The girl in his arms had her head resting on Oliver's uninjured thigh. Their faces looked ghostly in the eerie blue glow.

### Human (Stage II - Level 13)

She'd been wearing some kind of armor too, shiny and metallic. It looked like something a knight would wear. But her helmet was shattered so that it revealed her mousy face. Her cheek was sliced open. Jenny could see loose flesh moving every time the girl inhaled and exhaled.

Beside them, in a crude row underneath the whiteboard, lay more bodies. Three more girls and two more boys, none of whom Jenny recognized, but all wore some kind of armor similar to that of Oliver and the girl's. They ranged in level from nine to sixteen, but Oliver seemed to be the only one who was awake. A few were dead; their bodies didn't trigger a notification.

**You have fifteen seconds remaining.**

Jenny squeezed her eyes shut. Tears streamed continuously, and no matter how hard she tried to stop them, her breath caught in her throat, and her heart kept beating in a frantic panic as the remaining seconds whittled away. She'd found Oliver. But now what? Had she come all this way just to watch him die?

*Eve? Are we going to die?*

**Your fate is your own to create.**

A vision shimmered in her head: the three-headed figure, glowing golden and surrounded by liquid darkness. The faces flickered, but each one was stern. The lips moved. The eyes glowered. But Jenny couldn't understand any of it. She couldn't make sense of it. The middle face became her mother's again, scowling . . . crying.

*Are you just going to let me die? I thought you wanted me to give birth to you?*

Angry, she forced herself to inhale through her nose, trying to summon strength. The muscles in her right arm trembled as she strained, lifting herself off the floor. Golden light flashed between her fingers. She was breathing hard and sweating so much . . . but if she could just hit the angel with another Ignite . . . If she could just land one more blow with her hatchet . . . She glanced at Oliver, who stared back, eyes wide with concern. *It'll be okay*, she wanted to whisper.

But just as she managed to sit up, the light flickered out in her hand. Her hatchet didn't appear. Instead, she collapsed, her helmet clanging loudly as she stared up at the sacs wriggling on the ceiling.

**The potion is no longer in effect.**

She choked on her breath. Pain ignited first on her face, and she was excruciatingly aware of how the tip of her nose was smushed inward. The scratches in her throat flared up so suddenly, she wanted to scream at the top of her voice, but all she could muster was a weak cry.

Her neck throbbed. It felt as though someone had tried furiously to yank her head off her body. Her leg was crushed where the angel had grabbed her with its claws. Every single one of her bones felt broken, her muscles torn.

Agony stained her vision dark red. Oliver and the others blurred away, and she writhed uncontrollably, trapped in her ruined body, unable to summon the strength to even scream. A part of her wanted the angel to come back and put her out of her misery, crush her head like the flashlight and just end this.

Oliver whispered something to her. She saw his lips move, but she couldn't hear anything. Pain filled her head like wet gravel and cement rotating in a heavy mixer.

Her mind raced, trying desperately to figure out a solution, something, *anything*, to quell the searing pain. She just wanted it to stop. It made even her worst period cramps feel like a minor stomachache. It was as though someone had taken a sheet of printer paper and tried to see through her, one paper cut at a time.

Light burst behind her eyes, white and so bright that it felt like her mind was collapsing. She blinked over and over, shaking violently. She didn't have enough energy to get out of this one, but maybe . . . maybe if she could just eat something more significant than a tooth . . . she might be able to copy the wretched angel's skill. She'd have to eat flesh.

She cut her tongue on her ruined teeth, causing a fresh wave of pain, like electricity surging through her gums. Could she even bite anything in this state? Her lips were busted pretty badly, swollen and bleeding. Maybe . . . Maybe she could bite off a piece, saw through the flesh with the jagged bits of tooth sticking out of her gums. Or could she bite through the inside of her cheek?

But what if the skill didn't manifest? What if it was only something angels could do?

Frustrated, she bit down as hard as she could on her bottom lip. But without whole teeth, all she managed was to get her lips stuck to her gums, caught on the sharp edges of her broken teeth. She pushed her lip off with her tongue, and was about to try again when the floor shook.

Heavy footsteps approached. She saw Oliver's eyes go up, full of fear, as his arms tightened around the girl protectively. Jenny turned her head toward the ceiling, expecting to see the black-covered wretched angel. Instead, it was yellow with dark stripes, almost like a tiger.

### Wretched Angel (Level 23)

She saw the bottom of its foot. It was massive, and instead of toes, it had huge claws that extended forward like talons. It stepped over her, sniffed several times, then reached for Oliver.

*No*, she wanted to scream, trying to will her body off the floor. But then, she heard Oliver shouting. The angel hissed, smacking him hard, and his helmet bounced off the closet. The angel picked up the girl by her arm as Oliver lay still, an ugly red mark on one side of his face. It grabbed another girl, then dragged them both away.

Heart twisting at the sight of Oliver, Jenny forced her head to turn, trying to ignore the wave of dizziness. But she had to see what the angel was doing, and how many others there were.

The lab was a series of tables bolted into the ground. Each one had several sinks, gas dials, and ventilation hoods. Bodies lay in piles in between them, and in the centermost table, attached to the ceiling and floor by what looked like enormous blue cobwebs, was a giant blue sac.

This sac was upright and oblong, resembling a cocoon. Its blue insides shone brilliantly, and something floated inside of it in a fetal position as the light bloomed and faded rhythmically. The figure resembled an adult woman, long hair drifting. Jenny squinted, straining to see, and she recognized it as the female wretched angel who had bitten her fingers off. She recognized it by the two antennae sticking out of its head.

The notification made her stomach turn.

**Desecrated Angel (Level 30)**

# CHAPTER TWENTY-EIGHT

# THE COCOON

The cocoon radiated heat, making the lab room sweltering hot. The air was humid and thick with the metallic taste of blood. Bodies lay around it, piled in unsightly heaps. It was almost like some twisted sort of nest. Except the bird that had built this nest didn't collect little twigs and mud; it used flesh and blood.

**Desecrated Angel (Level 30)**

Jenny kept the notification in her head as she stared at it, vaguely aware of the striped, yellow wretched angel dragging the girls away. She remembered the stairwell, the first "nest" she'd seen. How those two wretched angels had kept that boy alive to drain his blood. These ones must be doing the same for all the sacs that covered the ceiling, and for this large cocoonlike sac. But why did the desecrated angel need such a thing?

The stench clogged her lungs. She had to cough, but knew coughing would set off even more agony, and she forced herself to remain as still as possible. Everything ached, burned, or throbbed. But with Oliver nearby, she refused to drift off into unconsciousness no matter how strongly the darkness tugged on the edges of her mind.

*Focus . . . Focus!* She connected thoughts. The creatures had dragged all the bodies here. These two male wretched angels must be serving the cocooned female. Did angels have a matriarchal society? Like bees and ants?

She ignored the pain, trying to remember things she'd read in books and seen in documentaries. One insect would become the queen, eating a special diet to grow large so it could lay countless eggs for the colony. Then they'd spread and seek out more food so they could lay more eggs and continue to grow.

The angels looked human, but the sacs they produced were not human at all. And the female angel reminded her of a worm or caterpillar gestating inside a cocoon before emerging with wings and . . .

She blinked in shock. Would the desecrated angel emerge with wings? Then it would look more like the angels from holy books, wouldn't it? How much stronger would it be?

She sucked in a warm, moist breath. Air whistled through her crushed nose and stung her bleeding gums.

The yellow wretched angel's covering turned green in the blue light before it faded, shining yellow again. It dropped one of the girls onto a pile of bodies and raised the other, cradling her limp form in its slim, muscular arms. This angel wasn't as wide as the one covered in black. It wasn't as monstrous, either. It had long white hair, and its covering was thin; Jenny could see the outline of its spine. The stripes were black, reminding her of a tiger.

It placed the girl on the table as though she were a slab of meat ready to be tenderized and slathered with spices. Jenny strained to see what the creature was doing, but it had its back to her, blocking her view. At least it wasn't Oliver's friend; she was lying on the floor, her broken helmet reflecting the cocoon's blue glow.

The bodies around the girl looked thin and drained . . . almost like tarnished angels. Some of them *were* angels, but even the humans appeared thinner and mangled, their faces ghastly. With a cold sweat, she realized they'd been drained of all their blood.

Once again, she tried to summon her hatchet, the muscles in her forearm straining. She clenched her teeth by accident, and renewed pains shot through her messed-up jaw. That's when she noticed the black wretched angel. It crawled across the ceiling between the sacs, touching each one with its clawed hands and tendrils.

A glimmer of golden light sparked in her hand, but she stopped trying to summon it. The light gave her the tiniest bit of comfort, but not yet. *Not just yet*, she told herself. If she summoned it, the angel would notice immediately, and she was in no condition to fight. She'd bide her time. Wait for an opening, any opportunity . . .

The other humans, the ones alive and lined up near her and Oliver . . . If she could somehow wake them up, if she could create a potion and split it between them all, just to heal them enough to fight together, maybe she could rally and—

A revolting crack cut through her desperate planning. Jenny winced, but she turned her head to see the yellow wretched angel on top of the girl. It crouched over her, pinning her arms with its hands. Her armor was torn open. The angel's face was pressed to her neck, and it started slurping.

They were long, wet slurps, with brief pauses to swallow as the girl cried softly. Jenny lay on the floor, wishing she could claw out the insides of her ears. She couldn't even tell if the girl was awake or crying helplessly in her unconscious state. God, she prayed the girl was unconscious. Nobody should have to suffer something like that.

The slurping went on and on, until finally, it was quiet again, except for the sound of her pounding heart.

The angel sat up, tilting its head back as it swallowed one last time. Its covering appeared green again before the light faded, then the creature slid off the table and stomped over to the cocoon, hissing as though it were speaking.

A crease appeared down the cocoon's center. From inside, something bulged against the protective skinlike layer, stretching it out before bursting through.

The desecrated angel's head appeared.

The bright blue glow faded to a dull gleam, as though from a dying lightbulb. The eerie hue stained everything in the room. Jenny didn't dare blink. The angel's face was dark, the covering no longer glossy and slick but instead looking metallic and woven. It reminded her of carbon fiber. Its face was thin and gaunt, with a pronounced jawline and cheekbones.

Its two antennae twitched as its golden hair spilled forward to cover the sides of its head. Gooey liquid dripped from its hair and chin while everything below its neck remained inside the cocoon. Its eyes were shut, but its mouth opened. A tongue stretched out expectantly.

Now a dull green in the dim blue light, the wretched angel bent slightly to kiss the other. Its throat convulsed, its chest heaved, and it gripped the desecrated angel's face with both hands.

As it swallowed, the cocoon's light brightened intensely, blinding Jenny. But the image of them kissing was seared in her mind. She heard the retching. She heard splattering. Swallowing. She pictured a mother bird feeding screaming chicks, their beaks open as they cried out. She'd throw up the worms and bugs she'd hunted after digesting them in her gut, and the young would eat it up.

When the light faded, Jenny blinked repeatedly, trying to clear her vision. She saw the desecrated angel staring.

A terrible chill sent goose bumps racing up and down her body despite the disgusting humidity and how much she was sweating beneath her armor.

The creature's antennae flicked. Its eyes were open, glowing violently blue, and Jenny realized it was no longer an empty stare.

Its eyes were no longer vacant whiteness. It had irises now, giving it a freakishly human appearance. Its lips curved into a smile, the carbon-fiber skin shimmering as it forced an arm out of the cocoon. Thick liquid glopped and splattered on the floor as it pointed with fingers covered in slime, hissing and shushing, not taking its eyes off Jenny's. Then it broke into a fit of coughing, hacking up blood and spittle.

The creature's breath was raspy and painful. Jenny got the sense it couldn't handle the air, as though its insides were still forming. What was it that caterpillars did inside a chrysalis? Dissolve into an organic soup before taking on a new shape?

The wretched angel's head turned, hissing something in response before helping the desecrated angel slide back inside. More gooey liquid escaped, dribbling down the side of the cocoon before the slit faded away and the large sac was whole again.

She knew what had happened. She knew the desecrated angel had declared its next meal. It wanted her.

Whimpering as pain shot through her skull, she again tried to get up, desperately flexing her core. If she could just get to her feet . . . if she could just stand, her head would stop spinning, she could summon her hatchet, and she might be able to do *something*.

But the yellow wretched angel was already stomping toward her, crushing limbs and hands beneath its feet. The other male was still working through the sacs, adjusting and stroking.

Her head dropped as she stopped straining. She turned to look at Oliver as the footsteps drew near. He was lying awkwardly, the red mark on his face glistening in the fading light. The sight of his twisted leg made her want to scream. He wouldn't be able to walk out of here, much less run. And if he'd had enough energy, then he would've tried to heal it already.

Maybe he could crawl? Maybe if she could create a distraction somehow, and he woke up . . . But would he leave his friend behind?

Her thoughts swirled as desperation threatened to suffocate her. No idea leaped into her mind. She wasn't the planning type—that was Susan. Jenny was the *rush-in-blindly-and-just-do-it* type. At least Susan was safe in the library.

The angel scooped her up with both arms. Something popped between her ribs, and her body writhed with pain as her limbs hung loose. Her shield bounced against its knees, but the angel didn't seem to care. Blood and drool glistened on its chin as it carried her to another table and gently, almost reverently, lowered her.

Her helmet clanged against the hard surface. She felt like a sack of potatoes. Her jaw snapped and crackled as she tried to say something, but her gums burned with pain, and all she managed to do was gape like a fish out of water.

On the ceiling, the black wretched angel moved further away, toward the back of the lab room. From this angle, it seemed like a fly exploring a bowl of flesh-colored grapes. The sacs wriggled, glowing faintly in the blue light as the angel caressed them.

Jenny's vision kept fading in and out; she was about to pass out. She was trapped in her useless body, her bones ruined by her own attacks, her face smashed in because of her recklessness.

But wasn't this how she'd always felt? Stuck in her own flesh. Trapped. All she'd ever wanted was to break free. To get away. To chase her dreams and wants and do all the things she wanted to do. It was almost poetic that this was how she died, then.

**You will not perish here, Jenny Huang.**

She scoffed, regretting it instantly as blood spurted out of her throat. *I thought you gave up on me.* She sensed Eve on the fringes of her mind, and she had a dozen self-pitying remarks, but before she could continue, the wretched angel knelt forward.

It was going to suck out her blood, wasn't it? Like a vampire, it was going to crack open her armor and bite her neck and then feed the desecrated angel. Jenny braced for the worst as the creature's hands explored her armor, but instead of attacking, it sniffed.

Its striped face hovered over her navel before working down to her feet. It paused where her armor was broken, where she was bleeding. Then it sniffed her left hand, turning her arm to move the shield out of the way. She felt the wetness of its lips against the stubs of her fingers, and she shuddered.

It sniffed her chest next, hissing gently when its lips brushed her crumpled nose, pain blossoming like a flame on her face. The hissing changed frequency, and then it climbed on top of her, its knees on the table, holding her hips. Its hands curled around her arms, and she stared into its empty eyes, saw the stained teeth, and inhaled the rancid, decaying odor of its breath. Its yellow covering shone green again, blue light glowing over everything as a drop of warm saliva hit her face.

*Ignite!* she thought. *Ignite!*

With all the possible strength left in her mind, she tried to summon the flames. She wanted to burn the dreadful creature to ashes, but her thoughts turned to mush. All the fight emptied out of her as the angel pressed its lips to her nose. She felt its teeth scraping against the exposed cartilage, felt its tongue—slimy and thick—run all over her face as though searching for something.

Then, it began to *suck*.

# CHAPTER TWENTY-NINE

# HESITATIONS

Once, on her way to school, a tragic incident disrupted subway services all over the city. Someone had jumped onto the tracks.

Jenny had waited nearly an hour at their station for a train. When it finally arrived, every single car was already packed. Yet everyone waiting at the station, to get to school or to get to work, forced their way inside. Nobody waited for the next train in New York City; it was always *rush, rush, rush.*

The swelling tide of people forced her into the subway car, and she struggled to find a pole to hold on to. There was hardly any room to breathe; she'd taken off her schoolbag and held it between her legs, praying desperately for the train not to stall underground. It was hot, bodies pressed her from every side, and she could feel their breath on her face.

She'd tried to listen to her music, eyes shut as the lights overhead flickered and the train thundered through the Manhattan underground. It swayed and rocked, and elbows bumped into her, arms brushed her shoulders, and people shuffled awkwardly. Everyone squeezed together to form a disgusting blob of limbs and sweat.

Someone grabbed her hip.

At first, she thought it was an accident. It had to be an accident. But the fingers lingered. They crawled up her sides, under her sweater. Nails scratched her gently. A moist palm massaged her lower back, the fingertips teasing the waistline of her jeans.

She'd wanted to scream. Wanted to turn and smash that person in the face with her phone. To tell someone. Anyone. But there had been hardly any room to breathe, let alone move away and escape.

She'd done nothing. She'd stood, unable to act, motionless except for the rocking of the train as it hurled through the tunnels and someone felt her up.

At the next stop, the commotion of moving people allowed her to escape. She pushed deeper into the train, no longer trying to be polite. A lump threatened to burst out of her throat. She found a spot beside one of the closed doors and leaned against it. She didn't look around. She didn't glance at anyone; she couldn't meet anyone's eyes. What if the person who'd touched her was staring back?

She kept her focus on her shoes, trying to delete the sensation of being in her body. The way her skin burned. She wasn't here; she wasn't real. She was just another fixture, a part of the train as it shook and screeched and thundered.

She didn't speak to anyone for the rest of that day. She didn't participate in class. She didn't eat lunch. She'd wanted to burn every skin cell that had been touched. Wanted to remove it with a potato peeler or cheese grater. It wasn't hers anymore; it belonged to that stranger.

And worst of all, she'd hated herself for not saying a word. For not fighting. For not shouting or screaming. But would anyone have heard her over the roar of the train? Would anyone have done a thing?

What should she have done?

What should she do now?

The angel's tongue slid into one of her nostrils. She felt the heat of her blood rising to her face; felt the sensation of it slipping out, as though a vacuum was attached to her nose. Her blood and its saliva dribbled down its chin and dropped into her mouth so that she could taste the rottenness of the angel's breath. She didn't shut her eyes, even as the sucking lifted her head off the table. All she saw in its white emptiness was the hopelessness and dread she'd always known.

She knew she could do something. She could hit it with her shield, push it off with her leg. She could exhale flames. The pain had faded; all she could feel was the draining sensation that burned the middle of her face. It only paused to swallow.

But her body no longer belonged to her; it wouldn't respond no matter how much she wanted it to. She was back on that train on that terrible morning, trapped in her flesh as someone else claimed it and made it theirs in the worst possible way.

Her blood left her body one suck at a time. She couldn't tell how much time had passed. How much blood did she even have left? Her mind went blank, and darkness overtook her before her eyes flew open and she was face-to-face with the wretched angel again. The way it hunched over her, it was almost like the creature was trying to resuscitate her with CPR.

When it finally stopped sucking and its lips separated from her face with a sloppy, wet sound, she was surprised to still be conscious. She couldn't feel her body. Couldn't move.

The creature slid off the table and stomped away, the tremors reaching her through the floor. She stared at the wriggling sacs on the ceiling, a dull silence ringing in her head. Then she heard hissing, heard retching. She didn't dare to breathe. She wanted to vanish. She wanted to not *be*.

**You must not surrender.**

The message burst through her thoughts like a ball of flame. Visuals accompanied it. She saw Susan, and she wasn't sure if she was imagining things or if Eve was revealing the present, but she was covered in blood. Fresh blood. Her nose was broken, and she was crying, clutching her cattle prod and sitting on the floor.

*No . . .*

Jenny's fingers twitched. She could still taste the angel's sour breath.

*What can I even do? What can I do? Is Susan safe?*

**Susan Brown remains an active participant in the Survival Challenge.**

*I'm going to die here . . .*

The next vision unfurled like dark angry clouds spreading wildly, rumbling with thunder and flashing lightning. The three-headed figure blossomed into the forefront of her mind, shimmering golden and transparent. Jenny was floating again in that darkness, in that other world where she'd met Eve.

Each of Eve's faces shifted, a blur of eyes and noses and lips. The center face settled, and Jenny recognized the exasperated look of her mother, the wrinkle on her forehead when her brows furrowed. It spoke with her mother's lips.

**I chose you for a reason.**

*Well, you chose wrong. I'm fucking done. It's game over*, she thought with ugly bitterness. She'd convinced Susan to think about this as a game; she'd tried to trick herself, too. But now, it was over.

Lightning flashed, searing her from the inside. The three-headed figure drew close—so close that her mother's face was suddenly right in front of Jenny's. She flinched, but couldn't float away.

**You are mine, Jenny Huang.**
**You are capable of so much more than you permit yourself to express.**

*What are you even—*

**Quiet.**

The force with which that word moved through her felt like a torrential downpour. Her mind trembled and came apart and reunited.

**At every turn, you choose to stop.**
**You sense your growth. You sense the possibilities of what you are capable of. But then, you hesitate.**

*I don't—*

**Your memories spill through me, Jenny Huang.**
**All your life, hesitation has been your response when anything goes**
**your way. You reject yourself. You push away every opportunity that**
**presents itself.**

The flurry of visions that burst like fireworks made her head spin. She saw
every crush she'd ever had. Saw her feelings for Susan. Saw herself attempting art,
attempting music, attempting to write stories. She saw the frustration, the fear,
the way she left everything half finished, half touched. From one thing to another,
trying and never completing. She even saw herself fighting, trying her new skills
and testing her new strengths, only to stumble.

**You bury your emotions and convince yourself you can feel them later.**
**You let yourself fester and fade and rot.**
**Why must you always wait to be free?**

The visions blurred. She was crying in bed, counting the days till she could
set out for college and move away.
*I don't know.*
In the next vision, she hovered in front of the library. She saw herself storming
down the hallway, cutting through the tarnished angels with ease, then saw the
fight she'd just lost to the wretched angel, saw what she could've done differently.
She saw her skills in action. Her throw. Her burst of speed. Her flames. Her hatchet.

**Your true self itches for release. Yet, you let yourself stumble. Buried**
**deep within your soul is a yearning desperate to be unleashed.**

Jenny held her tongue. She wanted to argue, to shoot back. She was worth-
less, incapable. She couldn't do this. She couldn't. She was only good at rushing
in blindly, and if someone wasn't there to hold her hand, to have her back, to pick
up her pieces, then she was useless. She just couldn't do it on her own. She was
not strong enough not—

**I have tasted your dreams, Jenny Huang. I have feasted on your night-**
**mares. I know the textures of your sins and prayers.**
**I have watched. I have listened. I have chosen you for my purpose.**

*But what if you chose wrong? I'm . . . All I do is mess things up. Whenever I try,*
*whenever I care too much, I just . . .*

**At your current stage, humankind can only evolve so many abilities before their minds collapse.**
**But you command several skills. Skills beyond the current prowess of your growing body, yet you have willed them into existence nonetheless.**

*I was just . . . just doing things I've seen before.*

**Have any of the wretched angels expressed such a number of abilities?**

She remembered the angels in the stairwell, the burst of speed she'd emulated. She remembered the other angel gorging on itself to heal. Eve was right. They weren't using many skills; they were relying on brutish strength and straightforward attacks.

*I thought . . . I thought that was because of you. Because you chose me or something. I thought you were helping me and making me stronger so I could give birth to you.*

But Eve ignored her.

**An average human at stage two would have one, perhaps two, whereas you have not yet been restrained by your capacity for growth.**

The other two faces stopped shifting. She saw Oliver with his glasses. Susan with her blue hair.

**The only thing stopping you, what has always inhibited you, is your self-doubt.**
**That is your eternal enemy. That is why your element is flame. You burn brightly then vanish, too afraid to continue burning.**

A hand touched Jenny's cheek. She looked at each of the faces in turn, stopping when she noticed the tears streaming down her mother's cheeks.

**I have chosen you because you are my best chance. I have made you mine, but in truth, I am bound by you.**
**If you fail, then I shall fail.**

*So you need me?* asked Jenny, a strange warmth filling her with the three-headed figure's golden light.

**Our fates are intertwined.**

Blue light flooded the space; Jenny opened her eyes to see the room completely basked in the glow, light pulsing from the cocoon, each beat brighter and brighter. Eve blinked out of Jenny's mind as the table shook, as though the earthquake had struck again. She turned her head, blood dripping down the side of her face, to see the desecrated angel moving inside the large sac.

The cocoon bulged and twisted and rippled as the wretched angel lumbered back, hissing. The angel on the ceiling hissed as well, but the cocoon kept pulsing. The floor shook, the sacs above jiggled, and a few of them dropped.

Jenny's blood had been an important ingredient. She wondered if it was related to what Eve had said, how she had a greater capacity than other humans. Did that make her blood special somehow? Was that what the desecrated angel had sniffed out when it pointed at her?

Her blood ran through that creature's veins now, and judging by the shift in light, the energy emanating from the cocoon, her blood had given the creature strength.

It would want more.

Jenny's mind filled with possibilities. She was still injured, still weak, still in agony. She didn't have enough energy for another potion of fortification, and without some sort of boost, even if she managed to get to her feet and fight, she'd die.

Her fingers clenched into a fist. Her shield scraped against the table. Every movement hurt, but at least she could move.

The wretched angel stomped toward her, her blood dripping from its exposed teeth. It was going to touch her again; was going to suck on her again.

Her heart raced. She felt faint. She felt weak. She didn't want to move, didn't want to be here, didn't want it to touch her again.

She pressed her tongue against her ruined gums, igniting more pain in her mouth to distract her from the paralyzing fear. As it approached, she sifted through movies and games and storybooks. Powers and abilities she'd always wished to have. Flight. Impervious skin. Regeneration. Fire. Lightning.

Her skills so far had been extensions of her own will. She'd wanted to throw harder and move quicker, and her body had responded. She'd wanted to explode with rage, and that had manifested as fire.

She wanted to research all of this, study it to the very last detail and plan out the best course of action, the best way to spend her energy. The best armor to build. She wanted to sit with Susan, preferably in Susan's bedroom, pouring over all the information until they came up with a crazy strategy, but Susan wasn't here.

Jenny would have to figure something out. In games, there were limitations that guided them; things they couldn't do or things they could abuse. But this guidance system . . . it was like being assigned a paper; like an essay she had to write on the beginning of *The Scarlet Letter*. Mrs. Rivera hadn't given them a question to answer. Instead, she'd wanted the class to propose a thesis and explore their own ideas. It had frustrated Jenny to no end.

The angel hovered over her, its face glistening. It was sniffing, licking its lips. It liked the taste of her blood.

Jenny retreated further into her thoughts as the creature grabbed her shoulders and climbed back up. *This isn't my body. I'm not here. This isn't happening to me. What delusion am I convincing myself of . . .*

She'd always escaped into stories, hadn't she? Lies she told herself before going to bed. Situations she imagined as she fell asleep. The books she read, the movies she'd watch, the daydreams she'd have about Susan, about the two of them venturing across fantasy lands.

Eve was right. Jenny had been *waiting* this whole time. Waiting for change. Waiting for some big meaningful action to change everything for her.

She'd always wished she wasn't who she was. Wished she wasn't trapped in her body, in this world, in this life. She'd always felt like a ghost possessing her body, desperate to break free but never willing to take the leap of faith.

All her life, she'd compressed herself into a pitiful little ball. All she'd ever done was rot . . .

Her lips curved into a painful smile as the angel's face drew near. *Rot . . .*

She remembered that biology lesson about the human body; how it was capable of such intense strength. Untapped potential that the brain suppressed to protect the body from itself. It was how mothers moved cars or people survived falls from burning buildings. A rush of adrenaline combined with an inhibition of thought; just emotion, just action, pain no longer part of the equation.

The angel's tongue found her nose again. Its teeth scraped her flesh, but she didn't care. Her body was broken and ruined. She was tired of rotting, but rotting was the answer.

Zombies, she thought as the angel began sucking. In zombie movies, the brain rotted away, enabling the mindless creatures to be stronger than they'd ever been as humans.

It would make the pain stop. Hurting was how living beings learned, but she didn't need to learn right now. She needed to survive. To kill. To break free.

This one bubbled up inside her. She sensed Eve's approval. The notification sent a gentle warmth radiating from the tip of her nose, and it felt like receiving a kiss she'd waited her entire life for.

<br>

**Skill Acquired!**
**Severed Spirit (Tier 1)**

**System Warning!**
**Severed Spirit (Tier 1) is a Restricted Skill.**
**While active, access to Energy and Skills is prohibited.**
**The body will begin to decay until deactivation.**

# CHAPTER THIRTY

# SEVERED SPIRIT

The wretched angel continued sucking Jenny's blood through her ruined nose. The lightheadedness intensified with each suck, and the taste of the creature's spittle made her want to retch as it slobbered all over her. This time, it didn't even feel like this was happening to her, like she'd detached already.

It didn't hurt. It didn't sting. She focused on the stripes on the creature's face, particularly the long one that curved from one cheekbone to its jawline. She'd lost too much blood.

It was now or never. Once she activated the new skill, she wouldn't be able to access her others, wouldn't be able to use her energy for anything. She'd be . . . Well, she didn't know quite how she'd be, but she imagined she'd turn into a zombie. She found the thought as curious as it was exhilarating.

But first things first. Golden light flashed, making the angel pause. Jenny's fingers closed around the now familiar firmness of her hatchet's handle while the creature's eyes bulged.

It held on to her arms, cocking its head, blinking, recognizing that something was amiss, but it wasn't attacking her. Its covering turned green as the blue light filled the lab room again. Blood dribbled down its chin and onto her chest. The angel seemed out of sorts.

Its cheeks appeared flushed, darker than the rest of its face, and its body swayed on top of hers as it sniffed her shoulder to shoulder; it kept readjusting its grip on her arms. The creature was unsteady. It reminded her of her mother and stepfather after they'd had too much wine.

Was it drunk off her blood?

But there was no time to wonder about that. The other wretched angel was still on the ceiling, carefully reattaching the sacs that had fallen earlier. Its tendrils streamed down, hanging loose but fluttering as it worked. It hadn't noticed anything yet.

The striped angel stopped sniffing her. It licked its lips, sucking the bottom one clean as it stared down at her, breathing excitedly. Just as it prepared to latch its mouth onto her face again, just before the darkness that clouded her vision threatened to overwhelm her, Jenny activated her new skill. *Severed Spirit.*

Like a bolt of lightning crackling through the night sky, a series of violent shocks stormed down her spine. She felt a *pull* in her tummy, right beneath her belly button, as though she was about to collapse in on herself. She cried out, gasping for air, spitting in the angel's face as it stared back, brows furrowed over its narrowing empty eyes.

A grin stretched her cracked lips. She ran her tongue over her gums. Her senses waned and wavered as she inhaled slowly, her nose gurgling but euphoria filling her chest. It didn't hurt.

Nothing hurt. It was as though a magician had snapped gloved fingers and said, *Voilà!* All the pain—all the stinging and throbbing and aching—had completely vanished. She was no longer trapped; she'd set herself free from the confines of her broken body. She'd cured herself of *herself.*

The angel's mouth opened as though it was about to ask a question. The edge of her hatchet flashed as her arm shot upward, swiping at the creature's face quickly, much more quickly than she'd intended. At first, she thought she'd missed. The angel released her, jerking backward and tumbling over her feet and onto the floor. Then its nose glistened for a second midair before bouncing off Jenny's armor and rolling away.

Her arm had followed through on the motion, her wrist hitting her shield, and she heard an ugly snap in her shoulder. Extended and bent awkwardly, her arm lay across her chest. She winced, but there was no pain. Nothing hurt at all, and she moved the arm without issue. She hadn't even let go of the hatchet like she would've if she'd felt the impact of her wrist against the shield.

She slid her legs off the table's side. The angel was hissing, crawling over bodies and trying to get to her, scrambling and slipping, unable to right itself. A wild exuberance made her heart pound, harder and faster than it ever had before, like a war drum amping up for battle.

Rolling her arm back into place, she took careful steps, half afraid this was a dream and the agony would come rushing back.

The concept of *feeling* itself had disappeared. Her body and mind were disconnected, like some invisible layer had squeezed between her insides and her conscious self. Her body still sent signals of pain, of texture and feeling. She knew of the humid heat that filled the room, the strange itch that crept up and down her spine, the throbbing pain in her shoulder and arm that mixed with everything else in her damaged body. But they didn't hamper her, didn't suffocate her.

It was like drowning in the ocean, except she could breathe the saltwater that filled her lungs and clogged her throat.

The wretched angel rose to its feet, swaying as it stumbled, clutching its face with one hand. It wasn't attacking right away. Did it think she wasn't much of a threat? Or was it actually drunk?

Jenny glanced at the ceiling again. The other one would notice soon enough, and she didn't want to get stuck fighting both.

Bodies squished underneath her boots as she closed in on the striped angel. She kept her shield up defensively, even though the angel didn't look like it would attack, and then she swung, trying to be mindful of how much strength she put into the strike.

If there was any resistance, she didn't feel it. Its yellow covering crackled first, before her hatchet snapped through its collarbone and chest, moving diagonally down to its hip. Its arms dropped to its side as blood burst out of the gash. It lumbered forward, unsteady and trembling, hissing softly. Jenny almost felt sorry for it, but then she remembered how it had hit Oliver, how it had broken that other girl's armor and sucked out her blood. And how it had *touched* Jenny.

She shoved the creature away with her shield. The top of its body separated from the bottom, and it collapsed in two heaps. Its guts splattered the floor, and Jenny wondered how much of that blood had been hers.

Its head lolled back onto Oliver's friend, who was still lying unconscious on the pile of bodies. Its white hair covered her face. The angel's heart slid out between exposed ribs, beating grossly and glistening in the blue light, still attached by flesh and sinew.

No notification appeared.

*Is it dead? It has to be . . .* But before she could get a closer look, before she could crush its heart underneath her boot and be certain of its death, a deafening roar made her look up.

Jenny stepped back, swallowing and raising her shield defensively, eyeing the large dark angel hanging off the ceiling by its claws. It looked like an enormous gorilla, its muscular legs swinging slightly. Its chest seemed larger than ever, and its tendrils slashed and whipped the air behind it.

Exhilaration coursed through her veins. Her heart seemed to beat even harder, the drumming in her head growing ferociously. *Third time's the charm*, she thought, bracing herself. This time, she would win. This time, she'd fuck it up.

It dislodged from the ceiling and dropped down with a terrible crunch. Something wet and thick splattered her shield, and Jenny's stomach turned. It had landed on the girl who'd been drained just before Jenny and who was still lying on the other table. Her head was completely flattened, and the angel's other foot had crushed her stomach. Blood and brain matter and viscera had splattered all over.

Some of the spray had landed on the cocoon, casting shadows across the room. But the blood dissolved with a gentle hiss, as though being absorbed, and the light pulsed. Something wriggled inside. For some reason, Jenny got the mental image of a baby kicking in the womb.

A bead of sweat ran down her forehead and into her eye. It should've stung, but all she felt was the wetness, which she blinked away, keeping her focus on the wretched angel.

It crouched down, grabbing the edges of the table with its claws. Its tendrils snapped in the air as it bared its teeth and hissed, its muscles bulging menacingly.

"C'mon," whispered Jenny, bending her knees and bracing for impact. She wasn't sure how her body would hold up. What if it just thrashed her again and she got trapped in a rotting, completely useless prison? Could she die? But she shoved the thought away, licking sweat and blood from the corner of her lips. When the cocoon's glow faded again, the wretched angel attacked.

It threw itself off the table, a dark mountain rushing up to meet her as it slashed the air, aiming for her head. Jenny ducked, one of her knees cracking loudly, and the angel flew over her, its large body feeling like a plane flying too close to the ground. But it couldn't stop, its momentum driving it forward, and Jenny used that to her advantage, remembering how it had swung its arm into her face when she'd tried to rush it before.

She raised her hatchet. The edge caught the angel's sternum, cutting into its black covering before catching on its flesh. She held the weapon firmly straight into the air, screaming with rage as blood splattered her shield from above, and the creature sliced itself open down to its crotch.

It tumbled onto the table where she'd been lying, landing with a thick, wet thump. Lying on its front, the creature retched violently, its legs kicking, feet inches from Jenny's face.

She wanted to set the creature on fire, to burn it to nothing and erase every trace of its existence. Rage and vengeance and a maddening, twisted pleasure struggled inside her. Before the angel could recover, Jenny stepped over a body and brought her hatchet down on one of its wriggling legs. The edge flashed through its meaty calf, and she felt a jolt when she struck bone, but the hatchet cut all the way through.

The angel let out a hideous cry as its large dark foot bounced into the pile of bodies. Thick globs of blood burst from its severed leg, spraying everywhere as the creature writhed in pain. Jenny's shoulder tingled. Her fingers were numb, but she readjusted the grip on her blood-covered weapon and readied to strike again.

She aimed for its spine this time. *If I can just paralyze it . . .*

But with a raging roar, the wretched angel whirled on the table. Its guts and blood squeaked beneath its abdomen as it struck her side with a large, clawed hand.

Sparks erupted from where the claws found her. Scales cracked and went flying, and Jenny was thrown back, her feet sliding on blood. She tripped over a body and flailed, her helmet bouncing off the edge of the other table, and she landed on her side beside Oliver's friend.

The cocoon glowed a few paces away, appearing even larger than before. The desecrated angel floated inside, seemingly undisturbed by what was happening in the lab room. But the creature seemed different—larger, with something extending from its back.

Jenny blinked repeatedly, her vision blurry. Her head spun from hitting the table, but something else caught her attention.

Oliver's friend was awake. Her face was screwed up with pain as she tried to sit up, flicking the dead angel's head off her. It rolled away, eyes staring blankly. The girl opened her mouth, shouting, but it sounded more like strained yowling. Her hand flitted up, and her fingers formed shapes, but Jenny couldn't understand what she was trying to say. And there was no chance to decipher it.

A gurgle came from the other table. The wretched angel had crawled over the bodies, leaving behind a disgusting trail of its insides to grab its severed foot. It bit into it like an apple, its teeth closing through the heel. The sounds of bone crunching reminded Jenny of their fight in the hall.

*Fuck that,* she thought, desperately searching for her hatchet. She couldn't give it a chance to heal. She had to act quickly.

Spotting the glinting edge when the blue light shone brightly again, she picked it up, climbing to her feet. One foot was stuck in the pile of bodies, and blood ran down her side—little rivers between her scales where the angel had ripped through her armor.

Golden light enveloped the wretched angel, its tendrils flashing. Jenny yanked her foot free from the tangle of limbs and stomped forward.

Her ankle popped. Her leg gave out, and she sank to her knees, eyes wide. But she wasn't going to waste the movement. With a wild cry, she brought her hatchet down on the angel's head, the edge sinking through the spiky black covering and landing with a satisfying *thunk*.

The golden light of its healing ability blinked out, and the angel went rigid, its back arched, its head still raised so that its eyes stared back at her. What was left of the foot dropped from its mouth.

A distorted squeal came from its lips. Jenny stayed on one knee, staring down at the dark blood gushing down the angel's face. She knew her lungs were burning, but all she felt was a dull aching in her chest. She sucked in a deep breath, wondering if the incessant drumming of her heart would ever slow.

How long could she keep the skill active? How much agony would hit her once she turned it off?

She'd need to make sure she had enough energy for healing. Her ankle was busted. She hadn't felt it break or anything, but that had almost cost her the fight.

If she'd tripped and fallen right into the angel's grip, it would've bitten through her neck instead of its foot.

But it was dead. The wretched angel was dead, and she couldn't help but feel relief. She'd gotten her revenge; she'd overcome this terrifying creature. Now, all that was left was to get Oliver and the others safely to the library.

She'd keep Severed Spirit active till then. There was still the cocoon and all the sacs above, and whatever else lay waiting outside the lab, but for now, this angel, this stupid creature that had given her so much trouble, was finally dead. Now she could—

With a roar that shook the floor, the angel pushed itself up and onto Jenny, its jaws wide open.

She fell backward, her legs folding beneath her. She couldn't tell if she was screaming or if it was the angel, but she managed to bring her shield up, jamming the edge between its teeth before it could bite her.

The creature bit down on the shield instead. Metal crunched, the edge of the shield cutting into the stretched skin on the corners of its mouth. The black covering on its face cracked, spiderwebbing over its nose and cheeks. Its eyes glowered furiously, wide and bulging and bloodshot, and blood continued to gush from the wound on its forehead. Her hatchet stuck out like a horn.

Screaming and hissing, it jerked its head from side to side, trying to rip the shield away. One of its clawed hands crushed her torso, while she blocked the other with her right elbow as the angel tried to claw her to bits and pieces.

Rage burned so hot in her throat, she almost thought she could breathe fire. *Just fucking die.* But instead of flames, she screamed back at the creature and relaxed her arm, just the slightest shift in force. The angel's grip loosened, and Jenny flicked the shield. The edge the angel was biting snapped downward. With a sharp *crack*, its bottom teeth gave away, raining down on Jenny's armor as the flat face of the shield sprang up to hit the creature in the face.

The motion knocked the hatchet deeper into its skull, and the creature slumped forward, its entire body giving out with a shudder. It landed on her shield with a heavy *thump*.

Jenny shoved it off, the angel flung back onto its feet before it stumbled backward, its body limp and askew, as one of its legs was still a bloody stump. Its lower jaw hung loose, clacking against the covering of its throat, its tongue limp and bouncing. But it didn't drop dead. It remained upright like a marionette from some nightmare.

It wailed at the top of its lungs, swinging its arms wildly, lashing out. Its claws whooshed through the air, and it turned this way and that, fighting countless invisible opponents, screaming bloody murder as it splattered everything with blood. It hobbled on its injured leg, making its entire body flail as its intestines spilled from the gash down its center. *How is it not dead?*

There was a motion to her left. Jenny turned to see the girl crawling forward, a knife in her hands. Jenny moved to stop her, but her legs were still folded beneath her, and she couldn't react in time.

"Wait!" cried Jenny, her voice hoarse. But the girl either ignored her or couldn't hear anything over the wretched angel going berserk.

Oliver's friend got to her knees and jammed her knife into the angel's hamstring as soon as it stumbled near her. It hissed and turned, swinging at the air over the girl's ruined knight helmet, but she'd held on to the knife, spinning around the angel's body so she could climb up its back.

Jenny rolled over and straightened her legs with her arm. The wretched angel stumbled into the cocoon as Jenny grabbed the table and used it to stand, the girl now on the creature's shoulders, her legs wrapped around its hanging bottom jaw and neck. She grabbed the hatchet, using that to steady herself as she raised the knife in her other hand.

But she never got the chance to strike.

Jenny saw it happen almost before it did, as though time had slowed and bent inward on itself. The wretched angel's claws found the cocoon. The blue skinlike casing tore open, and light blossomed into a blinding display, brighter than anything she'd ever seen before.

A jolt went through the floor, shattering every window and every light bulb overhead. Sacs rained down from the ceiling, a few bouncing off Jenny's helmet and shoulders.

There was a momentary pause, as though the entire world was choking on its breath. Jenny turned, trying desperately to find the spot where Oliver was unconscious. Dread seemed to condense inside her chest; she had to get away. She had to get Oliver as far away as possible from this thing.

The floor beneath her feet gave way. A terrible scream shuddered through everything around her, and for a blistering second, the bodies, the wretched angel, the bursting cocoon, and the girl seemed suspended in midair. Then everything went crashing down.

# CHAPTER THIRTY-ONE

# VALESCENT LIGHT

The wretched angel's teeth clacked in Susan's face, blood spurting from its mouth. She jammed her cattle prod into its empty eye socket, screaming as it collapsed on top of her. Something squished against the tip of her prod, and she let loose.

Lightning surged through the creature's orange head and burst from the back of its skull. Dr. Lee and Mrs. Monique dropped to the floor as bolts of lightning snapped and crackled over them to strike the library's ceiling over and over.

The lightning flickered and flashed. The angel writhed uncontrollably like it was having a seizure, its single arm flopping. Its palm bounced off Susan's chest and chin, but it had no fingers to claw her with.

She didn't stop until she was out of stamina, then Susan lay on her back, breathing hard. Her nose was bleeding, liquid streaming down her lips. Her cattle prod was still inside the angel's head; the creature lay on top of her thighs, unmoving, blood and drool staining her pants. Its hair was sizzled and sticking out, and strange veinlike patterns distorted the orange covering on its face and head. Smoke rose from it, and the stench of burnt flesh stung her nose.

She was barely aware of the others around her. She couldn't look away from the top of the angel's head, but notifications burst through her spinning thoughts.

**You've defeated Wretched Angel (Level 10)!**
**Experience has been awarded.**
**+50 Energy**

**Leveled Up!**
**Susan Brown, Level 9 → Level 10**
**+2 Stat Points**

**Ranking Bonus!**
Stage I → Stage II
**Congratulations on breaching the first threshold!**
**+30 Stat Points have been awarded.**
**+1 Energy Core has been awarded.**


**Skill Acquired!**
**Valescent Light (Tier 1)**

She couldn't focus on any of them, only catching a few details. The words didn't register in her mind. Instead, she saw Dr. Lee and Mrs. Monique crouched, a hand over their heads, staring wide-eyed. Leslie was on the floor too. She'd collapsed to her knees, shaking, and she looked at Susan as though she were also an angel.

Susan wanted to apologize, but how was she supposed to apologize for nearly frying them with her lightning? She hadn't meant to put so much into the attack, but she'd flashbacked to the two wretched angels from the hallway and the one before, in front of the boy's bathroom, that had bitten through her leg. She shuddered and yanked her cattle prod out of the eye socket.

The prod came away glistening, strands of mucus stretching from the creature's orange head. The burnt hair crumpled away, leaving it bald, revealing more of the flowery, veiny pattern burned into its covering.

Its head bounced down her lap as she squirmed back, trying to slide out from underneath it. The angel twitched.

Leslie screamed; Susan flicked her prod back on. It buzzed in her hand. Her heart thumped like mad; she knew she didn't have the strength for any more lightning, but she could still paralyze it, or she'd jam it into its head over and over until its brain was mush.

She was just about to strike the creature when it raised its head, blood dribbling down its chin. Susan's hand froze midair. The angel hissed softly, almost gently, and Susan looked into its eye. It wasn't vacant whiteness anymore; instead, an orange iris stared back, wide and frightened. A new notification accompanied it.

**Angel (Stage II - Level 10)**

The prod buzzed, her hand trembling as the angel blinked. It hissed again, the pitch adjusting slightly, and now it sounded more like a snake. Its tongue flickered underneath its top teeth, and its jaw moved as it let out a series of breaths and gasps and shushes.

Susan remembered the old-fashioned radio her father kept in his study. The angel sounded a lot like that crackling box as her father turned dials and tried to find specific signals. She wondered if the creature was trying to communicate.

It raised its one arm, hand shaking as it stared at the missing fingers. Its lips contorted as it moaned softly.

Susan didn't realize she was holding her breath till Dr. Lee shouted, "Stop!"

The angel whipped its head around to the source of the sound, blinking repeatedly, as though it had just woken up or emerged from a cave. Light illuminated the corner of the library from where the flashlight had rolled earlier, and several other students wandered over, some of them holding weapons, all of them terrified.

Dr. Lee had grabbed Mrs. Monique's spear. She had the tip pointed straight at the angel's neck.

"Why are you stopping me?" asked Mrs. Monique through gritted teeth. Her arms shook with rage, her metallic armor shining brilliantly in the light.

Despite bleeding from his arm, Dr. Lee held the spear firmly, refusing to let her attack. The sleeve of his lab coat was soaked red. His goggles were askew, but Susan spotted the frenzied look of excitement on his face.

"Can't you see?" he asked, his voice higher with excitement. His lips twitched and he licked them. "It was the *electricity*. Electricity did *something* to its brain. This is magnificent!"

The angel rolled off Susan's lap and collapsed on the floor, touching the shoulder of its missing left arm with a hand that had no fingers. The once exposed flesh and bone were now covered by a thick orange layer. Its chest and navel were uncovered, revealing brown skin and female anatomy, but if it had a sense of shame, Susan couldn't tell. Its legs were spread, and it stared at the scorch marks on the ceiling, gently hissing. Its one eye seemed to water.

Light moved. Leslie had picked up the fallen flashlight and was shining it on the angel, making the orange covering glisten vibrantly. But the creature didn't scream or hiss or try to cover its eyes. It squinted back; Susan could see tears streaming down the side of its head.

"Why's it different?" asked Leslie, staring at the creature. It blinked back, its orange eye darting from her to Dr. Lee to the tip of the spear then back to Susan.

Nobody addressed Alan's body, the boy whose neck the angel had bitten through once it broke free. Susan knew he was dead because no notification came up for him anymore.

She felt a pang of pity. He'd been terrified, and now he was dead. She had to remind herself to breathe again, her heart racing like mad as the others stepped cautiously closer. She was still holding her cattle prod; it buzzed in her shaking hand, but she didn't know what to do.

The angel showed no sign of aggression. It wasn't trying to grab her or bite her, but the sight of its blood-covered chin set her teeth on edge. That was Alan's blood. She almost agreed with Mrs. Monique; they should kill it and get it over with before it changed its mind and attacked again.

It was just lying there, hissing sporadically, its chest quaking as it spat up blood. Its face was covered in that strange dark pattern; Susan recognized it as what happened to people struck by lightning, the dark tattoo-like marking that became a permanent reminder.

Dr. Lee released Mrs. Monique's spear, his hands hovering in case she went for the attack. But she shook her head and stepped back, looking frustrated. He turned toward Susan and the angel, gesturing for her to move out of the way.

Leslie helped Susan up, muttering an apology for throwing the phone. Susan sniffled blood but didn't respond, instead leaning on Leslie as they hobbled away from the angel. It watched them go, blinking slowly, and it hissed softly again. She got the eerie sense it was saying goodbye.

Dr. Lee picked up his phone, inspected it quickly, then flashed a huge grin. "It's still recording." Holding his bleeding arm to his chest where red soaked the front of his lab coat, he continued recording with his free hand, narrating.

"And here we can see the specimen has transformed. We saw earlier examples of wretched angels, but they lacked irises and were extremely sensitive to light. This one . . ."

He paused and turned the phone onto Susan, who was leaning against Leslie. She still had the flashlight aimed at the angel.

"Move the light," barked Dr. Lee roughly under his breath. He looked angry and impatient.

Leslie's hand shook, making the light tremble, but she turned it to the floor, a hurt look on her face. Mrs. Monique sighed heavily before walking over to Alan's body, crouching down to close his eyes.

"Now," continued Dr. Lee, his face relaxing. "Susan. Would you mind explaining . . ." He trailed off. Squinting at her, he lowered the phone and removed his goggles, blinking.

Susan's throat went dry. Dr. Lee was staring at her the same way he'd stared at the wretched angel on the table as he was preparing to slice into it.

"What is it?" asked Leslie, looking from the biology teacher to Susan and back. Then she paused, releasing Susan's arm and stumbling backward, shining the light on Susan's face. She rambled incoherently, but Dr. Lee's voice drowned Leslie out.

"You're human stage two now . . . That's what it says." He spoke slowly, his voice low, as though he was processing the information as he spoke it. He let the goggles drop to the floor as his lips curled into an almost sinister smile. "Human stage two," he repeated. "So my hypothesis was correct. Jenny had a similar notification, but she left in such a hurry, and this was all so new to me, that I couldn't be sure."

"What are you talking about?" whispered Leslie. She was sweating even more now, and trembling. "Is she a monster too?"

Susan shook her head, her insides tightening at those words. "I don't know what this is. It just happened after that thing . . ." She nodded toward the angel. It had stopped crying and was following each of them as they spoke, its eye now focused on Susan.

"But this is everything!" said Dr. Lee breathlessly as he shoved the phone near Susan's face, as though recording her bleeding nose would give him new insight. "It means we can evolve too. Grow stronger like the angels and become . . . *more.* Think of the possibilities! The next stage in human evolution after millions of years. We just need to harvest more energy . . ." His voice trailed off again, and he moved the camera back toward the angel. "I wonder . . ."

Susan bit the inside of her cheek, discomfort making her stiff. But thankfully, that was when Mrs. Monique returned. She stood back, holding her spear with both hands, the tip pointed forward. She glared furiously with one eye. It was almost strange how her face and the angel's mirrored one another. Both missing an eye. Both unfamiliar.

"We should kill it," said Mrs. Monique firmly. Her voice was cruel and cold. The friendly librarian who was always cheerful and vibrant and sweet had vanished, replaced now by a tired soldier holding her spear, her entire body bristling to murder. "It was a mistake dragging that thing in here, and now Alan is dead."

There was a practiced ease to it that unnerved Susan. As though, somehow, Mrs. Monique wasn't unfamiliar with violent situations. And it dawned on her that Mrs. Monique had risen to the survival challenge and fought off several angels already to survive. She'd saved Susan and Jenny from the two wretched angels. How many others would jump into that kind of situation to help? Susan realized she didn't know a thing about the librarian beyond her friendly facade.

Dr. Lee shook his head. "It hasn't attacked anyone since Susan shot electricity through its brain. No signs of aggression. It seems more like a curious animal now." He paused to turn the phone back on Susan. "That was a mighty fine display, by the way. How did you do that with your weapon?"

"I'm not sure," Susan replied. She wanted to step away and sort through her thoughts, not answer a barrage of Dr. Lee's questions. "But I need to sit down. I feel lightheaded."

"Drained like a battery, I suppose . . ." muttered Dr. Lee under his breath, his face falling slightly. She got the sense they were wondering the same thing: if they could use electricity to alter the brains of other angels, turn them into harmless things like this one.

But what had it been altered to? Why did it suddenly have an iris? Why had its name changed? She wanted Jenny to see this. She wanted to know Jenny's thoughts on this.

With a heavy sigh, Dr. Lee knelt, bringing the phone closer to the angel. Its orange eye watched him with great interest, and it hissed again as though speaking, whistling through the gap in its teeth.

He began to narrate.

"Our brains send signals via electricity. They travel from neuron to neuron and conduct the processes of our central nervous systems. Susan's attack must have supercharged the brain. I only wish we could have recorded the visuals." He said this part gruffly, with a hint of annoyance that made Leslie click her tongue. "I wonder if the angel's strengthened form enabled it to survive the trauma, though its skin . . . Is that actually skin? Exhibits the telltale scarring of lightning victims . . ."

He was speaking too quickly for Susan to understand properly, but the little bits that reached her sent her thoughts spinning.

Were the angels just like humans, then? Trapped in this nightmare?

Susan sat near the entrance again, leaning against the librarian's desk, her eyes shut. She listened for any sign of Jenny outside, half hoping her best friend would return and bang on the doors to be let inside.

Mrs. Monique had walked her over and then returned to Dr. Lee's side. She was ready to kill the angel as soon as she could, but it still hadn't done anything other than hiss, repeating the same pattern of shushing and gasping, though nobody could decipher what it wanted.

Leslie stayed with Dr. Lee, holding his phone and recording as he made observations and tried to understand. The other students had moved Alan's body and covered it with a cloth. Several of them wept.

Sitting away from them, Susan wasn't sure how much time had gone by since Jenny had left. She didn't want to check; she wasn't even sure if the time displayed on anyone's phones would have any meaning when they weren't on Earth. But the reason she didn't want to check was cowardice. She didn't want to know how long Jenny had been out there alone. Guilt constricted her heart.

She kept picturing angels swarming Jenny and ripping her apart and . . . Susan sucked in a deep breath. Worrying wouldn't help. And she was a human stage two, just as Jenny had been when she left. She had a bunch of status points to apply and . . . She remembered the skill.

*Skill* . . . What did that even mean? Was it the same as when her cattle prod had gained an ability once it reached tier two?

She focused on the thought and brought up the notification.

**Valescent Light (Tier 1)**
**Generate purifying light. Draws heavily on Stamina to maintain.**

She held the notification in her head, repeating it over and over, trying to understand it as clearly as possible. Generate . . . a *purifying* light? Did that mean an ability to heal? She wouldn't have to spend energy on potions anymore?

Focusing again, she held up her hand, pushing her consciousness to focus on her fingertips; she could feel her blood pounding through her veins. Furrowing her brows and concentrating hard, she kept thinking *Valescent Light* as hard as she could.

Just when she thought she might pass out from thinking so hard, a shudder traveled up her arm, and a little sphere of warm silvery light flickered into being at her fingertip. A strange sensation tingled across her skin, and she felt a slight drain, as though the ball of light pulled on something from her chest to remain lit.

She felt the urge to press the light into her wounded leg. It was strange, but it felt like an extension of herself. As though her deepest wish had materialized. Trusting her instinct, she pressed the light to her ruined flesh.

An immense *tug* nearly overwhelmed her thoughts. Nausea threatened to make her retch. Her head spun. But the ball of light slipped into her wound and burst into brilliance.

Her jaw dropped as the searing pain vanished. The light, shining with every color of the rainbow, turned into strands, stretching up and down the ruined part of her leg. She saw blue and purple intertwining with white. She saw reds weaving in between and around. She saw greens and yellows and vivid oranges. The colorful strands seemed almost jellylike, almost like the way the angel's orange covering had burst from its spine earlier.

It connected one end of her wound to the other and solidified slowly, the glow fading away to reveal brand new flesh, pink and softer than the surrounding skin.

She touched it tenderly, her eyes widening with disbelief. But the pain was gone. Her leg didn't burn. Tears spilled down her cheeks, and she realized she could restore Jenny's fingers.

She wiped her face, excitement making her heart go wild. She wanted to scream with joy, though she wondered how far the skill would go. How much could she actually heal? And she was *exhausted*. She would definitely need to increase her stamina. Using it had *drained* her, much more so than using the lightning did, but once she figured this skill out, once she increased her stats and prepared herself . . . Maybe this was what they needed.

If she could heal herself and Jenny, they could spend their energy on more things than just healing.

She forced herself to take a deep breath. Partially because she needed to; she felt like she'd just run for hours and hours. But also because she needed to calm down. This could be big. Maybe she could convince Mrs. Monique to help her. They could go find Jenny, and maybe together, with this, they'd all have a fighting chance.

She remembered she'd gotten a bunch of points after she'd reached stage two. But before she could pull up her stats, a shock wave rumbled through the walls and windows of the library with such force that several people screamed. It felt like another earthquake.

Susan's heart leaped into her throat, and she looked up just in time to see the barricade come crashing down with a thunderous roar.

# CHAPTER THIRTY-TWO

# A Circular Steel Rod

A circular steel rod, roughly an inch in diameter and corrugated so that her blood glistened down its spiraling ridges, jutted out from her stomach. Jenny felt a sharp sensation in her lower right side; it reminded her of the random stabbing pains she used to get, wondering if it was finally appendicitis, but then it would turn out to be trapped gas in her intestines. It was seriously odd, sensing pain without feeling it.

She coughed up blood then rested her head back on the concrete slab she'd fallen on. Her feet hung off the edge, touching the tiles of the first-floor physics lab room. She was caked in dust, stuck to the slab, but at least it didn't hurt.

The sensation of her flesh around the rod was weirding her out. She knew if it weren't for Severed Spirit, she'd be dead. She might've passed out from the blood loss or pain, and she wondered now if that would've been better than this.

"Fuck," she whispered. Dust rose and spun all around her. She jostled slightly, felt her insides squish grossly, then gave up. About two feet of rod stuck out of her. She had to rip through her side to escape or climb up the entire thing and slide off. Her shield clanged uselessly against the slab.

She thought she'd dropped somewhere near the back of the room, but it was difficult to tell with all the rubble piled around. The physics lab was buried. The windows had shattered, and the swirling mistiness of the Veil floated inside. Its ghostly light shone through the clouds of dust.

Flashes of what happened kept popping up. The cocoon had exploded. She'd seen the floor give away. Saw the sacs tumbling around like enormous pieces of fleshy hail. The ceiling above had caved in.

Exposed pipes and rods and cement. The bodies that the angels had piled up fell like clumps of mud, their limbs and heads knocking into things. She'd glimpsed the girl and the black wretched angel, her hatchet still stuck to its head. But she hadn't seen what emerged from the cocoon, or if anything emerged at all. All she'd done was fall, trying to shield herself from chaos.

When she landed, there'd been a strange pressure in her back, and she'd seen the bar emerge from her insides, almost in slow motion. Her blood sprayed all over, and the thing kept extending until she slammed against the slab with an unceremonious clang.

She struggled again, grasping the rod with her right hand, trying to drag herself up its length. But no matter how hard she squeezed or how much she strained, she couldn't move more than a few inches off the slab before her arm gave out and she slid back down, frustrated. But without clear messages of pain, she was terrified of ripping her arm out of its socket. She didn't want her only arm with fingers still attached to be useless.

*This was stupid.* What bugged her the most was that she hadn't seen Oliver. Had he gotten dragged down too? Was he crushed under the rubble? Or was he still up there? She wasn't sure what the radius of the cocoon's blast had been, but there'd been other kids with him, too. Jenny hoped they'd woken up and were working on getting themselves and Oliver out, even if they didn't manage to get to her.

She laughed. *Fucking hell.* No, it would be stupid to give up now. Her body literally could not die until she disabled the skill. All she had to do was get out of this, kill a bunch of angels, and then . . . and then . . . She remembered how she'd poured the potion onto Susan's injured leg. Okay, so she wouldn't have to feel any pain. She could get someone to heal her body before disabling the skill, then she'd be just fine.

She grabbed the rod again and pulled, sliding a bit upward, wishing she could use both hands.

She got a bit further up, heard a *pop* in her arm, and stopped. There was still so much of the bar left to go. Her boots kicked at loose rubble, trying to find some footing to prop herself up, but something fleshy and soft gave way beneath her heel, and she stopped.

Exasperated, she slid back down to rest, slamming her shield into the concrete slab. Then she did it again and again, not caring that the sound was ringing out all over the ruined lab room.

Either she'd break the slab and free herself with the rod still inside her, or someone would hear her and come help. Or something else might find her . . . She used as much force as she could, picturing an angel devouring her while she was stuck here. Picturing the metallic, creepy desecrated angel she'd seen in the cocoon, its blue eyes . . . its teeth chewing through her face while it smiled at her.

She didn't have her hatchet; she couldn't summon it. But she figured she could smash any angel's face in with the shield, or grab onto them somehow and use their bodies to pull herself out. Or worst-case scenario, force them onto the bar as well, skewering them so she could take a few more of these assholes down to hell with her.

If it meant a bunch of angels would be distracted, then she would happily be a diversion while the others got out of the rubble. If they were alive . . .

She heard a crack beneath her, but the slab wouldn't give. She couldn't get the right angle. She didn't stop until she heard something wet, something squishy, as though a bowl of pudding had hit the floor.

Then she heard a giggle.

She turned her head. The sound had come from her right, where a pile of rubble formed a mountain over one of the physics lab room tables. Crushed bodies lay between them. An arm stuck out, almost as though it were reaching for her.

Then she saw what was making the sound. It was a pudgy baby crawling on all fours, its big head bobbing as its eyes wandered, an almost curious innocence shining in them. It wasn't like the angels' eyes. These weren't white and vacant; they had irises. Pupils. Large dark circles that moved until they spotted Jenny and paused.

The baby's face lit up. Gooey liquid trailed from its skin as it crawled over the debris, dust clinging to it. It tumbled and rolled, and Jenny almost wanted to shout for it to be careful, to not move, that she'd somehow get to it and help. But it paused to sniff one of the crushed bodies, and she saw several more babies wriggling around.

The first baby came up to her. Its palms struck the rubble, making fleshy sounds that Jenny thought would hurt, but the baby didn't seem to mind. Wet-looking black hair was stuck to its head; it must've just emerged from a sac. It was newly born, but it wasn't tiny like human infants, and it was already crawling, something human babies didn't do for like six months after birth.

She couldn't tell if it had emerged like this or if it was growing at an accelerated rate. And without the guidance system, she couldn't be certain of what it was. The eyes threw her off; they seemed too much like human babies. She remembered what Eve had said about the sacs having to be blooded, and wondered if that led to accelerated growth. Was that a way to ensure the infant would survive?

The baby crawled up to her, its chubby cheeks jiggling, its brows furrowed in concentration. It stopped by her boots and looked up with those large, curious eyes. They were brown like Jenny's, and full of life. A gurgle of laughter bubbled through its lips with spittle.

She almost thought it was cute. Almost. Cause right after clapping its hands, it slapped both palms down on the floor and lowered its button nose to where her blood had dribbled down her legs and pooled. It slurped.

"What the fuck?" whispered Jenny, her tongue moving awkwardly over her gums. She couldn't look away from the little creature; it almost seemed like it was nursing. Then she noticed the others wriggling toward them. They weren't as focused, and they paused to wiggle loose rocks and chew on loose limbs.

But they didn't have teeth. They couldn't rip into any of the flesh. The babies gurgled and giggled. One of them screeched. It was trying to bite into that arm sticking out from the rubble, the fingers unharmed between the baby's gums. It tried to grab the arm, reposition it, but when it still couldn't bite through the fingers, the baby screeched again.

Following its lead, others started to cry, too, wailing at the top of their lungs. It was like being in some demented nursery, except she was trapped, bleeding out, and one of them was drinking her blood off the floor.

Guilt panged inside her, a twisting knot in her stomach that she thought she shouldn't have been able to feel, but it was still there. She thought about the sacs she'd set aflame in the stairwell on her way to the second floor. Thought about burning the female wretched angel to ashes and bone, and remembered the little skeleton she'd found in the larger angel's embrace.

She'd consoled herself thinking that whatever was in those sacs was probably just as twisted and horrifying as the angels. But these babies, despite their cannibalistic instincts, seemed so . . . innocent. On top of that, they had eyes. Eyes that searched the rubble, spotted her, and lit up as though they'd found their mother in a crowd of people.

She wanted to throw up again. She'd never wanted any children, and now she swore if she got out of this, she'd have her uterus ripped from her body. Some part of her would always be terrified of pushing out a horror baby.

Swearing under her breath as the babies crawled over to her, Jenny grabbed the furthest part of the rod she could reach. She had an idea. Inhaling deeply, she positioned her boots beneath her, raising her hips slightly and arching her back. She was distorting her body quite a bit, and she tried not to think about how much this should hurt. Her right ankle was twisted and useless, but if she could just generate enough force, this could work.

Squeezing the bar, she pushed her feet against the slab, a cry of frustration escaping her. She paused after sliding up more than she'd managed before, exhilaration fluttering through her head. She glanced at the baby. It had stopped drinking blood and now sat back on its little butt, sitting and watching. It clapped its hands together, a wide smile on its face as Jenny struggled. The other babies drew closer, some on all fours, some sitting, all of them watching her with great interest.

She adjusted her feet and slid her hand up the rod. It was already slick with blood, and now, her fingers and palm were bleeding too, as the corrugated ridges cut her skin. Her insides squeaked and squished as she pushed off again with her feet, the angle of her body changing as now she was almost upright.

At one point, she almost let go and fell back, but she smashed her shield into the slab and used that as a crutch to hold on. Her body was out of breath, and even though she couldn't feel the pain or the struggle, she relaxed her shoulder for a second, squeezing the rod as hard as she could with her hand while she inhaled a lungful of dust.

"Stupid baby," she whispered, but without teeth, her voice sounded so stupid to her. She laughed, realizing she was missing teeth just like the angel babies. It was a gross, ugly laugh of desperation, exhaustion, and frustration. Her body was nearly all the way up the bar, her shield arm stuck behind her. It was such an absurd situation.

Gathering her strength once again, she kept going. Pulling with her hand, pushing with her legs and shield. Her insides shifted the further she climbed. At the tip, she quickly adjusted her right hand, letting go to grab the rod from behind. Her shoulders cracked, but this way, it was impossible for her to slide back.

She screamed for the last bit. Her insides struggled to let go, but as soon as she pushed herself off, she stumbled forward and fell right next to the first baby. Her helmet clanged against a piece of rubble, the breeze and dust teasing her insides. That couldn't be good . . . but what was she supposed to do now?

She wished she could use Ignite; use fire to close the wound. At least nothing really hurt, and she'd pulled herself back up. She turned to face the slab. It was covered in her blood, the rod sticking out like a beacon.

The babies watched as she hobbled back. Her right foot bent uselessly, and she stumbled again but caught herself. The first baby's lips opened, and it made a soft cooing sound, drooling.

Jenny licked her lips. She was a mess, but that wasn't new at this point. She'd managed to free herself from impalement, and that was an immense win as far as she was concerned. The babies hadn't tried to eat her; nothing had come sniffing her out. But there had to be other things out there. That desecrated angel, for starters . . . Where was it? What was it doing?

She pushed the bar forward, bending it near the base. Groaning, she adjusted her grip and pulled it back. Then she repeated the motion several times, the rod squeaking and stretching at the bend, and she relished her increased power as it snapped off cleanly. She had secured a makeshift weapon until she found her hatchet.

Holding the bar, she used it like a cane, hunched over and drooling as she bled profusely. *What happens when I run out?*

The other babies wandered around her. Some of them sniffled, sucking their thumbs or inspecting the blood on the floor. Her shield arm dangled loosely as she wondered what to do about the little creatures. *I could kill them and take their energy.*

# CHAPTER THIRTY-THREE

# CRAWLING OVER THE RUBBLE

Would the babies give more energy than the sacs had in the stairwell? After all, they were birthed already, and crawling about. She swallowed the lump in her throat. Her body was falling apart; she had to be very nearly without blood. Her heartbeat felt faint, and the gurgling babies wouldn't stop staring at her. *What if she ate them?*

She looked down at the first one and shuddered from that intrusive thought. Its eyes searched her own as it sucked on its bloody thumb. The sucking sound reminded her of the wretched angel earlier, the one with the stripes, its lips fastened to her crushed nose, and she grimaced. She raised the rod, swaying on her feet. She held it as though she was fishing. She could plunge it into the little creature's tummy, and it would be over.

*Do it . . . just kill it. Take the energy. You're going to need so much to heal yourself, and it's going to turn into a tarnished angel anyway. It would just mean more enemies to fight later.*

But still, her arm shook. The baby blinked back, completely unfazed by the steel bar. It didn't have the empty eyes of the angels she'd fought already, and even though these things liked blood . . . No, she couldn't do it. They seemed much more alive and innocent. She'd wait. She'd wait for them to turn into tarnished angels, and then she'd shove the rod through their throats. Besides, that way, she'd get more energy—guilt free.

Blood gushed from the gaping wound in her side. She tasted blood in her mouth, and it dribbled down her chin. She stepped around the kids, using the rod as a crude walking stick to rest her weight on. Her right foot was nearly useless; she couldn't put too much weight on it without her knee buckling, and it was irritating her despite the lack of pain. She had to hurry.

Two of the babies crawled after the bloody trail she was leaving in her wake. She scanned the bodies on the floor, trying to find Oliver or the girl, or any of the others who'd been up there. It bothered her that they'd all been unconscious or nearly dead. What had the angels done to them?

Jenny inspected her surroundings. The tables of the physics lab weren't as large, and they didn't have sinks or ventilating stations, but the tables from the chem lab were strewn about. Some were nearly vertical, crushing things underneath their weight. Some were upside down. But still, everything was covered in chunks of ceiling and tons of dust.

Bodies were crushed all around her, and between them were more sacs. Each one glistened like a giant grape; most of them were torn open and flat.

She stepped over mangled bodies, naked angels and clothed corpses alike. She stepped on fingers accidentally, crushed limbs. She grimaced whenever something squished, wondering if anyone had been down here when the explosion collapsed everything. If anyone had been hiding or dying here.

More babies joined the parade behind her, and she felt like a mother duck, hobbling, falling apart, and leading little bloodthirsty ducklings. Why were they so adamant about following her?

Her head felt heavy, like it was about to roll off her shoulders any moment now. She almost wanted to remove her helmet and let her sweaty hair cool down, but if anything else fell from above, she didn't want her skull cracked open.

She knew her body couldn't take much more, but she couldn't turn off Severed Spirit without ensuring she could heal. Oliver or one of the others could make something, or she just had to hurry up and find him then get back to the library; people there had energy to spare. She focused on that thought, of getting back to Susan. Then she could figure out what to do next. She was sure that once she was back with her, it would be alright.

Even though she felt like a zombie, her cheeks still flushed with a strange warmth at the thought of Susan. Jenny licked her ruined gums, wondering how her best friend would react to this messed-up body.

Feeling warmer and more alive, Jenny surveyed the exposed pipes, bodies, and rubble, squinting hard at everything, blinking dust from her eyelashes. She imagined other angels were on their way, attracted by all the noise of the explosion. And where was that desecrated angel? What was it doing? Was it stalking her through the dust-ridden gloom?

She heard coughing and froze, ready to fight. Something bumped into the back of her boots, and Jenny whirled around, stumbling as she raised her shield, ready to plunge the bar into whatever it was.

But it was only one of the babies, touching her feet and staring up at her, drooling spittle, as though it wanted to be picked up.

She fought the urge to kick it away. There was another cough, and something shifted and clattered. A large chunk of cement jostled loose off a table and crashed to the floor, and the girl from before emerged through the cloud of rising dust. Fresh blood dripped from her knife as dust caked her face and her ruined helmet.

The girl paused, her other hand resting on that chunk of cement, staring at Jenny. Her eyes went wide. She glanced down at the babies and then back at Jenny, as though putting two and two together. Before Jenny could say anything, the girl lunged forward with a bloodcurdling scream, kicking up loose rocks and debris in her wake.

Jenny blocked the knife with her shield. The impact drew up sparks, and she knocked the girl's arm away. She didn't attack with the rod, even though it would've been easy to jam it into the girl's exposed chest. Instead, she stepped back, shouting, "Wait!"

The girl wasn't listening. She yowled, a throaty, angry cry, as she circled Jenny, not caring about the limbs crushed beneath her feet. Her armor looked a lot like a knight's, with layers of metal, but it was thinner and didn't clink or seem stiffly uncomfortable like traditional knight's armor. Her helmet was cracked and broken, and the dark gray metal of her suit was scuffed and crumpled in several places, but Jenny thought it still looked very badass.

"Look," Jenny tried again, painfully aware of how stupid she sounded without enough front teeth. "I'm not gonna hurt you. I don't want to fight." Her words felt bubbly and too soft, consonants not forming properly, but she spoke slowly.

The girl spat and said something too, but just like Jenny's words, her voice seemed oddly shaped. A mixture of yowling and groaning, the syllables only somewhat recognizable. And as she spoke, her free hand went up, fingers forming shapes and patterns that Jenny recognized as American Sign Language. The girl was deaf.

Jenny lowered her shield in disbelief. A deaf girl had survived this long and was *this* strong? Though if Jenny hadn't arrived when she did, the girl would've been sacrificed to the cocoon. But still. Jenny had so many questions, wondering if the girl had a hearing aid, if her deafness was why Oliver was so protective of her, if she had a skill that would make up for it.

She dropped her rod. It clattered loudly on the rubble, and the babies crawled over to inspect it. Jenny didn't know ASL, but she knew the universal sign for *I don't want to fight*. She raised both hands, exposing her palms, showing the girl the missing fingers of her shield hand.

"I'm not going to fight you," mouthed Jenny slowly, hoping the girl could read her lips.

It seemed to work. She lowered her knife, glancing at the rod then back at Jenny. Her fingers moved in a fresh flurry of anger, her pointer thrust at Jenny as though accusing her of something.

Jenny didn't care. She just wanted to pick the rod up and lean on it again. Slowly, she squatted down, wincing at how her insides gushed and splattered the floor with blood. That shut the girl up. She made a new motion, slower this time, and trying to voice her words. Each one was elongated, a guttural grunt between them. "Are . . . you . . . okay?"

Jenny shook her head, grimacing as her fingers curled around the bar. She thrust the end into the floor and pushed herself back to a standing position. The babies all gurgled excitedly at the new blood, and some of them began to lick the rubble. She almost told them off; it was dangerous for babies to lick random things, especially covered in dust and grime. But then she remembered what they were.

The girl was still trying to talk to her. "Why . . . are you . . ." She paused to take a breath, her hand curling in frustration. She pointed her fingers at her own eyes and then at Jenny's. "Tar . . . nished . . . human."

A chill spread across Jenny's chest which had nothing to do with the sensation of cold. It was like her heart had turned to cement. *Tarnished human?* She blinked several times, desperately trying to contact the guidance system or Eve.

*What the fuck?* If she'd become a tarnished human . . . was she just like the angels? But how? *Why?*

Had severing herself from her body changed . . . She had the sudden desire to check her eyes. The girl had pointed to them. Had Jenny's become empty and white? Her heart pounded hard and fast, increasing the amount of blood flowing down her leg, to the babies' delight.

But before Jenny could ruminate on that horrible thought more, the floor shook. Debris rattled. Sounds came from behind the girl, but she didn't notice. She stepped closer to Jenny, cautiously, her knife hand trembling. Three figures emerged behind her, each one of them hissing and rushing toward them.

Jenny raised the rod, wishing she had her hatchet. There was no time to worry about her status. The girl saw the shift in Jenny's stance and raised her arms in a defensive stance as Jenny hurled the bar like a lance, mimicking Savage Throw.

The girl yelped as the rod rushed past her side and caught one of the angels in the chest. The creature was knocked backward off its feet, screaming as the rod burst through its body.

It collapsed on its back, the bar keeping its body raised off the ground as it struggled uselessly, its dark-green covering cracked open. It screeched, and the babies responded to the sound, screaming in unison.

The girl had turned to face the other two. She threw her knife at the nearest one, the blade plunging into the creature's throat. It dropped to its knees, trying to grab the handle and wrench it out, but the girl was already on the move.

She rushed over the rubble, moving light as a feather, and golden light flashed midleap as she jumped toward the third one. The knife reappeared in her hands while she brought the angel to the floor, its head cracking loudly as she stabbed it over and over, making mincemeat of its silvery covering, blood spurting out.

Jenny kicked off an angel baby that had been screaming and clinging to her leg. It landed on its butt, surprise on its pudgy little face, but she didn't care. She limped over and grabbed the rod, staring down at the wretched angel impaled on it.

It hissed faintly, hands wrapped around the metal bar protruding from its chest.

*Yeah*, she thought, stepping on its face, its teeth clacking uselessly against her heel. *Try pulling yourself out of it.* Using the rod to support her weight, she stomped down, and the creature's face crunched underneath.

When she was satisfied it was dead, she yanked the rod out of its chest. The babies had followed her, and they got to work on the angel's corpse as though Jenny really was their mother and had led them to a meal. She watched in twisted horror as they chewed through the dark-green covering and bit into flesh. They had teeth now, she realized. They were growing rapidly.

One crawled over to the crushed skull and began eating, the bones of the creature's face cracking and snapping between the baby's teeth. It slurped up brain matter, and that was all Jenny could bear to watch.

The other girl seemed repulsed as well. Her fingers formed words, and she shook her head, but she didn't try to speak again. A sense of comradery had blossomed between them now that they'd fought off angels together, and she even had a similar recalling skill for her weapon. Though Jenny couldn't help but wonder what the girl's other skills might be, since she was also a stage two human.

Then Jenny heard a shout. A clearly human shout, strained with desperation. "Help!"

She perked up, trying to discern the direction it came from. It sounded like a boy, but she couldn't be sure if it was Oliver or not. The girl, sensing Jenny had heard something, turned this way and that, probably assuming more enemies were approaching.

The babies wriggled. Another tried to crawl up Jenny's leg, but she shook it off.

The shout came again.

"Is anyone there? Please, we need—"

It ended abruptly, like someone was in excruciating pain, and Jenny's hopes faltered. It wasn't Oliver, but the voice was full of desperation. Whoever they were, they needed serious help and were willing to risk drawing the attention of angels to do so.

Either that, or angels were already upon them.

# CHAPTER THIRTY-FOUR

# A Cry for Help

Jenny pointed in the direction the shouting had come from with her shield. "Someone's there," she said.

The girl nodded and went ahead, moving lithely as she stepped over rubble and climbed over a table, her knife at the ready.

Still using her rod like a walking stick, Jenny followed as quickly as she could, hobbling around the tables and smashing large chunks of debris into bits with the metal bar. Empty sacs squished beneath her boots. The babies trailed behind her, sucking on their thumbs and gurgling as they tripped and tumbled. Nothing seemed to harm them.

Another shout came from ahead. She heard rocks clattering, and for a second, she wondered if the girl had run into an angel or fallen. Jenny dragged her ruined foot, used the rod to push herself over a few bodies and a rather large chunk of ceiling, then she saw what had made the girl shout.

The girl had joined a boy, who was struggling with one of the oversize tables from the chem lab room. It was upside down, and another one was jammed on top of it, as well as a large cabinet and a mountain's worth of rubble. She couldn't tell why they were trying to move it. The boy was large and muscular, and he had to be a human stage two because that was what she remembered from when she'd been dragged into the lab room.

His helmet was comprised of rectangular blocks that covered the top, sides, and back of his head, and he wore something thin and dark that hugged his frame and made his muscles seem more pronounced. He was groaning loudly as he tried to push the table; the girl helped as well, using her shoulder, her feet squeaking against the floor.

It wasn't until she stumbled closer that she saw the reason for their efforts. Jenny's heart nearly sank all the way down to the rupture in her side and burst out when she saw who was lying underneath the upside-down table, his legs completely pinned.

Jenny's chest pulled, like her ribs were collapsing. She'd forgotten to breathe. The boy was still trying to move the mountain, screaming as he failed, the girl screaming alongside him. But all they managed to do was knock a few chunks loose that rained down in a shower of dust.

Not caring for her foot anymore, Jenny rushed forward and collapsed by Oliver's side, the rod clattering loudly to the floor. The table had crushed his legs up to the knees, and blood pooled around his lower body and soaked into his pants. The greenish armor he wore like a jacket was caked in dust. She wiped his face, trying to clean it, but all she managed to do was smear her own blood on his cheeks. His glasses were shattered now, the empty frames clinging to his nose.

*Please don't be dead.*

It took her a frantic second to remember she couldn't see any notifications. Scrambling, she pulled off his green military helmet and cast it aside before pressing her fingers against his neck.

The other boy said something to her, but she couldn't hear him. All her focus was on finding Oliver's pulse. When she finally felt it beating against her fingers, she inhaled a shuddering breath, easing the pressure in her lungs. She wanted to collapse; wanted to drag him out from under the table; wanted to break everything and set him free.

His thigh was still ruined. The bone stuck out even worse than how it'd been earlier in the chem lab. The injury was covered in dust, the inner flesh exposed to all the dirt and grime. A helpless rage stirred Jenny's thoughts as she stared down at the brother she'd always ignored.

But the other boy was now shouting at her. He grabbed her shoulder, and she twitched with anger, turning to face him.

Now that she was up close, she saw how menacing he looked. He was dark skinned, tall and muscular, with a slim frame that screamed athleticism. She recognized his face; he'd been on the football team with Susan's ex, but she couldn't remember his name.

His armor was thin and metallic, like sportswear, but none of it was torn. Other than dried blood and dust, it seemed to have held up through however many fights he'd been in, as well as the fall.

As soon as he caught a glimpse of her face, he let Jenny go and stepped away quickly. Golden light flickered and flashed around his raised arms, forming red boxing gloves. His eyes narrowed with intense focus.

*Great*, thought Jenny. *There's no time for this shit.* She held up her hands again and shook her head. "I'm human."

"That's not what it says," he replied, licking his lips. His entire body seemed to bristle, like any moment now, he would burst into action and hit her with extreme force. Any moment now, he would punch her in the face. She thought she could skewer him before his glove ever reached her.

"I know," she said quickly. *Tarnished human . . .* She noticed red flashes of electricity gathering around his gloves, like he was charging them for something. "I'm human," she repeated, not caring how she sounded without teeth. "This is my brother. Oliver."

That finally got through to the boy. His stance faltered, the electricity snapping and blinking out. The girl touched his elbow, and he turned to see the words she signed rapidly. Jenny didn't care. She went back to inspecting the table and the rubble, trying to find some weak point, some way to get Oliver out. Maybe if they removed the stuff on top, bit by bit, slowly and carefully, they could work their way down without too much risk.

A giggle let her know the babies had reached them. She heard the boy and girl shouting, and she turned to see even more babies had joined her little flock. There were sacs in the rubble crushing Oliver, more sacs around them, and she wondered when they'd hatch, too.

"Don't hurt them," she said, not caring what they thought. She was eyeing the other rods and pipes sticking out of slabs of concrete. She reached for her bar and laid it across her knees, straining to remember something from physics. Something about basic machines . . .

But physics had never been her strong suit. She hadn't paid much attention in class, and now her brain felt like mush. Tears kept spilling down her cheek as she kept checking for the rise and fall of Oliver's chest. She wasn't trying to cry, the tears just kept coming, blurring her vision. She wiped her eyes with the back of her hand, the dirt and drying blood smearing wetly.

Oliver coughed, sputtering. Jenny touched his cheek. He felt warm . . . too warm. But was that because she was cold and lifeless or because he was running a fever? His eyes opened.

"Jenny?" he whispered, squinting. "Why are you . . . ? What happened?"

She shook her head, opening her mouth to speak, but she couldn't find the words.

"Are you hurt?" he asked before groaning, as though he realized how much pain he was in. He turned his head, eyes glistening wetly through his broken glasses. He focused on her mouth. "Your teeth . . ." He tried to sit up and flinched in agony.

"Don't move," she said quickly, resting her hand on his chest and glancing at his legs. He'd tried to pull them free. Some loose rubble had rained down, and she was terrified his legs would rip clean off.

Oliver cried out in pain, grabbing Jenny's arm and squeezing it, burying his nails in it, breathing hard. The other boy and girl hovered nearby, the babies crawling around them. Two of them wandered over to watch Jenny and Oliver, eyeing her brother as though he might be their next meal.

It was the boy who broke the silence. "Oliver?" he asked, crouching down and pressing one of his gloves into the dirt beside Oliver's head. "Are you good?" But he choked on his question.

"Is that you, Dulé?" whispered Oliver through gritted teeth. He let out a strained laugh. "I guess we're still alive."

The boy, Dulé, laughed. "Yeah. Yeah, I thought the striped one finally got us." He shook his head. Looking at Jenny, he added, "It had some kind of toxin or something that fucked us up." Then he swallowed hard, struggling to keep his voice steady. "This was . . . It's my fault. I wanted to fight them. I thought we could clear them out. And they had one of our friends . . ."

But Jenny had already tuned him out. *Toxins? They had toxins?* Was that why she'd felt so powerless when it grabbed her and sucked out her blood? She thought she'd just been afraid.

"I thought I was gonna have to watch them eat you guys one by one." Oliver coughed again, still squeezing Jenny's arm. Then he spotted the hole in her side, the blood dripping. He saw the baby that pushed its way to Jenny's side so it could stare at Oliver.

The girl shouted, and Dulé stood to see what was going on. Jenny couldn't take her eyes off Oliver's.

"You saved us, didn't you?" he asked quietly. His arms were shaking, but he stopped burying his nails in her arm. "Why are you so cold?"

She shrugged, blinking away tears. "I'm just tired." She tried to smile, to reassure him, but without teeth, it wasn't much more than a toothless grimace. Her nose rasped when she inhaled; she must look like a freak.

"Your eyes . . ." he whispered, reaching up to touch her cheek. "They're the same eyes as the . . ." Before he finished the thought, his eyelids shut. His hand dropped from her face, and his head turned, face relaxing as he exhaled.

"No!" shouted Jenny, her voice breaking. She was only vaguely aware of the girl and Dulé fighting off angels. The sparks of red light. The flashes of gold. She pressed her fingers back to Oliver's neck, blinking furiously through the tears, trying to see if his chest was still moving.

Thoughts of CPR went through her head; pressing her hand over his chest and pumping his heart for him, wishing Susan were here to shock his heart or something. Didn't the others have any energy? Anything? They could make potions or dream up something better and . . . But if his legs were still crushed, and he bled out . . .

She almost broke down, but then her fingers felt his pulse—a faint rhythm—and she wailed with relief. "He's alive," she whispered. Then she said it again loudly for the others, even though they were busy fighting. She spat blood, grabbed her rod, and hoisted herself off the floor.

The angels that had shown up—several tarnished and a handful of brightly colored wretcheds—lay dead or dying on the floor. The babies were crawling toward the bodies. Jenny looked at them for a moment, then she turned to the other two.

"Help me," she said, her voice quivering.

The rod scratched the floor as she limped over until she stood right beside the table. She tried not to think about the sheer amount of weight crushing Oliver as she grabbed its edge. Dulé and the girl did the same on the other side of Oliver, and together, they tried to lift it. A scream burst through her lips, all her muscles straining, trying to make the most of her separated mind and body. Blood gushed out of her wounds as though someone had squeezed her.

Crying out, she sank to her knees. They hadn't moved the table at all. It was impossible. They would have to lift a portion of the building.

"Fuck," she whispered, touching her wound and breathing hard to fill what blood she had left with oxygen. Dark spots blossomed in her vision, then she saw a loose chunk of concrete and remembered the lesson from physics class: a lever.

With a cough, she positioned her rod over the chunk, placing one end into the bit of space between the table and the floor. She kept picturing Oliver's flattened legs, thin as sheets of paper. But now, the metal bar stuck diagonally into the air. With the chunk of concrete under it, it looked almost like a seesaw. All she'd have to do was apply downward pressure and let the rod do the heavy lifting.

The others must have figured out what she was attempting, because they stepped forward to help, though the girl whisked away, crying out, as more angels appeared. Jenny caught Dulé's eyes. He hesitated for a moment, then hurried over to help.

Still on her knees, Jenny grabbed the bar with one hand and pressed her shield against it. Dulé's boxing gloves vanished, and he bent over to grab it as well. He counted down. "One . . . two . . . three!"

Grunting and screaming, they forced the rod down with all their might. The muscles in Dulé's arms bulged. The spots in Jenny's eyes nearly filled her vision. Just as it seemed like the table might shift and Oliver let out a groan, seemed like there was just enough space to drag him out—the rod snapped.

Its length flicked upward and spun away over their heads, nearly taking their faces with it. What was left of the rod was now trapped under the table. Dulé swore loudly.

Jenny stared helplessly at that tiny bit, blood dripping from her hand. Somehow, she'd thought the rod had been special, as though she'd found it for a reason. It had been inside her, hadn't it? How could it betray her like this?

Dulé's gloves reappeared as a tarnished angel sauntered over, hissing. Red light flashed, and a single punch completely obliterated the creature's head. Its body collapsed.

Breathless, sweat dripping down the side of his face, he turned to Jenny, his eyes filled with grief. "I wanted to use my Raging Strike and blow all the stuff away, but . . ." He shook his head. "It's not strong enough."

Jenny shoved her tongue against her gums, as though she was trying to force her teeth to grow. She was only half listening to his apology; she was trying to figure out a way to use his crazy punch.

None of her skills, even if she didn't have Severed Spirit active, would help. Frustration was building and building, and she wanted to scream until her throat went hoarse and all the angels in the building had found her.

Then she heard the babies gurgling loudly. A few of them were eating the angels the girl and Dulé had taken down while watching the rest of the fighting. Some of the other babies had wandered away from the group and were messing with something sticking out from the rubble not too far away from Oliver.

It was a large, muscular arm that ended in claws.

For the briefest of seconds, she felt motherly pride. She scrambled toward the appendage, limping terribly on her ruined foot until she collapsed on top of it. She pushed the loose rubble away, uncovering the black wretched angel that had nearly killed her. Its lower jaw was missing, and its insides were split open and exposed, covered in dust. Its tendrils were loose and unmoving. Smack in the center of its forehead was her hatchet.

An idea—a sick and twisted and horrible but desperate idea—came to Jenny's mind. She grabbed the handle of her weapon and wrenched it free as the babies chewed the angel's insides.

# CHAPTER THIRTY-FIVE

# OLDER SIBLING

She wanted to eat the dead wretched angel's flesh. Wanted to chew through the black covering of its skull and taste its brain matter. Her stomach twisted with a gaping, violent hunger; her mouth watered as she stared into its lifeless white eyes. The sounds of the babies tearing and chewing and swallowing only drove her ravenous insanity further.

Swallowing the excess spittle, she knelt slowly, her lips nearing the angel's ruined face. Its black covering had lost its shine; it seemed dull and lifeless now, covered in dust, but still delectable. She remembered how it'd turned gelatinous when it chewed on its own covering. Without its bottom jaw, she could see right into the pink darkness of its throat.

Blood ran down the side of its nose from the terrible wound on its forehead. A terrible wound that would give her access to a succulent meal.

Jenny stopped, her mouth hovering over its split-open forehead. Drool slid over her gums and out, a glistening drop that splashed on the dead creature's cheek. She was sitting on its chest, right in front of the spike, her knees on either side of its neck. One of the babies crawled over to see what she was doing. It cocked its oversize head, its bright green eyes shining. Then it pointed at the wretched angel's bleeding head as if to ask, *for me?*

Wiping her mouth with the back of her hand, the edge of her hatchet caught her eye. She realized it had changed—its appearance; its weight. Everything about it was different.

The metal part was now dark and smoky, glasslike with a textured pattern across its face that reminded her of molten rock. It was obsidian. She remembered that from Earth science, freshman year. The handle was a rich brown wood with shiny flowery etchings that climbed from bottom to top, as though someone had carved the intricate pattern into the wood and filled it with gold.

Her hatchet seemed more like an artifact from some ancient civilization now; something that might've been used ceremoniously rather than as a crude weapon or tool. It must be tier three now.

She wished she could invoke the guidance system to ask Eve for more information. What sort of abilities did it have now?

Not that knowing would help; she couldn't use her skills or abilities. Her hand shook, but she was grateful for the distraction; she'd almost given in and tasted angel flesh. Her fingers curled tightly around the handle, and she climbed off the dead angel. She ignored the baby. Half walking, half dragging, Jenny returned to Oliver's side, where she dropped to her knees.

Dulé and the girl were gone. She could hear their fighting: the hissing, screeching, scuffling, and occasional slam that sounded like a thunderclap. They must have led the angels away from Oliver. Since they were in a secluded corner near the front of the room, it was an easy place to protect.

*Smart*, she thought, inspecting the pile of rubble again. It reached all the way up to the large crater in the ceiling, blocking off the front door. They would have to fight to the other side and escape through the second exit. Dust and little bits escaped every so often whenever the floor shook. What if the whole thing collapsed?

One of the tables creaked precariously, and Jenny winced.

Something must have shifted, because Oliver awoke with a gasp. His chest rose and fell rapidly, and he stared at the rubble crushing his legs, eyes wide and frantic.

Jenny wanted to bite her lip, but that was impossible without teeth. She squeezed her hatchet; it seemed to glow now, emanating a faint golden aura which Oliver struggled to look at.

"Is that your weapon?" he asked weakly. He tried adjusting his glasses, but the lenses were long gone. They were just empty frames. "What you made? It's beautiful."

She nodded, almost wanting to laugh at the urge to say *"No duh."* That was how she'd usually respond to anything he'd say: with biting sarcasm.

"Mine was a knife," he continued. He raised an arm as if it was in his hands. "Got it to tier two, and I feel like I got close to tier three like yours. What does your hatchet do?" His voice was strained, but she got the sense he was talking to distract himself from the pain and to distract her from the situation.

Jenny turned her weapon over; the obsidian glimmered like metal from another world. The sound of Dulé's shouts filled the air, while the babies were still busy eating the delicious meal she'd left behind. "I can summon it back to me," she said finally, speaking slowly and hoping he understood her despite the lack of teeth distorting her words.

"Oh," whispered Oliver. He shut his eyes for a moment. "Just like Mackenzie. She copied my knife, but I got something else." He coughed violently and then groaned as the motion of coughing jarred his legs. Jenny dropped her hatchet to hold his hand.

The deaf girl's name must be Mackenzie, thought Jenny. She wondered what ability Oliver's knife got at tier two.

"Is she alive?" he asked softly, as though he'd already accepted her fate if she were dead. The last he'd seen of her, she'd been dragged away by the striped angel. The mark on his face was covered in dust, but Jenny could still see the red swelling.

"Yeah," Jenny replied, nodding and trying to smile, but then realized that wouldn't help much without teeth. "Still alive. And kicking ass."

Oliver started shivering like mad. His teeth were chattering. "Good," he said, his voice fading to whisper quiet.

Swallowing the lump in her throat, Jenny squeezed his hand. "Can't you hear her? She's right around this pile of shit."

He didn't seem to hear anything now. The shivering grew worse, and he stared at the gaping hole in the ceiling, his eyes watering. Tears ran down the sides of his face, clearing the dust. "It hurts," he said quietly, his voice layered with a moan of anguish. He squeezed her fingers so hard, his nails cut into her hand.

He looked like he was trying very hard not to cry and failing. He bit his bottom lip and turned his head slightly to look into Jenny's eyes, as though he were begging her to fix this, pleading silently.

Her heart broke; he'd never once looked at her like that before. Always it was curiosity or kindness or suppressed laughter, just whatever it was that little siblings did. She wanted to hug him; she'd never hugged him before. She wanted to console him and promise him everything would be all right. After all, that was her job as his big sister, wasn't it?

Shouldn't she know how to fix this? She was supposed to take care of him, wasn't she? A responsibility that had fallen on her as soon as their parents married. An obligation she'd resented and ignored, and now . . .

It was stupid. This was all so stupid. Struggling inside her was a disgusting hunger, a terrible heartbreak, and an aching that she wished would just *stop*. She forced herself to look at his legs again. If she could just get him out from under the rubble . . . they were on the first floor. She could carry him to the library, where he'd be safe.

But judging by the shouting and fighting, there were plenty of angels in the way. And somewhere, still in its cocoon maybe, was that desecrated angel, lying in wait.

She licked her lips, feeling the dust and dried blood stuck to her skin. His hand felt so warm in hers, and she listened to him praying softly, repeating the words her mother had taught him.

Jenny squeezed his hand back. "I'm going to get you out," she whispered. It was a promise. The first promise she'd made as his big sister. She'll figure *something* out.

His teeth chattered as he tried to speak. He was sobbing now. "Wait," he said, choking on the word. "Don't leave me here. I can't . . . I don't want to be alone."

"I'm not going anywhere," she said gently, repeating it as she let go of his hand. She was trembling now, too, trying to think. What could she use? The others had skills she didn't know about. She had this ruined body . . . There had to be something.

The hiss of an approaching angel cut through her thoughts. It must've slipped past the others. She turned to see a tarnished angel with long dark hair crawling toward them, an ugly gash going down the side of its face, blood dripping like wet paint, probably a result of Mackenzie's knife.

Oliver stared at it, his lips curling downward, his fingers balling into fists.

"It's okay," she reassured through the corner of her mouth, grabbing her hatchet's handle.

The creature moved slowly. It was injured in several places, and as soon as it got close enough, Jenny's arms snapped upward. The hatchet caught the angel's neck, streaks of golden light tracing the movement, shimmering.

The new edge cut through the creature so easily, Jenny almost released the hatchet in surprise. The angel's head landed several feet away, rolling, while its body seemed to hesitate, blood gushing out of the stump of its neck before it landed with a thud, bleeding profusely.

With a chorus of excited babbling, the babies crawled over as a group. They seemed even bigger than before, and she noticed several of them waddling on two chubby legs. Their eyes wide with excitement, arms held out for balance, they rushed to the tarnished angel's body. A few of them stumbled and fell, but then picked themselves up to hurry after the others.

"What are they?" whispered Oliver. "It says . . . It says *angel* . . . But yours . . . Why are you a tarnished human?" Fear shuddered through his question. His face was strained, turning pasty even with the healthy coating of dust. He looked like he was about to be sick.

"Don't think about that right now," she said quickly. Stress would only tax his body more. "Let's get you out first. Then I'll explain."

"But . . ." His voice faded. He sniffled, turning to watch the babies eat their next meal. They chewed through the tarnished angel's flesh, slurping and pausing to burp and spit up every once in a while.

Dulé stumbled near them, breathing hard, drenched in sweat. Jenny could still hear Mackenzie screaming and fighting, but there were other voices too. That gave her more hope. The more people they had, the better chance of getting out of there alive.

Wiping his brow, Dulé motioned toward the tarnished angel. The babies crawled all over it, chewing on fingers and elbows and shoulders. He made a face like he might throw up. "Sorry," he said. "That one got through."

"How many are there?" asked Jenny. She almost asked if they'd seen the desecrated angel, but knew that if they had, they'd all be dead. She didn't want to frighten Oliver by mentioning it.

"They keep coming," he replied, shaking his head and taking deep breaths. "But a lot of them are the weaker ones, and we have Alex and Tara helping now, too."

Golden light flashed. One of his boxing gloves disappeared, and he was holding what looked like a spray bottle of window cleaner. Jenny had no idea what it was without the guidance system.

"For you," he said, stepping closer and holding it out. "I'll make one for Oliver too. I would've made it sooner, but I didn't have enough energy. I'm guessing you don't, either."

Jenny shook the spray bottle; red liquid sloshed inside. It wasn't much different from her potions, but she thought it was interesting that others had come up with different means of healing. She glanced down at her wound. Blood still flowed from the hole in her side, but it had slowed down to a trickle. Her body was still moving—heavy and sickly but moving—and her heart continued beating, so she must still have enough blood to keep things running for now.

"How does it work?" she asked.

Golden light flashed again. "It's a minor spray of recovery," replied Dulé. "It'll close and heal anything. Saved us a bunch of times already."

She almost told him to wait, to store up more energy first so they could make something stronger, but Dulé already had another spray bottle in his hand. She pressed her lips together, straining hard to think.

Something about the way he said *close and heal* fluttered through her thoughts. These should work similarly enough to her potions, so as long as the wound closed and the blood flow stopped . . . Her breathing deepened as an idea formed. She glanced at Oliver's legs.

*Close and heal . . .*

She realized what she had to do. The only way to get Oliver out of this alive was to cut off his legs. She'd hold off from healing herself just yet; there was no way to know how much of these sprays they'd need, and if she could at least keep it together, keep Oliver alive, until they got to the library, then everything would work out.

"Okay," she said, her voice wavering slightly. She looked up at Dulé, realizing she was about to speak her idea out loud, making it real. "I'm going to cut off his legs."

# CHAPTER THIRTY-SIX

# POP

Jenny repeated the words silently to herself, trying to get them to sink in. *I'm going to cut off his legs.* She hated this. Hated she had to do this. Hated that she wasn't sure if she was trembling with hunger or disgust or fear. But it was the only way, and they'd be able to restore his limbs anyway, right? They would just need enough energy for the right potion or whatever else they could come up with.

More angels were going to show up. There would be more and more fighting until they eventually dropped from exhaustion or something really strong appeared . . . She shuddered, remembering her fight with the black-covered wretched angel. What would they do if something as strong as that crashed through the rubble?

On top of that, the desecrated angel was somewhere too. Was it crushed? Was it stuck? It hadn't emerged and killed them all yet . . . Maybe it wasn't fully formed. Earlier, while that striped angel was trying to feed it, the desecrated angel had seemed to struggle to breathe. Its insides could still be developing, or maybe it was like a butterfly, crawling out of its cocoon, waiting for its wings to unfurl and work before taking action.

Imagining that wasn't helping.

Jenny adjusted her goals, resolving to keep everyone alive. Nobody else would die—especially not Oliver, after all she'd fought through to get to him. She'd cut him free, heal his legs, then carry him to the library. Once there, Dr. Lee might be able to help. He must know stuff about this. Susan would be there, too; it would be safe.

Then, after recovering, she'd organize a group and come back. They'd find the cocoon or the desecrated angel and burn the entire thing to ashes. But right now . . . Right now, she had to cut through another person, her younger sibling.

"Are you sure?" asked Dulé, his voice cracking. He knelt on Oliver's other side, setting down the spray bottle and staring down at his friend.

Oliver nodded, but he didn't say a word. Instead, he turned back to watch Jenny, a frightened expression on his face, his lips pressed tightly together.

The air felt heavier. It stuck to the insides of her lungs. Other than the sounds of fighting and the babies feasting, all Jenny heard was Oliver's terrified breaths and her racing heart. At some point, she'd collapse too. Even with Severed Spirit, how much longer could her body go on like this? The quicker this was over with, the better.

She glanced at the headless tarnished angel. Its chest was wide open, and its heart stuck out, blood covering everything as the babies fed. Another flicker of hunger shot from her belly to her throat, but she swallowed it down. At least seeing the gruesome sight didn't make her want to retch, but this new feeling wasn't promising . . . Was she really turning into one of them?

She shut her eyes and prayed—a super quick prayer. To whom, she wasn't sure. Maybe to Eve. Maybe to Susan. Maybe to herself. All she could do was hope this would work, and that she wouldn't be responsible for the murder of her brother.

She opened her eyes when Oliver's fingers brushed hers. "It's okay," he spoke. His entire body was tense as if to stop the shaking, but he was struggling. Tears kept rolling down the sides of his head. "It'll be okay."

"That's what I'm supposed to say," Jenny replied. She was crying too. Snot mixed with blood and ran from her crushed nose down to her ruined lips. Maybe it was for the best she was in this strange state. If she'd been normal, would she have had the stomach to do something like this?

Moving on her knees, she positioned herself right beside the rubble. Her shield bounced off the desk, and debris rained down.

"Do me a favor?" she whispered to Dulé. "Take off my helmet."

She bowed her head, and he did as she'd asked. That felt much better. The air moving over her sweat-drenched hair felt good. Taking the helmet off made her feel like she could breathe easier.

Dulé set the helmet down beside Oliver, who touched the metal with a finger.

"Are you sure you're okay with this?" asked Dulé. "Do you want me to get Mackenzie?"

Oliver shook his head. "No, I don't want Mackenzie to see this." He paused and swallowed hard. Then, in a much softer tone, he added, "I trust Jenny."

Dulé glanced up at Jenny and seemed to accept it. He let out an exasperated sigh. "It's my fucking fault . . . I'm going to heal it right away, okay? It won't hurt one bit. You came up with these sprays, so you know."

"I know," said Oliver. "Yeah."

Jenny was bracing herself, combing through memories of TV shows and movies, stuff with big wars and battles, doctors and hospitals . . . The American Civil War. The Viking raids. There were so many injuries back then . . . and they used fire. Heated swords to cut the flesh, and fire to close the wound. She wished she could use Ignite.

She glanced again at the spray bottles to reassure herself. Knowing that Oliver was the one to come up with them gave her a bit more faith in their healing ability; she couldn't explain why. But as long as the spray could stem the bleeding, then they could eliminate the chance of Oliver bleeding out.

*What else? What else?* She tried to ignore everything but Oliver's legs and her hatchet, then she remembered all the pain. People screaming during amputations, biting off their tongues. It's not like they had any anesthetic, and they'd been through plenty of pain already, hadn't they?

Oliver's thigh was still torn open from the bone protruding, and who knew how many friends and teachers he'd witnessed die at the hands of an angel? She didn't have to imagine what Oliver and the others must've struggled through.

"Alright," she said. "Give him something to bite."

When Dulé didn't respond, she opened her mouth and mimed biting down on her arm then pointed at Oliver's mouth.

Oliver, sweating and shaking, nodded quickly. "Yeah, gimme something."

Dulé seemed flustered for a second, then he brought out his wallet. "Will this do?"

Jenny said yes, but she was studying the desk. It was halfway between Oliver's knees and his feet. She pressed her shield against his left leg, about the distance of a knuckle away from the desk's edge. She leaned in slightly, applying pressure that made Oliver squirm, but she wanted to make a dent in his armored pants. She repeated it for the other leg, minding his wounded thigh.

This way, the impressions of her shield gave her something to aim for. She wouldn't have to cut one leg then hesitate to size up the next while the first one bled. Two quick blows—that would be for the best. And she couldn't miss; this wasn't like cutting into an angel, where it didn't matter where she cut or how much she cut off. She had to be precise. It had to be clean. It had to be swift.

"Hold him steady," she ordered, pointing at Oliver's arms and chest. Couldn't have him jerking randomly in pain. "As soon as I cut it . . ." she continued, picking up her hatchet and wiping off the angel's blood on the floor. "As soon as both legs are free, drag him out, and we'll use the sprays."

She inhaled deeply, only vaguely aware of the others coming back. Vaguely aware of the babies finishing their meal and the rumble of hunger in her stomach. The fear and disgust and horror. She was cutting off someone's legs. *Oliver's* legs.

*It's the only way*, she told herself again. It was either that or stay here with him, fighting whatever came until she either fell apart or he died, or they both did. No matter what, she knew she'd never be able to abandon him.

She wondered what Eve would make of this. What would Susan do? Stop her or agree that there was no other choice?

Jenny steadied herself, shield against the desk, knee against the floor. "I'm sorry," she whispered, catching Dulé's eyes, ensuring he was holding Oliver down firmly. She couldn't bring herself to glance at Oliver's face; his entire body was trembling.

Jenny raised her hatchet and struck.

The weapon's new edge didn't just slice—it seemed to shimmer. Little sparks of golden lightning crackled around it, and it was as though she was cutting through the smallest particles of matter. She cut clean through his left leg, light flashing upon impact. Blood burst out, splattering the desk and floor, and she heard him scream. It was muffled by the wallet, but still a guttural, painful scream of agony.

She heard Mackenzie cry out, heard the scuffle of footsteps.

But Jenny couldn't hesitate. She couldn't falter now. She brought her hatchet up again, lightning crackling in its arc. Blood sprayed, and the edge sliced through his other leg with another flash of light.

Blood, thick and clumpy, gushed out of Oliver's severed legs as Dulé and Mackenzie dragged him back a few inches. Jenny grabbed the healing spray and squeezed, spraying it over and over. A red mist burst out of its nozzle, sizzling and bubbling wherever it touched Oliver's exposed flesh.

His muffled screaming seemed to make the very air vibrate, filling her head with heartbreak, and she thought she'd rather have that striped wretched angel suck her blood out through her ruined nose a thousand times rather than have to hear him like this.

But as Jenny continued spraying desperately, throwing the emptied bottle away as she grabbed the next, Oliver seemed to quiet. His screaming became whimpers. His wincing eased. His breathing relaxed, and when she was sure his legs had stopped bleeding, when the flesh had darkened and scabbed over, she stopped spraying.

Mackenzie reached for the wallet in his mouth, but Jenny shook her head. "Don't."

The girl flashed Jenny a furious look, but Jenny didn't care. She moved slightly, bending over to press down on the bone sticking out of his thigh. He screamed again. Mackenzie protested, and Dulé swore loudly, but Jenny was already spraying the wound down. She worked quickly and purposefully, and in a matter of moments, this injury was settled for now, too.

When she finally relaxed, setting the spray bottle down and noting that there was a tiny bit left, she motioned for Mackenzie to remove the wallet from Oliver's mouth.

The girl was still furious, but her expression changed to concern as she cradled Oliver's head with one hand and removed the wallet with the other. It came away with blood and was covered in saliva. His teeth were bleeding; he'd bitten on it so hard, the wallet was nearly chewed all the way through, but the leather had served its purpose.

Feeling dizzy, Jenny crawled toward Oliver's face. She gently moved Mackenzie's arm, then grabbed the spray bottle and used a bit of the healing spray on his teeth. The mist bubbled along his gums. He didn't need to feel any more pain than he had to.

"Oliver?" she whispered.

He wasn't responding. His eyes were open, glossed over like he was staring at something far off, but he wasn't responding at all to the spray, to Mackenzie's touch, or Jenny's voice.

She called his name again. And again. Dulé knelt, gloves appearing and disappearing in flashes of gold and red lightning. Mackenzie was trying to talk too, begging Oliver to get up, touching his arm. The babies wandered over as well, alarmingly bigger than before. They eyed Oliver with immense curiosity, and a few of them began to lick the blood around his severed legs.

"Get away!" shrieked Jenny through a choked sob. She threw the empty spray bottle in their direction. It bounced hard off the table, and the babies sat back, their eyes wide in utter disbelief.

Was this all for nothing? Was Oliver dead anyway? Mackenzie pressed her finger to Oliver's neck. Jenny watched, feeling as though time was stretching like thick strands of blood. Then Mackenzie's eyes perked up. She signed rapidly with her fingers while saying it too. "He's alive!"

Jenny breathed an immense sigh of relief. He still had a chance; they just had to get him out of there. "The library," she said, too tired for full sentences. Then, gathering herself, she repeated it. "Let's get him to the library. Someone'll help."

Mackenzie nodded, biting her bottom lip to stop sobbing. Jenny slipped a hand beneath Oliver's head as if to pick him up, but her shoulder cracked as soon as she tried.

Dulé grabbed her shoulder. "You need to heal yourself. I'll carry him."

There was a flash of light, and Mackenzie held out another spray. Jenny winced, wishing they wouldn't waste their energy, but she accepted it gratefully. She watched as Dulé picked Oliver up with ease, Mackenzie holding her knife at the ready.

The other two stood watch, both bleeding in several places, their armor dirty and bent. One of them, Tara, had a large hammer. The other . . . she'd already forgotten his name, carried a sword. The babies sat on the floor, waiting for her. What should she do about them? Could she just leave them here?

She sighed. They could follow her for now. They seemed mostly harmless, and she couldn't shake the feeling that they'd bonded with her.

*Just gotta get back to the library in one piece.* Jenny held the spray's nozzle to her side and squeezed. As soon as the mist hit her wound, a terrible flash of pain surged through her, as though she'd sprayed acid onto her torn flesh.

For a moment, she thought she was just imagining the pain. That, like before, she was receiving the pain signals but not actually feeling it. She opened her mouth but couldn't make a sound. The burning, the tearing sensation that a billion things were chewing her apart, was too much to bear, and a violent shriek filled her throat with enough force that she felt several *pops* in her chest.

# CHAPTER THIRTY-SEVEN

# WHAT WRIGGLES IN THE RUBBLE

Agony exploded through Jenny. She felt like she'd been punched in the gut then kicked several times before one of the large angels stomped on her. Her wound was *fizzing* like soda, but it wasn't a carbonated drink—it was her insides bubbling and hissing.

She coughed up blood; she'd screamed so violently that she was sure her lungs had ruptured or worse. The popping sounds in her chest were not promising, and a steady pressure spread throughout her chest. It felt like she was drowning.

She'd failed the swimming classes her mom had forced her to take one summer as a kid—one session of screaming and panic and choking on chlorine-rich water, and the instructor had thrown her out—but she'd never forgotten the feeling of water pressing all around her, threatening to steal away her ability to breathe.

"Fuck," she spat. Blood shot out of her mouth as she wheezed. Her breathing sounded and felt worse than before, and she clutched her wound. It was still fizzing. Something bubbled and burst against her fingers, and her blood felt sticky and thick, like boiling honey.

There was shouting, but her ears were clogged with blood or pressure, she couldn't tell; their words sounded muffled and distant. Her vision had filled with dark spots, and a sense of doom loomed over her thoughts even as the pain from the healing spray faded to a dull throbbing.

*I can't heal myself. I can't fucking heal myself . . . What the fuck?*

That had been her plan—to get someone, possibly Susan, to create a healing potion for her. She'd heal all her wounds and disable the skill and be as good as new. Then she could reap the rewards of all the kills she'd gotten so far. She thought she'd outsmarted the guidance system, but . . . She laughed, a pitiful laugh of self-hatred. A cackle of misery and woe and *holy shit,* fuck everything.

*It's my fault, isn't it? I was too brash. Too stupid.* Then again . . . If it hadn't been for that cocoon causing that explosion, she wouldn't be *this* badly injured.

Someone helped her up while the others continued arguing, their voices layered with fear and disgust. She looked up to see Mackenzie grabbing her shield arm. Jenny grabbed her hatchet and let the girl help her stand.

The others gawked at her. Dulé seemed worried and afraid, but the other two's lips twisted with disgust, eyes bulging with horror. She even detected distaste, like she'd stepped out of her skin and emerged a slimy mass of muscle and bone. It didn't help that the babies gathered around her, concern and curiosity on their chubby faces. They nuzzled her legs, and she was too tired to kick them away.

She knew the others didn't like the babies. She didn't like them much either, but right at that moment, she felt closer to them than she did the humans. They understood her. They couldn't talk, but their blood-covered faces and wide, hopeful eyes tugged on her heart.

She wished she could be as innocent and clueless as they were, blissfully unaware of everything but their immediate desire to feed and whatever they felt for her. Was that love? Was that need? Was she like a mother to them? Should she care about them?

All she knew was that she didn't want to be here, being scrutinized like this. She didn't want to be on display. She just wanted to hide away forever. She could almost feel their thoughts: Monster. Nightmare. What the fuck is wrong with her? Ugly. Fucked up.

*Yeah, yeah. Tell me something I don't know.*

She wished Susan were here. She wished it so hard that her heart seemed to clench like a tight fist, and she almost choked on the wishful thinking as another *pop* went off in her chest and she coughed.

Dulé was carrying Oliver in his arms, the stumps of Oliver's legs swinging as Dulé turned. He was saying something, but all Jenny heard was a ceaseless ringing, like something was screaming inside her head and refused to stop.

Judging by the others' reactions, they didn't trust her one bit. They didn't want her around; they didn't want to turn their backs on her. Like she might attack them. She couldn't really blame them. How frightening did she look? Her body was coming apart, she couldn't heal . . .

But hadn't she always felt like this? Even before this nightmare started? That nobody really wanted her around, that she was misshapen somehow, that her presence was unwelcome.

Conversations would fizzle out whenever she showed up, in person or online. Groups gave her anxiety, and she'd sit among classmates feeling like a ghost or an ornament or a shadow. Jokes would die down. She'd say something, and nobody would react. She hated the way people would turn quiet around her, even though they'd been laughing and cheerful moments before.

People just tolerated her presence until she left, didn't they? And as soon as she was gone, they'd return to the wonderful lives she'd interrupted.

All Severed Spirit had done was bring her truth to the outside. She truly was tarnished, wasn't she? What if this was her true form? A toothless, rotting creature covered in blood and falling to pieces. She belonged in a coffin buried six feet underground, away from the living . . .

Once the screaming in her head died down, she pressed her hatchet against her leg and nodded at Mackenzie. "I can walk."

The girl was vibrant, alive and fierce in a way Jenny couldn't be. She didn't want Mackenzie's friends to mistrust her for helping Jenny.

But Mackenzie shook her head. She opened her mouth as if to say something, and sounds came out that Jenny couldn't understand, but she got the sense that Mackenzie wasn't going to leave her behind. Was this because Jenny was Oliver's sister? Or because the girl actually cared?

"Alright," said Dulé, his voice laced with urgency as he motioned with his head. "We'll figure this shit out later. Let's get to the library like she said."

"But what the fuck is in the library? What if it's another nest?" asked Tara, fury distorting her face. Her helmet was similar to Mackenzie's, a knight's helmet, except she didn't have the visor. It looked like it had been ripped off, and her brown skin was cut in several places. She was missing the tip of her nose.

Mackenzie's fingers flashed, even as she held Jenny up, and Jenny could feel the girl shaking with anger. Why was she so determined to help?

But before anyone could respond, a tremor went through the entire lab room, making everyone stumble for balance. A bright blue light blossomed, bathing everything in its unsettling glow before fading. Jenny's heart raced, remembering how she'd been lying on the table and the same light had shone on everything.

The babies cried out. Some of them started wailing, and the others picked up on that. One of them grabbed Jenny's leg and refused to let go.

Another tremor jolted the floor. The rubble that had been crushing Oliver shook loose, and Dulé and Tara shouted and rushed away as it collapsed. Large chunks rained down like meteors, clattering and crashing, kicking up clouds of dust. The upside-down table, with Oliver's feet still beneath it, slid, and whatever blood was left in the severed feet gushed out disgustingly as they flattened completely. Tara screamed at the sight.

Then someone shouted, *"Run!"* and Jenny couldn't be sure if it'd been her or not. Mackenzie held Jenny's shield arm firmly around her shoulders, trying to pull Jenny forward, but what use was it?

"I'm just going to slow you down," wheezed Jenny as another large chunk of ceiling collapsed behind them, where they'd just been a few moments ago. It burst into countless pieces, exposed metal pipes clanging hard. One of the babies got hit, but it didn't seem to mind at all. It shook the impact off, then hurried after the others.

But trying to talk to her was no use. Mackenzie couldn't see Jenny's lips, so she let the girl help. Dulé jumped nimbly over the rubble as he carried Oliver with ease. Tara and Alex followed closely, dodging things falling from the ceiling and trying not to step on anyone, while the babies chased after Jenny, all of them crying and screaming.

Blue light surged every few moments, fresh tremors rumbling each time as the light seemed to shine longer now before fading away. Mackenzie was gasping and swearing as she pulled Jenny along.

The hole in the ceiling seemed to grow, with the edges crumbling and raining down. Jenny heard hissing from above, and kept bracing herself for a fight, but they'd nearly made it to the other end of the lab room, where the pulsing light shone brightest. It flooded her vision with bright blue and forced her to squeeze her eyes shut until it faded. That was when she spotted the cocoon.

It lay on its side underneath a fallen closet. The wooden doors were cracked, but they hugged the cocoon, securing it in place on the floor. Another upside-down desk, heavy and with the sink spurting dirty water, rested on top of the closet at an angle.

She couldn't see where the cocoon was torn, but the webbed outer layer of the sac wriggled, distorting and moving like a bug crawling underneath the skin, or like a baby trying to claw its way out of its mother's belly.

Blue light flashed again, more vividly than any of the pulses before. The entire building seemed to shake, as though the cocoon were a black hole and everything would be ripped and torn to bits, collapsing onto this central point. Dulé was already at the door, struggling to hold Oliver up in all the ruckus, shouting for someone to open it.

But it seemed that only Jenny had heard him. The others had stopped to stare at the cocoon, mystified by the light, even as debris rained and crashed around them. They almost seemed hypnotized. Even Jenny felt a curious, inexplicable *tug*, like they were about to witness something miraculous. Something otherworldly.

As though the sky had split open and a heavenly being was descending.

But this was no heavenly being. There was no sky. They were stuck in a crumbling physics lab covered in blood and dirt and surrounded by the dead.

The babies bumped into Jenny's and Mackenzie's legs, coming to a stop. She looked down to see their frightened expressions. A few of them sucked on their thumbs and stared at the cocoon with such palpable dread that a shudder ran up Jenny's spine. Wasn't that thing their mother? But the babies scrambled to hide behind Jenny's legs, and she got the sense that something truly terrible was coming. Jenny desperately wished she could ask Eve about this.

That desecrated angel . . . It was coming. There was no way they'd defeat that thing now. They had to run. They had to get away, regroup, recover, and then—

Another thought struck Jenny as though she'd used the healing spray again. Another horrible, disgusting thought. The desecrated angel had *eyes*; piercing blue eyes that looked so human, that had looked right through her and chosen her blood for a meal. It was just like the babies struggling around her legs. *Would light have any effect on these angels?*

And if light didn't work, they wouldn't be able to stop the desecrated angel, and they'd be leading it right to the others in the library. Right to Susan.

There would be no safe haven. Someone had to stay behind and lead it away; that was the best they could do for now: Distract it until the rest of them could make a plan. Someone had to remain, and Jenny knew without a single doubt in her heart that that someone would have to be her.

Another pulse of light, brighter than the ones before, burst out of the cocoon in shimmering bubbles, like rolling storm clouds gathering. Energy radiated violently, like the shock waves she'd seen in footage of bomb tests. The floor shook beneath their feet, and debris was blown back, clearing a circular area around the squashed cocoon. The desk above it creaked and fell to the floor with a heavy crash.

Jenny's eyes widened. The floor would break beneath them, just like it had done on the second floor. The cocoon's energy was too much.

Maybe that was their way out: The dumb angel would drop into the basement, and they could retreat to the library.

But at this rate, they'd plunge right down with it into hell.

It pulsed again, a furious wind slapping Jenny and Mackenzie as Jenny struck a table with her hatchet, keeping them from being blown all the way back to the other side of the room. The babies were knocked about this way and that, and Jenny lost track of them as loose rubble billowed around everything like they were in a tornado.

When it stopped, she heard a slam. Dulé had kicked the door off its hinges and stumbled into the hallway, shouting over his shoulder. Jenny was glad he was prioritizing Oliver's safety. The other two had been blown onto their backs, and they scrambled to their feet, the hypnotic spell broken. They screamed at Mackenzie to leave Jenny and run.

Mackenzie forced herself up, trying to drag Jenny, but Jenny wouldn't budge. She had to make sure the stupid cocoon sank, or she had to be there when the angel emerged. To do what, she wasn't sure.

The girl screamed in Jenny's ear.

"It's alright," Jenny whispered back. She saw the light flaring up again, and she gathered what strength she could to shove Mackenzie with all her might.

The girl's eyes went wide as blue enveloped everything. An ugly crack ran through the floor, and when the next pulse hit, the force pushed Mackenzie away, right through the doorway.

Jenny was flung against the wall, crumpling the exposed bricks with her shield. She cried out as the wind tore at her armor; it was growing fiercer and fiercer, the light expanding and contracting as it swallowed everything. A table slid toward her before twisting over another, like a car flipping over, and crashing into the doorway, completely sealing the exit off.

Her scales *melted* away. She felt her skin burning as she took the full brunt of the ejected energy, the cocoon no longer covered by anything. The closet had eroded away, exposing the dark gash like a lightning bolt through its center from where it had been torn.

Jenny pictured victims of atomic bombs—what radiation did to their skin and hair, making their blood vessels erupt and boil, the painful, miserable way they died. At least this didn't hurt, she thought. It wasn't like the healing spray.

The biting winds died, and the floor cratered around the cocoon. Dust and debris erupted, and she thought she saw a glistening, clawed hand emerge, reaching. She thought she saw the silhouette of something immense and fearsome with wings, with burning blue eyes that glowed in the dust-ridden gloom, rising. Trying to rise. But another pulse of energy blasted her right through the wall into the hallway as the room buckled.

The last thing she saw was the floor of the physics lab giving way. The glowing blue creature plunged into the darkness as the rest of the ceiling caved in, and the contents of the physics lab—the heavy desks, the bodies, and many of the babies— were sucked into the sinkhole that had formed.

# CHAPTER THIRTY-EIGHT

# BLOODED

Wheezing, Jenny crawled over a large chunk of ceiling, feeling like a struggling bug. Rods stuck out of the crumbling chunk's side, and she almost laughed. She'd been lucky to land where she did; lucky not to get skewered again. Though *lucky* wasn't quite the word she'd use right now.

The wall had buckled, as well as the ceiling, when the energy erupted. She'd been flung into the hallway, her armor and her skin searing as though struck by a burning wind. She'd rolled out of the way as tiles and concrete and whatever else made up the ceiling rained down, just conscious enough to raise her shield and use it like an umbrella. Everything bumped and jarred her body and fell away, and then it was still.

Through the gloom of the Veil, thick clouds of dust swirled and expanded.

She'd managed not to get crushed; she didn't even want to think about being crushed like Oliver. With Severed Spirit active, she'd still be in her flattened body, screaming and screaming inside her head.

*At least the others got away.* She hoped they weren't buried under any of the rubble, but she was sure they'd made a mad dash for the library as soon as they got out of the lab. Dulé seemed responsible and would put Oliver's safety above all else, but Mackenzie had been hesitant to leave her; Jenny hoped the poor girl hadn't been skewered by a rod or crushed and stuck under any of the rubble.

She touched her wounded side with her shield hand; her palm came away with jellylike brown blood the color of rust. She groaned, realizing that most of her armor was gone, burned away. The rest of it was burning and falling apart with her every breath. Whatever that burst of energy had been, it had *damaged* her in some way she couldn't understand.

Much of her chest and side were exposed, as well as her legs. Her pale skin seemed grayish, twisted grotesquely in several places and charred. The dark cloth that made up the underlayer of her armor hung loose where it was still attached to her, burned against her skin. Her arms were nearly bare.

One side of her face drooped slightly, feeling lopsided. That was the side that had taken the brunt of the cocoon's energy. She struck the floor with her hatchet, sending up sparks from the glowing edge, and pulled her body forward. Loose rubble came free and clattered around her.

The physics lab room was completely busted. The wall had given out, as well as the walls of the lab rooms to the right and left, so the hallway seemed much wider. One of the doors squeaked on its hinges, still attached to a part of the wall that remained upright.

In front of her, inside the lab room, there was a giant chasm. Like a gaping mouth with jagged teeth trying to swallow the entire school. The swirling dust even made it look like it was breathing. She'd seen sinkholes before, and it had been one of her random phobias that a sinkhole would open underneath her house one day and swallow her whole.

It was surrounded by an unmoving vortex of rubble and broken furniture and bodies. Several of the babies were crying and screaming, though none of them appeared injured, just caked in dust. She wondered what had happened to the ones that had fallen into the hole.

*Come to me*, she almost said. Her lips moved. Her breath slid between her cracked lips. But all she managed was a croak. Grunting, she smashed her shield into the floor and willed her body up. That was a mistake.

Her shield twisted awkwardly and snapped off the decaying scales around her wrist. Her palm slapped against the floor as the shield clattered.

She groaned, watching what was left of her armor glow like embers and burn away, leaving her arm exposed. She peeled the burnt bits of cloth stuck to her elbow, armpits, and sides off. They came away with skin, exposing her flesh. Sighing, she sat for a moment, nearly naked, her skin burnt and twisted, her legs folded beneath her. She sucked in a lungful of dust and then exhaled, the tickle in her throat growing with each breath.

At least nothing hurt. Well, her wound still ached from when she'd tried the healing spray, but nothing else bothered her. She didn't feel any of the burns or rot.

Her hatchet glowed behind her, that gentle golden color that shimmered across its obsidian face and made the flower patterns on the handle seem warm and alive. When she grasped it, she thought the warmth flowed into her chest and gave her strength, and she could pretend she wasn't a naked, bleeding, rotten corpse animated by the ghost of herself.

She tried to work out what to do as rubble shifted and collapsed. The babies wailed and cried, and everything seemed darker without the blue glow from the cocoon. Nothing seemed to be coming out of the hole. She kept expecting the desecrated angel to rise, massive wings beating and blowing everything away. She kept thinking it would want more of her blood.

What was below the physics lab? She raked her brain, trying to remember but struggling to come up with anything other than lockers and the offices of the guidance counselors. It was near the boy's locker room, she was sure of it, a part of the school she never ventured near.

Just when she made up her mind to crawl all the way to the library, blue light bubbled up from the hole and expanded to fill the lab room. It must have lasted only an instant before snapping out of existence, a sudden flash of light that left behind blue sparks and shimmers that crackled this way and that.

Something shifted while Jenny blinked hard—her vision full of spots from the light—readying herself for an attack. It was one of the bodies.

A tarnished angel, naked and thin, clambered out of a pile of rubble; a female with skin and hair so caked with dust, Jenny couldn't discern any of its features. Its eyes were shut, and Jenny wondered if it had fallen from above during the second collapse.

Then it opened its eyes—vacant eyes that were glowing a vibrant blue.

It cocked its head, staring at Jenny, who held her breath, mentally repeating *What the fuck?* over and over. Was it one of the *dead* angels? Had the desecrated angel *risen* the *dead*?

Drool slid down its chin as it opened its mouth and screeched, a throaty roar that sounded different from anything Jenny had heard before. It echoed all over the ruined hall. She saw several things shifting, and realized that screech wasn't just a battle cry—it was a *signal*.

Jenny grunted, preparing herself as best she could. The once dead angels pulled themselves out of the rubble, all of their eyes glowing blue. *This is some bullshit.*

The first one crawled over the rubble, moving quickly. Its bones snapped, and its skin tore on exposed rods and jagged edges. It didn't seem to care. The other bodies moved similarly, and Jenny was grateful it was only angels and not her classmates. She shuddered, trying to push that thought out of her head as the creature approached.

Jenny couldn't help but scream, some raw, primal fear rising up her throat. She wasn't just fighting angels now—she was fighting *dead* angels, and that somehow raised the creep factor exponentially.

She pushed off the floor with her left palm and struck the creature on the head with the hatchet. The edge bounced off its forehead, right above its eyes, leaving behind a deep gash with golden light flickering.

It hissed, writhing wildly before collapsing, the blue from its eyes gone. Another one leaped onto her. She felt its body against her own, felt its heat and touch, and she screamed like a madwoman, trying to untangle herself from its clutches as its teeth chattered next to her ear.

She managed to roll over, pinning it underneath her. It was already injured badly, bleeding all over, and Jenny slammed her hatchet into its chest, her other palm braced against the handle for extra force. Golden light sparkled briefly, and then another angel was upon her.

It spat and cried and tried to grab her shoulders while she tried to headbutt it on the chin but missed. She hit the creature right on its open mouth instead, feeling its teeth break the skin of her forehead. Wrenching the hatchet out of the angel beneath her, she lodged it into the belly of the other.

Blood gushed. Golden light shimmered. But Jenny didn't blink. The terror faded away, leaving only the desire to kill. To slaughter. And if they kept coming back, she'd just kill them again and again. That's all that mattered now. *Kill these fucking things.*

She struck again, and another angel fell beside her. She tried to crawl off, but a new one grabbed her feet from behind, and she fell forward. Her chin bounced off the floor and, screaming, she slashed the creature in front of her as best she could. She kicked the one behind, but its grip on her ankles was vise strong, and it crawled up her legs.

Feeling its breath on the back of her thighs, she lashed blindly with her hatchet until the edge connected with its scalp. Blood splattered her backside, and she pushed forward.

Three more reached her, teeth clacking, hissing, eyes glowing blue. One threw itself onto her back, pinning her down, while another grabbed her by the hair and pulled her chin off a body. She spat blood, all her muscles straining. "Fuck you," she gurgled, blood and spittle foaming between her gums. She didn't care how stupid it sounded without teeth.

But the angels didn't seem to care, either.

They whined and moaned and clambered on top of her. A knee struck her in the face, her arms still pinned down, and she lost her hatchet in the scuffle.

She was suffocating. The stench of blood and grime and sweat clogged her throat as she wriggled and squirmed, trying to escape, but more hands appeared. More fingers pulled her hair, clawed her skin, and found her throat. Fingernails scraped her broken nose. She smashed her head against one of them and realized it wasn't just tarnished angels in here. Her forehead struck the hard covering of a wretched one.

Raising her head, she looked into the glistening blue eyes of a wretched angel beneath her. She couldn't tell what color its covering was, couldn't even tell if it was male or female, only that her body was pressed on top of it. It must've been brutally injured earlier, and the wriggling mass of angels had dragged her on top of it.

Her thoughts flashed with the nightmare of being chewed to bits while her soul was still stuck in her brain.

It groaned, its mouth opened, and Jenny shut her eyes, bracing herself for the bite. But its lips never found her face. It didn't chew her while she watched helplessly; none of them were biting her. They weren't really hitting her either. They were trying to grab and hold her down. They were *dragging* her toward the hole in the lab room.

"No!" she shouted, and a finger entered her mouth. She tried to bite, but her gums closed on it harmlessly. Its nail scraped the roof of her mouth, and she spat it out. Squirming, she managed to wrench her left arm free, and she elbowed one of them, trying to find any leverage, but it was a sweaty, clammy mess of limbs and chunks of wall and blood. Teeth and eyes flashed all around her. Hissing and growling and grunts filled her ears.

Flesh pressed against flesh. She kicked and screamed and fought, then felt fingers find the hole in her side, felt teeth scraping her flesh in places she never wanted to be touched. All the while, she was being forced, closer and closer, to the desecrated angel.

That must've been what happened. The light. A command, a skill, or something to control these dead angels to do what the desecrated angel wanted. Maybe it wasn't fully formed yet? Maybe it still needed more blood.

She gasped for air but couldn't expand her chest. Angels pressed on her from every side, squeezing her, refusing to give her an inch of space; they were going to fall into the hole while clutching her, removing any possibility of escape.

The wretched angel was still underneath her. Its arms were wrapped around her waist, and they were actually dragging *it*, sliding the creature across the rubble and floor with her trapped on top of it.

And staring into its glowing blue eyes, she once again felt the hunger from before, the pang of incessant want, *need*. As though if she didn't eat right this moment, her body would swallow itself.

*Fuck it*, she thought. She thrust her face into its neck, trying to get as much of it into her mouth as she possibly could so that she could use her side and back teeth. Her lips stretched and tore, but she forced her jaw open.

The angel's covering cracked and gave way as she bit through. Cold blood spurted into her mouth and rushed down her throat, and a message struck her thoughts like a gunshot.

**Blooded.**

She barely registered it. She kept sucking, kept swallowing, as though replenishing her blood with the angel's the same way the angels had taken hers.

Her mind slipped into some dark recess, her thoughts flurrying like bubbles rising from her lips as she sank deeper. Her body didn't accept any of the signals she was trying to send.

*Stop! Stop sucking! Stop drinking!*

But at the same time, it was as though she made no effort at all to stop. Her body was taking care of its needs. She didn't resist. Couldn't resist. Wouldn't.

The light faded from the creature's eyes. The other angels were still trying to drag her, but her body moved over that angel's limp form. She felt its face bounce against her chest, her navel, her thighs, and then she was crawling on the floor and debris. She dug in with her knees, using friction to slow them down. They were inside the physics room now, only a few feet away from the hole, where she could feel the rippling heat emanating, beckoning.

The angels screamed, but it felt like she was hearing it from across a vast distance rather than while stuck beneath them. They strained hard. They pulled on her hair, and she thought her scalp might tear right off, but she held on. Somehow, she knew if she fell into the hole, if she fell into where the desecrated angel was waiting, she would die.

She didn't want to die.

As ruined and messed up as her body was, as twisted and fucked up as her mind had become, all the horrid things she'd done, and all the horrible things she'd lived through, and all the times she'd wished to die before this nightmare ever started . . .

She wasn't ready to die. Not yet. Not like this.

Tears welled up in her eyes as she felt the familiar sharpness of a metal bar cut her leg. Hope burned through her chest, and she swung her leg as hard as she could, forcing the rod through her thigh.

Several of the angels rolled off her. The rod was attached to a large chunk of ceiling, and the angels stumbled and tripped and flailed. They couldn't move her now—not without ripping her leg off first, and they didn't seem bright enough to figure that out.

*I don't want to die here. Please.*
*Am I praying?*
*Again?*
*Who am I praying to?*
*Fuck.*
*Fuck!*

Something sparked. For a second, she thought it was the blue light of the desecrated angel. Was it finally surfacing? Was it finally coming for her? Instead, a wave of warmth flooded the entire lab room. Rainbow-colored light spun every which way, blossoming with radiance all around her.

Her eyes widened. The angels crawled off her in a mad flurry, all of them screaming bloody murder as they scrambled into the hole to get away.

Collapsing, Jenny rested her face on the floor. Her leg was bent awkwardly, the bar jutting out through her thigh. Blood spilled from her mouth, and she heard footsteps scrambling to reach her. She heard voices, but her ears felt as though they'd been torn apart and filled with rotten flesh.

*The light,* she thought, her lips curving into a small smile as she struggled to maintain consciousness. It had pulled her back from that dark place. It felt like sunlight, like waking up before everyone else and claiming the quiet, cool calm of the morning for herself, opening the window to inhale the brisk air, fresh with the promise of a new day, and then witnessing the morning split the sky open.

# CHAPTER THIRTY-NINE

# I TRUST YOU

Susan carefully stepped over the bodies in the hall in front of the library. Behind her came Mrs. Monique, the only other person willing to inspect the large crash. Everyone had plenty of thoughts, but the other students were petrified, and Dr. Lee was obsessed with his specimen.

The angel seemed to panic, stressed out and hissing about something. It curled up into a little orange ball, hugging its knees.

Two boys stayed behind to guard the door, lights and weapons at the ready. Leslie wouldn't leave Dr. Lee's side.

In the hallway, Susan winced at the dried blood splattered everywhere. One of the angels was headless. The rest were cut up and brutally slaughtered. She glanced back at Mrs. Monique, who nodded, and Susan peeked around the corner, keeping to the bloodstained wall for cover.

Nothing had changed about the main lobby. There were still countless bodies piled up against the glass doors of the entrance, and none of them stirred. No notifications lit up in Susan's head. She glanced back at the math wing and saw all the bodies from when she and Jenny had fought them off, but didn't see anything alive or coming after them.

"The crash felt like it came from that side of the building," she said, motioning with her cattle prod. She clicked on the flashlight in her other hand; its beam cut through the swirling mist of the Veil and shone upon some faces. She quickly aimed it higher, unable to stomach the way the other students' eyes glistened in the light. She didn't want to recognize anyone.

She wasn't sure how much time had passed since the crash. She'd rolled away from the falling barricade and hid under the librarian's desk while the others freaked out. Once the shaking had stopped, she knew she had to see what it was. She had just taken a moment to figure out her stats, applying a generous amount of her Stage Two bonus to stamina. The rest she divvied up as best she could.

**Susan Brown**
**Human (Stage II - Level 10)**
**Age: 6,870 days**
**Stats:**
**Power: 10**
**Durability: 10**
**Stamina: 30**
**Agility: 11**
**Stat Points Available: 0**
**Energy Available: 182**

Making her way across the lobby, she wished she had more agility, wanting to get to the source of the crash quicker. She couldn't explain why, but she knew it had to do with Jenny. And even if her intuition was off, she couldn't just sit still.

She'd explained to the others that they had to find out what it was. If it was a strong human, then they needed to group up. If it was dangerous . . . better to know what was coming than to hide in the library like sitting ducks. The orange wretched angel that had become an angel stage two was no longer affected by light; what if other angels got that ability too?

She was trying to be brave like Jenny had been when she left the library, but Susan was already trembling. She'd put so much into stamina to ensure she'd be able to heal Jenny no matter what state she was in. She just had to be alive. *Please be alive.*

She had kept her blue armor from earlier, even though the scales were cracked. It was still some protection, and she figured it was best to reserve her energy for now. If anything came up, she and Mrs. Monique had their flashlights, and she had her thunder and light.

As they cut through the lobby, another violent tremor surged beneath their feet, making several of the bodies bounce and flop. Susan gasped as Mrs. Monique readied her spear, flashlight in her mouth, a look of focused fury on her face.

They heard what sounded like an explosion up ahead, and another vibration nearly knocked them off their feet. It sounded like a landslide, and Susan shone her flashlight down into the other hallway as a cloud of dust billowed out. Rocks and loose debris clattered toward them; something must have collapsed.

Before they could proceed, they heard shouting, and Susan's flashlight revealed a silhouette in the dust cloud carrying something in their arms.

"Oh my God," said Mrs. Monique, stepping forward quickly as three others showed up behind the first figure.

They stepped out from the dust cloud, but Susan barely registered the notifications. She saw they were human, wore armor, and were covered in blood and dust, but as soon as she noticed the boy in the larger boy's arms, that was all she could focus on.

It was Oliver, and the bottom half of his legs were missing.

"Oliver," she whispered. She'd bumped into him several times whenever she visited Jenny's house to do homework or watch movies or whatever. He was a sweet little kid who always wanted to hang out with them, but Jenny would turn him away and lock the door every time. Now, he looked pasty and sick, and his legs ended at his knees. Should she heal him?

The boy holding him was shouting something. Mrs. Monique was fervently calling them forward, instructing them to go down the hallway and get to the library. Their voices echoed around Susan's head, but she focused on the frantic girl. She kept trying to turn back, but the other two held her arms and dragged her forward.

Susan stopped them. "What's wrong?" But she already knew the answer by the sinking feeling in her stomach.

The girl's eyes were wide and tearful. She was holding a bloodied knife in one hand, and her armor reminded Susan of a classic knight, like something straight from the round table. The girl wrenched her arm free and signed quickly, her fingers in a flurry.

She pointed at Oliver, then signed, *His sister is trapped back there.*

After a quick glance at Mrs. Monique, who was confused by the sign language, Susan darted forward, the light from her flashlight bouncing all over the place.

Footsteps echoed from behind her. "Susan, wait!"

"You don't have to come with me!" she shouted, coming to a stop in the cloud of dust in front of the big lecture hall. The door was shut, and the shaders pulled down. To the left was the physics wing, from where Oliver and the others had emerged.

Mrs. Monique nearly stumbled into her, and she started shouting at Susan, but she stopped midsentence when she saw what had become of the physics labs.

The hallways had completely collapsed. The labs were blown out, their walls broken and scattered all over, with tables and chairs strewn about. Large chunks of the ceiling stuck out like stalagmites, many with rods sticking out of them. Lockers had spilled from the hallway above, and there were countless bodies. Dust and the stench of rot filled her nose and made her cough.

"What the fuck are those things?" whispered Mrs. Monique. Susan didn't even have a chance to be taken aback hearing the sweet librarian curse like that. She swore under her breath as well; babies crawled over the rubble, trying to climb over things, moving toward the room.

**Infant Angel (Level 0)**

They didn't seem to mind the flashlights at all. The beams drew their attention, and several of them exclaimed in glee. They looked like one- to two-year-old toddlers, some crawling, some walking on pudgy, shaky legs. The babies were covered in blood, too, and Susan almost thought they were injured from the collapse, but then she noticed that the blood ran down their chins and stained their hands and arms. Like they'd been making a mess of spaghetti and tomato sauce.

While they squinted and laughed at the light, the babies didn't seem interested in either Susan or Mrs. Monique. They moved into the lab room, climbing over the remnants of the walls, as she turned her flashlight inside. The light flickered over a door that remained standing, still attached to a chunk of wall. She saw the upside-down tables, the gaping hole in the ceiling, and then the bodies.

These bodies weren't dead; they were alive and wriggling, crawling over one another. Naked angels. They had to be tarnished, but no notification appeared in her head.

She stepped forward hesitantly, wondering if she just had to get closer. Then she noticed that several of the creatures were forcing others forward, dragging something underneath the pile by long dark hair, dragging other angels by thin limbs. An ugly crater waited in the center of the room—a large hole lined with debris and chaos. The angels were headed toward it.

She only caught glimpses of what was beneath them, but she was sure she saw someone struggling, and there was a trail of blood. A wretched angel lay dead, as though the others had steamrolled over it, but before Susan could figure out what to do, they screeched in unison. Several of them stumbled.

A pale leg stuck out from the wriggling pile, skewered through the thigh on one of the ceiling rods. The angels heaved, but they couldn't move now. That was when she got the notification.

### Wretched Human (Level 24)

*What?* That had to be wrong. There were so many angels; they must be messing up the notifications.

Her heart racing, she shone her flashlight right into their faces, but no other notification appeared, and none of the angels reacted to the light. Their eyes shone eerily blue, but they didn't even notice Susan or Mrs. Monique or their flashlights. They were hell-bent on dragging that someone into the hole.

"No . . ." Susan said softly. She knew it was Jenny. It had to be her. But she kept pushing the thought away, refusing to accept it. As if as long as she didn't see her face and couldn't confirm it was her, then it wouldn't be Jenny, and she would be safe.

Susan was shaking as Mrs. Monique caught up, cursing again and again at the sight.

She clicked her prod on, the buzz ready to turn into lightning, but what if she struck Jenny too? She saw the leg twitch, saw the bar slide and cut through her thigh, and that was all Susan could bear. Dropping her flashlight, she raised her arm, focusing on her hand, gathering herself. This had to work. It was definitely brighter than the flashlights. It just *had* to work!

A ball of light ballooned from her palm, expanding rapidly. It juggled for a moment before separating from her skin. *Valescent Light.* It was about the size of a beach ball, and rainbows splintered off, enshrouding the ruined physics lab with a shimmering brilliance.

The angels responded simultaneously. They went rigid, staring at the light, their teeth bared so Susan could see their spittle as they screeched. It was as though she'd splashed them with a bucket of ice water. Then, all at once, the hall went silent, the blue light fading from their eyes, and every single angel dropped, motionless.

Had she killed all of them? No, that didn't matter. Most of them fell on top of Jenny. What if she suffocated?

Susan rushed into the fray, nearly tripping on a piece of concrete. She got to the pile and pushed the bodies, ready to use her cattle prod on anything that even twitched, but there were still no notifications other than wretched human, and when she finally pulled off the last angel, she saw Jenny's face.

Her heart skipped a beat. "What?" she whispered, not sure what to freak out about first. Jenny's eyes were closed, her busted lips curved upward in a small smile. Her face was a mess, her once smooth, pale skin now burnt and peeling. Her nose was crushed, nearly flattened. Dried blood stuck to everything.

She was naked, but her skin was twisted and burnt and scratched in so many places. She looked shriveled. Then there was that hole in her side, right below her rib cage; a nasty, ugly wound where the blood didn't just look dry—it looked like she'd been splashed with acid. Rainbow light shimmered over her ruined body.

"Jenny . . ." whispered Susan, trying again. Her voice broke. The cattle prod slipped from her fingers and clattered to the floor. Her fingers trembled over Jenny's shoulder as though she might try to shake her best friend awake, but Susan was too afraid to touch her. Too afraid Jenny would crumble into ashes if she did.

Then Jenny's eyes opened, and Susan nearly flinched. She was staring back into the same eyes as the angels'—horrible eyes that lacked the gentle brown she'd grown accustomed to seeing lighting up on Jenny's face. Now they were bloodshot and white and nightmarish.

"Hey," Jenny spoke weakly. When she opened her mouth, blood ran down the side of her face, revealing her missing teeth. Her top and bottom front teeth were gone, and was she bleeding internally?

Questions raged in Susan's head. Razor-sharp doubts cut through her lungs. She didn't know what to do. She knew Jenny needed healing, but how much? What first? What did *wretched human* mean?

"Jesus . . ." whispered Mrs. Monique, who'd caught up. A baby hugged the end of her spear, and when Susan shot her a look of disbelief, the librarian shrugged. "I tried to kill one, but the stupid thing only giggled."

## Infant Angel (Level 0)

Susan eyed the baby. It was cute, brown skinned, and had a head of dark hair. Its eyes were green, and its pudgy, blood-covered fingers inspected Mrs. Monique's spear as though it was a new toy. At least they weren't a threat, she thought, turning back to Jenny.

She felt like she couldn't breathe, her chest was so tight. She didn't have enough energy for a substantial potion.

She glanced around at the dead angels. Why hadn't she received any energy from them?

She was terrified that she wouldn't have enough stamina to use Valescent Light to fix Jenny. This much damage was beyond anything she'd expected, but maybe if she could heal her just enough, maybe then a potion or something would take her the rest of the way. Yes. That was the best thing to do. Close the wounds, restore as much flesh as she could, and get her out of here.

Jenny grabbed Susan's hand. "You can't take me to the library," she rasped. Her words came out wrong; without teeth, she couldn't speak clearly, like speaking *hurt*.

"What—Why?" asked Susan, shaking her head, tears threatening to spill free. "What are you talking about? I have to heal you!" She thought about the sign language girl in knight's armor, or the boy carrying Oliver. They both seemed strong. They might have more energy.

"I can't heal," said Jenny, her empty eyes half closed.

And Susan didn't know where to look. She wanted to scream.

She'd been too slow. Too weak. If only she'd just killed that angel before and gotten to stage two. Instead, she'd sat around doing nothing while Dr. Lee studied it. She could've leveled up and gotten her ability and found Jenny and . . . But then that angel would've never changed . . . Did that count as taking an innocent life? She would've never known about that if she'd killed it right away.

Frustration welled up like a ferocious beast inside her. She wanted to smash something.

"What do you mean you can't heal?"

"I'm tarnished." Jenny's face twitched, moving the broken cartilage of her nose.

"No," said Susan. She blinked, and this time, tears did run down her cheeks. "It says *wretched*. Wretched! Jenny, what does that mean? Why did you think you were *tarnished*?"

"Oh," Jenny let out. "I guess . . . because I . . ."

"Because?" shouted Susan. "What did you do? What happened? Why can't I heal you?!" What was the point of her new ability if she couldn't use it to save her best friend? Its rainbow-colored light dazzled overhead, mocking them.

But Jenny's eyes shut. "If you take me to the library . . . If you take me to the library . . ." She cut off and went silent, a tremor going through her body.

The 'Wretched Human' notification in Susan's head flickered in a way she hadn't seen any notification flicker before. But just as Susan feared the worst, just as she prepared herself to force every bit of Valescent Light she could muster down Jenny's stubborn throat, Jenny spoke again. "Library . . . The Desecrated Angel will follow."

"Desecrated?" Susan repeated, breathless. She glanced around at the bodies and then at Mrs. Monique, who was inspecting the crater. The babies waddled over and gathered around Jenny and Susan. They eyed her nervously, some of them whimpering, but one sat beside Jenny's head and touched her forehead, leaving a streak of blood.

*What the fuck are these things?* Susan almost blurted out, but she swallowed the sob and glanced again at Jenny's wound.

"Jenny," she said, lightly shaking her friend.

Jenny's eyes flickered open.

"I have to try." Susan held up her finger, concentrating on its tip. Light sparkled into being, forming an opalescent orb that hovered over her nail. Its shine sent rainbows off in every direction, and the babies stared at it, mystified.

*If this works, I can call that big ball back.* The more she used it, the more aware she was, like flexing a muscle. All she had to do was heal Jenny, and then they could figure out this desecrated angel thing.

Jenny's eyes widened. "Is that . . . your skill? I can't see any of the system stuff like this."

"I reached stage two," Susan replied. "Just like you did. And this was the skill I got. It's called *Valescent Light*, and it fixed my leg. Look! See? It grew right back." She shifted on her knees, sticking out her leg to show Jenny.

But Jenny's eyes were shut. "It fixed your leg, huh?" Her voice was trailing off again. "That's good. I'm glad . . . I fucked up, Susan. I couldn't get enough energy. I suck."

Susan bit her lip. Was that why Jenny was being so reckless? "Don't even . . . Just let me try, okay?"

Her best friend nodded so weakly, Susan wasn't sure Jenny had nodded at all. But then her lips moved. "I trust you."

Susan sniffled. "I'm just going to use a little bit first, okay?"

There was no response. Mrs. Monique stepped over to watch, and Susan slowly lowered the little orb of light, bringing it to the terrible hole in Jenny's side. That seemed the direst, as the light revealed the ruined, twisted strands of flesh inside. Her hand shook.

As soon as the light slid into the wound, the colorful strands spread out. Hope filled Susan's chest; it was just like with her leg. Then Jenny screamed. She screamed so suddenly and shrilly that Susan fell back, the babies scattered away, and Mrs. Monique dropped to the floor, trying to find some way to help.

Jenny was panting, her hand slapping the floor until she found a rock and she squeezed it tight.

Susan was stunned. The light faded away, evaporating off the wound without having done anything. Her heart was shattering; her best friend was going to die.

"It's . . . okay," whispered Jenny, a strained smile on her face as she writhed on the floor. Her leg had slid up the rod, and fresh blood dripped onto the floor. "I'm—"

"No," Jenny interrupted her firmly, a sob chasing that word. "You can't hurt me. It's okay. The skill I'm using takes the pain away. You didn't hurt me, Susan. It just surprised me, okay? But it's gone."

Susan couldn't stop crying. Her light had failed. Her new skill had failed. She'd failed.

"I promise," said Jenny, who'd shut her eyes tight. Her voice dropped to a whisper. "But, Susan, I did it! I saved Oliver. So it's okay . . . Okay? I saved him. But now, you have to help him. You can heal his legs."

"No," Susan replied. "No. I'm not leaving you. I'm going to heal you." She summoned another ball of light, her arm shaking so badly that her teeth chattered. What was she going to do? Make Jenny scream again and again until she died?

Frustrated, she curled her fingers into a fist, squeezing the orb of light, and the light *blossomed*.

Her entire right hand shimmered brightly, shining stronger than the light had before, and Susan's eyes went wide. The light raced down her arm, nearly halfway to her elbow. Her flesh had become light. Every color of the rainbow pulsed up and down her skin, marking her veins. It wasn't blood flowing through them—it was her spirit. With every pulse of her heart, more and more of herself flooded into her arm, and the light shone brighter and stronger.

Susan stared, her thoughts swirling rapidly. She touched it with her other hand, and her fingers slid right through. It felt warm, like stroking a beam of light spilling in through a window.

She looked down at Jenny, who wasn't moving. And she knew what she had to do. Whatever skill had turned Jenny into this . . . it was keeping her from healing.

"Can you turn it off? That thing?"

Jenny was still shivering. "Yeah, but—"

"I won't let you die," said Susan. It was a promise. An oath.

Jenny shook her head. She opened her lips to speak again, but all she managed was a shudder. The whites of her eyes glistened as tears rolled down the sides of her head.

Susan grabbed Jenny's shoulder with her left hand, holding her light over Jenny's chest. It was a gamble, but if it worked, then maybe, just maybe, this was crazy enough to save her. Whatever it cost. Even if it cost Susan her arm or her life, she wouldn't let Jenny die.

"I'm going to stick my hand inside you."

# CHAPTER FORTY

# STRANDS OF LIGHT

*You're going to what?* thought Jenny, almost wanting to laugh. If Susan didn't look so damn serious saying that . . . *"I'm going to stick my hand inside you . . ."* C'mon. That was straight out of some kind of porno or something.

But her best friend's arm was glowing. It was made of light, hovering over Jenny's chest, translucent and colorful and beautiful. And Jenny . . . Jenny was terrified of it.

When Susan had tried to heal Jenny's side injury, pain had *ignited* inside her. It had been infinitely worse than the healing spray; she could've sworn someone had taken a chain saw and cut through her insides. The scream had burst from her throat before she could stop herself, but the look she'd seen on Susan's face— the shock, the horror, the heartbreak—had been enough to make her swallow the rest of the pain, to keep herself from screaming again. It wasn't Susan's fault—it was her own.

Jenny felt so far away; the healing attempt had plunged her deeper into the darkness. Was this what dying felt like? What should her last words be? Was this a good time to ask Susan to prom? Jenny nearly laughed this time, but her side still burned, and Susan was staring, looking terrified but confident in a desperate sort of way, waiting for her answer.

"Well?" whispered Susan. She was trembling, and even though she was nearly on top of Jenny, she seemed far away, like Jenny was watching her bottom lip wobble from the bottom of a well.

More darkness enshrouded her vision, threatening to conceal everything. But Susan remained fixed in her sights. The brightness of her arm kept the darkness at bay. Maybe this could actually work.

*Your arm looks beautiful,* Jenny wanted to say, but every time she tried to speak, every time she tried to form words at the base of her throat, it felt like she would retch instead. And she didn't want to throw up the angel blood—it seemed to be the only thing keeping her alive. What else could her heart possibly be pumping through her body?

*What would the side effects be?* she wondered.

She heard someone sigh heavily, but she didn't have the strength to turn her head.

"Let's get her leg off that thing first," said the voice, which Jenny recognized as Mrs. Monique's, the librarian's. "We need to be quick."

"What?" Susan turned, and Jenny wanted to cry out.

*Don't look away. Please. If you're not looking at me, I might die.*

Susan nodded. "Yeah, then I think I can just heal everything in one go." She paused to lick her lips, mumbled something, then repeated herself. "She won't feel the pain right now, so let's get her leg free." She was freaking out in that restrained, self-imploding way she always did when she was worried.

She was absolutely beyond the point of freaking out. Jenny had seen her nervous, anxious to the point of throwing up before an important presentation. She'd seen her terrified and frozen to the spot and wetting herself. She'd seen her take command on impromptu gym class teams, in debate classes, and in their online gaming.

She'd even seen her shy. Once. Susan had worn a pink robe with flowers for pajama day, and Jenny had tried it on. Jenny had told her she loved the smell, that it smelled like Susan, and Susan had blushed so much.

*Huh. That's a fun memory to think about.*

"On the count of three," said Mrs. Monique.

Together, she and Susan slowly slid Jenny's leg off the rod while Jenny's mind wandered. Three of the babies sat close to her face, whimpering and crying softly; they touched her cheek and stroked her hair. She wondered if they'd try to eat her if she turned off Severed Spirit, but since they hadn't gone after Susan or Mrs. Monique, maybe they wouldn't.

*Are they still going to follow me everywhere, though?*

She didn't think she'd mind. They were kind of cute, after all, and seemingly indestructible. She thought back to a few moments ago, when she was pleading with the universe not to let her die, that she'd do anything to stay alive. But she didn't want this.

She watched Susan and Mrs. Monique sliding her leg, trying their best not to damage her thigh any further. The look on Susan's face made her heart ache.

Susan shouldn't have to bear this responsibility. What if it failed? What if Jenny died anyway, and Susan had to go on knowing she'd killed her? How was that fair at all?

*I don't want to be a burden. Please just let me die.*

*But I don't want to die either.* Jenny couldn't reconcile these conflicting thoughts. There was no alternative to the situation, and she knew that Susan would try no matter what. No matter how much Jenny pleaded with her to get back to the others and heal Oliver. It was either Susan watched her die, or Susan killed her. Or Susan died, too, trying to save her.

Once they worked Jenny's thigh free of the rod, and it slid free with a gross, wet, sucking sound, they lowered her leg gently. There wasn't much blood. She thought most of it was in her mouth, down her throat, or in her stomach. And it wasn't even hers; it was the angel's.

### Blooded.

Now, what did that mean? How did she get a notification while in Severed Spirit?

She swallowed; the taste clung to her tongue, tangy and sweet, and she wanted more. Her stomach growled. The skin and flesh sticking out of the hole in her side flapped and trembled. Pain throbbed around her navel from Susan's healing attempt, and she dreaded Susan's plan, but Jenny thought she understood the concept: Keep her heart healed and beating while she deactivated Severed Spirit. They'd just have to pray it would heal the rest of her before she died.

And what about her brain? What if it shut down? But she hadn't sustained any damage to her head, other than her face. Maybe she had a concussion from her Instant Acceleration into the wretched angel's swinging arm. Would that be enough to ruin her brain?

Susan dropped beside Jenny's head again, her luminescent fingers hovering over Jenny's chest, over her heart. "Okay," she said quietly. She took a deep breath. "Jenny, are you ready?"

Jenny nodded.

Susan explained her plan again as the babies watched, wide-eyed and worried. "As soon as you turn it off, I'm going to stick my hand inside, okay?"

Jenny licked her gums, wondering if her teeth would grow back. She nodded again, then inhaled slowly. This could be the last breath she ever held in her chest. She watched Susan's lips move, counting it down.

*Three* . . .

*Two* . . .

Jenny reached for the skill in her mind, sifting through the clouds of darkness. She pictured pulling a lever; pictured herself struggling for a moment. Then, as soon as Susan whispered, *One* . . . the lever stopped resisting. She deactivated Severed Spirit.

It felt like she'd been wrenched from the world and flung into the sun.

Pain erupted across every inch of her body, like countless jaws sinking carnivorous teeth into her flesh and bones, chewing her to bits. As though someone was tearing her limb from limb, then jamming each appendage back into place, only to stomp on her and tear them off again. Every single signal her brain had ignored while the skill was active now rushed through her head. *Everything* hurt. She just wanted it to end.

She almost screamed, "Kill me! Kill me! Just let me fucking die . . ." Her feet jerked. Her hand scraped the floor, clawing till her nails snapped off. The babies wailed as Mrs. Monique held Jenny's shoulders down. Susan's brow was furrowed with sweat, her hand slipping inside Jenny's chest. Jenny could feel her fingers wrapping around her heart.

A gasp escaped Jenny's lips, and she pressed them tight, chewing on her lips with her toothless gums, trying and failing to cry. If this was it, she didn't want Susan to hear any sign of distress or pain. She clenched her entire body, her mind.

And just when she thought the pain would never end, that Susan's skill would force her body alive until the pain completely obliterated her thoughts, warmth spread across her skin, soothing and gentle, as though she'd been stabbed with cozy afternoon sunlight, forming an oasis of relief.

Susan's other palm rested against Jenny's cheek as strands of Valescent Light bounced like stones skipping across water all over her body.

For a moment, Jenny thought her heart had stopped, then she felt Susan's fingers *squeezing* it. Light pulsed with every squeeze, and Jenny couldn't tell if she was dreaming or not.

*Is Susan pumping my heart for me?*

This time, it was Susan who cried out, and she had to use her other hand to brace her shining arm. Rainbow light erupted from Jenny's chest, completely enveloping her, as the large, floating orb dropped down like a meteor and splashed onto her.

She tried to keep her focus on Susan's reddening face, tried to ignore the pain circling through her body. Then she blinked, and when she opened her eyes, she floated in a familiar, empty darkness.

It was the strange place she'd entered when she first met Eve. Another world. Water splashed as she straightened up, her toes finding the sandy bottom. The waves came up to her navel, and the lake trembled around her, endless ripples racing away.

She was whole. Her skin was no longer rotten and burned. Her wounds were healed. She even had her fingers back. When she touched her nose, she was surprised to find it exactly how it was supposed to be. She ran her tongue over her teeth and shuddered with joy. Teeth were such a precious thing to have; somehow, this was the detail that made her feel the most human again.

Other than the water she'd disturbed, nothing stirred. Nobody else was around, not even Eve. She'd expected the three-headed golden figure to emerge any moment now and chastise her again, but the sky was empty. The trees in the distance, of which she could still see every little detail with bizarre clarity, were all leafless. The branches stood as naked as Jenny.

Shriveled leaves blanketed the ground. Not a single bug crawled anywhere. The world was awfully quiet. The first time she'd been here, the quiet reminded her of the soothing calm of an untouched morning. But this was the eerie stillness of a graveyard. Cold crept up her thighs and filled her insides with dread.

Wading through the water, her feet kicking up sand, Jenny made it to the edge and threw herself onto the muddy bank. She tried to crawl out, but the lake refused to let go.

"What the fuck?" she cried out, straining to break free, but the waves gripped her tight. Droplets stuck to her skin. What felt like countless currents pulled on her feet, her thighs, her waist.

Grunting and digging into the mud with her hands, she kicked several times. The waves splashed and broke apart and collapsed, until Jenny managed to wrench herself free, climbing up the muddy bank to land face-first in the grass.

The grass was dead; she inhaled the bitter, ashen remains and nearly choked. Coughing and sputtering, she rolled onto her back and stared up at the emptiness, breathing hard. Mud covered her entire body.

"What happened to this place?" she whispered.

*What happened . . . happened . . .* The words flittered and echoed and came back to her, as though she'd spoken into a canyon, though there was no wind, no rocky cliffs.

"Hello?" she said, a little more loudly.

*Hello? Hello . . .* Again, the world responded, echoing the question back to her. She strained to remember what Eve had said about this place, but her memories were fuzzy, her mind filled with static; all she could see was the shock on Susan's face when they'd reunited.

"What do I do?"

*What do I do? What do I . . .*

Jenny got to her feet, dripping mud, shivering. Her fingers tingled from the cold.

Whispering filled the air. Jenny whirled around, trying to find the source, but nothing stirred. The trees stood unmoving. There was no wind. The whispering grew louder and louder, but she couldn't recognize any of the words. She couldn't even tell how many people or creatures were whispering. She raised her fists, ready for a fight, before she realized the whispering was coming from the water.

Waves rushed forward again, and Jenny scrambled back. Each wave was dark and bulbous, taking on the form of fish before crashing into the mud. The spray landed on her skin, and she felt countless tiny tugs. Was it trying to drown her? Had she broken some rule by trying to get out?

She rushed higher and higher up the bank, slipping and sliding on the mud and grass. The bank itself was giving way, crumbling and falling apart and disappearing into the water.

Frantic, she dashed into the trees, waves splashing at her heels. When she grabbed a tree for support, the bark disintegrated against her fingertips, throwing her off-balance, and she cried out, stumbling forward before tripping over a root. She landed hard, breaking the fall with her arms.

What was going on? Why was this happening? Was the world dying? Or was it rejecting her? Where was Eve?

Was this because of what she'd done? Because she'd given up her humanity?

"Eve!" she screamed, crawling forward till she could stand and run.

*Eve! Eve!* The world only threw her voice back at her from every direction. The whispering grew louder and louder as Jenny dashed through crumbling trees. The leaves crinkled and shattered out of existence beneath her muddy feet, and the waves roared and chased furiously. No matter how fast she ran or how many steps she took, the water gushed right behind her.

When she tripped again, this time because her foot sank into vanishing ground, the waves finally caught her.

She didn't even get to cry out. Waves slammed into her back and wrapped around her navel. She struggled, but how was she supposed to pull water off her? She smacked it, and all it did was splash. More waves grasped her legs and arms, the dark water surging into her ears and up her nose, bubbling and whispering. It rushed down her throat, worked its way between her legs, and seeped into her pores. It pressed her eyes. It had seized her. It had claimed her.

She sank into its enveloping darkness, raging quietly but desperately as the world swallowed her completely.

Then, it spat her back out.

Light ignited behind her eyelids, shimmering blue and red before intertwining, forming purple strands that stretched like vines and mixed with gold and silver. Yellow erupted like beams from the sun, each strand binding her, wrapping around her waist, raising her like a marionette, lifting her from the dark.

Jenny shuddered awake to see Susan's tear-stricken face. She was crouched over Jenny, her hand still buried in her chest, glowing so brightly that the tears on Susan's face shimmered.

The pain was gone. Nothing hurt anymore. Jenny only felt warmth.

She licked her teeth; it hadn't been just a dream. She had teeth again. She was alive.

"Hey," she whispered. Her voice felt hoarse. She remembered the tooth she'd swallowed, how it had scratched its way down her throat. How she'd tried to copy that angel's self-healing ability.

Susan rested her forehead on Jenny's, sighing so that their breaths mingled; their noses touched. Warmth rushed to Jenny's cheeks as Susan's hand slid out of her chest and the light faded.

"I'm really tired," said Susan softly. Her hand, now back to flesh, lay flat on Jenny's chest, as though she were terrified Jenny's heart would stop beating if she let go.

"Same," Jenny replied, making Susan laugh a gentle, little laugh, the tremor moving through both of them simultaneously.

A notification flickered against her thoughts, trying to surface. It was strange having thoughts that weren't her own again, but she welcomed it. It meant she was truly back. That Susan had saved her.

*I'm not dead.* She'd saved Oliver. They were back together. Now, all they had to do was get out of this stupid nightmare.

She imagined Eve had plenty to say as well, but she figured the first notification would be that of Susan's level. Staring back into Susan's warm eyes, achingly aware of Susan's hand on her bare chest, she let the thought emerge.

**Blooded.**

# CHAPTER FORTY-ONE

# HUNGER

Something's moving down there," came Mrs. Monique's voice through the clouds of swirling dust. She'd ventured toward the crater to give Jenny and Susan space and was shining her flashlight into the depths of the basement.

But Jenny barely registered what the librarian said. She kept replaying the first notification over and over. *Blooded. Blooded. Blooded.*

**Blooded.**
**You have tasted blood from another world.**
**+20 Stat Points have been awarded.**

*What the fuck is that supposed to mean?* The other notifications spurted rapidly, like fireworks bursting uncontrollably before fading away. She'd killed a bunch of angels, gained a ton of experience and energy, and had racked up a lot of stat points. But she was too afraid to ask the guidance system to elaborate, too afraid that she'd done something terrible.

That worry was lodged in her thoughts like a thorn. She kept thinking about how that other world collapsed and . . . hadn't that strange dark water caught her? She remembered *drowning.* How was she even here?

*Eve, are you there? Are you back in my head?*

**Yes, Jenny Huang. I never left. Congratulations on your blooded status.**

*Am I screwed up now? What happened?* She couldn't shake the unsettling feeling that something horrid loomed inside her. With Susan's light having dispersed, the ruined lab rooms filled with the eerie gloom of the void. Her best friend lay on top of her, her eyes shut tight.

**Susan Brown surrendered much of her spirit to resurrect you. She pulled you back into your body.**

*Resurrect?* Jenny's eyes went wide. *Resurrect?!*

A bead of sweat trailed down Susan's nose and landed on Jenny's face, then Susan started trembling, and that was all Jenny could concentrate on.

"Susan!" Jenny's breath caught in her throat. Her lungs burned, and the hole in her side—now healed and closed—ached, but at least now it felt more like she'd been punched in the gut rather than bored through with a rod.

"I'm alright," she said weakly. "Just feeling really tired." She lifted her head off Jenny and tried to sit up, blinking. Her eyes were bloodshot; dark bags hung beneath them as though she hadn't slept in days, and her face was sunken. What had she given up to heal Jenny? What had been the cost?

Jenny's body wasn't fully healed. She pushed herself off the floor, wincing as her shoulder cracked. She clenched her new fingers into a fist; they were pinker than the rest of her hand, and they felt strange, like she could feel her old fingers—her original ones—but saw these new ones now attached to her palm. The holes in her thigh and side were covered in pale, pink flesh, though the skin around the wounds was still red and angry.

Susan had done everything she could; Jenny even had her teeth back. The rest could be taken care of with potions or sprays or whatever else they could come up with.

But what about Susan? What was wrong with her? Susan's eyes were shut, and she was swaying as though she might collapse at any moment. Jenny grabbed her arm and held her steady, searching her best friend's face and trying to figure out what to do.

But the worst part? The worst part was, even as she fretted about Susan's exhausted state and what her best friend had sacrificed to save her, all Jenny could think about was how much she was starving. *Starving.*

The hunger that throbbed deep within her belly made her left eye hurt. She felt it in every limb, every muscle. Felt the saliva pooling underneath her tongue because Susan's body looked so soft . . . so sweet. Like her flesh would just melt in Jenny's mouth. And her blood! Her blood would be so warm and filling, and she wanted to compare the taste to the angel's. Wanted to know how different the flesh would feel ripping between her teeth.

Her stomach rumbled, and Jenny recoiled in horror, making Susan flinch as though Jenny had actually tried to take a bite.

"Does it still hurt?" asked Susan, her voice small, her eyelids struggling to stay up. She placed her hand over Jenny's, even though her arm was shaking from the effort.

Jenny bit her bottom lip with her newly grown teeth, blinking away tears. Her jaw ached, but it was nothing compared to the ache of hunger that made her teeth yearn to sink into flesh.

*What the fuck is wrong with me? No, I need to think about Susan right now. But not like that!*

*How can I heal her?*

*I've got enough energy. Maybe I can make something to restore her.* She reached for the system, trying to shape another potion with her thoughts; something that would restore Susan's stamina and take away her tiredness. It was like trying to use a muscle she hadn't in a long time, though it couldn't have been more than an hour since she'd activated Severed Spirit.

**I would not recommend this course of action.**

*Are you just saying that so I don't waste energy?* Jenny took a deep breath. She had to try something, didn't she?

**Susan Brown's skill drained her spirit to heal you. Not stamina. Not energy. Spirit cannot be restored by any means other than sleep.**

Frustration built up inside Jenny, so much so that she wanted to use Ignite and burn everything around them down. Feeling helpless, she pulled Susan in for a hug, terribly aware of how close her jaw was to Susan's throat. But she pressed her cheek to Susan's, both of them covered with dust and dirt and dried blood, and even though she was naked, she didn't care. She squeezed her best friend harder than she'd ever hugged her before. "Thank you for saving me."

Susan started to say something, but surrendered and weakly hugged Jenny back.

*Why?* thought Jenny. *Why'd you go so far, you big dummy? Just for me?* It wasn't a question she could voice yet. Maybe after all this was over.

"Fuck." Mrs. Monique scrambled back from the crater and rushed toward them, kicking up loose rubble and dust. "We have to get back to the library— right now. There are at least a dozen angels down there."

Jenny sniffled. Her nose felt crooked, but at least she had a nose again. Taking a deep breath, she let Susan go.

"Did they see you?" asked Susan, who scratched one side of her face, keeping her eyes on the floor. She seemed a little rejuvenated, her face flushed red.

Mrs. Monique put her flashlight in a pocket then knelt to help Susan to her feet. "I can't tell. There's too much dust and something *big.*" Once she had Susan standing, she turned to help Jenny and froze. "Jenny, your eye!"

Jenny blinked. She'd still been thinking about hugging Susan, but the heat from their embrace evaporated as Mrs. Monique's face morphed from shock to fear.

"But it says . . . No, it says you're human." Mrs. Monique stepped back and raised her spear, holding it with both hands and aiming at Jenny. The light from her flashlight stuck out of her pocket and made her metallic armor seem to shimmer.

The librarian reminded Jenny of a spooked cat, arching its back and baring its fangs, trying to determine whether an approaching stranger was dangerous. Jenny covered her left eye with her palm, realizing it had been stinging this entire time. She hadn't noticed because of her nose and her other injuries and the hunger . . .

She eyed the librarian, salivating at the thought of peeling off her skin and chewing through the exposed muscles, and then . . . *No! No, no, no!*

Susan raised her arms, looking between Mrs. Monique and Jenny. She opened her mouth to protest, suggesting this was because of what Jenny did to survive, but Mrs. Monique shook her head. She wasn't taking any chances.

"Eve?" whispered Jenny. "Am I still human?" She lowered her hand; her palm came away glistening with blood. She was crying blood.

"Who's Eve?" asked Susan, a note of alarm in her voice.

"Eve?" repeated Mrs. Monique, adjusting her grip on the spear. "Something's not right. Something's definitely fucked up."

*Shit. I said that out loud.* Jenny was about to try to explain, but Eve's words appeared in her head, and she hesitated.

**Your body remains human.**

*But why is my eye still . . . And only one of them?*

**When you severed your spirit, you perished, Jenny Huang. You died. You ripped your soul from your body, and it had to be ripped back.**

*Died?* Jenny blinked and wiped the blood off her cheek, unable to meet Susan's eyes. *No. I was thinking. I was fighting. I was—*

**Your brain continued to function, processing and reacting to sensory data.**

The visions of the other world falling apart, of the dark water consuming her, of the hollowed feeling when she'd been severed . . . She shuddered violently, then took a deep breath.

"Mrs. Monique," said Jenny when she felt steady enough. She looked at Susan and raised her blood-covered hand. "It's alright; I can explain." Her head spun as she looked between the two. Her stomach twisted with hunger and disgust and self-loathing. "But right now, there's something down there that wants my blood. And if I go to the library, it'll come after me. And if we stay here, you guys will get caught up in it."

"What thing?" asked Mrs. Monique, still holding the spear, still looking angry.

"A desecrated angel." Just saying its name made Jenny's heart race. "It can control the dead. It's—"

Mrs. Monique let out a frustrated scream. The spear shook, the tip coming so close to Jenny's nose that she could almost taste the metallic point, could almost feel it plunging through her head. Susan cried out, but Mrs. Monique didn't attack. Jenny hadn't flinched, either. She stared right back into the librarian's eyes. There was no time for this.

Mrs. Monique's shoulders relaxed, then she looked at the babies. They were sitting around Jenny, watching everything unfold quietly, sucking on their fingers or toes. Susan's hand was on the librarian's wrist.

Finally, she whispered, "I don't know what to do." Her voice quivered for a moment, and for that brief instance, Jenny saw a shadow of the familiar, sweet librarian who was always ready to help, to talk, to brighten anyone's day. But that vanished as quickly as it had appeared, replaced by that steel-eyed woman holding a spear pointed at her face.

Tears ran down Jenny's left cheek. She didn't look away. Mrs. Monique was only level three, and she had every right to be afraid. Maybe she even sensed the horrid thoughts coiling around Jenny's brain. A subconscious awareness that something was definitely wrong.

"So you're not one of them?" asked Mrs. Monique. "You didn't turn into one of them?"

Jenny shook her head no. She glanced at Susan, who lowered Mrs. Monique's spear then faltered on her feet. Jenny scrambled to catch her.

"Sorry," whispered Susan. "I'm okay."

Jenny picked up the cattle prod and put it in the girl's hands. "Where's your flashlight? You guys have to get back to the library." She figured if they used their lights, they should be fine. Nothing would bother them—the desecrated angel only wanted her.

"No," said Susan, mumbling and trying to steady herself. "I'm not leaving you alone again."

A heartbreaking warmth filled Jenny's heart as she stared into her best friend's eyes. Susan didn't hesitate for a second over Jenny's strange, bleeding eye. Her lips were pressed tight. She looked determined, but what good was determination if she was exhausted?

Before Jenny could say anything, that terrible hunger crawled up her throat again, and all she could think about was Susan's flesh and . . . Jenny was the one to look away first. Her strength returned with every heartbeat, and she couldn't help but remember Susan's fingers wrapped around her heart, squeezing it. No. Susan could not stay with her.

What if Jenny really was turning into an angel now? Or something worse? Who'd protect Susan from *her*?

They had to get to the library, away from her, with the others. Then Susan could rest, they'd be with Oliver and his friends, and maybe Susan could even heal his legs once she'd recovered.

In the meantime, Jenny could go find Miriam and the others in that room in the chem wing.

She sighed. She'd nearly forgotten about Miriam in all the chaos since. Was the poor girl still alive?

A tremor shook the floor. Everything rattled. Mrs. Monique whipped around to face the crater as Susan tripped into Jenny's arms. The babies cried out and latched onto her legs.

A beam of blue light shot out of the crater and through the hole in the ceiling. Wind battered them and sent rubble flying, clearing the dust, while Jenny dug her toes into the floor and held Susan tight. Her babies rolled and struggled, but they'd just have to fend for themselves.

The beam shimmered and surged—a lance through the entire building—then burst into radiant blue bubbles. Each one floated and sparkled like afterimages before fizzing out. Goose bumps raced up and down Jenny's body. She recognized that. Realized what was coming. And that light was much, much stronger than the flash she'd seen earlier.

She stepped forward and grabbed Mrs. Monique's shoulder, speaking as firmly as she could. "Take Susan and get out. Get back to the library. They only want me!"

The librarian looked *terrified*, her eyes wide. "What?" The librarian's gaze had changed completely. Her anger and steadfastness from a moment ago had vanished, replaced with nothing but abject fear. Had the light messed with her? Her lips were trembling, and she looked like she'd burst into tears any second now.

Jenny turned to find Susan petrified. Her arms were wrapped around her chest, and she stared at where the blue light had shimmered. It was the same as when the survival challenge began; Susan was rooted to the spot, terrified.

The rubble shifted, her babies squealing with fright as they half waddled, half ran back to her. A nauseating aura of dread crackled through the air, and her heart thundered. All the dead angels, the ones Susan had knocked out with her own light, twitched in unison, as well as all the other bodies strewn about the ruins of the lab room. The bodies of students and teachers—some of them crushed by tables and chunks of ceiling.

Every single one of them opened their shining blue eyes. Their arms and legs jerked, and they groaned, forming a chorus of undead voices that came from above, below, and behind them, echoing from the hallway leading to the lobby.

Panic spread through her chest like a whirlwind. Jenny pushed Susan behind her and shouted for Mrs. Monique to get a hold of herself, but whatever that blue beam of light had been, it hadn't only awakened the dead—it had messed with the living too, a sense of dread that felt like a night terror. Her heart pounded as the bodies crawled toward them. There wasn't a single notification for any of these things.

She thought about rushing into the pit. Would all these undead creatures follow her? They only wanted *her,* right? But what if they also went after Susan? What if that desecrated angel was after all of them now?

She couldn't take that chance. She'd have to protect her; she'd have to fight to the death. But the undead approached from every direction. What was she supposed to do?

Golden light flashed, and her hatchet returned to her hand. Its new obsidian face glistened, aching to slice. Her next thought was her nakedness. She was just about to spend energy to create new medium armor and possibly another shield when another notification burst through her desperate planning.

**Activate Exoskeleton?**

*Exoskeleton?*

*Yes*, she thought, eyeing the closest pile of undead angels—the ones that had tried to drag her into the hole. It was a mess of limbs. She glanced at the dead students, their torn flesh and clothes. They blinked and stared at their hands and wailed. So far, only the angels were crawling toward them. Maybe the humans . . . Maybe they were still in there?

Pressure erupted inside Jenny's navel. She cried out as the sensation expanded outward, pushing against her belly button and the base of her spine, like something was struggling to burst through her skin. Her muscles clenched. Her back arched as though she was seizing, and, looking up at the ceiling and making eye contact with another angel, the pressure released all at once.

A gelatinous red substance that looked like thickened blood spurted out of her belly button.

# CHAPTER FORTY-TWO

# EXOSKELETON

With each shuddering spasm, more gooey red substance shot out of her navel with enough force to make her step back. She swore her belly button had ruptured. Ropes and ropes gushed like geysers that curved in every direction before collapsing against her skin and splashing.

Jenny screamed.

Golden light swept across her like a shiver, bright enough to make the undead creatures pause and moan. It seemed to hypnotize them.

The red substance encircled Jenny's waist and dribbled up her sides before enveloping her chest. It rushed down her legs, up her back, and around her neck. As she struggled, as she tried to claw it off her cheeks and chest, the red stuff attached to her fingers and worked itself over her arms.

She bent over, clutching her knees as it slid through her hair and encased her scalp. It tightened against her thighs and covered the soles of her feet, leaving her navel bare, as well as her privates. She knew what it was. The shell-like casing that every single wretched angel she'd fought had been covered in. She looked like one of them, like the female angels whose bellies were also exposed.

*No!* she screamed with all her might. She pushed with her thoughts, thrust her consciousness into the substance, felt her racing pulse, felt the heat of her skin as the gelatinous red stuff hardened. She shaped it with her mind, picturing the first armor she'd made.

There was no way in hell she'd resemble these creatures; not when her mind was already crumbling, and hunger laced every single heartbeat. She didn't want Susan to worry. Didn't want Mrs. Monique or anyone—especially not Oliver— to hesitate because of her appearance.

The golden light, although it had dimmed, now crackled back to life. Scales blossomed across her covering, the substance receding from her face and rolling back on itself to her neck and down to her navel. It thinned slightly, covering everything she wanted to, before the light finally faded.

Breathing hard, spittle running down her chin, she touched her face with her armored fingers. Her face was still bare, but her scalp was protected, her dark hair untouched. With the covering, her arms and legs felt thicker. She felt bigger. The red darkened to a bloody shade of crimson as the scales shimmered, each one curved like the petal of a flower, and she was happy her navel was fully concealed. She couldn't see her scars or her belly button.

The new armor was like a bodysuit, fitting snugly, and perfectly conforming to her body. But it wasn't just a thin layer of cloth; this was hard like a shell, and it had a satisfying weight to it. She felt indestructible.

When her mind finally quieted, she exhaled, steam escaping her lips. Her exoskeleton bursting into existence seemed to have jolted Susan and Mrs. Monique from their terror, but now, their eyes were wide with shock.

"You look . . . beautiful," whispered Susan. She held her cattle prod with both hands, holding it over her chest as though she were praying. Her legs trembled. Mrs. Monique pressed her lips tight, her eyes twitching from Jenny to the creatures that had faltered around them. She seemed to be wrestling with the urge to attack.

Before Jenny could say anything, a violent twitch overcame her, and something shot out of Jenny's upper back—two tendrils, each one bursting out of her shoulder blades like streamers.

Susan stepped forward to help, but Mrs. Monique grabbed her arm. Jenny cried out, hugging herself and stumbling as two more shot out from her lower back. All four fluttered madly, forming an *X* that curved forward. They were flat and thin, about three feet in length, and made of the same material as her covering.

But as each one twitched and flickered, signals raced from their tips and rushed down into her spine. A tingling sensation climbed up her back, and Jenny sensed her surroundings in a way she'd never felt anything before.

Her tendrils whisked through the air, picking up on disturbances in the floating dust, the movements of the undead, and even Susan's quickened breathing. She sensed Mrs. Monique's anger, *tasted* it with her tendrils. It was like licking cold steel, and she shivered as a fresh wave of hunger threatened to rip out of her stomach the same way her exoskeleton had.

The hunger felt even more intense, ravenous now, enough to make her head ache. Through her tendrils, she picked up Susan's body heat. She felt Mrs. Monique holding her breath, and horrid images roped through her mind: Ripping them apart. Drinking their blood. Feasting . . .

She shut all that out. *Am I going crazy?*

**Your body is still adjusting. Your body will never be the same.**

Jenny swallowed the saliva pooling in her mouth, trying to focus on the tendrils instead of her stomach. They must have been similar to that dark wretched angel's from the hallway fight upstairs. It must've used these senses to intuit all of her attacks before she'd even committed to them. She remembered rushing right into its swinging arm, remembered how her face had crumpled. Had she copied it subconsciously?

Susan's lips twitched. She looked like she had a ton of things to say, like she wanted to touch Jenny's new . . . Was it skin? Or more like an outer layer of bone? But Mrs. Monique spun her spear and held it offensively. The undead were closing in. There wasn't a chance to discuss this.

Jenny turned to face them. Her classmates—their eyes empty and blue—raised their arms, many of them missing chunks of flesh and covered in dried blood. Their bodies were mangled, and they shuffled forward like zombies. Adding the undead angels between them, they all formed a herd of creatures with glowing eyes.

Jenny glanced down at her babies. Some were sitting. Some were standing and sucking on their thumbs. They all stared in awe and admiration. Was it strange that they felt even more like *her* babies now that she was . . . She pushed that thought away as well as she pointed at them to catch their attention. She then pointed at Susan. "Protect."

She wasn't sure if they'd understand her, but it was worth a shot.

Their brows furrowed. They pressed their lips together, then they waddled and crawled over to Susan. And even though dried blood stained their cheeks and arms and round bellies, Jenny was starting to find them cute in a way she hadn't expected. It helped that looking at them didn't make her salivate with hunger, and if they could keep Susan safe . . . then maybe she would have to readjust her decision to never have children. Unless they grew up to be something horrible.

She took a deep breath. The nearest group of undead was comprised of the ones that had tried to drag her into the crater, including the wretched angel whose throat she'd bitten through. Torn flesh flapped from its neck with its every step, its head permanently bent without support on one side. Jenny's tendrils whipped through the air, snapping like miniature crackles of thunder.

With a burst of light, she summoned her hatchet to her hand and, in the same motion, hurled it into the group. *Savage Throw.*

Three heads erupted in a row, golden light flashing each time. Blood and brain matter splattered her new exoskeleton as a series of notifications filled her head.

**+2 Energy**

**+2 Energy**

**+2 Energy**

*What?* The angels' headless bodies collapsed. Light streaked across the lab room as her hatchet snapped back into her hand, and Jenny sprang forward, slicing through necks and chests, each cut accompanied by a golden shimmer.

**+2 Energy**
**+2 Energy**
**+2 Energy**
**+2 Energy**

She ended by burying her hatchet in the chest of the last one, the wretched angel she felt intimately attached to after having drank its blood. Gold light sparked, and its ribs cracked, blood bursting out of the hole in its neck as the blue light faded from its eyes.

**+2 Energy**

With that, she inspected her hatchet, realizing she hadn't read through the notification of it reaching tier three.

**Hatchet (Tier 3)**
**Your weapon can now harvest Energy with every attack that invokes pain.**
**Energy harvested is doubled due to the effects of the Energy Core.**

She shuddered, remembering the same light shining when she'd cut Oliver's legs off. She'd gotten energy from that too, hadn't she? But she couldn't deny how helpful this was, and she was going to abuse the hell out of it.

The wretched angel beneath her was dead. Well, dead again. Another slice wouldn't invoke pain, so there was no energy to harvest.

She kicked its head, its neck stretching for an instant, its tendons desperate to hold on, but the crunch of her exoskeleton-covered foot connecting with its chin was too satisfying, and she felt even stronger than before. The creature's head jetted forward as though she'd shot a cannon, striking one of the undead students in the belly, forcing the boy to crumple forward in agony.

The boy screamed, and Jenny flinched.

*Are they still in there? Can they feel that?*

She stumbled back, her tendrils snapping with agitation. She tried to pick up on anything that might alert her to what the undead might feel, but there was nothing to be perceived from them. Their bodies were cold, and although they were breathing and their hearts were beating, they didn't emanate *life* the way Susan and Mrs. Monique did.

She sensed Mrs. Monique fighting, thrusting her spear through angels that wandered near her. She slashed through their bellies, shoved her weapon through their chests and necks, and punched any that managed to survive that. But the librarian wasn't getting any experience or energy from these kills; they were only tiring her out. She was still only level three.

The babies surrounded Susan, and split into several groups. It seemed like even more babies had joined them, and each one was completely focused on the task. Any angel or student who approached was set upon by a group, the babies dragging the person down and biting through anything within teething range. Jenny's stomach twisted with each human scream. Had the desecrated angel brought them back somehow? To endure this agony?

Rage built inside her like the charged winds ushering in a storm. More people and angels lumbered in from the lobby, so many that, for a second, it almost seemed like the middle of a normal day. After fifth period, when half the students were rushing to the cafeteria to be first in line for lunch, and the other half were exiting, trying to get to their classes.

Except, almost everyone here was already dead.

Jenny dashed away from Susan, Mrs. Monique, and the babies, hoping to distract the undead. Bodies rained down from the floor above. Glancing up, she saw angels and students dragging themselves to the edge then plopping forward, leading with their heads. Several of them smashed into the rubble and burst open. Others were skewered on exposed rods. And still others broke their necks from the fall, landing in a heap of broken limbs, moaning and crying.

But at least those ones weren't threats. Jenny tried to ignore their screams, tried not to think about the desecrated angel reanimating them with another beam of light.

She slashed through several more angels, gaining spurts of energy with each shimmering strike. She didn't attack the dead students. Their fingernails slipped off her exoskeleton as she bounded deeper into the ruined physics lab, leaping over desks and smashing rubble with her armored feet. She ran away from the crater, away from the others.

Her plan worked. Every single set of glowing blue eyes turned in unison, seeking her. She'd just reached the far end of the room and paused, feeling strangely cool. The crimson covering seemed to wick away heat without the need for sweat.

Bodies continued to rain down. Many fell right into the crater, screaming, but the undead on this floor had herded together, moving slowly as a large group in her direction. She noticed that the dead wretched angels weren't moving as they would've when alive. Was that another limitation to the desecrated angel's ability to raise the dead? Would that change if the creature grew stronger?

She took the opportunity to pull up her stats.

**Jenny Huang**
**Human (Stage II - Level 24) (Blooded)**
**Age: 6,801 days**
**Stats:**
**Power: 25**
**Durability: 15 (+30)**
**Stamina: 20**
**Agility: 20**
**Stat Points Available: 44**
**Energy Available: 422**

She'd leveled up *eight* times while Severed! And her exoskeleton seemed to boost durability immensely. She tapped her chest with her hatchet. This covering stuff really was crazy, wasn't it? Her exoskeleton felt even stronger than the ones the wretched angels wore.

Then she remembered the notification she'd gotten with Blooded. It had awarded her twenty bonus stat points, which was why she had so many available. She exhaled, eyeing the students and angels coming for her. There was no time to worry about what that meant.

She assigned five points to power, ten to stamina, and ten to agility, bringing them all to thirty. She then added five to durability to bring it to fifty overall, leaving her fourteen stat points in reserve. She'd save those for an emergency and throw them into whatever she needed to boost quickly.

A shudder swept through her as her increased stats resulted in a series of muscle spasms. Her tendrils went taut before relaxing, and she followed suit.

Her limbs ached to be used. Heat emanated off her hatchet as though it, too, ached for violence. If the undead students were gonna get in her way, then she would just have to make their second deaths swift. That way, they'd feel no pain, and she'd feel less guilty.

Ready to fight, ready to cut them all down so that Susan and Mrs. Monique could escape, she crouched low, and was just about to rush into the herd when a few more notifications appeared.

In the throng of undead, several *alive* angels pushed their way through the crowd, heading straight for Susan and the others, who were trying to cross the hallway. Susan was leaning heavily on Mrs. Monique as the undead ignored them, but the tarnished and two wretched angels were closing in fast.

The wretched ones were high-level. One was twenty-two; the larger one was twenty-five. It roared, throwing several undead students out of its way before bolting forward on all fours. This one was covered in green, male, with large, bulging muscles.

*Like hell*, thought Jenny, channeling her strength and drawing upon Instant Acceleration.

The room rippled, screams and moans curving around her like wind. Her tendrils trailed behind her as she burst through the crowd of undead.

Bodies burst open, flesh and blood turned to mist, and bones turned to shrapnel that bounced off her exoskeleton before she slammed into the wretched angel with the force of a runaway bullet train.

# CHAPTER FORTY-THREE

# WE HAVE TO KEEP FIGHTING

Jenny smashed into the wretched angel with her elbow and knee half a second before it reached Susan. The impact felt like an explosion, a jarring vibration running through her body as the angel's green covering cracked around its face, where her elbow had broken its cheek, and its side, struck by her knee. It rocketed away, blood gushing from its mouth, and crashed into the hallway wall with a satisfying boom that dislodged even more debris and dust from above.

Susan had fallen from the impact, the wind battering her, and Mrs. Monique just stared while holding her spear, unsure what to do. Jenny realized that from their perspective, she had popped out of nowhere covered in blood. Chunks and strands of flesh slid off her crimson armor, blood glistening on her scales and face.

She shuddered, realizing she'd accelerated through the herd of undead students. It wasn't like attacking an angel. The students were soft, human flesh, and each one had burst like a water balloon. But her biggest realization?

The Instant Acceleration and the impact hadn't *hurt*! Her increased durability was holding up.

The second wretched angel screeched as it lumbered toward them, its heavy footsteps thundering through the floor. This one was purplish black, strong—but it didn't matter. Through her tendrils, she sensed the air the creature displaced, sensed its every breath, and Jenny spun.

Light flashed in her hand. Her hatchet cut through the creature's side, and it collapsed in a heap at Mrs. Monique's legs. Its guts spilled as it writhed in pain, its body nearly split in half. It tried to get up and kept slipping on its own blood pooling beneath it.

**+2 Energy**

Jenny was about to finish it off when she realized Susan and Mrs. Monique should be the ones to do it instead. That way, they'd get more experience and energy.

The other wretched angel dislodged itself from the wall, its green covering falling apart where Jenny had struck it. It let out a weak roar before rushing Jenny, limping on all fours before pouncing, trying to claw her up. She stepped to the side, hatchet snapping upward, and disconnected the creature's arm with a flash of golden light.

It screamed in her ear, but Jenny struck again, removing the other arm at the elbow. The angel landed hard, armless and bleeding uncontrollably from its stumps, teeth mashing in desperation.

**+2 Energy**

**+2 Energy**

She grabbed it by the hair and dragged it over to Susan.

Jenny couldn't look them in the eyes. She wiped blood off her brow as it dribbled down over her left eye. Something squishy had bounced off her lips, and she could still taste it.

"You guys need to kill them so you can get stronger."

Susan didn't move. She just stared at the angel struggling in front of her. The creature was trying to wriggle forward like a worm, its teeth dangerously close to Susan's legs, but if it went for a bite, Jenny would behead it. Her tendrils would sense any dangerous movement, and they could taste the desperate hunger in the struggling creatures; it hardly matched her own ravenous cravings, and she had to look away from Susan.

Anger swirled like smoke in her lungs. It sizzled, and the urge to scream kept threatening to overcome her, but lingering between that furious desire was a strange *satisfaction*. She hated what she'd become, hated that she'd thoroughly enjoyed cutting the angels apart and rendering them helpless. Strength pulsed through her, and it was such a contrast to her helpless, falling-apart state that it felt euphoric.

She knew it was horrid, knew it was terrible. Knew she'd become something truly awful.

She'd *rushed* through a crowd of dead students, and she hadn't even flinched as they burst open. Student blood dribbled over her scales and made her crimson armor shine.

She shoved all those feelings down, compressing them into a little cube, the same way she'd do when thinking about her life, her mom, and all the bullshit.

*Once this is over, once I'm free . . . I'll figure my feelings out.*

She was much, much stronger now, and even though only a few levels separated her from these wretched angels, the difference was astonishing. With her increased stats, her powerful weapon, her exoskeleton, and her skills, she felt unstoppable. But she knew that if she stopped, the dark thoughts rumbling inside her head would become all too real; she had to keep killing and getting stronger.

Susan still hadn't taken any action. Her cattle prod lay dormant in her hand, and she was trembling. It was Mrs. Monique who finally finished the angels off after a moment of hesitation. She jabbed them through the chests, aiming for their hearts, and the creatures stopped hissing in pain.

The notifications appeared in Jenny's head.

**You have defeated Wretched Angel (Level 22)!**
**Experience has been awarded.**
**+100 Energy**

**You have defeated Wretched Angel (Level 25)!**
**Experience has been awarded.**
**+100 Energy**

"Holy shit," swore the librarian, letting her blood-covered spear clatter to the floor as she clutched her head, her one eye bulging. She looked like she was about to throw up.

**Human (Stage II - Level 12)**

Jenny almost did a double take. The librarian had leveled up so quickly off the two wretched angels; it was like farming high-leveled monsters in a game with a newbie friend. But why hadn't Susan struck the creatures? She could've leveled at least a few times as well.

Susan stayed on her knees, averting her eyes and clutching her cattle prod so hard her knuckles looked like they'd burst through her skin. It wasn't just exhaustion; something else was bothering her, and Jenny couldn't figure out what.

Mrs. Monique stepped aside to throw up. Her body was adjusting to the rapid leveling, and no doubt she was figuring out her stats and new skills. Jenny noticed her spear had gotten stronger, too. It now registered as tier two.

The mass of undead students and angels continued approaching, crawling over rubble and tripping over each other, many of them splattered with blood from Jenny's Instant Acceleration, but they were hindered by the large chunks of ceiling partially blocking the hallway—and Jenny's babies, who snarled and threw themselves at the students, pushing the crowd back.

Jenny crouched and touched Susan's shoulder, worry making her chest want to collapse.

"We have to keep fighting, remember? It's just like a game," she echoed the words she'd told Susan in front of their English class when all of this began.

Susan blinked away tears, the bags under her eyes looking darker than before. Her lips quivered, and she opened her mouth like she was going to say something, but all she managed was a weak, choking sob.

*Are you sure nothing can help her? Not even that fortification potion I used?* Jenny remembered how it had boosted all her stats. If it could help Susan even a little bit, then the cost of energy was more than justified.

**It will strengthen her, but without proper rest—**

Jenny's hand filled with golden light. The vial appeared with the creamy orange liquid, and she pushed it into Susan's hands, feeling pitiful. Susan had given up so much to heal Jenny, and this was all she could do in return.

"You guys have to get upstairs," said Jenny finally, searching and failing to find any words of comfort. They were surrounded by their dead classmates. The hallway had collapsed and looked like a warzone. And they were at their wit's end. There were no words of comfort for this, only survival. And she couldn't draw upon healing light in the way Susan had. She didn't think a hug would be effective either when she was covered in bits of human flesh and looked like a monster.

"Why?" asked Susan, her lips barely moving, her eyes fixed on the glowing orange potion in her hand.

Jenny realized she was smearing blood on her best friend's shoulder, but there was already so much dried blood on both of them. She helped Susan stand, half pulling her to her feet.

"I don't want to leave you again," whispered Susan, urgency cutting through her voice. "You need me."

"I need you alive," said Jenny. It was unfair. Unfair. Susan had saved her, found her literally dead and pulled her back from that horrid world, and all Jenny could do was repeat platitudes. "But right now, you need to get back to the library, and the only way there is upstairs."

Mrs. Monique marched toward them. Light flashed in her hand, and her spear returned to her the same way Jenny's hatchet did. The librarian seemed to be standing taller, her shoulders wider. She nodded at Jenny, then wrapped her other arm around Susan's shoulders. "You need to rest," she said. "We need to get you somewhere safe."

Behind them, the crowd of moaning and screaming students was slipping through. Despite the babies' best efforts, several people pushed forward and fell flat on their faces, then they raised their heads and began crawling toward Jenny, crying and salivating and not caring where they placed their hands or bodies in the rubble.

They moved like lizards, and Jenny's tendrils shuddered in anticipation, but one of the babies set upon them before it could get close enough. This wasn't going to hold much longer.

"Take that stairwell," said Jenny firmly, pointing to the far end of the physics wing, near the emergency exit that would've led them outside. "You can take it to the third floor and cross over." Jenny then remembered that Miriam was still on the second floor. "But you'll have to stop by the chem lecture rooms."

"The lecture rooms?" asked Mrs. Monique. She wanted to get to the library as soon as possible and come back with reinforcements.

Jenny took a breath. "I left someone there. Miriam. She's with some other students too, I think. We got separated in a fight."

Susan finally lifted her head. She was swaying on her legs, holding the cattle prod and the potion to her chest. "Miriam?" she whispered in disbelief. "Miriam's still alive?"

"I found her in a closet," Jenny replied, shaking her head. "But she's safe. I think. I don't know. It was room 223—the honors chem room in front of my locker."

"What are you gonna do?" asked Susan, looking over Jenny's shoulder with a miserable look to the wailing crowd.

Jenny knew what her best friend was thinking. How many more of their classmates would Jenny have to butcher?

**Human population remaining: 21**

She forced herself to keep from flinching. She'd ignored that notification for a while now, but almost reflexively pulled it up, and the number had dropped even further. Things were nearing the end. The number was counting down the inevitable, and it'd been stupid and childish to ignore it this whole time.

"I gotta end this," said Jenny quietly, half speaking to herself, then she forced herself to smile when Susan's face twisted with worry. Before her best friend could ask what "ending this" would mean, Jenny explained. "I think if I kill the desecrated angel that's doing all this, then it'll stop. The dead can stay dead."

It wouldn't end the survival challenge, but at least if she killed that thing, not only would she be even stronger but maybe it would provide enough energy to figure something out. An idea was brewing, taking shape; something she'd been thinking about since that other world collapsed and Susan had pulled her soul back into her body.

Jenny's tendrils snapped, sensing where the flashlight had rolled to a stop between a chunk of the wall. She picked it up and flicked it on, careful not to point it at her left eye. She didn't want to say goodbye, especially not while looking like this. "I won't let any of them come after you, so get somewhere safe, okay?"

Tears filled Susan's eyes. She nodded and sniffled, then inhaled deeply through her nose and downed the potion of fortification. Color returned to her cheeks, and she straightened slightly, though the bags under her eyes remained. She took the flashlight from Jenny's hand, their fingers brushing, and they stared at each other for a long moment before Jenny turned away.

Susan tapped Jenny's chest with the flashlight, the scales clinking like glass. She was breathing hard through her nose. "Stop that thing and hurry back."

Jenny nodded, not trusting herself to say anything more as she searched for the nearest baby.

It seemed to sense she wanted its attention, and it waddled over. This one had large yellow eyes and a shock of hair sticking out of its head, making it look like a pineapple. It was round and pudgy, though so caked in dust and dried blood that Jenny couldn't tell its gender. But it stared at her, eyes widening, waiting for her to say something, and she fought the urge to pick it up and squeeze it.

"Keep protecting them, okay? All of you guys." She pointed back at Susan and Mrs. Monique to emphasize it. "Don't let anything happen to them."

The baby gurgled then nodded. And she knew, by some instinctual, unexplainable pull, that it understood. That they all understood. They peeled themselves off the undead humans wriggling on the floor and away from the herd trying to get to Jenny.

Meanwhile, Jenny squared her shoulders and prepared herself for what she had to do. She backed away slowly, hatchet in hand, watching the herd's approach, watching them moan and crawl over one another and cut themselves open on exposed bars.

*This is for the best,* she told herself, even as her heart threatened to fall apart with each beat. *Susan pumped my heart.* But the girl couldn't fight in her current state. She needed rest. She needed to get somewhere safe. And this way, they could help Miriam too, and Jenny could focus on killing the desecrated angel.

After all, Susan was the good one. The sweet one. The one who cared about others and bettering the world, and all Jenny wanted to do was run away and be selfish and break things. Susan was the one who preferred playing support, but she would still be the shot caller, the navigator, wanting everyone else to be playing at their best.

And even in this hell, that innate kindness reflected in her abilities. Her weapon shocked and paralyzed. Her skill was to turn into literal light and heal at the cost of herself. She wasn't a killer, and there was no way she'd be able to fight the undead students.

Jenny heard the hallway door shut behind her. They were gone, leaving Jenny to face this part of the nightmare alone. She was alone again, but she was stronger; she'd become a monster, hadn't she? She'd come back from the brink of death, and now she could do what Susan never hesitated to do. Sacrifice herself.

Jenny would sacrifice whatever she had to. She would harness her anger and use it for something other than just crying and self-loathing.

She stared down at the approaching students, their moans and sobbing filling her ears like she was drowning in ooze. So many were covered in blood and viscera, missing limbs and parts of their faces. They were crying, and Jenny told herself it wasn't the same; they were already dead. She wasn't killing anyone—she was setting them free. If they could feel pain, then she'd end it as quickly as she could. She'd end their suffering.

But saying that was one thing. It was much easier to cut an angel who looked like a malnourished human than a student dressed in normal clothes, torn up and battered and wailing.

It had to be done. She wanted the energy, she wanted to set them free, and she needed to get to the desecrated angel.

Rage surged through Jenny before she ran forward, swinging her hatchet, and slashed through the first student—a girl with her hair tied back. Her left cheek was ripped open, her eyes wide with tears spilling down her face and mixing with the dried blood. Probably a freshman. Jenny's hatchet cut through the girl's head with a golden shimmer, and the blue light faded from her eyes before the body hit the floor.

**+4 Energy**

The undead humans gave more energy . . . Did that mean they felt more pain? She squashed that thought.

The next was a boy about a foot taller than her. She thought she recognized him from lunch or something. She buried her hatchet in his chest, slicing through his heart. Blood splattered her face, but she kept going, systematically working through the rest of them. Her tendrils snapped and twitched, sensing their movements, making it easier for her to step where she needed to.

She moved quickly and efficiently, slashing and slicing, each time with golden light shimmering and a notification in her head. She was working her way back through the lab.

**+4 Energy**
**+4 Energy**
**+4 Energy**

A furious scream built up inside her as more faces she recognized burst open, the moans and wailing surrounding her while she slashed through children and adults and the undead angels and the confused tarnished ones whose fingernails scraped Jenny's exoskeleton.

She stomped one of the angel's heads flat, its insides gushing out of every orifice. She wanted to explode with flame, wanted to burn them all to ashes, but she held that skill back. She kept picturing the boy in the stairwell, and she didn't want to burn a human—even if they were undead—like that.

### +2 Energy

"Eve?" she whispered, pausing as her fellow students tried to grab her, but they didn't have the strength to move her. Their faces were so close, and she caught her breath, trying to figure out the next step.

More gathered from the hall, while others rained down from above. She saw more tarnished and wretched angels among them; they registered notifications in her head.

"What does the desecrated angel want? Why's it doing this? Why's it so obsessed with me?"

**I believe it wants to end the Survival Challenge.**

# CHAPTER FORTY-FOUR

# FEEDING

Susan knew healing Jenny had cost her severely. She'd known it as she was pouring her soul into the light, the rainbows twisting and spiraling and encasing Jenny before seeping into her skin. She'd been squeezing Jenny's heart, and she swore she could still feel her fingers wrapped around it, desperately trying to keep her best friend alive.

She dreaded to think what might've happened if she hadn't increased her stamina before finding Jenny. Susan kept replaying that moment in her head: those empty eyes, the gruesome holes in Jenny's side and leg, her missing teeth, and those desperate, pained whispers as she begged Susan to leave her to die. Jenny's transformation, and the look on her face when she'd dragged the wretched angels over for Susan to butcher. What was her best friend turning into?

Susan felt like she was walking underwater, like her feet each weighed a ton. Her muscles burned from the effort as she followed Mrs. Monique through the heavy blue door, exiting the ruined physics wing, away from Jenny. The babies scurried through.

Pressure accumulated on her eyeballs. It hurt to blink. It hurt to turn her head and look at anything. She was thirsty and hungry and exhausted all at once; all she wanted was to climb into a comfy bed, rest her head on a pillow, and pull the blankets over her face. She didn't care how filthy she was—she just wanted to sleep.

Hell, she could lie down in this section of the hallway. It was a small, open space that the Muslim Student Association club used for prayers sometimes, a part of the school that was often forgotten. On the opposite end was an emergency exit, and to their right was the stairwell. There weren't any bodies here, but the walls and the door were stained with bloody handprints and smears.

The orange potion Jenny had made seemed to help. Susan had dismissed the notification and drunk it, not caring what it was, only that Jenny had made it for her. It tasted sweet and warm and delicious, and Susan almost wished she'd kept the empty flask just to sniff it. It had restored her strength to some degree, and her heart had steadied. Her body felt denser somehow, and breathing didn't make her head spin as much anymore. Though she was exhausted, she could at least move.

**Susan Brown**
**Human (Stage II - Level 10)**
**Age: 6,870 days**
**Stats:**
**Power: 10 (+10)**
**Durability: 10 (+10)**
**Stamina: 30 (+10)**
**Agility: 11 (+10)**
**Stat Points Available: 0**
**Energy Available: 182**

She could walk without leaning on Mrs. Monique, which was better than being a complete burden, and gave them more of a fighting chance if they ran into anything.

While the boosted stats felt somewhat good, there was a notification alerting her that it would be temporary. She didn't care. Even with the potion warm in her belly, she was still exhausted, but at least she was a little bit stronger so that in a worst-case scenario, she wouldn't be totally helpless.

She hated having to separate from Jenny again. Susan kept seeing her near death, eyes completely white, bleeding all over, buried under a pile of angels. Over and over, the thoughts attacked her, and she had to remind herself that she'd *saved* her best friend.

But Jenny was . . . Jenny was . . .

Susan couldn't understand what Jenny was. She'd only just begun to get a grip on their situation, the flesh-hungry angels, the school ripped away from the world, and all her dead friends and teachers. But now, even the dead were assaulting them? The other students were up and foaming at the mouth and trying to kill them too?

This was too much. Too much. She should still be with her best friend. Should still have her back. Why was she running away and leaving Jenny to fight them all alone?

"Third floor," whispered Mrs. Monique from ahead. She'd taken the lead once they entered the stairwell, taking each step slowly and carefully, as though the stairwell might crack open at any moment like an egg and drop them into the basement below.

That was where that monstrous thing Jenny'd described was waiting. Echoes of hissing and screams rose from the stairs leading to the basement, and Susan tried her best to ignore them, but her heart was beating so loudly. Surely that desecrated angel could hear it too?

She focused for a moment on the babies, pausing halfway up the stairs to catch her breath. They were freaking her out less and less, and Jenny had been the one to ask them to protect her. Somehow, that made her feel better. She remembered the fierce determination on Jenny's healed face.

*Okay*, she told herself. She had a job to do now: Find Miriam and get her to the library. If Miriam was still all right. Susan didn't want to delude herself.

Miriam always seemed sickly and out of it. For a while, Susan had thought she was a snob who pretended like she was better than everyone else, but then realized the poor girl was so used to being picked on and harassed that she preferred to keep to herself. Which Susan felt sorry for. But still, it was a miracle Miriam was alive. Maybe Jenny had found her and kept her safe.

Or maybe Miriam had gotten really strong somehow? Anything was possible with this system in their heads. But then, why wasn't Miriam with Jenny or the others? Susan hoped the girl wasn't injured or anything.

She thought about Oliver and his legs, the stumps swinging as the larger boy carried him. She sighed, grabbing the guardrail and pulling herself up. She was too weak; she wouldn't be able to heal anyone else for a while, no matter how much she wanted to.

She tried to focus and bring out her light again, but the most she managed was a tiny sparkle, a little tease of a glow that tickled at the tip of her nose and across her teeth, and she knew she was completely burnt out.

The babies seemed to notice her discomfort. One touched her hand, and she almost flicked her cattle prod on. They were tiny, like little toddlers, but caked in so much dust and dried blood they looked like little monsters. She remembered them moving through the rubble, and how they seemed indestructible. Nothing hurt them. She'd seen one bounce off an exposed metal rod without injury. She wondered if that was a biological thing, a natural defense mechanism for infant angels.

Roughly a dozen of them accompanied her. She wasn't sure about the exact count; they kept moving. They waddled up on all fours, climbing quickly and then waiting for her to catch up. Most of them led the way, but two of them held back and stayed right beside Susan, while three or four stayed farther behind, bringing up the rear.

*Angel babies*, she kept thinking. Why weren't they trying to eat her? Would they grow into tarnished ones?

Somehow, that didn't make sense, and she thought about the angel in the library, about how its iris had shown up, and how all these babies had irises. That couldn't be a coincidence.

And why were they listening to Jenny? They'd seemed strangely attached to her. Was that because of what Jenny had done? Were they her babies?

*No way.* That was an insane thought, even considering how insane everything was. But she couldn't help but remember how that red stuff had burst out of Jenny's navel the same way the angel in the library had transformed into a wretched one.

"Fuck," she whispered, and Mrs. Monique rushed back.

"Do you need to rest?"

Susan looked into Mrs. Monique's one eye and knew the librarian was only asking out of sympathy; she must look terrible. She shook her head. It was clear Mrs. Monique wanted to continue as quickly as possible, and Susan couldn't blame her. They didn't want to get stuck in a tight stairwell if something strong attacked.

As soon as Mrs. Monique turned away, the babies screeched and rushed ahead, then they heard footsteps. Lumbering, heavy footsteps and thuds.

One of the babies beside Susan gurgled softly. Mrs. Monique clicked on her flashlight and turned the corner, the sudden light surprisingly bright. The librarian swore under her breath.

The wails that echoed down the stairwell were much worse than the hissing and screeching of angels, because at least the angels were living things. The bodies of the other students and teachers? Their eyes glowing blue? The familiar faces she'd seen every day for years? That was a horror she couldn't wrap her thoughts around. How was she supposed to face that?

Mrs. Monique passed her the flashlight before rushing ahead with the babies. The sounds of violence echoed all over the stairwell, and Susan squeezed the flashlight and her cattle prod tight. It was like they were all Jenny. Beyond dead, their bodies torn and falling apart, driven forward by some desire that made no sense. No notifications. No levels. No way to discern them other than their blue eyes. They were actual zombies.

Susan climbed and turned the corner to see Mrs. Monique spear a student through the throat. A boy, probably a year or two younger than her. His face was already torn, his cheek flapping as he struggled. He clutched the spear feebly, blood gushing down his chin, until the blue glow faded from his eyes, and he went limp.

The babies dragged the next person down, an adult that Susan didn't recognize, and they bit through their neck. Susan flashed back to seeing Mrs. Rivera get chewed up in front of her.

She felt useless as they worked their way up the stairwell. Susan kept the flashlight ready in case an angel appeared, her cattle prod on if anything got past Mrs. Monique or the babies. They passed by the second-floor door, and Susan couldn't bring herself to look through the shattered window. They continued climbing.

They ran into four more students and another teacher, a large woman whom Susan recognized as the new assistant principal for the Biology Department. She'd only started this year, and Susan didn't remember her name. She'd been wearing a suit, but an angel had ripped through her chest and her neck.

Mrs. Monique gutted the sobbing woman, swiping the sharp end of the spear horizontally. The former assistant principal screamed in pain as her stomach split open, glistening intestines spilling out, but she was still trying to grab Mrs. Monique, who struck her again.

The woman stumbled back until her head smacked against the wall. Clutching her sides and gasping for air, crying, she slumped down, her intestines continuing to spill over her thighs. The blue glow faded from her eyes, and she lay still. Susan thought the assistant principal had a kind face, once rosy and full of life.

She knew it was pointless to feel guilty. They were already dead, but their screaming sounded too real. Their pain seemed too real. If she could just use Valescent Light, she was sure they'd knock out instantly. That's what had happened with the angels on top of Jenny, and she didn't want them to feel any more pain.

She especially hated their screaming as the babies chewed and ripped them apart; she cringed at the sounds of them chewing and swallowing. She'd almost forgotten they were monstrous.

When they climbed the final flight of stairs, Susan almost slipped on some blood while trying not to look at the girl whom Mrs. Monique had silenced with a thrust through the heart, her breath caught in her throat. Averting her gaze, she saw, right next to the doorway leading into the biology wing, a body dragging itself across the floor.

And Susan had to scream for the babies to stop just as they were about to set upon the boy, just as Mrs. Monique wrenched her spear free and was about to attack as well.

Miraculously, the babies listened. They tripped and scrambled, and one of them rolled into the boy on the floor before scampering away. Mrs. Monique held her breath, looking ready to strike, as Susan placed the flashlight on the floor.

The boy's eyes were glowing. His long brown hair, the hair Susan had stroked out of his eyes so many times, covered his face. His muscular build was clearly visible through his torn and stained varsity jacket. A chunk of flesh was missing from his shoulder, and his legs were chewed up in a nasty way, to the point she swore she could see his bones. His thighs were shredded to bits.

He clearly couldn't stand, and was trying to move forward on his arms, leaving behind a trail of glistening blood. One of his arms was bent the wrong way, the muscle of his forearm flapping against the floor. His other hand had no fingers.

It was Kevin, and he was sobbing.

Mrs. Monique said something frantically, but Susan wasn't listening. Her feet moved on their own, bringing her closer to Kevin as she clicked on her cattle prod. The static buzzing snapped soothingly in her hand. She wasn't sure what she was going to do, but she kept thinking about that angel in the library, kept wondering if people were trapped inside these undead bodies. Maybe she was just hoping. Maybe she was just stupid. But she was going to try.

This was the stairwell that she and Kevin used to sneak off to during free periods together. Where they'd hold each other, and he'd whisper in her ear, and his lips would find hers. He'd been so warm and confident and comforting . . .

This must've been where he and Leslie were hanging out when the survival challenge started. She tried not to picture them together, tried not to picture Leslie letting him feel her up.

The babies watched her curiously. Mrs. Monique touched her shoulder, but Susan dropped to her knees in front of Kevin, staring into his glowing blue eyes as he lifted his chin off the floor. His eyes were supposed to be brown and soft.

She felt the tickle in her belly as she prepared to send electricity through the prod. It wasn't the same pull she felt with Valescent Light. This seemed to draw on her stamina only, but she knew she couldn't overdo it. Passing out here would be even stupider than what she was about to do.

"I don't think it works like that," said Mrs. Monique softly.

"What if it does?" whispered Susan. "What if I can bring him back?" But she was speaking mostly to herself. She'd already made up her mind about trying.

Dumb thoughts kept surfacing: How she'd insisted on waiting till graduation before they got intimate. How she'd thought she might've loved him. How she hated the perverted jokes he and his friends would make about Jenny and other girls. How she was stupid for thinking he was the best guy ever because he'd been sweet to her.

How she was stupid because all she'd ever wanted was to be held and told she was loved.

She jammed her cattle prod into one of his glowing blue eyes. It burst, and he screamed, and she was pretty sure she screamed too. Liquid rushed down his cheek; there was a squelch, and the prod slipped deeper inside his skull, until she felt a rubbery resistance and let loose.

Lightning burst from the back of Kevin's head, frying his hair and striking the wall. Blue bolts flashed and crackled and sent shadows dancing all over the stairwell, and Susan stopped screaming as Kevin jerked and convulsed. She held on until she knew she'd collapse, trying to pour as much as she could into the attack, hoping beyond any reasonable amount of hope for another miracle. Maybe she could save others too. Maybe nobody else had to actually die and suffer.

Just before she passed out, she released her attack and let go of the cattle prod. The lightning stopped, and the stairwell darkened. Burnt hair and flesh stung Susan's nose, who was breathing hard, staring, trying not to cry. Kevin had gone rigid, his head still in the air, his back arched.

The blue light faded from his remaining eye. It was brown again. He blinked, and for a second, it seemed like he was about to say something. His eye widened;

Susan's prod was still buried in the other socket. His lips twitched. Tears and the mess of his ruined eye ran down his cheeks.

Mrs. Monique gasped, stepping forward to help, and Susan was just about to touch his face when Kevin collapsed. He hit the floor with a terrible bang, hammering the cattle prod deeper through his brain, and went still. No notification had come up at all. The stairwell was as silent as death.

Susan bit her lip; she'd expected as much. She raised his head, thinking how this would now be the last time she'd ever hold it; then, holding him by the forehead, she wrenched her cattle prod free; it was glistening and gooey. His other eye seemed to follow her, but it was a trick of the flashlight. He was dead. And there really was nothing she could do about it.

"I'm sorry," whispered Mrs. Monique, who helped her stand.

Susan shook her head. At least she knew for sure now. Whatever these undead things were, they were completely gone. There was no way to bring them back.

A hollow sadness settled in her chest. Somehow, this would all end, and everyone she once knew and cared about would be dead . . . if she didn't die as well. There was no point in mourning anyone yet. For now, she had to survive. *Then* she could mourn.

The babies left Kevin's body alone, and Mrs. Monique held the door open into the third floor. The Veil seemed thicker somehow, swirling like mist. An eerie quiet hung over their heads as the flashlight beamed around, revealing bloody stains and chunks of flesh and limbs.

There weren't any more bodies, so they quickly moved down the hall, expecting something to burst out of the bio labs at any second. Susan's breathing grew increasingly ragged, and she was worried now that the potion would run out and she'd collapse. But she didn't make a sound. She marched forward.

Every once in a while, she thought she saw movement out of the corner of her eyes, but it was the light bouncing off one of the babies. One of them had picked up an arm and was chewing the torn, fleshy end, the fingers dragging on the floor, until Susan asked it not to. Its eyes widened before it stopped sucking, then it dropped the arm and waddled ahead.

Anxiety filled Susan's chest. Something felt off in a way she couldn't quite explain. This was the floor Jenny and Susan had started on, on the other side of the building. She was trying not to think about Kevin, trying to think about Jenny, and trying to focus on crossing to the other stairwell and getting downstairs to find Miriam.

At the end of this hallway, Mrs. Monique slowly pushed one of the double doors open with her shoulder before freezing. "Something's moving out there," she said in a hushed tone. She'd pointed the flashlight at the floor, but she now slowly raised it.

With the door open, Susan thought she heard wind shushing through the halls. She strained to listen while the babies quieted as well, and then she heard what sounded like a faint wail, followed by whimpering.

"Fuck," spat Mrs. Monique.

Susan stepped past the librarian to get a better look. A bubble of green light shimmered on the other end of the hall, near the stairwell they'd planned on taking down to the chemistry wing. It was right in front of the music room.

The green light seemed to collapse and expand, as though constantly being generated and absorbed. Susan had to squint to see properly, but she saw someone in the midst of that bubble. When the green light faded for a moment, she recognized the pink helmet—the one she'd given Jenny.

She was sure of it. How many other pink helmets could there be in the building right now? It was on a girl's head; a girl wearing a denim shirt. She was on all fours, hunched over a body, and . . . it looked like she was *feeding*.

A notification burst through Susan's thoughts as she grabbed the door for balance.

**Human (Stage II - Level 16)**

# CHAPTER FORTY-FIVE

# UNSIGHTLY THINGS

Leslie was pacing. She hated pacing, but nervous energy turned her thoughts inside out, and she hated the discomfort throbbing in her chest. Everything felt tight; she didn't have her Xanax with her. She'd hoped Dr. Lee would've taken more of a liking to her, would've protected her—and at first, he did seem pleased by her attention, but as soon as he'd dragged that horrible angel into the library, he'd become obsessed with it.

She'd hated watching him cut into the angel. Hated how it screamed. Hated how it reeked of rot. Then it got free and killed that boy, and Susan shot it up with magic electricity. Now, the creature was suddenly . . . Leslie didn't know how to describe it. It wasn't violent anymore; it seemed to just weep softly, pitifully. And it kept trying to say something, but all she and the others heard was a strange shushing; incoherent whispering.

It made her so mad. Why was it so pathetic and weak, after all the terrible things these creatures had done? And what was going on with Susan? Lightning? Human stage two? The notifications in her head felt like she'd taken too strong of a hit from a joint, and she was on the verge of greening out.

Then it'd seemed like the world was ending again. The building shook. Leslie screamed—and she hated that she'd screamed again—and then Susan, who was looking suddenly stronger and braver with her leg somehow fixed, rushed out with Mrs. Monique. They left her alone with Dr. Lee and the angel, since the other students kept far away.

Dr. Lee hadn't seemed concerned by the rumbling or crashing. He'd continued trying to communicate, shoving his phone into the stupid angel's face and speaking notes out loud. Nobody had paid any attention to the dead boy. The librarian lady had dragged him into the corner and covered his face with a sweater.

For a moment, Leslie had felt bad she didn't know his name, but then she realized nobody was paying attention to her either, and she chewed the inside of her cheek. What should she do? She didn't want to die. She'd need to cozy up to someone. Maybe that girl, Jenny? She seemed like she knew what she was doing, and like the righteous kind of person who wouldn't let anyone else die.

Leslie paced away from the angel to watch the others nervously restack the tables to block the doors, but it was obvious they were waiting in case the others rushed back. Leslie chewed off a fingernail. It clicked between her teeth, and she sucked on it for a moment, then spat it away. It tasted like blood.

Someone made a face at her, and Leslie wrinkled her nose. *Like, bite me. I'm stressed.* She didn't want anyone to see she was trembling. She'd do anything for a joint right now. She and Kevin had been cutting class to smoke when this all started, and she was feeling anxious without her daily fix. Kevin was probably dead, though, the weed probably in his pocket. She sighed.

Shouting erupted in the hall. It sounded like a man, and Leslie perked up. She waited, her arms crossed, as the others pushed tables aside. Two people shone light into the hallway just in case, but it wasn't more angels—it was four students begging to be let inside.

No, wait, there were five of them. The biggest one was carrying the fifth, a boy with his legs cut off.

They stumbled into the library covered in dust and scrapes and bruises, each one with their own helmet and armor. Someone showed them to a table where they could set the injured boy down. A girl was arguing with the biggest boy, whom Leslie recognized as Dulé from her tiny crush on him last year. Except he'd turned her down, so she'd told everyone he was gay.

She didn't approach the new group like the others, bursting with questions and worry and concern. She watched Dulé and the girl argue about going back. He was the only one talking, on the verge of shouting, and she was making sounds of rage but speaking with her fingers. She was deaf.

Leslie couldn't help but admire what the girl was wearing. A knight's shining armor? Even though it was battered and broken and caked in dust, Leslie wanted something like that.

They were arguing about someone's sister stuck back somewhere, but Dulé didn't want to leave the boy. The other two kept saying there was something wrong with the girl they'd left behind. That she had to be an angel or something.

The deaf girl wasn't convinced. She looked sadly at the boy on the table before barging out of the library. Dulé swore loudly, asked the others to keep the injured boy safe, then rushed after the girl.

That all seemed so dramatic. Why didn't they just wait here?

Leslie chewed off another nail, thinking about the photo shoot she had scheduled. It was for a big sneaker company, and she'd been excited to try on their new footwear. Her father was going to pick her up, and she was going to get that big burger after work, and then she was going to throw it up. After that, she'd meet with her tutor.

She'd been struggling with calculus, and her guidance counselor had warned her that if she didn't pass the class, she'd have to take the remedial course over the summer, and there was no way in hell she was giving up her three-week trip to Bali.

She kicked a book on the floor; it slid away and slammed into a shelf. This was all so stupid. She'd been trying to figure out whether or not to take Kevin on the trip, or if it would be better to go single and bump into other cute boys. But what did that matter now? She was stuck in this library, covered in blood, and feeling icky.

In her absentminded pacing, she'd returned near the creature, where Dr. Lee stood and caught her attention.

"Leslie," he said. "Would you mind staying with the angel for a moment? I don't want her left alone."

"Excuse me?" asked Leslie. She looked at him and the angel in disbelief. Why did he care so much about its feelings?

"I want to speak to them," he said, motioning with his blood-covered arm at the new students who'd walked in. "They might know things. And they're high-level." His lips twitched into a smile. His eyes bulged slightly.

She nodded slowly, fear panging in her stomach in a way she couldn't explain. Her teacher seemed like he was staring through her, his mind already working on whatever he had planned, and she barely mentioned one of them was injured before he shuffled toward the others, a skip in his step.

"Okay," said Leslie, squatting down—several feet away from the angel—to look it in the eye. Disgust and anger rolled into a swirling mixture of hatred, and her lips curled. She wanted to kick the ugly one-eyed thing, but she didn't want to break her ankle or something on its orange armorlike skin. What even was that, anyway?

The angel stared back, its orange eye trembling, tears glistening down its orange cheek. The other socket was empty and red, and looking at it made Leslie sick. At least its torn shoulder was covered; she'd hated seeing the exposed flesh and bone. Its remaining arm had no fingers, the same way Jenny's had none.

Leslie inhaled deeply. "What are you?" she asked, knowing it was futile, knowing it was stupid. She knew what it was—an angel. But it had changed twice. First, it had gone from a skinny zombie thing to a more fleshed-out orange thing. Then it'd turned into this: angel stage two. Jenny and Susan were human stage two. What did that mean? Could Leslie reach that, too?

As the angel shut its eye, Leslie tried to concentrate on her thoughts. On herself. On what she was to this system thing. It came to her head like a random daydream.

**Leslie Garcia**
**Human (Level 1)**
**Age: 6,425 days**
**Stats:**
**Power: 2**
**Durability: 2**
**Stamina: 7**
**Agility: 5**
**Stat Points Available: 0**
**Energy Available: 0**

Her eyes went wide. "Are you seeing this shit?" she asked the angel. She shook her head in disbelief. It was laid out so . . . so easily. Like the screens at a cosmetic surgery page where she could choose what to enhance, what to improve. She could change herself and grow as she wanted to!

But she needed to level up like the others had. She needed more of this energy stuff. But how?

"If I kill you, will I get stronger?" whispered Leslie. She bit her lip and shuddered. She'd never killed anything before. While her family freaked out about spiders, if she found one, she'd carry it to her window and set it free, even as her father screamed bloody murder. Roaches and centipedes and moths—she didn't kill them. She just helped them be on their way.

While she didn't want them crawling on her, she didn't think it was right to deny them their lives just because some people thought them unsightly. After all, that's what she'd heard all her life, hadn't she? "Don't eat so much, Leslie." "Leslie, you're turning into a chipmunk." "Leslie, you can't shop in this aisle anymore. None of these will fit you."

Nobody ever expected the overweight girl in middle school to become a model by high school.

She knew most other girls hated her, like Jenny and Susan. They were just jealous, weren't they? *Toxic bitches.* They'd bullied her relentlessly for not fitting their standard of beauty, and now that she'd exceeded theirs, they couldn't stand it. So, when she was fat, nobody liked her. Lose some weight. Eat less cake. Leslie's face is a big mistake. And now that she was thin, she was too pretty; guys wanted her, and girls hated her.

She grimaced, dropping to her knees beside the angel, daring to move closer. "I guess you're like me, then. No matter how much you transform, you're still . . ."

The angel seemed to relax now that she was closer. She couldn't really tell, but it had stopped sniffling and shushing. The angel raised its fingerless hand, the stumps glistening in the light, and Leslie had the strange sensation the creature wanted to touch her.

Its orange palm found Leslie's cheek, and she closed her eyes, leaning into the warmth. Something shifted—somewhere deep inside her. The oddest, strangest sensation.

It was the way she felt about bugs, except in reverse. As though she were the bug, and the angel was admiring her. She shuddered. She'd never felt like this before; never felt someone touch her cheek with such curious gentleness . . .

Then she remembered this angel had bitten through a boy's neck in front of her.

She was about to pull away and run to the other side of the library when the floor rumbled again. Blue light flashed through the air, sparkling and shimmering.

For a second, it looked like Susan's lightning, but it didn't crackle; it didn't sizzle. It simply flashed and vanished, and Leslie felt her face twisting in horror. Her eyes widened. Her nose and lips curled, and a wail escaped her throat. Goose bumps crawled up her arms and the back of her neck, and she couldn't move. She was frozen to the spot—and so was the angel, its one eye wide, its palm still against her cheek. That freakish flash of light had done something to them.

A moan came from the corner. She turned her head, her neck stiff, and saw the dead boy struggling with the sweater draped over him. He clawed at it then rolled onto his belly, the sweater falling away. He twitched. His neck was torn, blood spilling.

He twitched again, and he was looking right at Leslie. His eyes were glowing blue, and Leslie whimpered as he scampered toward her. His arms and legs moved like a spider's, and he was wailing as he stomped over books, wailing as he barreled down on top of her.

She heard shouting. Something shattered and exploded. She heard someone rushing toward her, and then the angel threw itself off the floor and lodged its orange arm into the boy's throat just before those glowing eyes and snapping teeth reached Leslie.

Horrible choking sounds filled the library, his blue eyes frantic. He grabbed the angel's orange arm, but it was buried to the elbow, and blood gushed from his ruined throat. His limbs jerked wildly, and then he went still. He was dead. Again.

Leslie sobbed, staring at the boy, his face warped. He was stuck to the angel's arm; it couldn't shake him loose, and she couldn't bring herself to help.

It was Dr. Lee who wrenched the boy's body off.

He seemed shaken as well, muttering to himself. He threw the boy's body away and then stared down at the angel even as another explosion shook the entire library. "We have to kill it."

That snapped Leslie out of her fright. "What? Why?" She glanced from him to the angel. It seemed to be cowering, looking at something past Dr. Lee.

Dr. Lee drew his katana, a menacing look in his eyes. Leslie glanced back toward the others and saw that much of the library floor had given way. It was falling apart as she watched, the floor bursting as though something was trying to dig out of the ground. She blinked, and one of the students was dragged underneath.

The others rushed through the exit. One of them shouted at her, but she couldn't hear him. Her heart was pounding too hard, and without all the lights, it was much darker. They only had the flashlight beside the angel.

"Don't you see?" spat Dr. Lee, only half his face illuminated. He didn't seem aware at all of the commotion behind him. "The dead are rising. Something horrible is coming." He was shaking like mad. "And those kids explained it perfectly. If we kill them, we can get stronger and stronger, and I want to evolve. I have to be strong. I have to survive this challenge. I have to—"

Holding his katana with both hands, he drew it back, ready to jab it into the angel's chest.

Before she knew what she was doing, Leslie screamed and threw herself on top of the angel, spreading her arms, trying to protect it. Surely he wouldn't stab her?

"There's something coming!" she screamed. "We have to get out of here!"

Dr. Lee glowered and stamped his foot. "Fine," he replied. "You wanted to help me no matter what, right?"

Leslie shook her head, tears spilling down her cheek. She glanced between his legs. Something was cutting through the floor and getting closer, and she was torn between running away and stopping Dr. Lee. "Not like this," she said. "Don't kill her."

That seemed to give him pause. The floor rumbled again, and more of the library gave way. Dr. Lee didn't even flinch as a shelf collapsed beside him. Maybe if she could stall him enough, they could fall downstairs and . . . She wasn't a fighter. She was pathetically weak and helpless. What was she going to do?

When Dr. Lee spoke again, his voice was steely and low. "I want to see how much I'll get for you," he said.

"What?" she whispered as he thrust forward, the point of his katana plunging into her.

It felt like she'd been punched. Hard. She didn't even cry out, just looked over her shoulder at the blade protruding from her back, looked at the bloody hands holding it. Looked at the twisted, ugly look on Dr. Lee's face. She felt its length inside her with every beat of her heart. Every breath.

A roar filled her ears. It sounded like the world was splitting into pieces. The light near them flickered and flashed, and Leslie felt like she was being photographed. She could be on a horror magazine cover: The girl stabbed through by her science teacher.

Dr. Lee withdrew the blade, and Leslie felt every inch of its metallic length slide out of her. "Not dead yet," he noted.

He raised it again, this time aiming higher. Aiming for her heart. And she couldn't even move, let alone say a word. The floor shook. Dr. Lee grunted.

Before he stabbed her again, a dark arm shot out from the floor, fingers coiling around her thigh and squeezing so hard that blood gushed from the wound in her back. She heard what sounded like giant wingbeats, a hissing that made the angel cry out in fear, and then the floor erupted as she got wrenched through.

Whatever was holding her squeezed her leg so hard that lights burst in her head. She was only vaguely aware of the angel and Dr. Lee falling with her. The flashlight spun all around them, and Leslie thought she glimpsed something dark and gigantic with burning blue eyes before everything went dark.

# CHAPTER FORTY-SIX

# LIKE A NAIL HAMMERED INTO WOOD

What does the desecrated angel want? Why's it doing this? Why's it so obsessed with me?"

**I believe it wants to end the Survival Challenge.**

Jenny shuddered like when she was a kid, crawling out of bed in the middle of the night—anxiety making her want to throw up—and the floor would creak. And she'd be terrified she'd wake her mom, who was exhausted from work.

Students crowded around her like a tidal wave of sobbing bodies. They scraped her chest, fingernails snapping off on the red scales of her exoskeleton. They grabbed her arms and legs, but couldn't budge her at all. All they could do was moan and wail and scream in her face, breaths reeking of rot, as though begging her to just do what that angel wanted so they could rest.

*End? End the survival challenge?* She switched back to thinking the thoughts, too afraid to voice what that could mean. *What does that have to do with me? How can an angel end this?*

She wrenched her arm away from a boy who'd wrapped himself around it, groaning and grunting and sliding on the floor as he tried to pull her away. But she wasn't the severed, dying person she'd been before. She wasn't weak and falling apart.

When she wrenched her arm away, he went spinning, tumbling through several bodies. His head bounced off a chunk of rubble with an ugly crack, but he didn't seem to care as blood rushed down his face. He blinked his glowing blue eyes then crawled toward her as others rushed to fill his space.

**Your blood flows through the desecrated angel. I believe it sensed your potential and your spirit. With enough of your blood, with enough living human blood, it can complete its metamorphosis and**

**become a true contender for the Survival Challenge. Your blood is more potent.**

*Its what? Metamorphosis? Like a butterfly? So, if it does that . . . if it finishes that . . . it can kill us all and win?* Jenny flashed back to the cocoon, the blue light surging within it. The way the striped angel kept bringing it more and more blood to drink, all the bodies piled around.

**We witnessed this behavior only once before. The very last Challenge, two thousand years in the past. That was how *He* first entered your world.**

A vision struck Jenny like a nail hammered into wood. She glimpsed a man in long white robes. He was bearded, and his beard and hair were dark and long and flowing as he levitated off the ground, arms extended. His skin was gray and metallic and shifting in that gelatinous way her exoskeleton had when it first formed. Two enormous wings unfurled from his back, white and porcelainlike in appearance.

She knew his name. Billions of people knew his name and worshipped him. A pillar of light engulfed him, connecting from the earth beneath his floating feet to the heavens above, and the desert around him erupted.

With that, the vision ended, leaving Jenny shocked even as two notifications surfaced, one after another.

Two wretched angels shoved their way through the crowd, launching the undead students over their shoulders or crushing their skulls without a second thought. They didn't even pause to bite or anything; they seemed to be barreling through without care, both covered in dust. One was large and female, with brown hair bouncing on top of yellow-green covering.

**Wretched Angel (Level 21)**

The other was male and much smaller, covered in white with blue stripes, and bulging with muscle. Its head ended in a large spike instead of hair; it almost looked like a shark fin cutting through a sea of dead.

**Wretched Angel (Level 25)**

Several tarnished angels ducked in and out of the throb of wailing students. They seemed utterly confused, and Jenny licked the blood off her lips. Stepping back, she pushed through the moaning crowd, toppling whoever was behind her.

Her tendrils snapped, slapping people across the face and shoving them back. Eyeing the approaching angels, she kept thinking about the vision. About *Him.*

She had even more questions for Eve now, but her goal remained the same: She had to stop that desecrated angel; if it got her blood, it would kill everyone else and win. It would get to her world.

But even if she dove into the basement to face the desecrated angel right now, all the undead students and angels would just follow her down. And the thought of suffocating under a pile of her undead classmates—sweaty limbs and desperate and wailing—while also trying to fight that powerful creature that wanted her blood . . .

She inhaled deeply, allowing her chest to expand, fire swirling in the back of her throat.

First things first. Kill the wretched angels—they'd be the most trouble.

Just as she readied to launch herself at them, she realized they hadn't come after her. They were moving further inside the ruined physics lab, toward the crater. She lowered her hatchet, dumbstruck, as the creatures jumped into the basement.

"Christ," whispered Jenny, then she bit her lips. Could she even swear by His name anymore? Fear struck her, like when she'd felt the blue light flash, and the dead came back to life. The church, everything her mother had pushed onto her, the world's largest religions . . . Everything she'd learned and researched in history—it was all crashing down. What did it all mean?

*Okay*, she thought. New plan: Clear the hallway, end all their suffering and put them to rest, and make sure they can't keep coming after her. Then kill that piece-of-shit angel.

With that decided, Jenny dove into the throng of screaming students, hatchet swinging, tendrils swishing through the air.

Jenny recognized some faces. Each one made her stomach twist, but she refused to look at them longer than it took to slash them. She refused to remember their names. She made their deaths swift and easy, her hatchet flashing gold with each strike, removing limbs and slitting throats.

She could use Ignite and end this quickly, but Eve had advised against that. Her hatchet attacks generated energy, while just killing these undead creatures gave her nothing. She'd need all the energy she could collect. Begrudgingly, she'd agreed.

Undead humans gave plus four energy. The angels, either dead or undead, gave plus two regardless. She tried not to think about how she was harvesting pain.

When she came upon tarnished angels who were still alive, she didn't hold back. She slashed them repeatedly, chopping limbs off one at a time before kicking them away to die slowly in the rubble. She wanted them to suffer, to scream in agony, limbless and bleeding out, if only to fill the hallway with something other than the wailing of her fellow students.

She got notifications of their deaths and received energy and experience, but she didn't care. It was the tear-stricken eyes radiating blue light that bothered her. She worked systematically through the crowd as more and more bodies and angels jumped down from above or spilled in from the lobby. She noticed several more wretched angels diving below, and her curiosity and dread grew and grew, even as the numbers racked up in her head.

**+4 Energy**

**+4 Energy**

**+2 Energy**

**+4 Energy**

It felt like the entire school population was wriggling through the ruined hall, even though she knew that couldn't be true. Many of them were already eaten. Many of them were ripped apart, their bodies spread all over the building.

It was a flurry of clothes, colorful and covered in blood. She couldn't meet their eyes; their sneakers were easier to look at. She tried not to think about how they were all really just kids, how they'd all been killed already, torn and chewed to death by angels, and then here she was, killing them again.

Worse still, she kept thinking about biting into them. Their soft, tender flesh, though dead for a while, would still be delicious. Their blood would fill her body so nicely, would satiate her growing thirst.

With horror, she felt a *slurp* through one of her tendrils, and recoiled.

The tendril had burst through a boy's navel, through his hoodie and into his belly button, and it had *slurped* just as the striped angel in the lab room above had with its lips latched onto her ruined nose.

A rippling shiver went through her exoskeleton, as though it was absorbing the blood, making it a part of itself, of her, and growing. A vibration began between her legs that climbed inwardly through her, and it felt *good*. She tasted the metallic sweetness with her entire body, as though every single one of her cells were drinking it in.

Her knees almost went weak; she couldn't stop herself. She kept sucking more and more, the blood coursing through her tendril as the boy dropped to his knees, eyes wide with fright, mouth agape as his face thinned out. He couldn't move at all, and she stood in front of him, tendril fastened to his navel, sucking. Sucking. *Sucking.*

Another one reached for someone else, and she cried out, grabbing the first and wrenching it free from the boy. The blue in his eyes shuddered, and Jenny slashed his neck. Golden light shimmered, blood squirted all over, and she struggled with the urge to latch on to more.

She could latch on to four people at a time and drink her fill, and her exoskeleton would only grow stronger. Shouldn't she do that? Shouldn't she make herself as strong as possible before facing the desecrated angel?

Before she could react, she caught sight of Mr. Wilkins, her guidance counselor. He was a large, round man who wore colorful Hawaiian-print shirts. His glasses were missing, but even with his eyes glowing blue, even with his nose hanging by loose skin, there was a kindness to him that quelled her rising nausea.

She'd only spoken to him a few times, but she missed sitting in his office while he explained her college opportunities and what she could do, interviewing her, trying to learn more about her so he could write a proper recommendation letter. He was always smiling, always prepared to figure things out, and now, his chest was torn open.

Flesh was missing from his neck and sides. Her tendrils latched on to the wounds even as he stomped closer, moaning and reaching for her. His blood would taste so good . . . and he was an adult. Surely that was less guilt inducing? Her tendrils buried into his flesh, all four of them, holding him in place as his arms swung madly for her.

She inhaled noisily through her nose, forced herself to regain control of her tendrils, and tore them off Mr. Wilkins. She ducked as he burst forward, dodging his arms, and swung upward, catching him on the chin with her hatchet and slicing through his face with a burst of golden light.


### +4 Energy


The front of his head split in half as he collapsed. Several students tripped over his large body, and Jenny dashed away from them with a burst of Instant Acceleration to steady herself. To keep her tendrils away from the others.

She was disgusted with herself. Disgusted by how good it felt. Disgusted with how she didn't even feel sick. It was more like she'd just had a delicious meal after a long day at school.

She clenched her fists, her tendrils compressing.

She'd rushed deeper into the collapsed lab room. Rubble crushed into dust beneath her red feet as the undead humans moaned and wailed, clambering and tripping over Mr. Wilkins while trying to get to her.

*No*, she told herself. *No!* She couldn't have their blood. She wouldn't. Not them. Maybe an angel . . . Maybe if she came across another angel . . .

The hunger and thirst twisted into an ugly feeling; she thought she'd rather have another metal rod or two rammed through her stomach. She had the creepy sensation her exoskeleton was growing on its own. Did it have its own needs? This thirst hadn't existed when her tendrils first formed. Was this new? Was she still changing, or had she just not noticed while Susan was here?

*I really am turning into a monster . . .*

The hole in the floor gaped nearby, but the presence she'd sensed down there, that deeply rooted feeling of death, had dissipated slightly. The desecrated angel must be on the move, and Jenny still didn't have a plan.

And there were still so many people left on this floor. The moaning and crying were relentless. She just wanted it to stop.

Someone in a blue uniform stumbled toward her—one of the few adults that stuck out from the crowd. She had a blue hat on, and her face was clawed up, blood gushing down her legs from the ugly gash across her hip. Jenny didn't know the woman by name—she didn't know any of the security guards by name—but she knew their faces.

She knew their smiles as they welcomed everyone every morning and checked for ID. They kept the lines for the buses orderly and neat. And if there was any trouble, they were swift to respond. She'd always heard bad things about uncaring school staff, but she'd never gotten that feeling from anyone here.

Bitter, ugly rage surged through her, and she stomped forward. Her exoskeleton-covered foot cracked the floor, and several chunks around the hole collapsed into the basement, but she didn't care. Jenny launched her hatchet, her tendrils snapping backward to generate more force for her throw.

Her weapon rocketed away from her fingers, and she shut her eyes. She heard the first gruesome *crack*, then heard several more. Blood splattered everywhere, drops landing on her face and scales, and she wiped them away with her tendrils without opening her eyes. They sucked in the blood, and she shuddered, but without being able to see, she realized something.

She could still *sense*. She could still feel the movements in the air and track the locations of the undead hobbling toward her. Sound wasn't just sound that reached her ears—it was vibrations that quivered through her tendrils and into her spine. Taste and smell blended into one sense, and with all that information, a strange image of the hallway formed in her thoughts. The rubble and metal rods and tables, the holes in the ceiling and floor. Even the sweat and drying blood on all the bodies around her.

Jenny threw herself forward, drawing her hatchet back to her hand. Then she swung. And swung and swung and swung. Without vision to distract her, she flexed her consciousness through her tendrils and kept them from latching on to anyone again. No more drinking the blood of innocents.

Breaths and spittle flicked against her face and exoskeleton. Blood splashed her scales, and her armor absorbed every drop. She worked faster than before, each step quicker than the last, each attack flowing into the next. Her tendrils flashed, grabbing arms and pushing students out of balance so she could strike them down with ease.

On and on it went, a cruel and bloody dance. Her lips pressed tight. She hardly dared to even inhale, trusting her every movement to her expanded senses as one by one, the screaming died down.

**+4 Energy**
**+4 Energy**
**+4 Energy**

And she didn't stop until she was sure not a single pair of eyes were left glowing blue. A stifling silence hung over the hallway, and Jenny finally exhaled properly and looked around her. She breathed in through her nose, a sob threatening to break free, but she shoved the emotions down. If she ever got out of this, she knew she'd spend the rest of her life going through the yearbook over and over, counting every student, every teacher and staff member, she'd just cut down.

It was one thing to fight off angels that resembled humans, but to slaughter an entire hoard of dead children forced back to life? Her classmates? People she'd had lunch with and walked to school with from the train station? What if one of them had been Susan or Oliver? What would she have done if they were the ones with glowing blue eyes?

She spat blood, her head throbbing. Her hatchet struck the floor, and she walked away, feeling dizzy, trying not to step on any severed body parts. Golden light filled her hand, and a bottle of water took shape. She remembered Susan's thing: Hydrate.

That brought her some comfort, until she drank too deeply and remembered how it'd felt when blood gushed up her tendrils and into her body. She coughed up water, choking, blinking away tears.

She spotted a girl's head lying near her, accidentally making eye contact. The girl had red hair. Tears were still fresh on her cheek, and she was staring unseeingly into the distance. Her brown skin was marred with blood. She was probably a junior or sophomore, but Jenny couldn't even tell which of the bodies were hers.

But at least it was finally quiet. No more demented crying. They could finally rest.

But Jenny couldn't. Now, she had to get downstairs; had to find that horrible creature responsible for resurrecting the dead and put a hatchet through its face.

It wanted her blood, didn't it? But what if *she* drank *its* blood?

Even as she downed more water, her thirst didn't quench. Her tendrils jerked this way and that, and she knew she wouldn't be properly satisfied from just water.

"Eve," she whispered, thinking again about the vision she'd seen. *Jesus Christ.* The way Eve had mentioned Him, what could that mean? How was this all connected?

Before she could figure out what to ask, blue light flashed again, lightly this time, as though from a distant source. But the same dread sank through her chest like ice. She backed away from the crater, glancing all around her, searching with her eyes and her tendrils for any sign of trouble. But surely everyone was too cut up to be dangerous? Surely the angel couldn't bring them back to life *again?*

As if in response, all the bleeding body parts wiggled. Warbled screams started up like a chorus, and Jenny's face fell. Her heart snapped into pieces.

That red-haired girl's head turned. Her eyes were glowing blue, and she bared her teeth, spitting in Jenny's direction. Severed arms and legs twitched. Several people dragged what was left of their bodies over each other, over rubble, toward her, and it was more than she could take.

Heat blossomed in Jenny's mouth, tendrils whipping through the air as she roared.

"Ignite!"

# CHAPTER FORTY-SEVEN

# ASHES AND PRAYERS

Flames flickered all around Jenny. Smoke and the sulfuric stench of burnt hair and flesh stung her eyes. She'd stopped screaming, stopped trying to burn down the entire world, and all that was left were ashes and scorched rubble and quiet.

She choked on the air, and her exoskeleton shifted. The red armor slithered up her neck to cover her mouth and nose, forming a mask that filtered out the smoke and ash. All the while, she remained on her hands and knees, trying to catch her breath. Her tendrils, now large and more pronounced, swished overhead, whistling through the air. Her insides ached like she'd just thrown up uncontrollably.

The tendrils had grown. They looked more like tentacles rather than thin extensions of her skin, and she realized they *were* tentacles now, glistening like exposed flesh, red and dark and ending in sharp points. She was trying very hard not to think about how they'd grown after sucking blood from that boy, and she definitely didn't want to think about how that had been *her* desire. These things just reacted instinctually, the same way her covering had shifted into a mask so she could breathe without issue. They were remarkably intuitive.

Jenny was in the hall again. She only vaguely remembered standing in the midst of fire, only vaguely remembered billowing flames on everything that moved until she'd run out of strength and collapsed again, catching herself with her tentacles before lowering herself to the floor.

Smoldering bits of cloth drifted down and fizzled out. Like a thick blanket of dark snow, ash covered the hallway, the rubble, the melted steel bars, and everything else. Strewn between the ashes were bones. No skeleton was complete. All the bones were blackened and crumbling, and Jenny tried not to picture the students and adults they belonged to, that she'd cut down only moments ago.

A notification reached her through the dark clouds of her thoughts, and she sighed, her throat aching. She let it fade away.

**Ignite (Tier 2)**
**Generate flames from any part of your body.**

*That's nice*, she thought. *But I just set fire to a bunch of people from my school that I chopped into bits so I could get the energy . . .*

**Jenny Huang**
**Human (Stage II - Level 24) (Blooded)**
**Age: 6,801 days**
**Stats:**
**Power: 30**
**Durability: 20 (+30)**
**Stamina: 30**
**Agility: 30**
**Stat Points Available: 14**
**Energy Available: 1048**

That was . . . so much energy. She shuddered. Plus four for every attack on a human; plus two for every angel. Harvesting their pain. On top of that, there'd been several tarnished angels thrown in the mix, and all the numbers and notifications had become a mess in her head.

She only felt hollow. She should feel worse, and she felt terrible that she didn't, but there was only so much despair and horror she could feel before it turned to rage. There was nothing left to bury, no real way to assess whose ashes were whose. Nothing to put into urns. Nothing to return to their families. She thought it was truly sick that the ashes of the angels were mixed in with the ashes of the humans.

"I'm going to murder that thing," she swore, eyes shut tight, tentacles swishing. Fury swelled hot and bright as though she'd used Ignite and swallowed all the flames.

Explosions shook the building; distant booms rumbled through the walls and floor, but she couldn't be sure where they were coming from.

From above, where Susan had gone? Or below, where the desecrated angel was on the move?

It had to be from below, she decided. Most of the upper floors should be cleared by now, with everything coalescing here. And even if something should attack Susan, Mrs. Monique or Jenny's babies would protect her. Her babies seemed indestructible, and she was glad she'd sent them with her. All she had to do now was finish off the desecrated angel so it could stop forcing the dead back to life.

She didn't want to think about Susan or Oliver or one of her babies with glowing blue eyes, their minds warped by whatever the angel had done. Could she kill any of them? Would she let them rip her to pieces? Was that how the desecrated angel planned on winning?

Again, she pictured what Eve had shown her: the religious figure worshipped by so much of the world . . .

It wanted her blood, didn't it? The angel was trying to win and get to her world, that much was clear. And it had some connection to Him. Some enemy of Eve. The reason Eve was here at all.

*Make it make sense.*

Light flashed. Her hatchet returned to her hand, and she stomped back into the ruined lab room, kicking up ashes, smoke swirling around her.

Eve wanted Jenny to birth it into her world. The angel wanted Jenny so it could . . . become more human and qualify to win? Was that similar to how she'd become less human? How she had these tentaclelike things now that responded like limbs?

There were so many things she wanted more answers for, but what kept surfacing in her thoughts were thoughts of God, the expansion of the West, and all the detrimental effects of colonialism. The civilizations and peoples and histories plundered and lost.

Did it all tie back to Him? *For Gold, God, and Glory . . .*

Her heart raced at the thought. She felt like she was back in Sunday school, questioning the lady trying to teach them lessons from the Bible, questioning how so many things didn't quite match, even though she'd taken comfort in the good.

She'd always thought of God not as the disastrous, vengeful figure in the texts but as a force for good. As the universe. Even though Jenny had hated the church and her mother's preaching and how everyone acted so hypocritically. How could you preach kindness and still find space in your heart to hate?

They'd made her feel different, asking questions about where she was from and what she ate and the language she spoke. But she had been born in the same city, she ate the same foods, and she literally spoke the same language. Still, they ostracized her until she questioned herself and was unsure who or what she was supposed to be. It'd only gotten worse when she started having feelings for Susan.

But how could she reconcile that with what Eve had shown her?

Things sort of clicked into place. "*Whoever eats my flesh and drinks my blood remains in me, and I in them.*" It was one of the few lessons that had stuck with her, mostly because it was creepy and gross and seemed to stick out of the entire message of peace and love.

She wondered if that was why her prayers had never been answered. All she'd ever prayed for, cried all night and pleaded for, was peace and love. For her mom to be less stressed. For things to be less hurtful at home. And that had never come true. God had always let her down.

Had she been praying to an angel this entire time? What even was He? Was He like Eve?

**He has permeated through your world for thousands of years, gaining the most over the last two thousand. He has rewritten your histories, scorched civilizations and rooted out their victors, and declared Himself the one single truth.**

This time, it wasn't visions that filled her head but things she'd read and imagined. Important things from history classes: the cultures lost to war and disease, genocides spanning the globe; the explorers claiming lands for themselves and God . . .

Eve had shown her gods and goddesses before, and she realized every single culture's beliefs were based on some truth. These were the challenges that had led to the gods she loved reading about. They had truly existed in her world; they had been humans, just like her.

**The Survival Challenge's existed for millenniums long forgotten; before Him, before even the worlds had taken shape. It is a means to nurture change and nurture growth. A means for the spiritual to become flesh. Gods and monsters and all the stories that have shaped and expanded your world.**
**But He has perverted the Survival Challenge. He wishes to rule every world, and with yours in His possession, with the material world finally under His control . . . there will be no end. All will be subjugated to His will . . .**

*But didn't He already win, though? The vision you showed me? The last survival challenge?* She pictured Him again, the flowing hair and beard . . . the pillar of light as countless bowed before him. *He made it to my world. He's everywhere. People all over worship Him.*

**The man whose mind he consumed—the man your mother worships pinned to a cross—he fought. He defied Him and sacrificed himself to stop Him.**
**The part of Him that reached your world was separated from the flesh, trapped as spirit in a material world. Permeating. Adjusting. Shaping your civilization for two thousand years in preparation for this Challenge.**

*Shouldn't He be here, then? Is He here?* Dread filled her all of a sudden. The same dread she'd get from church, from her mother. That she was doing something wrong; that she had sinned and was being watched.

**I am here. I have protected you.**

That didn't really comfort Jenny. She kept thinking about that other world, the one she'd woken in twice. The first time, meeting Eve as the three-headed figure. The second, when she'd died, and the world had tried to swallow her whole. Eve was only using her too, just as He had used the man she knew as Jesus. It was all a game to them, but there was even more weight on Jenny's exoskeleton-covered shoulders now.

It was all on her back, wasn't it? Not just keeping Susan and Oliver safe, but her entire world. Wasn't that too much? She was just a kid! All she'd wanted was to get out of the city and live her life. All she'd wanted was to tell Susan how she felt. But that all seemed so far away and pointless now.

*Even if I stop this thing . . . then what? It only ends when one person is left, so everyone has to die anyway. But what happens if I die?*

**Then we fail, and He will reign across all worlds till the end of time. Our fates are intertwined, Jenny Huang.**

*But I'm stuck here. That means you're stuck here, and I'm not just going to . . .*
She pictured it: Her tentacles reacting before she could help it, snapping through the air. She saw herself cutting everyone down, everyone in the library. Susan's hurt face. Oliver, who was already nearly dead. It wouldn't be too difficult to rip them apart. After all, she'd just cut down nearly a hundred students.

She could win. She could emerge as a goddess in her own right, something to rival the legends of the ancient world, something to stop Him. Was that what Eve wanted?

Eve didn't respond, and Jenny wasn't sure how to push the question. She'd wasted enough time. *I'm going to find a way,* she thought to Eve, afraid to voice the words. Afraid she might fail.

So she spoke them to give them more weight, to generate some false confidence that she hoped would turn real. "I'm going to save them. I don't give a fuck about your challenge bullshit or Him. If Susan's not there . . . then fuck the world."

She shook with rage and cold determination, trembling. The new fingers of her left hand, the fingers that Susan had grown for her and were now covered in the red exoskeleton, curled into a glistening fist. She squeezed so hard, picturing Susan crying as she stuck her shining arm into Jenny's chest, that her fist caught fire. Flames licked up her entire arm, illuminating the ruined lab room and burning hot and ferocious.

*This is going to be useful.* Jenny glanced back at the hallway, half hoping Susan would come back. That her babies would rush back to her side. She was preparing to jump into the basement, and she found herself feeling alone.

There was no point in feeling alone.

She focused her attention on her feet, and her exoskeleton shifted, melting and spreading forward till five vicious claws formed around her toes. She did the same for her fingers, the ones curled around her hatchet as well as the ones on fire.

With her tentacles, she tasted the air below, but nothing lay waiting beneath her. The angel had to be up to something, but what? Why had more blue light flashed? Where had the wretched angels gone? Her babies, the ones that had fallen during the cocoon's eruption, weren't down there either, nor were the dozens of bodies that the angel must've woken back up.

All she felt when she reached with her tentacles were her own wants, the twisted mixture of hunger and thirst that thrummed through her muscles and made her belly ache. Her throat was parched, and there was an ache in her tentacles like she desperately needed to work them out.

She was glad Susan wasn't here. The desire to kill. To hunt. To feed. It was nearly overwhelming, and she remembered how soft Susan's skin had looked . . . What if her tentacles latched on to Susan?

Would she be able to stop herself?

*Kill. Kill. Kill.*

She wanted to kill something. Needed to. Not another undead creature, but something living. Something trying to eat her. She could just about feel herself stabbing through an angel with a tentacle and sucking and sucking and slurping all their precious blood. It would be *so* satisfying.

The cravings threatened to overpower her. If it weren't for her makeshift mask, she'd be drooling. Stranger still, she found it nearly arousing. Her body seemed to be reacting to her bloodlust, and finally, she understood. *Bloodlust Ecstasy.*

Jenny understood why Eve might have chosen her. Why Eve kept pushing her this was who she'd been all along. A vicious, bloodthirsty monster pretending to be human.

She took a step forward and plummeted down into the basement, landing with a heavy crash as she broke through a desk below. She prayed earnestly for something to attack her—so she could quench this thirst.

# CHAPTER FORTY-EIGHT

# THE BASEMENT

Her tentacles whisked around her, smashing desks into pieces, slamming against the metal filing cabinets that lined the walls, and slapping rubble into dust. She was searching. Seeking. Sounds and scents and vibrations climbed through their lengths and into her spine, giving her a rough mental vision of her surroundings even before her eyes could adjust. Shadows scattered everywhere as she raised her burning fist.

She knew where the ruined office desks and chairs were, where the rubble-crushed things lay, the metal bars sticking out. She even felt the cocoon, and she stepped off the desk to crush it beneath her feet. It crunched, something thick and creamy oozing out like melted cheese, and the scent reminded her of how everything had tasted like batteries when she'd messed around with an electromagnet and shocked herself.

Nothing was alive; that much was clear. Nothing she could slaughter; nothing she could drain. There had been bodies here—she saw the smeared streaks of blood, the bloody handprints glistening by her firelight—but there were no signs of her babies.

She was sure she'd seen them sucked into the crumbling floor, and had been hoping they'd be waiting for her. Which was strange, because they weren't even really her babies, but still, she'd hoped. It would've been comforting, and now she wondered if proximity to the desecrated angel had turned their allegiance over.

The door of the office was off its hinges, cracked and on the floor like a broken bridge between the room and the hallway. The surrounding wall was mostly collapsed, and cracks jutted through whatever was left standing. The mist seemed to be thicker down here, swirling all around her and shrouding her vision just as the smoke had upstairs.

Jenny moved slowly, leaving the wreckage of the office behind her. To her left were more offices, the guidance counselor rooms, and the health office where they handed out free condoms. The hall curved around the building, leading into the gym locker rooms.

To her right was the rest of the hall beneath the physics hallway, and at the end of it was the stairwell Susan, Mrs. Monique, and her babies had taken to the third floor. Directly ahead was the large central hall of the basement. It was lined with lockers, but large doors on the right side opened into the cafeteria. Along the left wall was the entrance to the gym.

She adjusted her grip on her hatchet, tentacles at full alert for any sign of danger. She saw bloody streaks, footprints, and handprints, and the eerie quiet reminded her of the second floor, when she'd been searching for Oliver and found bodies missing before discovering Miriam stuck in the closet. But this time, she knew the bodies in the basement hadn't been dragged away. They'd gotten up themselves.

But to where? Shouldn't they be coming after her? Wasn't that why they'd been resurrected?

Her tentacles expanded as far as they could go, undulating as they sensed for any sign of anything. Any disturbance in the thick air of the Veil, any sound, any scent. But all that came back was the metallic scent of blood, the ashes clinging to the blood drying on her scales, and . . .

A strange feeling she couldn't quite place at all. It was like walking into your apartment, and there being a hint of an odd odor, or maybe a sound that didn't belong, or something was out of place. Like the feeling she'd get when she knew her mother had been through her bedroom, shuffling through her stuff. She'd known right away something was wrong. Her stomach would tighten, and her heart would quicken, anxiety sinking into her chest.

It was like when back in middle school, she'd come home from school, and there'd be an empty bottle of something foul smelling. Her mom would be waiting with a hanger or a wooden spoon, and Jenny would know she'd done something wrong.

Her mother would devolve into screaming fits and attack, and Jenny would try not to cry or scream because that'd only make things worse. And all the while, Jenny would go through everything in her mind, desperately trying to figure out the problem, trying to fix it in any way possible.

That was how Jenny felt, frozen in the hallway, eyes shut, using her tentacles to their fullest. Running her tongue over her new teeth, barely daring to breathe, she squeezed her hatchet's handle. She wasn't powerless, she reminded herself. She was a monster now. A monster who wanted blood. *I'm the one hunting. They should be terrified of me.*

Her heart wouldn't stop thudding violently. Something was definitely wrong— but what?

The feeling emanated from her right, from the cafeteria. Something terrible. She knew the desecrated angel must be in there, but by now, she'd memorized the dread she associated with it—a mixture of disgust and anger. No, this was something else. There was something else in there; something the angel was doing or creating. It was trying to end the survival challenge, after all.

Her scales bristled. She was feeling more and more tense, expecting something to attack any moment now, and then a faint cry shivered through the tension.

It was so faint she'd only felt its slight vibration through her tentacles—a cry laced with agony and fear. But it wasn't coming from the cafeteria; it came from the opposite direction, from behind her, in the gym.

Focusing every sense, her tentacles reached for the doors. For a second, she thought it was the angel messing with her, making a sound to draw away her attention before it attacked, but she knew she'd have to check. What if someone was hurt? It hadn't sounded like the moans or wails of the undead; she'd heard those enough times to know exactly what they felt like.

It was just like with Miriam. A little sound. Something out of place. What if someone was hiding in the locker rooms, or under the bleachers? She knew there was a secret space inside them when the teachers rolled them up against the wall; she'd dropped her phone in there one time. Someone could easily be hiding in there.

Making up her mind—and trying to convince herself she wasn't chickening out from facing the desecrated angel—she pushed the latch and stepped into the declining hall that led to the gym.

Her burning hand revealed the bloody smears on the wall. Again, no bodies, but she saw an arm wriggling, the fuzzy pink cloth of some cute sweater wrapped around it. Red flesh glistened on the opposite side of the fingers crawling toward her.

Jenny knelt and held the hand. She would never know whom it belonged to. The fingernails scraped the red covering of her burning palm as flames devoured the severed limb till nothing remained but ash. Jenny kept going, descending further underground, until she got to the double doors that opened into the gym.

The doors had glass windows in them, and her heart nearly stopped at the sight.

It was utter destruction. The bleachers that lined the leftmost wall were torn apart and smashed in several places. Craters covered the walls, cracks spreading between them. There must've been a massive fight here. Were these the explosions she'd heard earlier? The hardwood floor was littered with debris, chunks of ceiling, and bookshelves, but what made her want to scream was the sight above.

The gym was right beneath the library.

The gym was built deeper into the ground than the rest of the basement, giving it higher ceilings, but something had managed to tear through them anyway.

Ugly gashes left lights swinging from their cables like vines and exposed the library above. She could still see some bookshelves and tables that hadn't fallen through, but no sign of any of the people who had been there.

Jenny shoved the door open so hard, the glass shattered and the heavy metal door sailed across the basketball court to lodge itself into a crater on the opposite wall. Dust rained down.

Tentacles swishing like mad, Jenny rushed through the gym, stomping debris into nothing with her claws, searching for any sign of Oliver or Dr. Lee, or any of the others. She came to a stop halfway across the gym, turning this way and that. The large windows were shattered, and there was a body stuck in the glass, wriggling and failing to get free.

Jenny stared at the bloody creature, realizing it was an undead angel, since it was naked and no notification turned up. Blue eyes shone against the gloomy backdrop of the Veil, and the pathetic sight only made Jenny angrier.

She sensed a shift in the air behind her, a slight breeze, and turned to see a gaping hole in the wall near the corner to her right. Something had burst through the bricks, exposing the weight room, where dumbbells and equipment were twisted and scattered. And through the opposite wall of the weight room was another hole leading into the hallway Jenny had just stepped into the gym from.

If she'd walked further down the hallway, she would've seen the hole from the outside. Something had come through the walls to get here, and Jenny knew it had to have been the desecrated angel. It had dug its way through the basement to get to the library, the biggest source of remaining living human blood in the building. That's what she would've done, too.

Her heart sank, and she smashed a bookshelf into bits of wood with a tentacle. The library was supposed to be a safe place! She'd sent Oliver and the others there . . . but there was no sign of them here. And had Susan made it there with Miriam? What if they'd died from the fall? The gym was double the height of any hallway or room. What if they'd been dragged into the gym and butchered, only to awaken with glowing blue eyes? Had her worst fear come true?

She cried out in frustration, but it was muffled by her exoskeleton mask. The basketball nets were broken, the glass backboards shattered, and the pole was bent backward, as though the angel had used it to climb higher before reaching the ceiling. She grabbed a table, recognizing it as the heavyset librarian's desk, and chucked it at the windows. It twirled, spilling books and paper before colliding with the undead angel and rocketing into the Veil, vanishing from sight.

She heard the faint cry again; this time with her own ears. Breathing hard and trying not to panic, Jenny scanned every inch of the debris. Maybe someone had survived. Maybe the desecrated angel hadn't been able to get everyone. That was when she spotted something bright orange and glistening, and her blood ran cold. It was the covering of a wretched angel.

It was trapped under a chunk of ceiling, a metal rod piercing through its back. The creature was missing an eye, but it reached for Jenny with a fingerless hand, crying and covered in blood.

Jenny approached it, fuming with rage. Her arm burned harsher and harsher till the flames towered over her. Her tentacles writhing, she was just about to smack its head into the floor and crush its skull when the notification registered.

### Angel (Stage II - Level 10)

She stopped walking and glared at the creature, a tentacle hovering over its orange forehead. Its eyes weren't blue. And the notification made no sense. An angel? Stage two? But it looked exactly like the wretched angels . . . And then Jenny noticed that its one eye wasn't white and empty. An orange iris stared back at her.

Was this . . . Was this like the opposite of her Severed Spirit?

The creature struggled, raising its arm again, and Jenny got the distinct feeling it was begging for help. Pleading. But its struggling caused the rubble to shift, and the creature cried out, banging the floor with its palm before spitting up blood. Fresh blood.

The scent hit Jenny as though she'd slammed into it with Instant Acceleration. Saliva pooled in her mouth, and her stomach twisted. She tried to keep away, even as her feet moved on their own. Her tentacles drifted forward, curious, hesitant despite the unceasing hunger clawing at her insides. A small part of her was struggling to hold back. *Don't kill this one. It's different.* She could feel her heart throbbing in her brain, like her mind would fall apart if she didn't have at least one slurp of blood.

And then the angel spoke.

A hissing shush, which sounded more like a snake spitting, cut through the agonizing thirst like her hatchet through flesh. A shudder flickered up her spine; she'd heard the angel with her ears, her eyes, and her tentacles. A language that spoke with its entire body.

Jenny dropped to her knees, the hardwood cracking beneath her from the impact. The angel had touched its palm to Jenny's trembling tentacle, and the hissing climbed like electricity, like she'd touched a live wire. Color and light burst through her head as if she'd been hiding in the dark for hours and hours before stumbling into daylight.

She found herself falling. Falling from the sky . . . No. She was falling *toward* the sky. She was flying!

She was flying. Her tentacles were gone, replaced instead with enormous wings that shimmered in the warm sunlight. She counted four wings in total, two on each side, each one about as large as her upper body, and beating in sync.

Little scales fluttered away with each heavy wingbeat, catching the light and sending rainbows circling every which way. She ascended higher and higher, nearing the clouds, and that's when she saw them: towers of glass. Except they weren't like any of the towers she was accustomed to seeing walking around Manhattan.

These weren't built upward. Instead, they hung from the underbellies of clouds, jutting downward, rows upon rows in neat geometric patterns. This must be the world of angels. These must be their structures, their cities.

But how was she seeing this? *Feeling* this?

This wasn't anything at all like the times Eve had shown her visions. This was . . . *real*. Like she was actually there, the wind curling beneath her wings, the sun soaking into her . . . it wasn't exactly flesh. She looked down to see her form—womanly, but instead of skin, there was only shifting orange light. Her arm looked like Susan's had when she'd been brought back to life. Her red covering, her scales, everything was gone.

Warm wind rose from underneath her, propelling her higher and higher. The nearest city, the nearest group of towers hanging like stalagmites, grew closer and closer, and Jenny realized she was inside the angel's mind. She was seeing what the angel saw, feeling what the angel felt.

Countless other angels fluttered around the towers, climbing into hexagonal windows and vanishing inside. It was almost exactly like watching crowds of people crossing streets back home. The towers seemed to be made of glass, but they weren't see-through, and she wondered about their community. Their culture. Did angels have to go to school too?

Every single one of them shimmered, and as Jenny drew nearer, she noticed that their light was always shifting. Sometimes green, sometimes blue and purple, changing as they beat their large wings and flew around the towers.

Joy bubbled inside her. She was home. *This* was home.

And then a shadow swept across the cities, churning them into dark, angry storm clouds. A sound like a blaring trumpet, loud and painful, then the sound of the sky ripping apart, shook everything. Towers crumpled and collapsed, sinking away from the clouds, and Jenny glanced down to see the world open beneath them like a mouth. Angels plummeted like shooting stars, their lights trailing behind them in fading sparks.

Her heart broke. Her ears bled—the blaring sound continuing to assault her. Her wings beat desperately as she struggled to stay afloat. And that was when a voice, a voice with the texture of sandpaper scraping against her skull, forced its way into her head and demanded she *fall*.

# CHAPTER FORTY-NINE

# THROUGH THE EYES OF AN ANGEL

*Fall.*
*Fall.*
*Fall . . .*

It wasn't a phrase or word in her head. No thoughts, no notifications, nothing like that. It wasn't at all like how Eve communicated; it was more like instinct, like watching the streets from the top floor of a skyscraper: the tingling in your feet, the sinking feeling in your chest. An obsessive pressure, a tug, that kept repeating over and over, growing more and more forceful. A little voice in the back of your head that asked what would it be like?

Clouds spilled like lakes collapsing into waterfalls. Jenny strained hard, beating her four wings furiously, trying to resist the pull. But how do you resist gravity?

It seemed to swallow light itself. The bright blue sky, the clouds, the angel cities, and the angels themselves. Everything darkened.

All the while, the urge to *fall* rampaged through her body—a wordless incantation, a demonic mantra made entirely of manic thoughts.

Angels plummeted, screaming, their wings tearing, the light of their bodies streaking like the tail of a meteor burning in the atmosphere. Their buildings collapsed into vapor as electricity crackled out of the shadow below, shattering what was left of the clouds, shattering the world.

And Jenny, as well as billions of angels, tried as best as she could to resist. Her instincts, the angel's instincts, told her to go up, to break the surface of the sky and escape this pull, this horrid, wretched pull, but it was more than Jenny could handle. Her body succumbed.

Gravity won. Her form gave out, twitching and fracturing, and she dropped face forward, feeling as though something had jammed its hand in her mouth, grabbed her bottom jaw, and was trying to wrench it off. Her feet kicked behind her as her wings beat over and over, but the air itself betrayed her. Tornado winds blew her toward the darkness, and then she heard an ugly snap behind her neck.

A searing, burning sharpness ran down her shoulder blades accompanied by the sound of fabric tearing, and she screamed as her wings were ripped from her back. They disintegrated into feathery sparks of light, the bright orange light of her body shimmering uncontrollably until, finally, she dropped into the gaping darkness with a splash.

It was just like jumping into water. Everything muffled. Everything blurred. She opened her mouth to scream, and darkness bubbled down her throat.

Slowly, she realized the other angels were with her, all of them sinking through the dark abyss, their various colors shining and mixing and out of focus, and it was like staring at pictures of distant galaxies, of nebulas. So many colors blurring into one another, shifting.

A crackling sound emanated, like ice cracking. At first, she thought it was all around her, then she realized it was coming from within. Her body was solidifying, the orange light turning gooey and jellylike. She couldn't breathe. Pressure closed in around her chest, her neck, and a jolt ran down from between her eyes to her navel.

Her bones had taken form—that had been the crackling sounds—before flesh blossomed from each one. Her body felt as though she'd been tossed into a blender. Agony twisted through her as veins and arteries wrapped around her muscles. Her stomach burst into throbbing existence, followed by all the other organs popping into her chest like flowers unfurling. Blood gushed through her as soon as her newly formed heart started beating.

Her light faded, swallowed up by her flesh, and one by one, the surrounding lights faded away as well, leaving her and all the angels lost, falling through the darkness, blind. She couldn't breathe. She was choking. There was no air; she had lungs now, but there was no air. She clawed at her throat, her eyes bulging, her heart pounding. Her chest was going to implode.

Something opened underneath. Another jagged, ugly thing, but light erupted from it. A welcoming light that brought sensation back—but no. That was cruel. Brutal. Her body ached with agony. Her flesh boiled on her bones. She wasn't sure if she'd heard the others screaming first, or if she'd started screaming from the pain, but countless angels screamed and screamed, and then she saw it.

The new hole wasn't just a tear through this empty world—it was a mouth. Two rows of shining white teeth emerged. Two eyes without irises opened, bloodshot and massive. Long white hair floated all around the dark face, and Jenny was swallowed whole.

Teeth snapped shut, jetting her deeper into the mouth. Darkness once again embraced her, and she was floating, as though this new darkness were water, not just emptiness. But if she didn't get some air, she would burst. She would die.

Every single muscle burned till she was sure they would all snap off her limbs. Light emerged from above her, shimmering brightly, like she was at the bottom of a pool. Blurry figures emerged at the top, and she kicked hard, trying to escape, trying to reach the top.

When her head finally broke the surface and she could suck in a desperate breath of air, light flashed all around. Light that hurt her eyes so much, it felt like someone had plunged daggers into her sockets. The screaming only grew louder, and she blinked and struggled as the lights flashed and flickered, breathing hard. Something was bubbling inside her—a terrible, dangerous feeling that she could only describe as malice. A hunger so wretched it threatened to consume her.

And that presence. That incantation in her head. It wasn't *fall, fall, fall* anymore. Now it was *eat, eat, eat.*

Everything rumbled as she pulled herself out of the darkness. Her hand found the surface solid; it wasn't at all like water. She got a distinct feeling that climbing out meant she could never return. It was a one-way entrance.

She'd climbed out halfway when her blinding surroundings shook violently. Her face fell flat against the dark surface, and then the lights went out. It no longer hurt to open her eyes. She could see. She could breathe. And now, she must feast.

But where was she?

Blinking, she looked up and saw crowds of students clambering to get away from her. Tear-stricken faces, screaming and shouting in terror. Climbing onto the large tables of the cafeteria.

She was in the cafeteria! It was dark, the lights had gone out, but she could see the orange-and-white walls. And there were so many people still alive!

She opened her mouth to beg them for help, but all she managed was a warbled scream.

Her limbs felt hollowed out. She was just skin stuck to bone. Decaying flesh. Where was her light? That glorious, beautiful, shimmering orange that her body once was?

She tried to stand, her bare feet on top of the darkness. She had no balance, and she stumbled. She'd never walked before; she'd never had to use her feet to support her weight. She couldn't remain upright, and she fell forward, catching herself with her palms. Her fingers didn't sink into the hole beneath her, but she saw her face reflected in its rippling surface.

Her ugly, ruined face. Her teeth sticking out, her gums receding. Her brown skin marred. And her eyes . . . Her eyes were empty. Her wings were gone, and she'd been forced to become something she wasn't.

And the hunger . . . the violent, revolting hunger that told her if she just had more blood, if she could just get more flesh, she could be complete. She could recover and be strong again, and maybe her wings would grow back.

Children surrounded her. Students. Lunch aides. People were crying, and many of them were staring in utter shock and disbelief, still holding trays of cereal and milk and fruit.

On instinct, she lunged at the nearest child, throwing herself at him and landing on his chest, knocking his tray over. Her teeth closed around his throat before he could even protest.

## Blooded.

Something filled her head. A thought. A word? A message. Was it from Him? Was it His will? She wasn't sure. She didn't care. All that mattered was the hunger. All that mattered was the burst of sweetness as soon as his hot blood spurted into the back of her throat.

Milk mixed with blood on the tiled cafeteria floor. As she chewed through muscle and swallowed, she felt strength coursing through her. She looked up to see other bodies. So many meals, just waiting to feed her, to replenish her.

The other angels crawled out of the darkness and rushed into the crowd, then it became a feeding frenzy—a storm of screaming and blood. Her mind throbbed violently. The blood tasted better than anything possibly could, and she knew she'd need more. The agony. The pain. The unrelenting promise that pushed her forward. *Eat. Eat. Eat.*

It became a blur of flesh. Thoughts filled her head with every kill, every bite. Every time she swallowed, words and numbers appeared. She was only vaguely aware of them. Her level climbed. She gained stat points. But what could that matter when it couldn't fill her belly?

She chased the rushing crowd up a flight of stairs, leaping from one body to the next: Boys screaming as she buried her fingernails in their faces and bit a chunk off their shoulders. Girls whose chests split open so she could lick their still-beating hearts. How soft they all were, the little ones. How easy they were to pin down and bite.

She fed all the way to the main lobby. Students pounded on the glass doors, screaming for them to be let out, but the doors would not open. And beyond the glass was only the Veil, the swirling darkness where she'd been unable to breathe. Now, they were trapped. Now, she and her kind could feast. Could heal. Could recover. And maybe He would free them once they'd eaten. Maybe He would allow them to return home.

Why were they crying? She tore at their clothes, reached for their faces. Their bones snapped with such ease. Their guts spilled so freely, just begging her to slurp them up. But they kept struggling, kept fighting back. Punching her. Grabbing her hair. Screaming in her face as she salivated and spit and hissed, but she and the other angels worked quickly through the terrified group.

Didn't they understand? She needed them. She had to do this. If she didn't eat, she'd perish; she'd die. It was His order. He wanted this. They're His people too. Why couldn't they just obey?

The feast in the lobby was an uproar that ended too soon. She nudged a woman, stroked a boy's hair. Blood was stuck in her nose. She puked and tripped over a pile of dead. Dead meat was still. Still blood didn't taste anywhere near as sweet.

She clawed at a twitching body, and then she heard sounds. The others hissed loudly, and there *she* was. She recognized herself, bent over beside Susan, adorned in shiny red armor. She'd puked as well. It was her. She was staring at herself.

Jenny's mind shattered. Caved in. Expanded. Hurt.

Everything hurt. She saw the fight. Saw the struggle. Angel after angel hissed and screeched and went after her and Susan.

How dare they? How dare they hurt her? Jenny the angel threw herself at the nearest attacker and bit into their throats. She leaped to another, moving ever closer to herself and Susan, and was just about to turn, to help herself fend off the attackers, when a blinding surge of pain tore through her side like a wildfire. She screamed and limped away, collapsing, clutching her shoulder with her one remaining arm. She'd hurt herself. She'd slashed off her own limb. Why?

How could she do this to herself?

The fight continued, and she watched from the floor, bleeding profusely, until she heard a roar. An order. A command. From another angel; a stronger one. Her vision faded when she sensed the Greater Ones approach. They were strong—too strong. They were going to kill her!

The blue covering flashed as the blonde Greater One bit her fingers off, and the larger black one launched itself forward. They'd hurt her! They'd hurt Susan!

And she was powerless. Something stomped on her back, and she heard a disgusting crack from her lower spine. Blood gushed out of her cut shoulder, and she lost all sense of self.

It wasn't until light flooded the hallway, light that burned her eyes and made her want to scream, that she woke up. A bunch of blurry silhouettes moved around her; she heard voices, shouting.

She tried to stand, pushing herself up with her one arm, but her legs wouldn't work. Pain burned at the base of her spine, and she collapsed, her nose striking the floor. She threw up again. But she saw. She saw and recognized Mrs. Monique carrying her limp body out. She saw one of the boys picking up Susan. They turned the corner, vanishing down the hall where the library was.

Why were they taking her away from herself?

Crying, hissing, and screeching, Jenny pulled herself forward. She slapped the floor with her one hand and dragged her body, sliding on her own blood, crawling over students and angels alike.

She moved at a snail's pace, passing in and out of consciousness. *Eat. Eat. Eat.* The feeling raged in her head, and she licked blood off the floor. It did nothing to ease her. There was only one hope. Only one way to become human again: She had to eat herself. She was sure of it.

She'd managed to drag her body near the library when the doors opened and light hit her again. She shut her eyes, hissing and convulsing, and when she opened them, she saw herself. She saw herself towering over her, a look of hatred and rage on her own face. She wore the pink helmet, the flashlight duct-taped to the top shining into her eyes.

She swore she felt them sizzling, but she couldn't look away; she couldn't blink. She stared back at herself, hissing, pleading for just one bite, anything to end the horrible, cruel feeling in her head. *Eat. Eat. Eat.*

And then her shield came down onto her one hand with a decisive thud, slicing right through her fingers, and the connection between herself and the angel faltered.

Jenny, in the angel's body, was dragged into the library by her hair, screaming, struggling. But she couldn't grab anything; she couldn't fight. Her legs refused to work. Then she was on a table, and Dr. Lee was on top of her. He wanted a tooth; he wanted an eye. She strained, trying to break free. Couldn't they see it was her? Didn't they know? She was in here!

A soft voice cut through the malice. It was Susan, her sweet scent. Jenny picked up on that and held it firmly between her thoughts as she stared at her: the blue armor, her blue hair, her tired face. Maybe—just maybe—if she ate her, then she could break free. She'd be rid of Him. She could just be.

Light flickered. Someone shouted. Her eye slipped out of its socket, and the grip on her loosened, giving her enough leeway to move. She twisted her body as soon as someone was near, and she bit through their throat. She wasn't sure whose, but it wasn't Susan's.

**Ranking Bonus!**
**Tarnished Angel → Wretched Angel**
**Congratulations on breaching the first threshold!**
**+30 Stat Points have been awarded.**
**Exoskeleton Activated.**

Orange light burst out of Jenny's—the angel's—navel, covering her completely, solidifying, protecting her, strengthening her. With hot blood soothing her parched throat, she threw herself off the floor and onto Susan, who screamed. Who screamed and screamed and screamed.

Something was jammed into Jenny's head, and another light erupted inside her, followed by a blinding, furious surge of energy that enveloped everything. The connection between her and the angel shivered again, violently.

She blinked forward through time. With each blink, a new face appeared: Mrs. Monique looking furious with her spear pointed at Jenny's—the angel's—face. Dr. Lee holding up his phone and talking softly to her, as if trying to win her over, as if she were a wild animal that needed to be tamed.

And all the while, she was crying. She was . . . sad beyond measure. Like she'd lived a lifetime and had nothing to show for it. Like she'd blinked, and all her life had been a waste. She couldn't speak. Couldn't communicate. Nobody understood her as she begged to be put out of her misery.

The feeling was gone. His presence was gone. There was nothing driving her thoughts. No more hunger, nothing pushing her forward. *Nothing, nothing, nothing.* She was empty and hollow and terrified. What had she become? Why was she like this? She just wanted to go home, to feel the warm breeze beneath her wings. To find a partner and melt her light with theirs . . .

In another blink, she saw Leslie, who was squatting down and talking to her. Jenny reached for her, feeling sorry, feeling sad, and just wanting to be touched.

Blue light flashed—light that filled her with dread and panic. *Run, run, run . . .*

She blinked again and again. The dead boy, the one whose throat she'd bitten through, got up and attacked. She saved Leslie, then Dr. Lee was upon her. He wasn't talking soothingly anymore; he had his katana, ready to kill her. She knew that look in his eyes; she'd seen it on her own face. A desire for blood. A hunger that would never be satiated.

He was shouting, stepping forward to stab her, but Leslie got in the way. Leslie? Why was Leslie protecting her? But that didn't matter. The dreadful feeling grew worse and worse, and the floor of the library gave way, then everything was falling.

Heavy things landed on top of her, crushing her already ruined back, and she saw the creature responsible: The desecrated angel, even greater than the Great Ones. The Matriarch with a body made of molten, navy-blue metal. Eyes with blue irises gleaming brighter than stars.

The Matriarch knelt and grabbed the bleeding Leslie, who was crying and kicking, and Dr. Lee, who'd passed out. It knelt and licked Jenny, licking the blood off her face and back, then it grinned. "*You are useless to me,*" it said. It spoke. It hissed. The language moved through her like a shudder.

And then it was gone, and the next thing she saw was herself again, covered in red. Covered in red in the way she was covered in orange, with large tentacles swirling around her. Her face was twisted with anger and hunger, so furious that she felt it emanating through every single step, through the vibrations in the air.

And she accepted it. She surrendered to herself. She could rest.

Jenny stumbled back in shock. She was back in the gym, her heart racing, her head pounding. Her tentacles swished in agony, wrenched free from the angel's touch.

"What the fuck?" she whispered, swallowing hard. There was a lump in her throat, like she'd been crying. She couldn't stop shaking, and she stepped away from the wretched angel. It looked deflated, the lips of its wrinkled face curved in a smile.

Its one eye stared right through her.

**You've defeated Angel (Stage II - Level 10)**
**Experience has been awarded.**
**+800 Energy**

**Leveled Up!**
**Jenny Huang, Level 24 → Level 25**
**+3 Stat Points**

# CHAPTER FIFTY

# A MORBID NEST

Panic-stricken, Jenny rushed away from the angel she'd just drained as it lay there, an orange, mummified husk.

The gym spun around her. The debris. The loose writing. The books and furniture scattered across the hardwood floors. She tasted blood.

Her tentacles swished wildly; they'd grown even thicker and longer than before. A tingling persisted in the back of her head and ran down her spine in a continuous waterfall of sensation; shudders that never quite became shudders. She wanted to throw up.

She wanted more blood. She wanted to die. She'd *died*. She was sure of it.

She'd lived an entire existence as an angel, fleshless and full of light, with her wings beating and the sun of another world shining on cities hanging from clouds. She'd breathed through her skin; she'd been light.

Then flesh had been forced upon her. That life had only lasted a short while before she'd been transformed, mutilated. Sentenced to drown in the ravenous, all-consuming hunger. A hunger she knew all too well.

But she knew what this meant. She knew all the angels in the building had been innocent, had been creatures of light minding their own business, forced into this survival game.

"Gah!" she screamed, stumbling into the weight room. Her tentacles slashed through every weight and machine, crumpling metal and knocking things away.

Breathing hard, trying desperately to bury the agonizing sadness—the weighty feeling that she'd died—she grabbed a barbell with two tentacles and snapped it in half. She threw the pieces over her shoulder. Her world wouldn't stop spinning; she wasn't sure if she was real. What if the angel had been the true Jenny? What if she was just some afterthought haunting what was left of her fucked-up body? How could this even happen?

**Angels exist beyond the parameters of linear time. Perhaps your actions—your severing—and the actions of Susan Brown's healing took advantage of the schism between worlds.**

"I don't care!" shouted Jenny. Her voice was muffled in the weight room. She wanted to keep screaming, keep shouting. Just to feel alive. Just to feel like she hadn't killed a part of herself.

She was sick and tired of Eve's nonsense. She couldn't quiet her mind. Everything raced all at once.

The flashes. The students she'd attacked and ate. The way she'd ran into herself. Wanted to eat herself. Was convinced she *had to* eat herself. How she'd cut her own fingers off. The faces. The hunger. The agony. Susan.

Jenny swallowed the lump in her throat, remembering how the desecrated angel had licked her. She could still feel its tongue, slimy and wet, the breath reeking of rot and flesh. It went down her head and down her back. But she'd been the angel; it wasn't *this* body. Yet the sensation remained. The disgust. The gross feeling that she'd been claimed.

She cried out again, shaking. Sweat beaded on her exoskeleton like condensation before rolling down the scales, gathering dried blood and dust. She leaned forward and grabbed her knees—but she didn't have fingers like she used to. She had claws that encircled her crimson-covered legs, and that feeling only made things worse. She wanted to touch someone, to feel someone else, just to make sure she was real.

*Linear time* . . . She sucked in deep breaths and realized she wasn't just breathing through her mouth—her exoskeleton could breathe as well. Her tentacles drew in air, and every little detail was only making her nausea worse.

"Fuck," she whispered. Golden light flashed, and her hatchet returned to her hand. Squeezing its handle gave her a sense of stability.

She'd come to that conclusion already: She wasn't human. She had to be a monster. She *had* to be. That was the only way to survive, to keep the others alive.

The others. That angel had the others. She'd seen Dr. Lee and Leslie, and everyone else who'd been in the library. Oliver, Mackenzie, and Dulé had to be with them, too. And Jenny understood why. She couldn't even blame the creature; it was exactly the thought that had crossed her mind dozens of times in the pangs of hunger: The library was the biggest source of fresh food left in the building.

If the desecrated angel wanted to become "complete," to become wholly flesh, then that was exactly where it would hunt.

She willed herself forward, taking shaky steps, using her tentacles to balance herself. She took the steps up to the gym equipment storage room; it was built higher than the weight room, and she knew it was adjacent to the hallway.

Bins with basketballs and volleyballs and footballs were knocked loose. The lacrosse sticks were scattered. Dried blood covered a bunch of things, but she didn't pay it much attention. There were doors leading to the gym teacher's office, and she knew she could go through them to get back to the hallway, but there was a quicker way.

Switching the hatchet to her left hand, she punched the wall as hard as she could. It crumpled under her blow, and Jenny stumbled through the collapsing debris, standing in the hallway again as she tried to harness her rage.

Like *hell* would she let the creature have Oliver after all she'd been through. And like hell would Jenny leave the creature alive to go after Susan.

But just as she was about to wrench the cafeteria doors off their hinges, she forced herself to pause. She needed to ground herself, center her convictions. Burying her claws in her palm, struggling to puncture the exoskeleton, she shook with a tumultuous wrath, but knew it would be stupid to rush in there. She'd done enough stupid things. She'd been unhinged, irresponsible, and downright impulsive, and she'd almost died too many times to count.

No. If she wanted to do this, she had to go in with a cool head. She had to be focused.

Straightening up as best she could, Jenny squared her shoulders and shut her eyes. A static image flickered in her head, and she had a vague outline of the hall-way, the doors, and the holes in the wall. But she put everything out of thought and focused on her breath.

"Calm down," she whispered. "Calm the fuck down. Don't go rushing into another fight. Not this fight. I can't mess up again."

*I have to destroy this thing. I have to figure out what to do before it kills everyone else, and this comes down to a one versus one anyway.* She didn't think anyone else in the school would be able to handle the desecrated angel. It had to be her.

An ugly thought formed in the back of her mind. Maybe it was her own; maybe it was Eve urging her to win. But if she let the desecrated angel kill everyone else, all she'd have to do was defeat it and win guilt free. It was not like she'd have killed anyone, right?

*No,* she thought. *No!* The guilt would eat her alive no matter what. And "everyone else" included Susan and Oliver. She would not allow that. She couldn't.

But what if it came to that, anyway?

*Fuck. I'll figure it out. Right now, I just have to stop this thing.* She inhaled as deeply as she could, her tentacles stretching to the maximum, filling her body with oxygen. Her head stopped spinning. *Drown everything else out. Focus on this.*

She pressed the tips of two tentacles against the cafeteria door, feeling the cold metal, trying to perceive the vibrations and get some sense of what lay ahead. But all she had was a pit of doom in her stomach; a relentless dread. Her subconscious screamed at her to run, to escape. It was a primal response. Whatever lay ahead was *bad*. It was *wrong*.

She couldn't see through the doors; she'd need to get inside first. Slowly, careful not to make a sound, she pushed the door open the tiniest sliver. The mistiness of the Veil was much thicker in the cafeteria, tendrils of steam curving out like she'd taken the lid off a pot of boiling rice.

Sliding through the opening and holding her breath, she carefully shut the door behind her. If she needed to, she'd tear the doors apart to escape. If she could.

The first thing to hit her was the stench. Rotting food, spoiled milk, vomit, blood. Even through her exoskeleton mask, she smelled it; she tasted it through her tentacles, each one swishing, trying to make sense of these disturbing vibrations and the smells and the looming terror that spread through her like ice.

She couldn't see more than a few feet ahead. The mist swirled, thick and congested, and the lighting was gloomy but surprisingly colorful. Spread throughout the cafeteria, as if from multicolored lightbulbs, were colors. Greens and yellows. Oranges and blues and purples. But the mist swirled, and things faded in and out of view. The lights grew bright then dulled before brightening again.

Her tentacles were overwhelmed, and the static image in her mind was hazy, showing only vague silhouettes and the shapes of tables and pillars. Nothing that could be the desecrated angel.

On the far left were the large windows of the cafeteria. Most of them were shattered, but they let in the pasty glow of the Veil. As Jenny moved deeper into the lunchroom, she found what looked like spider webbing: silky, glistening threads stretched between pillars from floor to ceiling. And stuck to them, stuck all over, were wriggling bodies—humans and angels and even some of her babies.

Some of their eyes glowed blue, and they lay silent, blinking and struggling helplessly. There were tables caught in the webbing too, stuck upright and stained with bloody handprints and smears.

She remembered a lesson about spiders; how they sensed vibrations through their webs to know where prey had been trapped. She'd have to avoid touching it.

Stepping slowly, carefully, eyes and ears and tentacles on full alert, Jenny crossed between the tables. She was terrified one of the phones or trays of food or something would crunch under her feet and give her away. Liquid pooled all over the floor—milk, water, blood, urine. She stepped over them, not trying to splash into a puddle. It wasn't until she approached the people stuck to the webbing that she saw the sacs.

They were enormous, just like the cocoon from the chem lab, wriggling and suspended in the air. She counted almost a dozen near her, her heart sinking with each one.

'Cause each one came with the notification she'd dreaded this entire time.

## Desecrated Angel (Level 30)

They were all dripping blood, glowing with specific colors, and she realized they were the sources of the blooming, colorful lights. And they were lighting up the cafeteria just as the cocoon in the chem lab had.

Something crunched beneath her foot—a spilled bowl of breakfast cereal. Jenny froze, her tentacles going still. She strained every sense, trying to figure out if anything was onto her, but nothing stirred other than the creatures stuck to the webbing. Nothing made a sound.

She moved slower, creeping around the cocoons and the pillars. It wasn't until she neared the center of the cafeteria that she saw it: the world-tearing gash, like an open eye in the middle of the cafeteria floor. It was about the length of a cafeteria table, and about as wide as she was tall.

She'd seen it from the inside before, when she'd surfaced for air and blood, and crawled out of it. But seeing it now, spread across the floor—a swirling, unblinking darkness—her stomach lurched like she'd climbed up very high and was now looking at the street below. A part of her wanted to fall. A part of her still remembered that instruction, His will, beaten into her psyche.

*Fall. Fall. Fall.*

An arm burst from the floor. The darkness rippled around it, and Jenny held her breath. The emaciated arm, just skin stretched over bone, reached forward, and the palm slapped against the dark surface. A bald head appeared, the eyes as empty as every angel's she'd fought. It bared its teeth, saliva dribbling down its chin as it screeched.

## Tarnished Angel (Level 1)

Jenny remained motionless, hiding behind a pillar as the tarnished angel dragged the rest of its sickly form out. It plopped on the darkness, huffing, straining. She was just about to rush forward and snip its head off when a soft shush came from above.

Too soft. Unsettlingly soft. It sounded almost motherly—nurturing and kind. A soft, gentle shushing that made both Jenny and the tarnished angel raise their heads.

Something shifted. Two giant somethings unfurled, and Jenny realized with racing horror that they were wings: transparent and silky like butterfly wings. As they folded back, their tips nearly reaching the floor, wind battered the cafeteria. The mist swirled and cleared slightly as a chill washed over Jenny, and everything stuck to the webs shook.

On the ceiling, it looked like an enormous insect, but the notification in her head confirmed the lurch of fear.

### Desecrated Angel (Level 44)

A shiver that seemed to go all the way into her bones seized Jenny. She couldn't look away. The angel kept shushing, and it was almost songlike as it raised and flattened its wings again, stirring more air. With the wings flat against the ceiling, it almost vanished into the tile design; it reminded Jenny of how chameleons or octopi camouflaged.

Every signal in her body screamed, *Danger!* The angel had four arms sticking out of its sides, two legs, and twin antennae jutting out from its head, where blonde hair shimmered, golden and bright, full of life and energy. Its exoskeleton was no longer shiny and blue; it was strangely metallic, almost fibrous, and it made Jenny think of denim more than anything.

But it was much bigger now, taking up a huge portion of the ceiling with its limbs spread, directly over the gash in the floor. When it and its mate had attacked Jenny in the hallway by the library, it might've been a foot taller than her. Now, it was several feet bigger; she thought each of its arms were longer than she was tall. Definitely thicker.

Most importantly, it hadn't spotted her yet.

Jenny rushed to the side, careful to avoid the webs, and hid behind another large pillar, ducking near a cafeteria table. Chocolate milk was spilled across the orange surface, and a crushed tomato lay beneath it.

On closer inspection, it wasn't a tomato. It was a lung or something.

Her tentacles stretched lengthwise up the pillar, and she held her breath, peering carefully from the side while using the table as cover.

The desecrated angel dropped slowly. It held on to the ceiling with its upper arms while reaching for the new angel with its lower ones. When its feet hit the floor—its large claws striking the surface of the darkness—everything rippled.

The desecrated angel stood with the top of its blonde head nearly touching the ceiling above. But now that it had moved, Jenny could see what it had been hiding.

She spotted Dr. Lee first, his bloodstained lab coat ripped open. He was struggling, but his limbs were stuck to the webbing that held him and others to the ceiling. Beside him was Leslie, whose eyes were shut. And around them were the other faces from the library.

Jenny strained, squinting through the gloom, but she didn't see Oliver or Dulé or Mackenzie. She saw the others from the chem lab, but that was it. Her heart racing, she pushed the terrible thoughts out of her head and refused to check how many humans were left alive.

A murmur drew her attention. That giant creature was humming, the sound generating vibrations that sent waves of pleasure through Jenny. Her tentacles shuddered as an odd, strange pull wrapped itself around her heart and tugged as if to say, *Come closer.* Clenching her teeth, she stayed as motionless as possible, squeezing her tentacles flat against the pillar.

The tarnished angel made a raspy, hissing sound, and then the desecrated angel lifted it, a metallic, clawed hand on each of the thin angel's hips. Lifting it up as though it were a baby, as though the desecrated angel was a mother raising her newborn to kiss it on the forehead. But instead of a kiss, it put the creature's head in its mouth and violently jerked to the side, snapping the head right off the neck.

Jenny shut her eyes, swearing silently as blood rained down on the table beside her. There was a *crunch*, followed by chewing, then she heard the unmistakable noise of slurping. Her stomach lurched again, but she kept still, even as the desecrated angel started chewing and swallowing, smacking its lips and eating noisily.

Forcing herself to look, Jenny saw the legs of the tarnished angel disappearing inside the larger creature's mouth. It raised its face to the ceiling and swallowed again, a sizeable lump moving down its throat to its belly. Its middle wasn't exposed like before, when it was just a wretched angel; it now wore the metallic denimlike covering like a full-body suit.

Blue light surged from its navels to its wings, lighting up the mist and cafeteria before fading away.

She took the opportunity to dash to the next pillar, using Instant Acceleration out of fright. Once she'd hidden herself behind it, she checked around the pillar to see steam rising from the angel's face. Two more arms shot out of the darkness below, and the desecrated angel lowered its gleaming blue eyes to its next meal.

Jenny searched every inch of the ceiling she could see through the shifting colors and mist, squinting at all the webbing stretching around her, trying to find Oliver or anyone else. But too many creatures wriggled; too many things were trapped in the webs, and the danger emanating from the darkness kept throwing her off.

Her tentacles kept homing in on the biggest threat—the desecrated angel— and the majority of the static vision in her head was just that. Just the oversize, four-armed angel as it chewed through the newcomers.

She dashed to the next pillar. Now she'd gone around the desecrated angel from where she'd started. There was another exit in the back of the cafeteria, and she could take that upstairs if she needed to escape quickly. But there was still no sign of Oliver, though she saw more of her babies, curled up and suspended in a web. Asleep.

One of the cocoons was a few feet away, letting off pulsing purple light. She could just make out the silhouette of the creature inside, and she wondered if she could burn it alive while it was still in there. Before it and the others could hatch. Maybe create a distraction.

That was when she realized the desecrated angel had stopped eating. The cafeteria was silent, and Jenny held her breath, slowly turning around the corner.

It stood there, arms spread, blood dribbling down its front, covering its breasts, and spilling over its belly to flow down its legs. Then it turned to face the purple cocoon, and Jenny went completely rigid. It stomped over slowly and crouched down on one knee, bringing its face to the sac. Its blonde hair bounced as its wings folded back, glowing brightly.

Jenny could reach out and touch the angel with her tentacles if she wanted to. She didn't even dare to blink.

It slit a hole in the cocoon using a fingernail bigger than Jenny's face. A slime-covered purple angel screeched and raised its head from inside, but the desecrated angel pressed its oversize lips to the smaller creature's face.

Jenny's stomach twisted as the crunching and swallowing ensued, and she turned away, trying to decide which pillar to rush to next; how best to avoid the webs. She wondered if she could climb up to the ceiling with her tentacles, cut the others free, and get them out.

Or would it be better to fight the desecrated angel right now? While it was feeding? To take it by surprise and chop off its enormous head?

What was it even doing here? With all the cocoons and all the angels, undead people, and babies trapped in the webbing. It was like a morbid nest. Was this why the wretched angels had ignored her and jumped into the hole? Had they been called by the desecrated angel? Were they all going to hatch and become just like this creature?

The desecrated angel made that creepy, gentle purring sound, and once again, Jenny felt drawn to it. Like she wanted it to pick her up and press its lips to her mouth and regurgitate blood and flesh so she could swallow it till she was full. It was calling to something deep and primal inside her; it was calling to her angelic needs. It was calling to her like the mother Jenny had always wanted.

*Wait.* Eve had said this desecrated angel was trying to win the survival challenge, trying to become more flesh, more complete. And it was raising all these angels to become desecrated.

It was trying to amass an army so that when it won, when the survival challenge ended and the school returned to New York, it could surface with an army. And Jenny knew all too well the will that pulsed inside the creature's head. *His* will. *His* desires.

That wasn't even the worst thought in Jenny's head. She pictured her city; pictured the millions of people that walked its streets and clogged its buildings. An endless supply of flesh and blood; something that might finally quench the hunger.

# CHAPTER FIFTY-ONE

# BEYOND HELP

Susan bounced in Mrs. Monique's arms, feeling like a useless rag doll as the librarian carried her, rushing down the third-floor hallway. Behind them, the walls erupted with dark-green energy. Another bubble of light and sizzling heat blew up the lockers, battering them with debris.

Mrs. Monique ran, her face strained, with Susan held to her chest. She'd dropped her spear somewhere in the chaos, and Susan felt awful weighing the librarian down. She should just leave Susan and escape; she was just dead weight.

They reached the central area where Susan and Jenny had found Harry Kim's dad, where they'd fought the first wretched angel. Those bodies were nowhere to be seen. A series of *cracks* caught up with them, and green light exploded right over their heads.

The explosion threw the librarian forward, and Susan tumbled out of her arms. Both of them rolled across the bloodied floor before coming to a stop near the double doors of the English Department.

Her vision blurry, pain radiating through her side and up her neck, Susan squeezed her cattle prod, blinking over and over to get the dust out. Down the hall, hunched forward and limping, came Miriam. She sauntered slowly, grinning maniacally, her eyes bulging. Maybe it was the pink helmet, but her head seemed too heavy for her body, lolling to the side, and the grin was too wide. It showed all her bloodied teeth, and it looked like the corners of her lips would rip.

"C'mon!" called Miriam. Her voice echoed all over the hall as debris rained down from the scorched ceiling. Crumpled lockers slid off the walls and clattered to the floor.

Susan glanced at Mrs. Monique, trying to figure out what to do, but the librarian was out cold.

**Human (Stage II - Level 12)**

At least there was still a notification, thought Susan, wincing again as she grabbed the wall and pulled herself up. She focused what strength she had left, harnessing it into what felt like a coiled spring inside the cattle prod. There was no use trying to reason with Miriam anymore; the girl had completely lost it.

Two of the angel babies emerged from the destroyed hallway they'd left behind. Screaming, they threw themselves at Miriam, who turned to face them and screamed right back, a demonic, ugly scream. She swatted them away like flies. Susan guessed Miriam had put all her stat points into speed and strength, because the crazed girl moved so quickly, and each smack sent a baby smashing into a wall.

Miriam stumbled closer once she'd knocked the babies away. The entire front of her shirt was stained dark with blood, and she was drooling uncontrollably to the point that fresh saliva ran down her chin, glistening over dried blood.

The sound was the worst part. *Shlip.* With every inhale, she sucked up the excess saliva. "Fresh," she said. "Fresh, fresh, fresh. I have to eat you while you're fresh. That's what the voice says. Fresh is best. I'll get really strong. I can win!"

Susan braced herself, but Miriam whirled around with rage when more babies emerged. The pink helmet flashed; Miriam's arms swung. A fist broke one baby's face, breaking its little nose. Susan blinked, and Miriam kicked one more baby into the ceiling before opening her mouth and releasing another dark-green bubble.

It exploded like a supernova, blinding Susan for a moment, and she cried out, hearing the babies scream in pain. Bits and pieces of the ceiling splattered the hallway. Pushing herself off the wall, she stepped toward Miriam, readying her cattle prod as another baby attacked the girl's legs.

*I have to kill her.* An ugly thought. She hated it. But the girl was unhinged, and she kept mentioning Jenny.

Susan had already tried talking to her. When they found Miriam, she'd been eating the undead body of the music teacher, his rib cage torn open and a chunk of flesh slipping from her mouth.

Susan had called out that it was alright, they could help. She wasn't alone. This could stop. But even as she'd said those words, even as she'd tried to do the right thing, she knew the girl was too far gone. And even though the notification said human, even though Miriam *looked* human, she scared Susan more than any of the angels so far.

Even the babies had seemed completely unsettled. They'd hid behind Susan's legs, holding on to her, all of them shaking; like wild animals sensing a terrible presence. The horrid feeling in Susan's gut had twisted; something was definitely wrong, but she'd tried again anyway, hoping Miriam could be reasoned with.

"Miriam? It's me, Susan. I don't know what happened, but—"

Miriam had wiped the blood from her lips then raced down the hallway, laughing. A green bubble had burst from her lips, and the hallway had erupted. The floors, the lockers, the doors; it was a storm of debris. Miriam had rushed right through the mess and attacked Mrs. Monique before either of them could say anything else.

The librarian had fought, exchanging blows. Miriam's arm had bounced off Mrs. Monique's reflective armor, and she'd even taken a slash to one arm, but it hadn't been enough. Miriam had laughed and kicked the librarian away.

"I have to stop her!" screamed Miriam, manic glee twisting her once pretty face. She was covered in so much blood, her eyes glistening green. "I have to stop her. The voice . . . It's the *voice*! I swore I'd stop her. Jenny's going to ruin *everything*!"

"What the fuck?" asked Mrs. Monique, clutching her side and backing away as Miriam stared at both of them, as if trying to decide who to eat first.

Susan shook her head. "What are you talking about? Why are you doing this?" She readied her cattle prod. If she could stun the girl, Mrs. Monique would have the upper hand.

"It's Jenny," said Miriam quietly, hunching over and staring at Susan. She licked blood off her arm. "Jenny's going to ruin it. I have to stop her and win, or we're all fucked."

"Ruin what?" said Susan, but that was all Miriam had to say. The pink helmet had flashed, and Miriam was barreling down on Susan. The babies had pounced and thrown the unhinged girl to the floor.

Miriam had screeched as they bit her thighs and her hand, kicking and punching and trying to throw them off. Another bubble formed inside her mouth, the light pulsing as it grew, and then Mrs. Monique had grabbed Susan and rushed off right as another explosion took out that entire section of the hallway. The roof had collapsed, the tiles on the floor had ripped apart, and it'd felt like they were rushing out of a war zone.

But the librarian was out cold now, and Susan couldn't run. She could feel the potion Jenny had given her fading. Fatigue spread through her with every heartbeat, and she knew she'd only have one real shot. She couldn't miss. One burst of lightning to the head, and Miriam would be out for the count.

As the smoke cleared, Miriam picked something off the floor. A baby. She held it with both hands, like she might throw it in the air and catch it, like it was an innocent game. The girl smiled even wider, then turned to catch Susan's eyes. Her smile showed off all her bloodied teeth.

The baby struggled and wailed, scorched from the explosion, and before Susan could even cry out, Miriam sank her teeth into the little creature's neck.

An ugly crunch, followed by a slurp. The baby let out a squeak, its pudgy arms and legs wriggling desperately before going rigid. Holding the baby to her mouth, Miriam dropped to her knees, sniffling and sucking and moaning.

"So good!" Miriam exclaimed loudly after one long, final slurp. She dropped the limp baby and raised her hands in prayer, blood gushing from between her teeth, tears running down her face. "Thank you . . ."

Lightning burst out of Susan's cattle prod, rippling through the air till it hit Miriam in the chest, blasting the girl back. Electricity snapped up and down the blood. The pink helmet puffed up and shattered.

Miriam spasmed uncontrollably, her limbs twisting as more and more bolts of lightning struck her. Susan stepped forward, overflowing with anger and disgust and horror. She'd seen enough horrible things. She'd seen enough people attacked and eaten by the angels. But to see someone she knew do that? To a baby, no less?

Susan held the cattle prod with both hands, feeling the drain as surge after surge of lightning shot out, flashing and filling the hallway with crackling blue light. But even as Miriam spasmed and her shirt caught fire, she laughed.

Miriam was laughing and screaming, several green bubbles spreading from her lips, rising. Susan's lightning curved toward them as if drawn to the bubbles, and the instant they touched, there was a flash of light and another explosion.

The walls and floor around Miriam fell away, plummeting her to the second floor. Susan was flung backward, and she fully expected to slam into a wall or something, but instead, it was Mrs. Monique who caught her, softening the impact. Her cattle prod had been thrown from her hand, and she coughed loudly, leaning on Mrs. Monique for support while blinking away tears as smoke and dust stung her eyes.

What was left of the lockers peeled off the walls to crash loudly below. A portion of the roof had come down, blocking the central stairwell, and the thick mist of the Veil swirled overhead, slowly seeping into the building. It was like looking up at a stormy sky, except there was no rain or wind, only an endless, empty feeling.

Light flashed, and Susan flinched. But it was only Mrs. Monique summoning her spear. The librarian had blood running down the side of her face from a nasty wound, and she opened her mouth to say something, but a bloodcurdling scream rang out from the second floor.

"Please!" screamed Miriam. "I need to find her! Where is she?"

Susan looked frantically through the rubble, trying to find her cattle prod. Her head ached and pounded, but fear throbbed through her limbs. Jenny had enough to deal with; if the crazy bitch attacked Jenny while she had to deal with the undead . . .

It was Mrs. Monique who found the cattle prod and placed it firmly back into Susan's hand.

"The babies . . ." whispered Susan. She forced herself to take deep breaths. If she passed out, it would be over.

"I don't see any of them," said Mrs. Monique. She sounded just as exhausted as Susan felt. The librarian stumbled, touching her forehead, her fingers coming away with blood. "Why does that girl keep screaming about Jenny?"

"I . . . I don't know."

Mrs. Monique shook her head. "This is all sorts of fucked." She motioned for the stairwell in the back. "Let's go down that way and get back to the library or something. We need backup."

Susan couldn't argue with that. The two of them didn't stand a chance, and she wondered about the kids who'd been with Oliver. They were strong. Maybe together, they could stop Miriam and help Jenny.

She let Mrs. Monique lead the way, glancing repeatedly over her shoulder. But all they heard was Miriam screaming and crying, and the impacts of a fight that must be the remaining babies struggling. She shuddered, trying to suppress the image of Miriam sucking the baby's blood.

As they crossed down the hall, she noticed the puddle of dried blood from when the first wretched angel had chewed through her leg. She saw the cracks in the walls and the floor from Jenny's battle with it. And when they walked past the boy's bathroom, her blood froze; she heard banging.

Multiple people were banging on the door, moaning and crying, trying to get out, and she almost went to help—to push it open—before she realized they must be the undead. Undead who couldn't figure out how to pull the door open and kept trying to push through. The librarian glanced at her, and Susan shook her head.

When they got to the stairwell door, Mrs. Monique grabbed Susan's shoulder. Her one eye was frantic and bloodshot, and more blood ran down her dark face. "Susan. How do I use my ability?"

"What?" asked Susan, taken aback by the sudden ferocity.

The librarian was breathing hard. She licked her lips and glanced toward the rubble again. "When I killed those angels Jenny wanted me to, I leveled up and got an ability. I don't understand, but it says *Barrier*."

Susan blinked, finally getting what the librarian meant. It was just like how she had Valescent Light, but she wasn't sure how to explain it; it had felt so natural to her, as easy as breathing or extending her arm and making a fist.

Then she remembered that not everyone had even noticed the system right away. Maybe it was more difficult for some people.

"You just . . ." She hesitated. "You kind of just focus on it. You imagine what it would feel like, and it's like exhaling. You bring it into existence."

Mrs. Monique nodded, clenching her teeth as if thinking hard. "I'm trying," she said. "Fuck. I'm trying." She opened the door, and they spilled into the side stairwell and headed down for the library.

They moved quickly. Going downstairs was easier than climbing, but Susan held the railing tightly and wished the babies were with them. She didn't want any more of them to get hurt or worse. Then Mrs. Monique stopped abruptly again, and Susan glanced around her to see why.

Ashes covered the entire stairwell. Scorch marks stained the walls, and part of the stairs had collapsed, as if by some terrible impact. Skeletons of various sizes lay on the floor, all the bones blackened, and many of them just piles of ash. The tiny ones gave Susan pause, and she shuddered, but past them, wriggling and crying and struggling, were about a dozen bodies with glowing blue eyes. Humans and angels, and someone rushing through them.

A girl, slashing and screaming, cutting the creatures down with a knife. It was the girl from downstairs; the deaf one who'd told Susan about Jenny, and behind her came the tall boy in boxing gloves, Dulé, carrying Jenny's brother on his back. Oliver's face was red and drenched in sweat.

"Why aren't you at the library?" Mrs. Monique shrieked. She stepped forward and plunged a spear into one of the undead. Before long, all of them were motionless, the blue light faded from their eyes as blood trickled down the steps. She helped Susan climb down till everyone stood near the second-floor doorway. Through it, they heard faint screaming, and the walls shook from another explosion.

Mrs. Monique stepped toward the other kids and touched Oliver's forehead. "The boy's burning up." She glanced back at Susan, worry and concern twisting her face.

But Susan didn't know what to do. Would Valescent Light work on a fever? She could maybe regrow his legs if she had a chance to rest, but . . .

She stepped forward, ignoring every single ache in her body while trying not to trip on an arm. Another explosion rocked the floors, and the deaf girl signed something at Dulé, who asked, "What the hell is that?"

Susan didn't pay attention as Mrs. Monique explained the Miriam situation. Instead, she pressed her glowing fingers to Oliver's flushed face, her hand shaking uncontrollably from the effort. She shut her eyes, concentrating, willing every ounce of her spirit to flow from her chest and through her arm to gather at her fingers. There wasn't much left, but maybe it could help. Maybe it would be just enough.

Someone gasped, and she relaxed slightly. It must be working. But the drain proved too much, and after a few seconds, her head tilted back. She would've collapsed if someone hadn't wrapped an arm around her waist and caught her. When she opened her eyes, she noticed Oliver's face seemed less troubled. He wasn't that sickly color anymore, and he was breathing easier.

"I'll restore your legs as soon as I can," she promised quietly.

Dulé shot her a look like "You can do that?" But then he noticed the deaf girl signing and nodded at Susan. "Mackenzie says thank you. And so do I."

Susan returned the nod weakly, leaning against Mrs. Monique.

But Mackenzie shook her head. She was trying and failing to speak, distorted syllables coming from her mouth. She let out a frustrated sigh, and then Dulé continued for her. "The library collapsed. Something . . ." He shook his head. "Something's down there, and . . ." He stopped again and took a breath. "And we have friends on this floor." He motioned toward the second floor with his chin. "Martin, Janice, and Anna. They were hiding somewhere in the chemistry hall, and—"

Mrs. Monique cut him off. She exchanged a glance with Susan, who shook her head sadly. Then the librarian explained: if they were in the chem wing with Miriam, they were dead. She left out the part of them being most likely eaten.

Dulé didn't say anything. He stared at the bodies on the floor, and Susan recognized the look on his face. He was studying each one, trying to find someone he knew. Students and teachers he'd shared classes with or seen around school. How normal everything had been only a few hours ago. He was trying to bury the news he'd just gotten. Mackenzie looked furious, the knife shaking in her hand, and she kicked one of the dead angels.

"What happened to the library?" asked Susan. She got the sense they were beyond terrified.

Dulé shook his head as Mackenzie touched his shoulder, then Oliver's face. And then finally, Dulé spoke. "It's gone. Something came from underneath and . . ."

Susan's eyes went wide. "From underneath?"

Mrs. Monique exhaled loudly, but before anyone could say another word, another explosion rocked the building. Dust rained down from above, and chunks of stairwell clattered all around them. And that's when they heard Miriam's voice, loud and shrill, coming right from the second-floor hallway.

"I can smell you out there!"

"Run," hissed Mrs. Monique. She was the first to react, readying her spear and taking a defensive stance. "We can't fight her in here. You guys go; I'll hold her back."

"No," said Dulé, adjusting Oliver's weight on his back. "Whatever's down there . . . We have to go *up*." He tried to push by Mrs. Monique, his feet sliding on blood, but before he could make any headway, another explosion burst through the wall above. The stairwell cracked, and a large chunk struck the floor beside Susan before breaking into bits.

Mackenzie shouted something incoherent and held up her knife. Susan glanced at the door; they heard laughter, growing louder and louder. She didn't know how the deaf girl could sense what was coming, but there was nowhere to run.

All of a sudden, there was quiet, heavy and thick. They all held their breaths, except for Oliver, who was still unconscious. Dulé took a few steps back, carefully descending the stairwell with Mackenzie standing in front of him, facing the doorway to the second floor.

Mrs. Monique motioned for Susan to leave, but she couldn't even bring herself to move. The cattle prod shook in her hands.

The door creaked open. The pink helmet—its plastic melted and peeled and curled upward—appeared first. Miriam's eyes were next, gleaming a bright green, then bloodied fingers emerged to wave. "Found you."

# CHAPTER FIFTY-TWO

# A Fire in the Cafeteria

The thick mist of the Veil was suffocating, seemingly to threaten Jenny from every angle, obscuring her view. All her senses were on high alert, but the static image in her head was useless. Her tentacles homed in on the desecrated angel's presence, and the gut-twisting feeling emanating from the darkness in the center of the cafeteria only confused her more.

The enormous angel held the purple cocoon with two arms, retching so the angel inside would drink through a revolting kiss.

**Desecrated Angel (Level 44)**

It was almost twenty levels higher than her. Stronger, with abilities she didn't know of yet, and gigantic. How had it managed to grow so big? It hadn't been that much bigger than her when it had come out of the cocoon.

**The desecrated angel focused on size in a similar manner to your tentacle's growth, converting blood and flesh into physical development.**

Sickened, Jenny slid away from the cocoon as the feeding continued, purple light radiating through the mist. She was careful to step over a puddle, careful to avoid the webbing that glistened inches away from her face, and careful not to make a sound when the desecrated angel shushed the creature in the cocoon back to sleep.

A shudder traveled down her spine, and she ducked under a table to watch. The giant angel's body convulsed, letting out a hiss, then something gooey shot out of its navel and slapped around the sac. That was how it produced its webbing, and Jenny couldn't help but find it eerily similar to her exoskeleton spurting out of her belly button.

Trying to keep from throwing up, Jenny shut her eyes and strained her tentacles. The humans on the ceiling were the only other living beings in the cafeteria. One of them was fading fast, and she knew there was no time to waste if she wanted to help them. The desecrated angel seemed to be saving the humans for itself while feeding newly born tarnished angels to the angels in the cocoons.

What she needed was a distraction. Something to lure the desecrated angel away so she could get closer to the ceiling.

It didn't take long for it to feed the cocoon, and when the large creature turned to face the darkness again, more tarnished angels hissed and emerged.

Brown napkins covered this side of the cafeteria floor. The dispenser had been smashed, and the napkins spread across an area, soaking up spilled milk and blood. Jenny crawled over them until she emerged from the opposite end of the table, nearly stepping into a web headfirst. Fortunately, she caught herself and straightened up, coming face-to-face with one of her babies that had fallen through the physics lab.

It was limp, suspended by the webbing and caked with dust. Its eyes were wide and lifeless. Its belly was torn open, the insides hollowed out like a hole in a tree.

There were no notifications; none of them stirred. A pang of sadness filled her as she counted almost a dozen babies. Some of their eyes were wide and unseeing, some shut tight, mouths open. Pudgy arms and legs stuck to the web stretching between two pillars, all of them with their insides ripped out; the desecrated angel had given birth to them to eat them. It hadn't been like the mother angel in the stairwell, who had clawed out its eyes to fight Jenny.

Following the web, Jenny stopped when she reached a green cocoon attached to the metal kiosk where students inserted their student IDs and filled their balances with cash. Up ahead, attached to the other end of the web and stuck to a pillar, was another cocoon. This one emanated a white glow that she couldn't tell apart from the mist without being close.

She heard the desecrated angel retch on the other side of the cafeteria. Her heart pounding, she glanced again at the dead, disemboweled babies and remembered the ones she'd burnt to death before they could hatch. She walked slowly, her face right next to the webbing so that when she exhaled, droplets of condensation stuck to the silvery, sticky stuff. She wondered if it was flammable; she wondered if the cocoons were flammable.

*Only one way to find out.*

Keeping low to the floor and trying not to slip on a napkin, Jenny crouched behind the closer cocoon. Its green light shone brightly as she drew nearer; she could see the gestating desecrated angel within, curled up in a fetal position. Waiting to be fed.

She passed a mess of wriggling undead angels and humans, their eyes glowing blue, their limbs stuck to another web. They were quiet, unlike the moaning, crying hoard she'd fought above.

When she got to the green cocoon, she hid behind its bulk as the giant angel lumbered around the cafeteria. The kiosk for refilling lunch cards was busted open so that cash covered the floor beneath the cocoon. It was odd, staring at all that money; odd thinking how she'd always wanted and needed more, yet here, in this hell, money held no value at all.

She readjusted her hatchet in case the fire wasn't enough and the angel inside burst free to attack. Praying this would work, praying it would draw the giant angel's attention and cause a big enough distraction, she inhaled deeply through her nose. Then, once her lungs were fully expanded and she'd slid a few feet away from the cocoon, she let it out. *Ignite!*

She was careful this time, controlling the fire. Softly and gently, the burning sensation in the back of her throat grew hotter and hotter, then the flames blossomed, curling and blooming before engulfing the green cocoon.

It began to glow vibrantly, reminding Jenny of burning copper over a Bunsen burner in chem lab, and she had to shield her eyes with a tentacle as the light flashed brightly. She stopped using her skill and watched as fire covered it completely. Flames licked up and spread across the web, lighting up the space between the kiosk and the pillar, and catching the dead babies.

Jenny didn't stay to watch. She dropped on all fours and moved away. Behind her, white light flashed just as vibrantly as the green cocoon had, and she knew it was on fire too.

A scream tore through the cafeteria as the floor jolted from heavy steps; her spectacle was working. She dashed away with Instant Acceleration, turning to hide behind a pillar by the windows as flickering orange, red, and yellow flames turned green and white, a show of light illuminating the back half of the cafeteria. The giant angel stood in the midst of it all with its four arms spread helplessly.

More webs caught flame, and screams echoed all around; the undead were on fire now, too. Jenny held her breath as the angel moved through the burning web, hunched over and reaching for the white cocoon. The haze cleared from the flames, and Jenny saw the cocoon melting like molten glass. The desecrated angel clawed it open, but the angel inside slumped out, limp as the dead babies. Its body was covered in the melted white exoskeleton, still gleaming from the heat, oozing like thick liquid.

**You've defeated Desecrated Angel (Level 30)!**
**Experience has been awarded.**
**+500 Energy**

The giant angel howled as Jenny covered her ears, wincing. It beat its wings furiously, air rushing through the cafeteria, causing the fire to spread. The napkins burst into flames, lighting up along the floor, and fire jumped to other webs.

The angel roared, swiping at the burning webs and shooting more like fishing nets. These muffled the flames for a moment, and Jenny imagined they were wet when the angel produced them, but the new webbing caught fire within seconds, and the blaze continued. She couldn't help but grin. *Fuck you*, she thought.

Her other guess had been correct, too: Desecrated angels were vulnerable while cocooned. Their insides must not be fully developed, and whatever change they were going through, whatever the purpose was, all Jenny had to do was set them on fire before they hatched.

As the giant angel screeched and tore at the burning webbing and bodies and cocoons, Jenny rushed for the center. Without thinking, she ran over the darkness, and only realized it when a hand burst from it and she nearly tripped.

### Tarnished Angel (Level 1)

Before the new angel could fully emerge, Jenny shoved a tentacle into its mouth, shooting out the back of the creature's head. Its body slid, as though suddenly it was no longer allowed to cross through the darkness, and its upper body slumped forward, blood and insides gushing. Whatever hadn't made it across was lost.

### You've defeated Tarnished Angel (Level 1)!
### Experience has been awarded.
### +20 Energy

Jenny flicked her tentacles even as they sucked up the blood. But there was no time to feast—the desecrated angel would only be distracted for so long. She leaped onto a table and then launched herself at the top of a pillar, her tentacles slapping around it. From the other side of the cafeteria, smoke swirled through the mist, cloaking her even more, but she could still see the silhouette of the giant angel amidst the flames, screaming with rage.

Using her claws, she climbed up then slammed her tentacles into the ceiling so she could hang from it. Dr. Lee stared at her with wide, bloodshot eyes. His glasses were gone, and his arms and legs were spread, stuck to the webbing like a helpless bug. The distinctly sharp odor of urine emanated from him.

Beside him was Leslie, lying face up with her cheek against the ceiling. Her breathing was shallow, and blood dripped from her back. Blood—warm and fresh and delicious. It made Jenny's tentacles twitch, and her core tightened. She could suck them both dry; they'd never even know. Surely, she looked just as monstrous to them as the desecrated angel had? And why should *it* be the only one to feed?

Leslie's blood smelled so good . . . Jenny shuddered, remembering her time as the angel. Remembering how Leslie had spoken to her, had tried to protect her from Dr. Lee. And how the science teacher had stabbed Leslie. The girl was about to bleed out, judging by her faint heartbeat. There were several other bodies wriggling about, as well as a few faces from the library that remained motionless, eyes wide and unseeing.

She grabbed Leslie first, and after a quick glance to make sure the desecrated angel was still distracted trying to stomp out the fire, Jenny dropped, smoke and mist swirling around her. She cradled Leslie against her red exoskeleton and took the impact of the fall with her tentacles, lowering her feet gently so that Leslie wouldn't feel a thing. She didn't want any more blood spurting out; didn't want to lose her mind. Jenny didn't even dare breathe.

She carried Leslie over to the janitor's closet. The door was bolted shut, but a locked metal door wasn't going to stop her. Prying it open with her tentacles, she carried the unconscious Leslie inside. The place smelled of ammonia and cleaning fluids, and it wasn't a big space. There were buckets and mops, a sink, and an extra janitor's uniform.

With Leslie resting on the floor, leaning against a shelf of rat poison, Jenny focused. Golden light took shape in her hand, and then she held a major potion of recovery to Leslie's lips. The dark red liquid matched Jenny's exoskeleton, and Leslie drank it greedily.

**Perhaps it would be best to end her suffering. She is weak, and you can harvest her energy and experience, and secure your victory.**

*You want me to kill her?* thought Jenny, already struggling with her bloodlust. There would be no witnesses, and Leslie would die anyway if Jenny failed to stop the angel. Why not take her strength and use it?

But no. She bit her lip and stopped that train of thought. It was only Eve trying to end the survival challenge; it wasn't Jenny. She repeated that over and over. *It's not me. I'm not going to kill someone who's innocent. Because where would it stop?*

Steam rose from Leslie's torso, and she slumped back, eyes fluttering. As soon as she saw Jenny, she opened her mouth to scream, but Jenny was prepared for that. She wrapped a tentacle around Leslie's face and held her till she stopped squirming.

Jenny could taste the wound healing, and as much as she wanted to kneel and tear through Leslie's neck and suck and suck and suck, she forced the urge down and kept her tentacles in check.

"It's me," she whispered. "It's me, Jenny. It's okay."

*Yeah,* she thought. *Totally okay. Every muscle in my body isn't straining from the effort of not eating you.*

Leslie stared for a moment, eyes wide and brimming with tears. Her usually flawless skin was caked in blood and dirt, and any facade of the perfect girl was gone. She started sobbing and shaking, and Jenny slowly unfastened her tentacle.

"It kept licking me," whispered Leslie. Her eyes went out of focus as she touched the bloodied hole in her shirt where the wound used to be. "It was licking me right here." Then she turned over and threw up, and Jenny looked away, feeling like she might be sick herself.

"You'll be safe here," said Jenny, turning. "Just be quiet." She rushed back to where the others were. The flames were still raging, but the desecrated angel was stomping them out. Jenny was running out of time.

**You've defeated Desecrated Angel (Level 30)!**
**Experience has been awarded.**
**+500 Energy**

**Leveled Up!**
**Jenny Huang, Level 25 → Level 26**
**+3 Stat Points**

The angel in the other cocoon must be dead now, too. She climbed back to the ceiling, scanning the rest of them. Other than Dr. Lee, two people from the library, and the boy who'd been with Oliver and the others, everyone else was dead, holes in their chest, their faces sunken as though they'd been hollowed out. A part of her was relieved that Oliver wasn't among them, but that only left her with the worry of *where* was he?

Eve had confirmed that he was alive, but it couldn't seem to locate him. Or Susan. Or any of the others. What had happened to them? But she couldn't stress about them; not till she'd cleared the immediate danger.

She carried the students to the janitor's closet without saying anything to them, and they were too terrified to resist. She let Leslie explain that they had to be quiet and hide. In the back of Jenny's mind, they were just an emergency food supply. At best, she was preventing the desecrated angel from getting any stronger off them.

She'd saved Dr. Lee for last. She wasn't sure if she even wanted to save him. What if he went after the others? But it didn't matter. The flames were dead, the flickering light gone, and the smoke was dissipating, as though the Veil's mist was clearing it away.

The cafeteria was quiet and unnerving, and the mist thickened, threatening Jenny once again. Another hand burst out of the darkness, and a new tarnished angel clambered out, hissing. Jenny held her breath as the desecrated angel approached.

A series of tremors went through the floor as Jenny slid away, darting behind a pillar near the ceiling, trying to keep out of sight.

The angel held the half-melted cocoons in its arms. It set them down, and one of them crushed the tarnished angel below. Its blue eyes seemed to shine more brightly than before. Rage, like waves of heat, emanated from the desecrated angel, an invisible force that squeezed Jenny's chest and made her heart pound. It was pissed, and it spread its wings as it raised its head, a cry of rage gurgling in its throat.

But it stopped mid-outburst. It had noticed the ceiling and the missing people. Looking right at Dr. Lee, it blinked, the blue light of its eyes vanishing for a moment before reappearing brighter and sharper than before.

Jenny held her breath, clinging to the pillar with her claws, trying to find an opening. Should she attack? Should she grab Dr. Lee? The angel stretched till its nose was pressed against him, and it sniffed. Then it sniffed again, deeply.

*It knows. It knows I'm here.*

The creature plucked Dr. Lee from the ceiling and brought his wailing face to its mouth.

# CHAPTER FIFTY-THREE

# FACE OFF

With the angel's large dark claws wrapped around his bloodstained lab coat and squeezing him tight, Dr. Lee looked so small. He was crying and sobbing. "Please! Please, just let me go. I mean you no harm. I can help you. Don't . . . Not again. Please! Don't!"

Jenny licked her lips. Dr. Lee wasn't worth saving, but she couldn't let the angel eat any more humans; she couldn't risk it getting any stronger or larger. The melted cocoons lay on the floor, and more tarnished angels crawled out of the darkness, hissing as they took their first breaths.

She couldn't let it get any stronger. She had to stop it and save Dr. Lee.

What she needed was another distraction. Inhaling deeply, she used Ignite again, this time on the webbing on the ceiling, where the drained human bodies were still suspended. Quietly, she apologized as their clothes caught flame, lighting up the cafeteria from above.

The angel shrieked as Jenny dropped and immediately used Instant Acceleration. She streaked down the front of the cafeteria, right where students would line up with trays to get their meals, while more and more flames erupted from her arm.

Webbing caught fire. The blue-eyed undead screeched and hissed, and a moment later, she ran her hands over another cocoon, which erupted with yellow light. It was almost as bright as the sun up close, but it was enough. The desecrated angel released Dr. Lee and stomped toward the sac, its wings beating like mad.

Burning bodies rained from above, free from the web. Dr. Lee was between them, limbs wriggling, about to splatter onto the darkness where the newly born tarnished angels hissed and salivated, desperate for their first meal.

She considered letting him die, letting them eat him alive while he screamed. But she'd already gone through this much trouble, and she didn't want the desecrated angel to feed off stronger tarnished. Reflexively, she used Instant Acceleration again, knowing she'd have to shoot right by the desecrated angel to reach Dr. Lee.

She rushed so close to it she could feel the warmth of its body, the feeling of doom as it stomped toward the burning cocoon. She knew it had sensed her. By smell or by feeling, it had recognized her.

Slapping her tentacles against the floor and leaping, Jenny caught Dr. Lee mid-air before landing, not caring to soften the impact for him. She kicked away one of the tarnished angels, then didn't stop running until she'd shoved him outside the cafeteria and told him to flee.

He landed on his ass, squinting hard and blubbering, as her tentacles whipped through the air. For a split second, she justified her horrid thought. She pictured herself tearing into him, sucking the blood from his heart and chewing his muscle and taking his strength. She'd get a ton of energy and experience, wouldn't she?

He was vile and sadistic and selfish, and he'd tried to kill Leslie, who was annoying but innocent. He looked so pathetic like this, having wet himself and panic-stricken. Jenny left him in the hall; his death would not be on her conscience. At least the others were safe. For now. How long till the desecrated angel sniffed them out?

The only thing standing between the creature and a huge meal was Jenny.

**You've defeated Desecrated Angel (Level 30)!**
**Experience has been awarded.**
**+500 Energy**

She shuddered from that notification. A part of her had hoped it was *the* desecrated angel, but that was wishful thinking.

As Dr. Lee scrambled up the hall and toward the main stairwell, Jenny summoned her hatchet back with a flash of light. She had twenty stat points to use now, and 3,368 energy. Her tentacles swished with anticipation while she squared her shoulders.

Ten into stamina, she decided after looking over her stats. If she tired out while fighting that creature, she was dead. She twitched as a tickle ran up her abdomen; her lungs expanded with new air, and her muscles relaxed. The remaining ten points, she split evenly between power and agility, and another surge went through her limbs and tentacles. With a deep breath, she released the tension and surveyed her stats.

**Jenny Huang**
**Human (Stage II - Level 26) (Blooded)**
**Age: 6,801 days**
**Stats:**

**Power: 35**
**Durability: 20 (+30)**
**Stamina: 40**
**Agility: 35**
**Stat Points Available: 0**
**Energy Available: 3368**

*Okay, one more thing. If I want to win this fight, I have to bet everything. It's win or die.*

**A Major Potion of Fortification will cost 1,250 Energy.**
**Sufficient Energy.**

A familiar excitement swished through her; it was that reckless desire to kill, kill, kill. The minor potion had buffed her significantly; what would the major potion do?

Golden light sparked in her outstretched hand. Ribbons stretched and wrapped around, forming the rounded glass container. It was just as orange as the minor variant, with silvery metallic traces, except there was something new. Little dark bubbles that reminded her of boba, and she couldn't help but smile before downing it all.

**It will restore your Health and Stamina, as well as temporarily boost your Stats immensely.**
**Lasts 10 Minutes.**

Warmth enveloped her like she'd used Ignite within. Her head cleared, and an urgent electrical feeling surged behind her teeth. She exhaled steam; she felt like she could climb any mountain, stop a raging river all by herself, or even lift the entire building. A glance at her stats revealed why.

**Jenny Huang**
**Human (Stage II - Level 26) (Blooded)**
**Age: 6,801 days**
**Stats:**
**Power: 35 (+35)**
**Durability: 20 (+30) (+20)**
**Stamina: 40 (+40)**
**Agility: 35 (+35)**
**Stat Points Available: 0**
**Energy Available: 2118**

The major potion *doubled* her stats, though she wished it doubled the boost in durability from her exoskeleton too. But that was just being greedy.

With that, she felt as prepared as she'd ever be. She adjusted her hatchet, admiring the obsidian face and sharp edge as her red-covered finger clinked against it. Then she stepped back into the cafeteria.

Smoke, accompanied by a sulfuric stench, filled the space. This time, the angel had put out the flames much quicker, and the only source of light were the glowing colors blooming from a few corners—red and purple and a grayish one. Only three cocoons were left.

She knew the desecrated angel had sensed her. She'd already saved everyone she could. All that was left was defeating the creature; all she had to do was kill the giant bitch.

Her mouth had gone dry. *Too late now to create a bottle of water*, she thought. Stupid. But adrenaline pumped through her limbs, and she strained all her senses, her tentacles spreading in four directions.

Even if the creature was several levels higher, she'd won these odds before, hadn't she? Her first wretched angel? She'd defeated that before she'd even reached level ten. And now she was much stronger with her skills, exoskeleton, and tentacles, not to mention the boost from the potion.

The desecrated angel stood waiting in the center of the cafeteria, its giant form towering through the hazy mist and dissipating smoke. The sulfuric stench of burnt flesh stung her nose, but she didn't shift her exoskeleton to mask herself again; she might need to breathe fire.

It glowered at her, its shining blue eyes following her as she walked. There was no use in hiding. It was locked onto her scent just as all her senses were locked onto it.

The angel's blonde hair covered part of its dark metallic face. It was hunched over so its four arms relaxed by its side and its breasts sagged, but as Jenny moved closer, the creature bent its knees, looking coiled to leap.

Jenny stopped and braced herself, hatchet at the ready, tentacles swishing. She stood about a cafeteria table's length away. Torn and burnt bits of webbing drifted by her; she was waiting for the angel to make the first move. If she rushed in there, it would just grab her with one of its arms and snap her in half. Something from Sunday school came to mind: David and Goliath. But she was just as monstrous as the angel was; she wasn't afraid.

Some more tarnished angels burst from the darkness below with hideous screams, and Jenny glanced down. That was when the desecrated angel pounced.

Its wings unfolded with a *snap*. Wind battered everything, and the creature rushed straight for her.

Jenny didn't blink. She ducked low, and the angel flew over her. It was like watching an airplane overhead coming in for a landing: large and powerful, and so close that if she reached out her hand, she just might touch it.

It slashed at her with razor-sharp claws, but Jenny rolled away, and the angel landed with a huge crash. However, it was on its feet before Jenny, coming at her swinging. Jenny swiped an arm with her hatchet, the edge bouncing off the creature's metallic skin with sparks, and blocked another arm with two tentacles, straining against the sheer strength of the larger creature. But its third arm managed to hit her on the waist.

Claws left deep grooves in her exoskeleton, and Jenny cried out as searing pain went up her side. With her other tentacles braced against the floor, she twisted and kicked the angel in the thigh, using the force to throw herself back and away, desperate for space.

She skidded over the darkness as though it were ice, sidestepped a hissing tarnished angel before stopping on the other side. Her tentacles whipped overhead; Jenny was sweating like mad. Her side throbbed with pain, and blood dribbled down her scales. Its claws had broken through to her skin, but not deeply enough to do serious damage. She applied pressure and watched the giant creature steady itself.

It was too large. Up close, she barely came up to its navel. Her hatchet couldn't even cut into its arm.

The desecrated angel lumbered forward, hissing, steam rising from its jaws. It smashed everything in its path away—the molten sacs, the tarnished angels—upending cafeteria tables and tearing through its own webbing. A scream filled the room as the creature reached for Jenny, beating its wings to swirl up the mist and smoke.

Jenny saw her opening right away. Grasping her hatchet with both hands, she braced herself before bursting forward with Instant Acceleration. Everything rippled around her, and she willed herself to go faster and faster as she shot for the space between its thighs, her hatchet raised so she could slice into the creature.

She imagined cutting through its innards as she'd done to the black-covered wretched angel—this creature's mate. She cried out just before the edge of her hatchet met the angel's navel.

But her weapon bounced off the metallic skin, snapping her backward as she was stopped abruptly. Her legs rushed forward, and she went tumbling, her momentum sending her sliding forward. Her head bounced off the angel's leg so that she went spinning, crashing into a pillar.

The lower portion of the pillar crumpled, burying her in rubble, while her hatchet skidded away somewhere. Jenny groaned. If this had been before her exoskeleton, her head would've been bashed inward by the impact, and her arms would've come right out of her shoulders. She was more dazed than hurt, the breath knocked out of her lungs.

Before she could clear the rubble and stand, the angel was upon her. Its claws wrapped around her torso, squeezing the tentacles against her back, and she heard a faint *crunch*.

Lifting her out of the ruined pillar, it held her upside down. The angel glared, and she knew what it wanted. It was pissed she'd ruined its plans: the chem lab and all its eggs and babies; the humans it had collected. And now this. She'd burned several cocoons and killed off the other desecrated angels before they could emerge.

*It's okay*, she thought. *I'm pissed too.* Jenny forced breath into her chest, her insides straining against the claws, and used Ignite with her entire body. Every bit of her exoskeleton caught flame like she'd become a bonfire. The angel screeched, opening its hand with surprise and stumbling backward. Falling, Jenny concentrated the fire to her mouth before releasing it all at once like a flamethrower.

Fire shot out, bursting forward. She'd aimed for the creature's chest and face, hoping to burn it seriously, but the angel raised a hand and blocked it. The flames licked its palms and wrapped around its claws as Jenny caught herself with her tentacles before hitting the floor.

With a roar, the creature reached for her again, smoke trailing from the hands she'd burned. Jenny slammed two tentacles into its face. One found its nose, squishing right up into a nostril, while the other bounced off the creature's cheek.

It roared and struggled with her tentacles until it grabbed a hold of them and yanked them furiously. Blood spurted out of its nose as the tentacle slipped free, and Jenny sucked it in.

A shudder of energy pulsed through.

Just as she was trying to pull herself free, she saw the crack on the angel's navel, right below the creature's belly button. A crack like she'd taken a hammer to a piece of wood in shop class.

With a flash of light, her hatchet returned to her hand, and Jenny stepped forward, letting her tentacle coil around her body as the angel held firm. She was just about to swing again, thinking for sure her hatchet could cut through the weakened point, when the angel jerked to the side, lifting her off the floor by her tentacle and flinging her body with a roar.

Jenny jetted across the cafeteria at almost the same speed as her Instant Acceleration. Webs tore, and she burst through an undead angel, sailed over the scorched area she'd burned earlier, and was about to slam into the far wall when she latched on to a table with her tentacles, raising it off the floor and cracking it in half. It slowed her down just enough to bury her claws into a pillar and force herself to stop.

Dropping down quickly, she hid behind the table she'd destroyed, trying to catch her breath. Blood, guts, and bone fragments stuck to her, and she peeled torn skin off her scales. Something was in her mouth—a chunk of muscle from that dead angel. Jenny chewed and swallowed before swiping her blood- and sweat-soaked hair out of her face.

Rumbling jolted the floor and walls as the desecrated angel came toward her, and Jenny leaped onto the splintered table to face it.

It rushed across the cafeteria floor, knocking away tables and collapsing another pillar. Jenny's eyes went to the red cocoon attached to one of the vending machines. Remembering the screech of agony and rage when she'd burnt up the previous cocoons, she took aim and stomped forward, launching her hatchet with a Savage Throw.

The hatchet's obsidian edge glistened in the red light and, just before the desecrated angel reached her, burst through the red cocoon and sank into the chest of the angel inside. Gooey red liquid splashed, and the giant angel stumbled to a stop to whip around.

Beating its enormous wings savagely, it generated enough force to lift Jenny off the table and slam her into the wall, then rushed right to the ruined cocoon and the injured angel.

Jenny grinned, blood dripping down her chin as she slid to the floor. She'd been right. The desecrated angel *needed* these cocoons; its response was almost maternal. But why did it care more for these things than the babies?

She didn't care. All that mattered now was killing it, and with the creature distracted, Jenny had the perfect opportunity to hit it hard. Kicking off the wall with both feet, she combined the motion with Instant Acceleration and struck the angel on its back with as much force as she could, slamming into it with her exoskeleton-covered arms.

She connected with its spine, right between its wings, where its shoulder blades met. Metallic skin and bone crunched, and the creature rocked forward, slamming face-first into the vending machine where the red cocoon sat.

The glass of the vending machine shattered, and the cocoon gushed. Gooey red liquid splattered the packs of chips and cookies and chocolate.

**You've defeated Desecrated Angel (Level 30)!**
**Experience has been awarded.**
**+500 Energy**

A terrible moaning sound escaped the four-armed desecrated angel, but Jenny wasn't done. She leaped onto the angel's back, tentacles wrapping around its arms, trying to keep it from getting back up. The creature lay on top of the vending machine, the sac squished underneath it. Spread across its metallic-blue back were dozens of cracks, meeting at the center.

She'd been right. The angel *could* be damaged—it just took a lot to break through its skin.

Light flashed, her hatchet returned to her hand, and she slashed over and over at the cracks. Sparks burst like fireworks as the creature screamed and struggled to push off the floor. Its wings folded and beat desperately, but each of Jenny's relentless strikes caused the creature to convulse with pain.

Her weapon shimmered with light, and notifications filled Jenny's head.

**+50 Energy**
**+50 Energy**
**+50 Energy**

She screamed as the angel screamed. Jenny slashed over and over, grasping her hatchet with both hands as blood shot out and splattered everything. She only stopped when she struck bone, her hatchet getting stuck.

**+50 Energy**

The desecrated angel roared so loudly, it was like thunder right in Jenny's ears. Before she could wrench her weapon free and attack again, a blue light flashed. The angel's entire body lit up, as bright as any of the cocoons had when Jenny had set them on fire.

For a second, she was dazed, blinking and trying to restore her vision, trying to see with her tentacles, but a chill moved through them. Fear bubbled up through her thoughts and gripped her just as the angel had. It was the same flash of blue light that had arisen the dead.

The angel pushed off the vending machine, gooey red liquid splattering in every direction as it whirled around to smack her away.

Jenny's hatchet flew out of her hands from the impact. The angel twisted and stomped toward her as she bounced off the floor and slid till her head struck a table.

Something bright shot out of the creature's navel, catching Jenny like a net. Before she could tear it off, the angel towered over her, shooting more and more webbing from its navel until Jenny was trapped. She couldn't struggle; it was like having several weighted blankets pinning down her limbs.

**You have five minutes remaining till your potion loses effect.**

*Fuck,* she thought. She'd lose her boosted stats, and she needed every single drop to do any damage at all to the desecrated angel. Without it, she'd be a rag doll. She had to be quicker; she had to do more damage before it ran out.

But just as she was about to use a full-body Ignite to burn herself free, she heard a chorus of moaning and hissing. She couldn't turn her head, but she could see them in her peripheral vision. The half-melted desecrated angels, their bodies distorted and grotesque.

They stalked nearer and nearer, their eyes shimmering blue, their exoskeletons melted and drooped so they looked even more freakish and nightmarish than usual. They crawled on all fours, wheezing for every breath and clambering straight for her.

The enormous desecrated angel started to hum just as it had when lulling the tarnished angels that had emerged earlier. Jenny recognized that humming. Soothing and sweet; it was an order.

It was feeding time.

# CHAPTER FIFTY-FOUR

# FIGHT FEAR WITH FIRE

Moaning and whining swirled around Jenny as she struggled with the webbing. The strands weren't thick, but with several layers stacked, they might as well have been steel nets. She didn't have enough space to use her full strength; they pinned her firmly down, the side of her face stuck against soggy bread and a foam tray. It crinkled uncomfortably with her every attempt to escape.

The desecrated angel lumbered forward, hunched over, its lips curled back in a snarl. It beat its wings furiously, and the wind battered Jenny, but it also knocked away the undead angels, which toppled over each other as another flash of blue light illuminated the cafeteria. This one was so bright that Jenny felt her bones recoil.

Fear shot straight through her, and she struggled to catch her breath. Her lungs emptied and refused to refill. Her heart couldn't stop hammering against her chest, and Jenny let out a frustrated cry, trying to tear through the webbing with her exoskeleton-covered fingers.

The desecrated angel's power was getting stronger and stronger, and she was surrounded by the undead, with their melted, twisted forms. On top of that, her potion was running out. She didn't stand a chance; she kept picturing the worst. The angels were going to tear her apart; they were going to eat her. And there was nothing she could do about it.

Fright and panic twisted like knives in her stomach, wave after wave making her head hurt; her eyes ached like they'd pop out, and a scream suffocated in her throat.

She strained every muscle, trying to tear and kick and cut through with her tentacles, but even as she managed to peel off one section, another web slammed into her, catching her in a new uncomfortable position. All she managed to do was get more and more tangled, like a moth stuck in a spider's web. Everything was closing in, and she was the prey.

She felt Eve trying to communicate, felt her stats and her skills within reach, but the thoughts kept getting lost in her frantic need to escape. She'd never been good in cramped spaces. All she wanted to do was get up and breathe; every thought was laced with a new flash of blue light.

This time, her scream turned into a whimper. She remembered the time she'd hurt her back. She'd had to have an MRI done, and that machine had freaked her out so much.

But she'd managed to stay still. The technician had warned her if she moved, she'd have to do it all over again, so she remained as motionless as she could, staring at the white panels enclosed around her, feeling like she was in a coffin as the sounds of the machinery grew louder and louder. She found it funny that she'd hurt the angel in pretty much the same spot, hitting its spine with her hatchet.

Picturing the angel in an MRI machine snapped her out of the fight or flight response.

She didn't have to lie there and take it. This fear wasn't hers; it was a response to the angel's ability—and she had abilities of her own. *Ignite!*

Flames flickered down her entire body as the first of the undead creatures reached for her. It was the green one, its melted covering hardened over its eyes and nose, leaving only a gaping hole for a mouth visible.

When it grabbed her arm, its fingers caught fire. The creature screamed as the webbing melted away and Jenny twisted toward it, pressing her burning hand against its face. The green metallic covering turned gooey and slimy, melting further over its mouth and clogging its throat so that its scream choked out. It felt like squeezing jelly, but Jenny focused her fire into her palm and blasted through the creature's skull. The body fell away, smoke rising from its scorched neck.

With a cry of rage, Jenny whirled around. A flash of light returned her hatchet midswing, and she sliced through partially melted torsos and arms.

**+16 Energy**
**+16 Energy**
**+16 Energy**

They screamed as they fell, and Jenny noticed undead humans and angels scrambling from around the cafeteria, rushing toward her. An undead wretched angel reached for her, and Jenny cut through its ribs. Something dense struck her shoulder, and as she toppled over a cafeteria table, several creatures piled on top of her, snarling and moaning, their fingers tearing at her exoskeleton.

She swore loudly and pushed off the floor. For a second, she marveled at her ability to not just do *a* pushup but to lift several bodies as well. Her tentacles shot out, grabbing two of the angels and hurling them away, giving her just enough space to squeeze out of the tangle of rotting limbs.

Sweating, covered in blood and slime, Jenny leaped to her feet and squared her shoulders. Fear from the blue light still tried to undo her, but she couldn't pay it any attention. She had to focus and ignore everything else as best she could.

She inhaled deeply, eyeing the injured desecrated angel towering over all the others. The crowd of undead swarmed toward her, and Jenny screamed, letting loose a large stream of Ignite.

Fire billowed forward, mushrooming, expanding, as Jenny stomped closer and closer to the undead. Each one shrieked in turn as they caught flame. The cafeteria roared to life with a flickering orange-and-red glow, and warmth enveloped Jenny, clearing out every trace of fear from the blue flashes. The burning, screaming bodies stumbled through the flame, their dark silhouettes fading in and out as they reached blindly.

But before they burnt away completely, Jenny broke down into a coughing fit, a terrible hacking cough, like she might spit out her lungs; her throat felt like it had been scraped raw. She'd overdone it.

Her mouth tasted like ashes; her eyes watered from the pain and from the stench of burnt flesh as the creatures wriggled on the floor, still smoldering. But they weren't ashes like the ones she'd attacked before. These still crawled, half melted, half scorched. Demented cries escaped their ruined forms.

Jenny snarled, slashing off their heads with a spin of her hatchet. She slew them as quickly as she could, making her way to her target.

**+16 Energy**
**+10 Energy**
**+10 Energy**

The numbers lit up her thoughts, one after another, as she sidestepped, slashed, and stormed through.

**You have two minutes remaining till your potion loses effect.**

She slapped several undead away with her tentacles then threw herself forward, moving in close now that the giant creature's back was hurt so badly. It struggled to remain upright, its footing was unsure, and Jenny wanted to take as much advantage of that as she could.

The angel raised an enormous arm. Jenny's hatchet bounced off its wrist, and she spun, lashing out with her tentacles. Two struck the creature on the face, one of them splattering against an eye. The angel howled and stepped back, one of its legs nearly buckling, but it spread its wings wide, flapped them fiercely, and stabilized.

In the flickering firelight, the crack on its navel glistened. Jenny zeroed in on it. It was the crack from when she'd tried to burst through it before, but just like with the angel's back, all she had to do was attack it again and break the exoskeleton to get to the flesh.

When it swung again, trying to grab her, Jenny stepped closer instead of farther away and drove her tentacles, all four of them, into the creature's chin. Its head snapped back, the gigantic creature stumbled, and Jenny swung her hatchet from the side.

She focused all her power into the attack, making use of every drop of her boosted stats. The edge struck right on the mark, exactly where the crack had formed; the metallic exoskeleton shattered like glass, exposing the pale belly, and the creature roared so loudly, it sounded like a thunderstorm breaking over her head. It slapped its clawed hands over its stomach, beating its wings to remain upright as it backed away, breathing loudly.

*Kill, kill, kill* . . . Jenny couldn't suppress the grin this time, sweat dribbling down the side of her face as she looked up into the angel's blue eyes.

Its face was twisted in pain, its breathing labored. But Jenny wasn't about to let up. There was no need for mercy; this was the angel who had bitten off her fingers and eaten them. The angel who had gathered Oliver and his friends for food. Her insides burned with want; she could smell the sweet blood drying on the angel's back. Desecrated angel blood . . . strong and powerful and so sweet it made her tentacles swish recklessly. Her heart pounded with anticipation.

That exposed belly . . . so pale and soft; much more appealing than the tarnished angels'. She wanted to peel its skin off. Wanted to cut all the way through, till the angel was right on the verge of death, and then, only then, she wanted to eat. She wanted the creature to watch as she ripped it to bits and swallowed.

And maybe after that, she could be full. She wouldn't feel so hungry around Susan and the others. She wouldn't accidentally hurt anyone.

The scent was stuck in her head like a song she couldn't forget, and now she was humming too, mimicking how the angel had done so before.

"What's wrong?" she asked, stepping closer. Her tentacles shuddered. Blue light flashed, and a fresh wave of fear swelled up, but she dismissed it right away. With victory so close, how could she be afraid?

The angel bared its teeth, hunched over and protecting its navel with two hands. Its other two arms reached forward, but Jenny was quicker. She flung her hatchet with a Savage Throw.

She'd aimed for its neck, but the creature tried to duck. If its spine weren't injured, it probably would've managed it, but the obsidian edge caught the creature on the nose. Jenny heard a crack, followed by enraged hissing, but it had raised its arms instinctively to grab its face.

Jenny was already racing toward it, all her focus on the exposed belly. Golden light flashed, and she slapped an arm away. Just as she reached the creature, just before she could bury her hatchet into its flesh, the angel beat its wings.

Wind as powerful as a hurricane's slowed her down, pushing her back. A closed fist slammed down, and Jenny blocked it with both of her arms. The impact jolted through her shoulders and down her back, and she grimaced. Then another arm shot out before she could throw off the fist, and oversize claws wrapped around her chest and waist, plucking her right off the floor.

"No!" she gasped. The creature squeezed, hissing loudly.

Jenny struggled and squirmed. She heard a series of cracks; the sharp tip of the angel's claws dug into the grooves it'd left earlier, puncturing her skin. Screaming with rage, Jenny slashed and slashed, her feet kicking, her tentacles whipping the angel feebly, unable to get enough momentum with the claws wrapped around her torso.

Her weapon bounced off its metallic forearm. Sparks shot up, but the angel ignored these attacks and grabbed Jenny's legs with another arm. It was breathing hard, its nose crooked and rattling, taking its time as it glared at her with those cruel blue eyes. They seemed so large up close, jaws large enough to swallow Jenny's head whole.

Then it opened its mouth to roar, revealing large, stained teeth, and the warm stench of decaying flesh and vomit hit Jenny in the face.

Suppressing a cry, Jenny took aim as best she could, mustering up enough for another Savage Throw. If she could just pierce through the inside of its throat, it would be over. She raised her arm, and the angel twisted forward, turning its head in the blink of an eye. Its teeth flashed, its eyes glowed brightly, and Jenny's arm was in its mouth.

The angel's pupils dilated. Everything seemed to happen in slow motion: Its teeth connected with her exoskeleton; Jenny blinked, realization spreading through her like lightning as the creature's jaws closed shut with a *crunch*.

Her exoskeleton snapped. Her elbow popped, bursting between the creature's teeth, and the angel *slurped*. Its entire body lit up with blue light when it swallowed the first rush of her blood.

The hatchet dropped from Jenny's hand, but just as it clattered to the floor, she summoned it back to her left. Her new fingers—the ones Susan restored for her—they curled around the handle, and Jenny swung underhand as best she could, unable to see clearly through the tears. It bounced off harmlessly the first time.

Sensing something, the angel hesitated before sucking out more blood, but Jenny knew the frenzy in its eyes. The bloodlust. Her blood gushing into its mouth was all it could focus on. The overwhelming thirst.

On her second attempt, she heard a crack. On her third, the hatchet's edge slid deliciously into flesh.

**+50 Energy**

A choked cry escaped the angel, muffled by Jenny's arm. It spat her out. Strands of blood and saliva connected her ruined arm to the creature's lips as Jenny fell away. The angel grabbed its navel, where the hatchet was buried deep, and this time, when it flapped its wings, it crashed back, stumbling through one of its own giant webs to crash against the wall. Blood spilled down its legs, running freely through its claws.

Jenny landed hard on the floor. Her head spun, and she winced, trying to move her right arm. It was still attached, at least, but she could barely raise it. Pain throbbed, but it wasn't as bad as she thought it would be. She still had the potion's effect.

Gritting her teeth, she forced back a sob and focused her anger on the angel. It had drunk her blood, but she'd cut it open. And now, its blood was spilled too.

It kept crying out in agony, blue light flashing repeatedly. Strobing. Striking Jenny with fear every second, injecting fear right into her thoughts. But she kept her focus. She bit her tongue. She squeezed her injured arm repeatedly, pain making her salivate.

She could barely stand looking at how her exoskeleton cracked and splintered, but she couldn't stop here. She couldn't rest. She couldn't let the creature rest. She had to kill it *right now.*

# CHAPTER FIFTY-FIVE

# COLLAPSING STAIRS

In the blink of an eye, Susan saw Mrs. Monique dive forward and spear Miriam's waving hand. The tip connected with the girl's palm, punctured through, and struck the wall beside the door with a loud clang.

"That's enough!" shouted the librarian.

Miriam stared at her skewered hand. It was pinned to the wall. Blood dribbled from the wound, and her green eyes blinked. The corners of her lips twitched, and her face distorted like she was about to cry. She let out a loud, haunting wail, turning slowly to look at everyone, her eyes wide and full of tears as if silently asking, "Why would you do this to me?"

She pulled on her hand, and Susan winced, because it looked like the girl was trying to rip her hand free of the spear. The skin stretched—the *fingers* stretched. More blood gushed out and ran down the wall, but Mrs. Monique yanked the spear free before it could get worse.

Miriam hiccupped, wiped her eyes with her ruined hand—smearing fresh blood across her cheeks—and then smiled. She pursed her lips as though she were blowing a bubble with chewing gum, and another dark-green bubble expanded outward. Mackenzie dashed forward, about to follow up on Mrs. Monique's attack, while Susan tried to grab her arm.

"Wait!" she shouted, but she was too slow to catch her. The bubble snapped free of Miriam's lips and exploded with a dazzling flash of green light.

Screams echoed up and down the stairwell. The shock wave threw Susan down the flight of stairs as the dead bodies erupted, limbs and pieces scattering all over. She couldn't see where the others had gone, landing on top of something large and hard.

It took her a moment to pull herself up, then she realized she was on the chest of a wretched angel. Its head was split open nearly down to its mouth. Its purple covering was cracked. Susan scrambled to get off, breathing hard. Her body ached all over, but it could've been worse. Her ears rang. Her head spun. But at least she wasn't badly hurt. She'd even managed to hold on to her cattle prod.

Leaning against a partially collapsed wall, she stared up the stairwell to the second-floor door. The walls had been blasted so that their insides spilled into the stairs. What was wrong with Miriam? Why had she become like this? Why did it remind Susan of what'd happened to Jenny?

Had the girl lost her mind? The way she'd attacked the babies . . . The way she'd eaten one of them.

Miriam had always been quiet and reserved, keeping to herself to avoid getting teased or harassed. One time, some kids from the football team had taken to yanking on her hijab, pulling it back and ruining the folds, and Miriam had snapped, swearing at them in Arabic, but that had only made them tease her more. Susan had always tried to be nice to Miriam, but it wasn't like she'd stepped in to stop the harassment. And what was she supposed to do now?

Dust swirled. Something creaked overhead, and Susan heard coughing. Dulé emerged. His helmet was missing, and a nasty bruise had formed on his forehead, but he held Oliver in his arms. He opened his mouth to say something, but all he managed was more coughing. He had to place Oliver down, propping him up against the dead wretched angel that Susan had landed on.

From the corner of her eye, she saw some bodies move, and her heart sped up instinctively, panic surging through her. But it was only the dead.

Mackenzie pushed several bodies off her and sat up, summoning her knife back with a flash of light. Her ruined armor had crumbled away, revealing a torn gray sweater. She looked murderous, but her face softened when she spotted Oliver and Dulé. Susan noticed her arms were mostly bare now, burnt looking and raw, and she imagined that was how Mackenzie had protected herself from the explosion.

But where was Mrs. Monique?

As Mackenzie tended to Dulé, Susan searched the rubble, fear spreading through her with each feeble step. She tripped once or twice, and stepped on a few things that squished under her feet, but there was no sign of the librarian until she heard shouting overhead, followed by wretched cries that had to be Miriam's.

Mackenzie shot Susan a look before dashing up the stairs two at a time. The steps were clear of bodies, and Susan followed slowly, trying not to twist her ankle on any loose chunks of the wall. She clicked her cattle prod on so that it crackled and vibrated in her hand. She might not be able to shoot lightning again, and she didn't particularly want to after that reaction with one of Miriam's bubbles, but if Susan could stun the girl, maybe the others could stop her. Permanently.

**Humans remaining: 12**

"Oh," she whispered, pausing and squeezing the railing. It had come up sub-consciously; she didn't want to know. Didn't want to see it drop by another number. Was Jenny one of the twelve left? And if they didn't stop Miriam, then *their* numbers would be subtracted from the total and . . .

Strength she couldn't explain flowed through her. It was like a second or third wind, and she climbed as quickly as she could, reaching the top steps just as Mackenzie slashed Miriam's leg.

Mrs. Monique jabbed toward the girl's face, but the tip of the spear only caught the helmet and knocked it off. It clattered to the floor and rolled toward Susan. The pink coloring was scorched to an ashy black. It didn't look anything like the helmet she'd originally made, the top plastic peeled and curled so that it resembled an ugly, twisted crown.

Miriam slapped Mackenzie hard enough to knock her into the door. The girl's face struck the heavy metal, and she crumpled without a sound.

With a laugh, Miriam whirled around and tackled Mrs. Monique's legs, bringing the librarian down with a heavy crash, then tried to pin Mrs. Monique's arms and bite her, looking oddly similar to the first tarnished angel that Susan had seen.

But before Miriam's teeth could connect with anything, Mrs. Monique managed to roll to the side and knock her away. Miriam cried out in frustration, her head turning this way and that as if trying to find a way out, but when she caught sight of Susan, her eyes lit up. Shoving the librarian, she scrambled toward the steps, reaching out with stained hands.

Susan was shaking badly, but she let go of the railing and was just about to hit Miriam with the cattle prod when Mrs. Monique grabbed the girl's hijab and tugged hard. Miriam's head snapped back. She twisted and wailed, but the librarian attacked with her spear. The tip sliced through Miriam's shirt, leaving a groove of red in her exposed pale skin, but that didn't slow her down.

She leaped onto the woman and pushed her against the wall. Her fingers found Mrs. Monique's face, and this time, it was the librarian screaming uncontrollably as nails raked her cheeks and lips and clawed her empty eye socket.

"Stop!" cried Susan, diving for Miriam. She slammed the cattle prod into the gash Mrs. Monique had made, an ugly cut that went down her side toward her navel. There was a brief instance of resistance, and then the prod slid inside Miriam.

Electricity surged into her thin body, and she started convulsing. Her fingers curled into fists, latching onto Mrs. Monique's face. She shook violently, her eyes rolling into the back of her head till she looked just like the angels, a warbled scream lodged in her throat.

Mackenzie appeared next, shouting something that sounded like "Stupid bitch!" The side of her face was a mess, an ugly purple mark forming around her cheekbone. She was about to thrust her knife into Miriam's throat when green light bubbled out of Miriam's open mouth.

There were a series of *cracks*, and the light blossomed and shot upward, illuminating the underside of the stairwell above for a hideous second before erupting. This time, the explosion went off overhead. All they felt was wind and searing heat, and then the steps came crashing down.

Large chunks struck the floor beside them. One clattered over Mackenzie's head, and her knife went flying out of her hands. In the chaos, Susan's grip on the cattle prod slipped as well.

"It leveled up!" shouted Miriam. "It got stronger! *I* got stronger!"

As stuff crashed down around them, Miriam pointed at the floor. Green rings of light traveled down her arm in waves, gathering at the tip of her finger as her hand shook. It looked like a weapon charging up, and Miriam was struggling to hold on. Then, it all released at once with more force than anything Miriam had shot at them before.

For a moment, Susan thought she was dead. The floor erupted, and everything went dark. Or was it too bright? She couldn't tell, but she was sure her face should have been burnt away. Her ruined armor should have evaporated, and there should be nothing left of her skin or bones.

Instead, all she felt was a dropping feeling, like she was falling, then she hit the stairwell below, breaking through those steps as though the entire building were collapsing. When she struck the floor, all she felt was the sudden shock of coming to a stop.

Opening her eyes, she found herself encased in something that looked like glass. Square panels of silvery light shimmered and encompassed her in a cube. A similar silver cube was around Mackenzie, who was out cold and lying on her side, blood around her head. Rubble bounced off the protective cubes and clattered away.

Then she saw Mrs. Monique inside of her own cube, a strained expression on her face as the veins throbbed on her forehead. Her arms were raised with the palms facing Susan and Mackenzie, and Susan realized what had happened.

The librarian had figured it out. Her skill. The barriers!

With a gasp, Mrs. Monique dropped her hands, and the barriers flickered away, leaving the librarian gasping for breath, sweat and blood running down the sides of her face.

Sound rushed back to Susan. Pieces of the stairwell clattered down around them in clouds of dust. Her heart thundered. Then she heard a wheezing and rasping coming from behind, and Susan turned to see Miriam stretched out on her back.

Her face was darkened. Her body had been hit by a large chunk of the stairwell, several steps still attached together, and it lay over her hips and thighs. Her hijab had come nearly undone, trailing from her head like a cloth river winding through rubble.

"What the fuck?" Dulé appeared, covered in dust and looking desperate and frantic while holding the unconscious Oliver in his arms. Susan exhaled a sigh of relief. She'd been half afraid they'd crushed the boys in the fall.

Before Susan could respond, Miriam started laughing. It was a choked, painful laugh, but the girl shifted the rubble off her and struggled to sit up. "Isn't it neat? I can do *this* now." Green light surged back to her fingertip, and she pointed at Susan's face. More rings of light flashed up Miriam's arm as her eyes widened with glee.

Susan braced herself for the worst, but Mrs. Monique raised her hand, and a silver sheet of light shimmered in front of Susan and the others. The librarian looked completely drained; generating the barriers must cost as much stamina as Susan's lightning. And how did impacts affect the ability?

Miriam didn't fire again. Instead, she cocked her head, blinking over and over. Then a blue light flashed, making Susan wince before she realized it wasn't green. It wasn't another exploding bubble, but she recognized it. Fear flared to life in her head, and a desperate need to *run* seized her.

But it didn't seem to affect Miriam the same. The girl's smile widened as she got to her feet. Her legs were shaking, and her torn shirt flapped so that Susan could see the gash down her side; the cattle prod was stuck in the wound. Her hijab trailed behind her, revealing her dark hair. The cloth was still attached by a clip, but she didn't seem to notice. Instead, she licked her lips and lowered her glowing green hand.

"They're here," she said softly. "Right here." And she pointed ahead, through the blasted doorway and down the hall. "In the lunchroom."

Miriam straightened up, squeezing her eyes shut as she lifted her nose to sniff. "And there are more . . . kids . . . weak and easy . . ." She laughed and shook her head. "Forget you guys," she said as she walked by them, her glowing hand raised as a warning.

The barrier moved around Susan, keeping a separation between her and Miriam as the girl left them behind. They heard rumblings and shouts. Something screamed—a hideous, ugly sound—and a jolt shivered through the entire building, knocking more rubble and dust loose.

Blue light flashed over and over, and each time, a fresh ripple of fear cut through Susan's chest like a shard of glass. She wanted to throw up. She wanted to rip out her heart and make it stop. She kept seeing the worst happening. Kept picturing Jenny's death in every way imaginable. Decapitation via teeth. Claws buried in Jenny's stomach. Her limbs ripped apart. Her jaw torn off. On and on it went, and it hurt each time, even though she knew it was the light causing this.

It hit the others just as hard. Mackenzie cried out as she woke up, covering her ears with her hands. Dulé dropped to one knee, his head bowed, tears leaving trails down his dust-covered face as he struggled to breathe. Mrs. Monique dropped her barrier and slammed a fist against her armor, the sound ringing down the basement hallway.

Only Miriam seemed completely unfazed by the light. She approached the cafeteria doors and turned to look back at Susan. "Just in case," she said. "I want to level up some more."

Then she pointed with her glowing finger and released another blast of green light.

# CHAPTER FIFTY-SIX

# REVENGE

Using her tentacles to lift herself, Jenny got to her feet and summoned her hatchet. It slipped out of the angel's belly with a satisfying gush, and the creature buckled to its knees, screaming and howling. Her left hand squeezed the handle, and she grimaced as the angel screamed again, in a pitch so high that it felt like being stabbed in the ears.

She'd been so close. If she'd hit the angel with her right arm, that blow would've been immensely more powerful, and this would've been over. But still. This was good. The angel couldn't stand, so all she had to do was land one more solid attack.

Even on its knees, the angel was enormous. It took up almost all the space between the ruined pillar and a broken table. Red goo from the crushed cocoon glistened on its neck and chest, and blood rushed out of its navel despite its best attempts to stop the flow with two hands. A third arm held onto the pillar; the other was pressed firmly on the floor as the angel sucked in deep breaths, hissing and drooling and glaring. Its wings fluttered pitifully.

Jenny's right arm hung loose. It was useless from the elbow down, but she ignored it and marched right toward the creature. A Savage Throw to the head. She'd follow that up with Ignite and boil its eyes, and then attack again and again and again.

**The potion has run its course.**

All of a sudden, whatever was holding her up was cut off, and she cried out, losing her footing. Every ache—the hurt of every bruise and every scratch—hit her simultaneously. Her head spun, and she slipped on the glistening floor, catching herself with her tentacles so that she hung like a rag doll. Bile rose to her throat, burning her insides. Her arm hurt so much she almost wanted to tear it off.

She hissed, trying to stifle the pain. Tears streamed down her face and clouded her vision. She'd been so close. *So close.*

**You need energy, Jenny Huang. To heal. To reinforce yourself. Victory is within reach.**

"How?" she whispered, straining against the pain. "The only angels left are the undead. And they don't give me shit."

Eve didn't say the next bit, at least not in words, but Jenny understood. The three-headed figure flickered in her thoughts; she saw her mother's face, then Susan's, then Leslie's. She saw Leslie in the janitor's closet, hugging her legs, huddled with the others Jenny had saved from the web. They were right there. Waiting in the closet. Ripe for the picking. All she had to do was kill them.

**Victory is within reach. You must claim it.**

Jenny shuddered. She squeezed her eyes shut, tears escaping from the corners. Hunger rampaged through her, and she knew one bite would replenish her. One human kill would give her everything she needed.

She swore at herself. Swore at Eve. Cursed this stupid game. Cursed what she'd become. What she'd always been. All she could think about was soft flesh between her teeth, biting and chewing and swallowing, and again she remembered how soft Susan had looked, drained of all her strength and leaning against Jenny . . . How good she'd smelled.

But something else caught her attention. Something immediate. Something right next to her.

It was sweet, and the more she focused on it, the more her tentacles went into overdrive, whipping uncontrollably. So *this* had been stirring her hunger and pulling apart the edges of her mind. She opened her eyes and raised her hatchet, staring at its obsidian face as her hand shook; she swore she could feel her every heartbeat. She'd caught this scent before. When she'd attacked its spine, but it had slammed her away before she could indulge.

The angel's blood was stuck to the obsidian like paint splattered across dark glass. It dripped from the sharp edge, and she shuddered when a drop hit the floor. She could hear it. Feel it. And she almost gave into the instinct of dropping on all fours and sucking it off the dirty tiles, but why would she do that when there was still so much left on her hatchet?

Inhaling deeply, Jenny flattened her tongue against her weapon and licked all the way to the top. She ran her tongue side to side—from the handle to the sharp edge—and slurped when she'd drooled too much. A tingling spread from her tongue down to her chest and through her entire body; from her forehead to her toes, to the tips of her tentacles. Sweet, like biting into a freshly peeled clementine; the burst of flavor.

All the world faded away, and all that mattered was picking up that next piece and popping it into her mouth. This wasn't enough. It wasn't nearly enough.

She smiled as the angel howled again in anguish. It was moving away, crawling and limping, spilling more precious blood. No matter how strong it was—no matter how many levels it had on Jenny—a hatchet to the belly wasn't something it could just shake off.

It was heading for the darkness, from where more tarnished angels were crawling out, hissing and hungry. But the desecrated angel was even hungrier, and it grabbed them and fed.

Jenny groaned. The angel was doing what Eve had wanted her to do: Eat the others. Grow strong enough to win.

Jenny willed herself forward and stumbled as pain shot through her ruined arm—pain that burst into her head like fireworks, forcing her to stop and hyperventilate. She'd been through worse, but that didn't make this any more bearable.

"Okay," she said, spitting. She pulled up her stats, glancing at how much energy she had left.

**Jenny Huang**
**Human (Stage II - Level 26) (Blooded)**
**Age: 6,801 days**
**Stats:**
**Power: 35**
**Durability: 20 (+30)**
**Stamina: 40**
**Agility: 35**
**Stat Points Available: 0**
**Energy Available: 2952**

Hope wasn't lost. She'd been lucky. Killing off the angels in the cocoon had given her so much to work with, she could've laughed with joy. Another major potion of fortification shimmered into existence in her left hand, and she downed it in one go.

Throwing the container over her shoulder, that familiar surge shuddered through her, and again, she felt like she could do anything. Pain dulled slightly, but then it spiked all of a sudden. She gasped and nearly face-planted. Pressure formed in her lungs, a tightness that caught her breath, and she choked. She smacked her exoskeleton-covered chest, then hit herself again—harder this time—hard enough to make a crack, and she coughed up blood and whatever was in her stomach.

**Using performance-enhancement creations without rest
will result in bodily rejection.**

"No shit," hissed Jenny, wiping the spittle off her chin and trying to ignore the lump in her throat. "You couldn't tell me that before I made it?"

**You have five minutes remaining till your potion loses effect.**

*Five?* She blinked repeatedly as her body relaxed. *Five minutes? Half of what I got last time, but all right. All I have to do is kill this thing, and then I can relax. Then I'll have all the energy I need to do whatever I want.*

She looked at her ruined arm. The whites of fractured bones jutted out from her torn skin, her elbow crushed to nothing. Looking at her own exposed tendons made her feel even sicker. At least the pain had faded to a dull throbbing. She had enough points to heal it, but it might be better to keep the points in reserve, in case she needed something else. She'd spent too much on the major potion of fortification, but she was sure it would be enough to kill the angel. And somehow, that idea tickled some deep recess of her mind: *I can beat you with one arm tied.*

Concentrating, she shifted her exoskeleton, peeling it back slightly from her forearm to thicken around her elbow. The red covering melted and jiggled around, sealing in the cracks and reinforcing it before hardening once again, making her shudder as it took hold in her ruined flesh and bones. She didn't bother with the scales this time. It looked as monstrous as she felt.

Satisfied that it would hold her arm together, she snaked one of her tentacles from her shoulder down to her wrist. By moving the tentacle, the arm moved well enough to at least defend herself, and her fingers still worked. She closed and opened a fist, but it didn't feel strong enough to hold her hatchet, much less attack. She'd have to keep using her left for now.

*Alright. I'm losing time.* With one cursory glance at her stats to make sure they were actually doubled and there weren't more adverse effects from using the potion again, she set off, rushing toward the desecrated angel, whose enormous form took up the center of the cafeteria.

Excitement filled her thoughts like a beehive, an endless buzzing. She wanted more of its blood with every fiber of her being. She quickened her pace, half running, tentacles swishing. The angel turned; it was hunched over the darkness, and its blue eyes flashed. A tarnished angel was in its mouth, feet first, its arms swinging as its back arched. The frail angel let out a final scream, reaching desperately before vanishing behind the desecrated angel's lips.

Once it swallowed, the creature roared, shaking out its wings. It spat up flecks of blood and flesh and bone. Blue light flashed, and its navel wasn't bleeding any more, but it was still a mess—raw pink-and-red flesh, torn open and exposed.

The angel's piercing blue eyes met hers, and she stared back, wondering if it could sense Jenny's bloodlust. Wondering if it was afraid. Wondering if it even understood. When she'd been an angel, her mind had been an incoherent barrage of despair and hunger, but this angel had irises—eyes that looked almost human. It had tended to the other cocoons. It understood rage.

She remembered back in the chem lab when it had chosen her for feeding. How it'd wanted her blood, and now, how she wanted its blood. She licked her lips. She wanted more than just blood. She wanted to bite through its fingers and chew and swallow. She wanted to bite through its throat and drown its final scream in blood and watch the blue fade from its eyes. Every inch of her tentacles wanted more.

The angel roared and flapped its wings, rising to tower over Jenny, guarding its navel with one hand and attacking with the other three. Blood spilled from its torso, and with its back injured so badly, its movements were even slower.

Its size was still a problem, enormous and furious. Jenny slapped away two arms with her tentacles, twisting and turning to dodge the third. She rushed right for its belly, trying to get another strike in, but the angel didn't move the hand over its core once. Blue light flashed. It hissed with rage and swiped her legs, and she realized it was trying to catch her again. Eating her was the only way it could win now. The tarnished angels must not have given it nearly enough to recover fully.

Jenny switched up her approach, painfully aware of how little time she had before her potion ran out again, then it would be game over. She couldn't exhaust herself in a futile fight, just dodging and failing.

She kicked off the floor and launched herself backward and away.

The angel blinked; it hadn't expected that, but it soon bared its teeth and spread its wings, knocking through a ruined pillar and pushing a table away. Another tarnished angel emerged from the darkness between them, but neither of them glanced at it. Jenny was locked onto the desecrated angel, and it was solely focused on her.

Jenny launched her hatchet at its oversized head. Before the handle even left her fingertips, she was dashing forward with Instant Acceleration. Arms crossed in front of her face, she burst through the tarnished angel and slammed into the desecrated angel's hand-covered torso as hard as she could. Her hatchet bounced off its face, leaving another crack on its nose, then skittered away.

The desecrated angel bellowed in pain, nearly doubling over as blood spurted out from underneath its palm and claws. It swiped viciously for Jenny, but she was ready. Her shoulders ached from the impact, and her reinforced right arm felt like it was about to tear off, but she caught the creature's large arm with both hands and used it to hoist herself up.

She leaped into the air and was already swinging her left arm as light flashed and her hatchet appeared. Before the edge could make contact with the angel's face, the creature raised a hand and blocked her attack.

But this was the hand Jenny had burned before; she'd attacked it several times already. Cracks lined its metallic covering, and her hatchet sliced through its four fingers with ease.

## +50 Energy

The angel's forearm struck Jenny on the chin, and she was thrown away, landing on her back and sliding across the floor. Her jaw and neck hurt, and she heard a crack as she straightened up. Her injured arm hurt even more, but she couldn't help grinning.

Her attacks felt more decisive. She was getting quicker and quicker, and it was all becoming second nature: Maneuvering. Twisting. Attacking. And all the while, the angel was getting slower and weaker.

It was huffing hard, dropping again to its knees with enough force to shake the entire cafeteria. Its blonde hair fell in front of it, and Jenny remembered when that angel had attacked her before. When it had been wretched, it'd bitten into her thigh, chewed off her fingers. And it would have killed her and Susan if it wasn't for Mrs. Monique and the others from the library.

But she'd gotten her revenge, hadn't she? She'd cut off *its* fingers now. She only wished she'd done it slower, one finger at a time. Good thing there were still three more sets left.

"Is that all you've got?" shouted Jenny, her throat hoarse, tentacle tightened around her right arm. She heard an ugly *click* where her elbow used to be attached, but that didn't matter. This was about to end soon, and then she could heal up with all the energy she'd get from killing this bitch.

Now that it had dropped, Jenny was almost level with its massive head. Even if she couldn't get to its belly, she'd already cracked its face. She'd thrown a table at it. She'd hit it with her hatchet. She just had to puncture its exoskeleton again, break through, and slash and slash and slash.

The angel beat its wings. Wind shuddered through the cafeteria, and it snarled, leaping at Jenny. It kept low to the floor, staying on its knees and two arms like some sort of giant humanoid insect. Its claws scratched the air, inches in front of Jenny's face, as its fingerless hand swung at her. Jenny misdirected that arm by knocking it back with her tentacle, giving her an opening to swing.

She wanted to catch it on the cheek or cut off its nose, but it hissed and slammed another arm on the cafeteria floor, destroying it and causing Jenny to lose her footing in the explosion of tiles.

The angel slammed its head into Jenny's chest, knocking the breath from her lungs. It kept its head pressed to her, and pushed her back and upward, lifting her body off the floor. Her hatchet bounced harmlessly off the angel's ear as it flapped its wings so hard that everything around them—rubble and tables and bodies— blew away in a storm of mist and dust. It smashed Jenny into the ceiling with enough force to crater the entire thing.

She threw up blood.

Her weapon slipping from her hand, she saw stars bursting behind her eyes. The three-headed figure appeared and blinked away, darkness rising like twin tidal waves from each side and spilling through her head.

Out of desperation, Jenny grabbed a fistful of blonde hair and yanked. Hair tore off, ripping out of its scalp, sticky with sweat and blood. The angel screamed and snapped its head from side to side, tearing at Jenny. Claws raked her exoskeleton, piercing her tentacles and leaving deep gashes. It was trying to rip her apart while pinning her to the ceiling with its giant head.

Trying not to scream, and trying not to pass out, Jenny forced air into her lungs, breathing through her bleeding tentacles as well as her nose, storing up as much as she could before expelling it all with one rageful shout. *Ignite!*

The angel shrieked as its hair caught fire, flames engulfing its head completely to its shoulders. Its onslaught of attacks slowed as it grabbed its face with multiple hands, trying to pat out the flames, giving enough space for Jenny to slip away.

She was falling, just barely holding on to consciousness, but her body reacted the split second she saw her opportunity.

A flash of light brought her hatchet back to her hand. This time, she did what she'd been aiming for all along: She buried the weapon into the angel's navel and swung upward. The sharp edge sliced further into its belly, slid up its navel, then through the creature's sternum. Its exoskeleton crackled and split, and Jenny collapsed as blood spurted out and sprayed all over her.

### +50 Energy

Blood which she accepted with an open mouth, like trying to catch raindrops at the start of a storm. Her tentacles swished as the angel's cries vibrated through the floor and through each of them until she couldn't hold them back anymore. There was no stopping the impulse, the absolute *need* that took control.

Each tentacle, even the one she'd wrapped around her ruined arm, latched onto the angel's belly. Each one slid through the wound and squished through the angel's insides and began to *slurp*.

She pumped the angel's blood into herself, four greedy swallows at a time. If the precious few drops she'd licked off her hatchet had been a surprising gush of flavor, this was a supernova. Her eyelids grew heavy and dropped. Her breathing deepened, and her heart rate slowed as new blood flooded through her, swirling into her bloodstream and pumping through her heart.

It ached. It ached in the way a bruise would ache, but she'd still press down anyway. It ached in the way she'd touch herself and try not to make a sound but come completely undone. How she'd claw at the sheets and wonder if she'd ever feel someone else's lips pressed to her own. How badly she wanted to feel loved and whole. This agony was sweet and delicious, and wave after wave of shuddering pleasure spiraled up and down her spine.

Warmth spread. Pain faded and blurred into joy, and she dismissed the notification that her second potion had run out.

She didn't need any more potions now. She didn't want anything else. This blood was richer than the other angels'. The lesser angels. The undead angels. This blood had power to it—something ancient and remarkable. Something divine. And it was inside her. Moving into her.

A whimper escaped her lips. She pressed a fist against her belly button as the urge grew stronger and stronger. She felt it with each breath she took. She felt the angel's breath on her face, felt its needs and fears, and it felt *good*. Its breathing was ragged. Smoke rose from its burned scalp as it collapsed onto the floor, right over the darkness that connected worlds.

Some blood spilled into the darkness below, and it soaked up every drop like a sponge. Jenny gnashed her teeth and adjusted her tentacles. She wanted it all; it was all hers. She'd done all this work, come all this way.

She spread the angel's belly open further, the skin tearing like cloth. The muscles snapped apart, and the exoskeleton cracked like an eggshell. It was losing all its strength, all its durability.

One of its wings lay flat. The other was half unfurled. Up close, it looked like thin, stretched skin. Veins ran through them like webbing, and they were slightly translucent. Its leg twitched. The blue light of its eyes dimmed, and she knew it was almost over. It was dying, its power flowing into her, and as soon as it was dead, she would level up tremendously. She would gain enough energy to do whatever she wanted.

Its large head was starting to remind her of a deflating beach ball. The blonde hair was almost completely gone, only a handful of ashy strands clinging to its ruined scalp. Pressing her hand to the creature's chest, she pushed the angel onto its back. Its breathing was shallow and quick, its chest rising and falling as it struggled for each breath. A whimper slipped out of Jenny's lips as a new pressure took hold of her.

Her exoskeleton shimmered and grew, and the scales reemerged. Dropping to her knees beside its head, her tentacles attached to its navel like several umbilical cords. She was losing it. Losing control. Blood wasn't the only thing she wanted. Just a drink wasn't enough to sate this hunger.

Her legs went weak, her shoulder blades cracked, and two more tentacles exploded out of her back to latch onto the angel, worming deeper into the abdominal space and sliding and squeezing everywhere they could.

Blinking away tears, she stroked the angel's skin before pressing her palm against it, her exoskeleton retracting so she could touch the creature directly, skin to skin. So she could feel its racing heartbeat. Jenny couldn't stop salivating.

She pictured biting through its chest, imagining the angel's breasts to be soft under the exoskeleton. Where she could split its ribs open, get to that frantic heart, and sink her teeth into it as it pumped blood into her mouth and—

It raised an arm as if to attack, but it dropped helplessly with a thud. She looked into its eyes without blinking. The strange, blue eyes. Blue and glistening. The irises shook as they stared back into Jenny's, unblinking. Was it crying? Was it suffering? She didn't care.

She was hungry. Maddeningly hungry. Like she hadn't eaten in ages.

But just as she was about to take her first bite, a series of cracks snapped through the air. Green light flashed from the direction of the entrance, and she heard screaming. Many people screaming.

The front of the cafeteria exploded just as Jenny turned her head. She glimpsed Leslie and the others from the janitor's closet, running and shouting. And then someone stumbled toward them, a big, toothy grin on her small, blood-covered face.

Jenny's jaw dropped. It was Miriam. Her shirt was cut and torn, and she was bleeding from a gash in her side. Her hijab had come undone and fluttered behind her. And she dragged a boy by the arm. He was limp on the floor, his head lolling, hanging onto his shoulders by a bit of skin.

Miriam smiled, and red-stained saliva dribbled down her chin. "Hi, Jenny. I was looking for you." Then she pointed a finger at her, and a green bubble of light took shape at her fingertip. Light surged around Miriam's arm.

"Run!" came another scream—a voice Jenny recognized. A voice that made Jenny's tentacles stop slurping. She turned and saw Susan, covered in dust, limping toward them with a frantic, fearful look on her face.

She was just about to call back to Susan when green light flashed. Something hit Jenny right in the chest—a burst of heat and force, an explosion that shattered her exoskeleton and flung her away. Her tentacles were wrenched out of the desecrated angel, and her head bounced off the ruined pillar before she rolled to a stop on the floor.

# CHAPTER FIFTY-SEVEN

# LASAGNA

Everything was dark. Jenny wasn't sure how far she'd been thrown, or if she was even whole. Her body felt absent—*she* felt absent. Where was she?

*Where am I? How did I get here?*

The first sound to penetrate the deafening numbness was chewing.

Ripping.

*Swallowing.*

Someone was eating, but Jenny didn't hear these noises with her ears. The sound waves traveled through the air to reach her greedy tentacles, blood still moving through them, gushing into her body as though she were a cave flooding in a storm.

She accepted and drank, allowing the baffling sensation of liquid heat to flow through her, swirling and spiraling. Her body needed this. *Craved* every precious drop.

When she blinked, she caught blurry visuals of the chaos around her. Large steel shelves were knocked over, and oranges were everywhere, many of them crushed by falling rubble. Cooking utensils and giant pots littered the floor.

It took her a few moments to realize where she'd landed. She'd been blasted through the wall and into the kitchen, where she must've hit the large metal refrigerator door. It was crumpled behind her, but she didn't remember the impact.

Her eyelids felt so impossibly heavy. It wasn't until she inhaled through her nose and filled her lungs properly that pain ballooned inside her. The sleepiness vanished with a single shudder, and Jenny coughed and threw up blood. She retched again, and blood—thick and gooey and darker than it seemed possible— spilled from her lips

Trying to sit up in the rubble, she clutched her aching chest. Jenny was hyperventilating, her eyes bulging. Her memories flashed—a green bubble had struck her. Shot out of Miriam's finger.

*Miriam!*

Gingerly, she lowered her head to glance at the damage. She winced so hard that she cried out in pain.

Her exoskeleton had burnt away, exposing her bare chest where the skin was burnt so badly, it looked like hardening lava. Each breath was accompanied by a whimper, and each whimper only made it hurt more.

*And the chewing.* Teeth snipping through flesh. Saliva, and the sounds of swallowing. A moan of delight followed by a wail of ecstasy. *Who the fuck is eating my meal?*

Jenny rested her head against the bent refrigerator door, trying to ignore the pain and steady her breathing. It hurt like hell, but she tried to distract herself from it.

Looking through the broken wall into the cafeteria, she extended her tentacles forward like radio antennae, trying to find out what was going on. Images fizzed through her head, static that snapped and crackled like she was struggling to get a connection.

But it was Miriam. Miriam was bent over the desecrated angel, pinning down the creature's wrists as it hissed and tried to flap its wings against the floor. The girl was chewing through the angel's arm. She peeled the metallic exoskeleton away with her teeth and dug into the exposed muscle. All the while, the angel shrieked and shrieked.

*Fuck . . . that's mine. That's my meal. I nearly died to claim that. What the fuck is she doing?*

Jenny retched up more blood. She whimpered at the loss, the dark liquid pooling in front of her and running down the tiled floor to mix with some kind of spilled sauce. From the smell, she realized lunch was going to be lasagna.

Lasagna was about the only school lunch she thought was decent. Sure, the pizza days weren't terrible, and sometimes the tuna sandwiches were good, but the lasagna never missed.

*I could kill for some lasagna . . .*

Jenny's tentacles dropped heavily to the floor, crushing chunks of the wall and cartons of milk, which burst. Her tentacles slurped up the liquid, and she shuddered. Her mind was a mess of hunger and hurt, and every time a tentacle slurped, her focus went right to it.

They were thicker now—heavier and fleshier—and she had six. *Six tentacles.* Drinking the angel's blood had furthered her transformation, and she touched her left eye, wondering if her right eye looked the same now. Wondering if her irises were gone. She'd become so monstrous . . . but what good was that if she was lying here in the ruins of today's lunch, barely daring to breathe?

Her ruined arm was limp and bent backward and to the side. She looked at it for a long minute, but no matter how much she tried to will it to move, the most she managed was a twitch, and all that accomplished was more pain. Her good arm struggled against the floor as she tried to position her feet underneath her, and leaning against the refrigerator, she tried to force herself to a standing position.

Only to slide back down when her muscles gave out; her ruined chest hurt too much for words, and everything ached. Hadn't she been through enough already? She'd fought and fought and fought. She'd won! She'd won that fight.

*I fucking won. So why am I . . .*

Jenny slammed her fist against the floor. The tiles cracked and burst as the entire kitchen trembled. Pots and pans banged, loose rubble rained down from the ceiling, and then she heard footsteps.

*Food.*

*Sustenance.*

Ready to strike whatever it was with her tentacles, Jenny turned viciously, lowering herself forward onto her arm so that she felt like a three-legged cat crouched and just waiting to spring forward onto prey. She would rip whoever it was apart and bring them piece by piece to her teeth. It was *exactly* what she needed to regain her strength.

She smelled the person first; tasted them with a shiver that rushed through all six tentacles as Susan stepped into the kitchen.

Excess saliva mixed with blood and ran down Jenny's chin. The taste of the angel's blood was nothing compared to the warm, homely, and inviting scent of Susan.

Susan was limping. She was injured, her shoulder *bleeding*. Beautiful, rich blood spilled down her arm, down her back. Blood. Gentle and human. Susan's blood . . . delicate and inviting and warm, not as thick as the angel's but much more sweet smelling.

Jenny felt an itch she couldn't possibly scratch with her fingers. It grew and grew and grew, spreading from her brain down into her stomach before worming through her intestines; if she didn't scratch it right this minute, she would *explode*.

A lump formed in her throat. Her stomach twisted, her chest aching and burning as she watched her best friend struggle to reach her, climbing over a fallen metal shelf to collapse at Jenny's feet, staring with wide eyes.

A meal delivered straight to her. Who was she to refuse?

*No. No. No. No. No!*

Jenny stopped breathing. She didn't dare blink or move a muscle. Her tentacles were zeroed in on Susan's frantic heartbeat, and the sounds of chewing and swallowing and Miriam's relentless glee kept shooting through Jenny. Wave after wave of hunger. Anything might set her off; she'd lost control. All she wanted to do was rip Susan open and lick every inch of her from the inside.

Susan didn't say a word. She was on her hands and knees, breathing hard, staring at Jenny's ruined chest. Tears cleared streaks down the dust on Susan's face, and her hair didn't even seem blue anymore. The blood on her shoulder was drying, and she was clearly injured badly beyond her exhaustion, but a rainbow of light emanated from her hand. She reached for Jenny's face.

*I don't deserve this.* Jenny seized Susan's arm with a tentacle, halting the beautiful light inches from her chest. She shook her head, only to cough up more blood.

"Jenny!" whispered Susan, struggling against the tentacle.

"No," said Jenny, doubled over to the side as she vomited more dark blood. "Don't worry; it's not mine." She glanced up at Susan, expecting her to look horrified. Disgusted. Freaked out.

But Susan only looked more worried. Her lips wobbled, and even though they were covered in dust and grime, Jenny wanted to kiss them so badly it ached. It was either that or the desire to rip them off with her teeth.

Susan deflated, the rainbow light flickering. "I tried to help her," she said, motioning with her head. "Miriam . . . I don't know . . . She's lost her mind. She ate the babies and . . . Oh, please, Jenny. Please, just let me heal you! You're hurt so bad." Her eyes lingered on Jenny's bare chest, and she tried again to yank her arm free of the tentacle.

"No," Jenny repeated firmly, trying to stifle another cough. It would feel so good, she thought, to have Susan heal her chest and clear the pain . . . But Susan had already given up so much to heal Jenny before, to bring her back from the brink of death. What would another round of healing cost an already exhausted body? No. She wouldn't put this on Susan.

And the babies . . . There was another ache in Jenny's chest that she couldn't explain. Miriam had *eaten* the babies? They'd seemed indestructible . . . Innocent and cute, and just a little bit bloodthirsty, but they'd been *her* babies. And now they were dead, too.

Maybe they weren't dead. Maybe Miriam hadn't gotten them all. Jenny promised herself she'd go looking for them after all this. Take care of them. Raise them? *I don't know.*

*This is my fault.* She should've killed the angel quicker . . . but she'd lost herself, hadn't she? The blood had tasted so good . . . and now, her tentacle was wrapped around Susan's arm, and she could feel Susan's racing pulse, and feel her delicious warmth, and . . .

Jenny exhaled slowly. Once she finished that angel bitch off, she'd level up a lot, then she'd have all the energy she needed to heal herself. Besides, it was just her skin that was burnt; the damage hadn't gone all the way through. It hurt, but it wasn't immediately life-threatening, so there was no need for Susan to waste what stamina she had left.

But while Jenny tried to clear her head of the furious desire to bite into her best friend, Susan had kept talking, pleading, trying to get free of the tentacle. But even as she did that, another one inched toward her.

"Why aren't you saying anything?" Susan whispered frantically.

Forcing herself to swallow the excess saliva and another wave of blood, Jenny summoned her hatchet back with a flash of light, slamming it into the floor with so much force that the kitchen shook. Susan flinched but watched silently as Jenny got to her feet.

She stabilized her tentacles. Her injured arm clicked and clacked against her side, swinging uselessly and drawing Susan's attention to it, but Jenny held her back gently, as gently as she could manage despite all her instincts screaming.

She shut her eyes and felt for her exoskeleton, forcing it to soften and shift. It grew warm, glowing red hot as it turned gelatinous and spread over her burnt skin. Tilting her head back, she felt the angel's blood pumping through her muscles and covering. She'd drank so much, but had vomited too much before she could process it. Otherwise, it would've added to her exoskeleton, and she could reinforce herself further. But this would have to do for now.

She was glad Susan was here—relieved and happy—and desperately hoped those feelings weren't just out of hunger. But seeing Susan had given her the final piece of the puzzle forming in her head. The idea she'd had. How to get out of this bullshit *without* killing everyone else.

**Human lives remaining: 10**

Susan inhaled sharply. Jenny bit her tongue. It hadn't just been an accidental thought to check the count; it was the system letting everyone know the survival challenge was winding down to a finale. Whatever Jenny was going to do, she had to try it soon, or else it wouldn't matter anymore.

She knelt, feeling better now that her exoskeleton covered her chest wound. It worked like a compression shirt, keeping the pain minimized, and letting her focus.

She'd been forming the idea ever since Susan had saved her. Jenny had *died*. She was sure of it. She'd crossed worlds not just once but twice. She'd been in Eve's world. She'd been an angel. She'd killed her angel self.

And she'd seen how the angels were brought to this space. That darkness slashed through the worlds; the same darkness that had sucked the school into the Veil. She remembered falling through it, transforming from flesh to light and back again, muscles and skin growing across her bones. Disintegrating. Reimagining.

In Eve's world, that darkness had risen like water and swallowed her whole. That must've been when she'd become an angel.

That was the key. Invoking that darkness, making her own cut with energy or light or *something. Somehow.* That was the way back to Earth. And she was sure Susan's power could do it. A healing light to pierce the darkness.

**The only way out is victory, Jenny Huang. No other means is possible.**

*Nah,* thought Jenny. *You keep telling me that, and I think it's bullshit. Maybe that's how they did it for a billion fucking years, but fuck that.*

**What makes you think you are so special—**

"Susan," Jenny spoke out loud, straining as a headache formed through her head. "I think I have a plan, but I'm not sure."

Her best friend blinked. Her hand had stopped glowing, and she opened her mouth to say something, but Jenny grabbed one of her tentacles and squeezed it as hard as she could.

*You told me we were all special, and anything was possible. You kept saying that. So why can't* this *be possible?*

**We had an agreement, Jenny Huang.**

*The one where you just appeared in my head? The one where you showed me all those things and made me think I could save everyone?*

Susan wiped her cheeks, smearing tear-soaked dust. "What are we gonna do?"

"First," Jenny said through her teeth as her headache worsened. "I'll stop Miriam."

"You mean, kill her?" mouthed Susan.

Jenny nodded. She didn't hear any more chewing, but the angel was still alive. Was Miriam taking a break? Was she full? Jenny didn't care. The girl was too far gone—eating other students, the babies, the angels. Miriam wasn't any better than them. Her life was forfeit as far as Jenny was concerned.

Susan lowered her head and sniffled, but she nodded as well.

Eve, however, had a few choice words to say.

**You cannot end the Survival Challenge by any other means. It has been a contest of champions since the dawn of time itself. Even before the angels. Before the demons. Before the humans.**

*Before the angels?* Jenny felt even sicker. *So you just forced people to fight to the death?* At first, she'd thought herself blessed. A supernatural entity choosing her during this nightmare? Helping her? Protecting her? But things were rapidly coming to an end, and she remembered what Eve had asked of her. To birth her into the world.

**That is what humans do. Suffering is the human condition.**
**I have observed you since you crawled out of the oceans. Since you**
**discovered tools and made weapons and seized power and—**

A shudder like she had a terrible fever struck Jenny. It felt like an avalanche of ice cubes rolling down her spine. An onslaught of thoughts rampaged through her head, and she realized Eve was lashing out. Eve was frantic. *Desperate.*

Whatever idea Jenny had, *it could work*. And Eve didn't want that.

As if realizing Jenny's realization, everything calmed. The ache vanished.

**This matters not, Jenny Huang.**
**The Survival Challenge only ends through one singular means. And YOU shall rise victorious. YOU SHALL BIRTH ME INTO THE MATERIAL WORLD.**

Jenny stumbled forward and lost her footing, catching herself with a tentacle and dropping to her knees. Eve's words hit Jenny like a brick wall, and too many visuals of gods and creatures and blood flashed through her head to make any sense.

"Jenny!" Susan's voice pierced through the onslaught.

"And what if I don't?" spat Jenny, breathing hard. She couldn't meet Susan's eyes, but she didn't care anymore. "WHAT IF I DON'T?!" she screamed. "What if I let Miriam or some angel get me? What if . . ." She took a breath. "What if I kill myself? Then what? THEN WHAT WILL YOU DO?!"

She felt a violent tug on her tentacle, and Susan was suddenly in her face, grabbing her shoulders. A hand found Jenny's cheek, and there they both were, on their knees, in the ruined school kitchen, noses touching. Jenny's tentacles spread behind her, each one burning as though she'd used Ignite.

Susan's breath was shallow and quick, the warmth caressing Jenny's cheek. Her eyes were wide and tear stricken. "Who are you talking to?" she asked softly. "Why would you say something like that?"

# CHAPTER FIFTY-EIGHT

# BROKEN

Jenny shook violently as she stared into Susan's eyes, glancing once, only once, at her lips. Too many emotions fought for control: Desire. Love. Sadness. Anxiety. Hunger. But the worst of all was Eve's presence. It didn't seem fazed at all by Jenny's outburst; instead, Eve seemed to be laughing.

**Should you fall, then Miriam will feast on your beloved. She will rip Susan Brown to pieces and gorge herself.**

A vision appeared of Susan blasted into a wall. Her stomach and legs were burnt and peeling, blood running down her chin as she gasped for breath. And then Miriam, holding Susan's face with two hands, moving in to chew off Susan's bottom lip while she was too weak to even scream.

Jenny thought her head would explode. Eve was right. She was trapped; she had no choice. Giving up would ensure Susan's and everyone else's deaths.

Tears escaped her right eye and rolled down her cheek, and she looked away from Susan.

"I'm sorry," Jenny said. She took a breath as Susan moved closer, but it was a mistake. Her tentacles shifted forward, and she almost acted out of instinct and grabbed her best friend, but she bit the inside of her cheek until blood burst into her mouth, and she kept herself in check.

"Remember what you said?" whispered Susan. "How we have to keep fighting? We have to—"

Using her good arm, Jenny pushed Susan gently away, unable to bear the painful expression on her face.

"I remember. And I have a plan." She took another shaky breath. "I gotta stop Miriam first, then we can try it. I think if we use your healing power, we can . . . Maybe we can cut through the worlds and go home." She wasn't making sense. She knew she wasn't making sense, but how else could she explain it?

Susan's brows furrowed in confusion as her arms fell to her sides. "You mean how the floor's all weird? I don't know if I can do that."

This time, it was Jenny's turn to touch Susan's shoulder. She squeezed gently, still holding her breath. "We're gonna do this. We're gonna get through this. Fuck this whole thing. Fuck Eve. Fuck Miriam. Fuck everyone."

When Susan didn't say anything, Jenny continued, trying to figure out the best way to move forward.

"Miriam's going to move soon. She might come after us or the others, but I'll distract her. You get to them and . . ." That was where her plans fell apart.

"I'll keep them safe," Susan declared, a defiant look on her face. "Oliver's unconscious. Mackenzie got knocked out. But Mrs. Monique and Dulé can still fight."

"Okay," said Jenny. Dulé seemed strong, and Mrs. Monique . . . Jenny was glad the librarian was still alive.

She helped Susan up. The girl looked smaller than before, fragile. Jenny wanted to hug her, to pull her in and hold her tight and . . . But Jenny knew if she did that, she would never let go, or worse.

Susan grabbed Jenny's arm. Her fingers slid between the broken exoskeleton to touch her exposed bone and flesh. Rainbow light swirled, and before Jenny could protest, her ruined arm was woven back together.

New flesh formed like multicolored wiring before hardening. She looked up to see Susan falter. There was a smirk on her dust-covered face, even as she looked like she was on the verge of passing out.

"You idiot," whispered Jenny, crying freely now. "Why would you do that?"

"You're going to win," she said. "*We're* going to win." Then she squared her shoulders, and even though her breathing was labored, she nodded and turned away. Judging by her straightened back and strained gait, she was trying very hard not to appear weakened. She exited through the far door of the kitchen.

Jenny rolled her healed arm, her tentacles smashing through everything in the kitchen. Boxes burst open, revealing stacks of oranges and peaches. Milk sprayed into the air. Metal trays crumpled. *Focus*, she told herself. *Focus! I can't bite Susan. But Miriam . . . Yes. Miriam. I can bite her. I can sink my teeth into her. And it'll feel so fucking good.*

*And then we can all get the fuck out of here.*

*And then I can try to make sense of how broken and hurt and fucked up everything is.*

She stomped forward, her exoskeleton shifting again. It renewed the covering on her healed right arm, and she brought her hatchet back to her with a flash of light. It felt much better in her dominant hand.

For her left, she extended her covering to form newly sharpened claws, then used what extra she'd generated from the angel's blood to expand a layer of armor over her tentacles, hardening them.

*Kill the Desecrated Angel. Kill Miriam. Kill the Survival Challenge.*

Her eyes shifted focus from one thing to another as she stepped out of the ruined kitchen. A table. A pillar. A burnt cocoon. A body. Miriam.

**Wretched Human (Level 24)**

The notification sawed through her, and she paused. Miriam didn't move. She was lying on the floor, right over the darkness that seemed to bubble and froth around her, with her bloodied hands folded over her tummy and a content smile on her face.

She was *wretched* now. The same thing Jenny had been after Severed Spirit. Had Miriam done something similar?

Wouldn't that work in Jenny's favor? If Miriam had severed her soul, then she couldn't access her abilities and skills. She was a sitting duck, so why was the girl so relaxed?

Eve wasn't responding. Jenny's head felt almost empty, like Eve had abandoned her. Was it mad? *Fuck it.* Jenny had her plan. She was going to see it through.

Right next to Miriam was the desecrated angel. There wasn't much left of the giant, fearsome monster that had torn through the cafeteria. It lay gasping for air, only the right side of its face intact. Its teeth were exposed, opening and closing its mouth slowly, and its eyes were a dull blue as it stared aimlessly at the ceiling.

Its legs were mostly gone. Miriam had eaten through its thighs and into its navel, where its ribs were splayed open. Its lungs sat inside like two dying birds taking their last breaths. And beside them was a blue heart, still beating. Still connected to its body by a bonelike casing and a system of veins and arteries.

Jenny stared at the gruesome sight, half aware that Susan was rushing down the windowed side of the cafeteria. She'd be at the exit soon enough, and then, she'd be safe from this nightmarish scene.

One of the angel's arms was mostly whole, though she could see the bone. It raised its hand as if reaching for Jenny, but the creature couldn't sit up. It didn't have the strength to do anything. The arm slammed back to the floor.

Miriam burped and opened her eyes, her head turning to face Jenny. "I guess it's almost over."

Alarm bells rang in Jenny's head. Something had shifted in Miriam's eyes. She didn't look frightened or anxious or wary like she'd looked before, when Jenny'd stumbled upon the girl locked in the closet. She looked relaxed. More relaxed than Jenny had ever seen her before.

Her shoulders were low, arms open. Blood stained her chin, her throat, and her torn denim shirt. Her dark hair was loose, and what was left of her hijab was a long, blood-soaked piece of cloth. Miriam had never come to school without her hijab; she even wore a sports scarf in gym class.

Miriam licked her fingers clean and sat up. She stroked the angel's burnt hair and pinched its nose. Her hand looked so tiny on the giant head; she was on her knees beside the creature, humming. "It was your voice I kept hearing, wasn't it?"

"A voice?" said Jenny. *Voice? Like Eve's?*

"Yeah," she said, smiling. She stroked the angel's forehead and then poked its exposed cheekbone. The angel shuddered. "Every time there was blue light, I felt her pull. She kept calling me. *Come help me. Help me stop her. Help me grow strong . . .*" She looked up at Jenny. "Your face kept appearing. She said you were ruining everything: Her plans. Her dreams. Her children."

She rubbed her tummy. "But you know what, Jenny? I figured out a better way to get stronger. And apparently, I'm really good at it . . ." Another burp, louder than the one before, escaped her lips. "Excuse me," she said, then she turned to the side and vomited.

With that, Miriam collapsed and began to seize. Her head snapped back, her limbs bending and moving in random directions. Her mouth was wide open as her throat formed choking sounds, and her shirt flapped wildly, revealing her thin form and an ugly gash running down her side with what looked like Susan's cattle prod buried almost completely inside.

Green light expanded from her belly in radiating waves. Heat and force repelled Jenny as she struggled to move. She could just kill the girl now, bury the hatchet in her neck and end the madness, but then, with twin crunchy sounds, something burst out of Miriam's back. Wind slammed into Jenny, and she was forced to step back, bracing herself with her tentacles.

Miriam had grown *wings*. Leathery and huge, as dark as Miriam's hair, they unfurled. Wings shaped like clawed hands with skin webbed between each hideous finger. The palms were attached to Miriam's back so that she looked like a monstrous butterfly. Her shirt fell, torn to bits, revealing her bony form.

Her ribs showed. Her navel was sunken, and she covered her chest with her thin arms, shaking. The wound in her side trailed blood down her pale skin. She looked up at Jenny, eyes wide and red, as though she were asking, *What the fuck?*

She opened her mouth to say something, but another seizure took over. Her body arced, her hands dropped away, and something shot out of her belly button; something gelatinous and liquid, a thick white substance that spread every which way. It slathered over her chest and up to her neck, dribbled down her legs, and took shape. Miriam fell on all fours, panting and crying. Her hand-shaped wings spread wide, lowering to the floor to reveal knucklelike bones on their backs.

Saliva glistened, stretching from her lips to the darkness below. She'd transformed just as Jenny had, but her eyes hadn't changed. They still had irises, and though the notification still said "Wretched Human," Jenny got the sense that she'd transformed through a different means. It wasn't a skill like Severed Spirit.

"Miriam," Jenny spoke. "What the fuck did you do?" She adjusted her hatchet, trying to find an opening to attack. The girl's white exoskeleton was *thick*. It completely disguised Miriam's frail body and gave her a muscular, powerful appearance that reminded Jenny of the brutal black-covered wretched angel she'd fought on the second floor.

The girl slowly got to her feet, hunched forward, her white-covered arms swinging like they were too heavy. Raising her head, spittle dribbled down her covered chin, her eyes gleaming with green light. She flapped her wings, and her hair bounced every which way. The cloth of her hijab danced all around her, and she yanked it out, snapping the clip that had held it in place.

"Do you wanna know who was up there in that room?" she asked.

Jenny didn't respond. Her mouth had gone dry; the look on Miriam's face was pure rage. This was nothing at all like facing down an angel, even the desecrated angel. She was staring at the monstrous form of another *human being*.

*Is this what I look like to everyone else?*

"You know who was in there?" spat Miriam. She took a shaky step forward, but when her heavily covered feet hit the floor, the darkness shifted, and the cafeteria trembled. "*Martin*."

"Martin?" repeated Jenny, backing away. *Who the fuck is that?*

Miriam took another heavy step forward, stomping on the darkness and causing it to ripple. "Fucking *Martin* and his stupid, whiney whore of a girlfriend, *Janice*."

"I thought you'd be safe there." Jenny held her ground, trying to find an opportunity to attack. Miriam's wings looked cruel and evil, like they might grab Jenny.

"Do you know what they used to call me?" Miriam asked, holding up her hijab. The cloth trailed down to her legs and wrapped around a thigh, leaving bloody stains on her white exoskeleton.

This part, Jenny did know. She'd heard all the jokes. The teasing. The toxic bullshit.

"A *terrorist*." Miriam stepped over the desecrated angel and moved even closer. She crushed the angel's hand, and it screamed, but she stamped down on it again. "They would always . . ."

For a second, her anger broke. Her face looked shocked. Afraid. Alone.

"Miriam," whispered Jenny, praying she could get through to the girl. She looked so desperately sad and heartbroken. Maybe there was a way to stop this. Maybe there was still some hope for her.

But Miriam's brow furrowed. She snarled and shook her head, then inhaled loudly before holding up the cloth. "Well now, I can do exactly that!" She threw it into the air, spread her arms, and screamed a terrible, gut-wrenching scream. A green beam of light burst out of her mouth, incinerating the cloth of her hijab. The beam carried on, burning into the ceiling, and judging by the force and heat, it must've gone through the entire school.

Miriam turned her head, still screaming. The beam followed her movements, cutting countless paths of devastation through the cafeteria as it zipped in every direction.

The remaining pillars burst. Tables erupted. Jenny flattened herself on the floor to dodge the beam, then rolled out of the way as it sliced back through. It left the darkness unharmed, but the floor exploded as soon as it hit the tiles behind where Jenny had been standing, and she cried out as it cut through two of her tentacles.

"All my life!" screamed Miriam, stopping her attack with a snap of her jaw. She held up her hands and seemed to choke the air, strangling an invisible enemy that she couldn't stop arguing with. "All my fucking life. Get higher grades. Be prettier. Be smarter. I have to be a doctor. I have to marry a good man. I have to have children! I have to do this. I have to do that! I have to be *good*. And yet . . ."

She dropped her hands and turned to face Jenny. Her wings beat several times, blowing away the falling debris from her attack. "Nobody ever just wanted *me*." She stumbled on the word.

Jenny was on the floor, holding her two burnt tentacles and only half aware of the sliced-off bits wriggling nearby. She cleared her throat, trying to think of what to say to Miriam. That it was okay. That she could help. That there was still hope. But nothing made sense. There was no getting through the ferocity of Miriam's rage.

With a flap of her wings, Miriam leaped forward and screamed again. Another beam of destructive light shot out, and Jenny launched herself at Miriam, diving for her legs.

# CHAPTER FIFTY-NINE

# TO SPREAD YOUR HIDEOUS WINGS

Jenny whipped Miriam across the face with an exoskeleton-covered tenta-cle. The red coating crackled, leaving an ugly groove on Miriam's white armor. The girl's exoskeleton was almost as strong as the desecrated angel's. It was dense and thick, but Jenny already knew the secret to breaking through: Multiple attacks.

It helped that the girl wasn't as strong as the angel, though the impacts of Miriam's attacks still hurt. Jenny was falling apart from prolonged fighting with the angel and the surprise explosion she'd taken to the chest.

But that terrible beam . . . whatever it touched, it incinerated. It was like Jenny's *Ignite* *but* concentrated to a lethal point that burned through steel, concrete, and even her exoskeleton-reinforced tentacles in a flash. Which meant, if the beam landed on her body, it was game over.

This wasn't going to be as easy as she'd hoped. Miriam wasn't just some human; she was transformed like Jenny, corrupted by the survival challenge. Blooded and fueled by a deep, ugly rage, and Jenny wouldn't be surprised if the other girl also had a Bloodlust Ecstasy bonus.

Where Jenny tried to channel her rage into fighting the angels and surviving, Miriam had completely surrendered to it. Jenny could sense the cruel, cold intent through her tentacles as she whipped around, dodging Miriam's ugly, clawed wings and explosive bubbles shot out of glowing arms.

Every time she closed in, ready to sink her weapon into Miriam's neck, a wing slammed Jenny away. If this were a fair fight and she hadn't just fought the des-ecrated angel, if she hadn't been caught off guard by Miriam's exploding bubble, she was sure she could take the other girl down easily. Even with her white exo-skeleton and those creepy, nightmare wings.

But Jenny was exhausted. Her throat felt like it had been scraped raw, and her muscles were already pushed beyond the point of exhaustion. She needed rest.

She wanted another potion, but enough time hadn't passed. Trying that again would backfire and leave her weak and vulnerable.

Crying out in frustration, she struck Miriam over and over with her tentacles, even the shortened ones, in a cyclical barrage. Like she was spinning her arms on the playground and threatening to walk into someone.

Miriam slapped each one away, screaming and snarling, swiping with her hands and her wings. Jenny shifted gears and focused on the desecrated angel. That stupid thing was *still* alive. If she could just kill it, stomp out its pitiful existence, then she'd level up. She'd get all the energy she needed, and even though Miriam would too, Jenny had the advantage of a higher level. She could stop her before the girl could make sense of what had happened.

Miriam grabbed a tentacle with her teeth, ending the barrage. Her lips curved into a gruesome smile, and she bit down.

Before Jenny could scream with rage, Miriam slammed a fist into Jenny's chest. The impact set off so much pain that her vision flashed white.

"I knew you weren't healed!" shouted Miriam gleefully through a mouthful of crackling tentacle. "I could *smell* it."

"You bitch," spat Jenny, raking Miriam's scalp with her claws. Her sharpened tips scraped the exoskeleton, but she curled her fingers and grabbed a fistful of Miriam's hair. She tugged as hard as she could.

Miriam *shrieked*, so loud and shrill that Jenny covered her ears with her shortened tentacles as the girl struggled to get away. The ugly wings snapped forward and shut, crashing against Jenny like a pair of cymbals over and over, but Jenny only held on tighter.

Green light blossomed between them. Wrenching Miriam's head back, Jenny slammed her elbow under her chin just as another beam erupted from the girl's lips. Heat and energy blasted into the ceiling as Miriam screamed, clawing at Jenny's chest and straining to lower her head to hit Jenny in the face with the attack.

Rubble rained down from the ceiling, smoke, ashes, and molten bits. The wings kept beating, hitting Jenny again and again as she struggled to keep the beam pointed firmly upward.

*Just one swipe*, she thought. *I could slash through her throat.*

Snapping her teeth shut, the beam vanished, and Miriam's eyes shone bright. Pursing her lips, she exhaled a bubble instead.

*Not this shit again.* Jenny kicked off the floor, throwing herself backward as she crossed her arms and tentacles in front of her body. The bubble snapped, and the explosion sent Jenny flying.

She crashed into the vending machine where the red cocoon lay mushed and stuck in shattered glass. Miriam got knocked away as well, but Jenny couldn't see where the other girl had landed. With the ceiling still falling apart and all the smoke and dust, Jenny could hardly see a thing.

Groaning as aches trembled through her tentacles, she pulled herself out of the vending machine, dripping red goop down her legs as shards of glass bounced away. The exoskeleton covering her arms and tentacles had burnt away, the crimson now a rusty, brownish red. The rest was either weakened or crumbling, but at least she'd protected her chest this time.

She made a mental note to hug Susan extra hard to thank her for healing her arm. It would've been blown off by now.

Her head rang from the repeated wing attacks, and her face hurt from exposure to the beam up close. The shimmering light had looked like a pillar right in front of her, and if even just a little bit of it had reached her forehead, her skull would've been incinerated.

*I have to get the angel.*

Trying to shake off her exhaustion, Jenny snapped her tentacles like whips. Rolling her head, she sucked in deep breaths and used her tentacles to sense the angel's location. As soon as she found it, she launched herself in its direction. The creature was crawling across the darkness to where a few more tarnished angels had climbed into the cafeteria.

She ran as quickly as she could, leaping over a debris-covered table and one of the ruined cocoons, but just as she saw the angel pulling its bones across the floor, Miriam emerged from the side, her wings flapping, hair trailing. With her glistening white exoskeleton and wings, she looked more angelic than any of the monsters they'd faced.

Jenny was forced to turn and meet the attack head-on.

They collided in a shower of sparks. Jenny slammed a tentacle into Miriam's jaw, forcing the girl's mouth shut as green light bubbled. A wing reached for Jenny, but golden light flashed, and she struck it with her hatchet, slicing through what felt like stretched skin and drawing blood.

Miriam howled and backed away, clutching her injured wing, her eyes wide and teary as though accusing Jenny of hurting her. She inhaled deeply then let loose another beam of sizzling green energy just as Jenny dashed in for another strike.

In a desperate attempt to dodge and reach the angel, Jenny used a burst of Instant Acceleration to cross the cafeteria floor while throwing her hatchet in the opposite direction, hoping its reflective face would draw attention away.

It worked; Miriam turned her head, trying to catch it with her beam.

Jenny came to a stop right behind the desecrated angel. She could see through its back; flaps of meat stuck to its spine. How was it still alive? It was pinning a tarnished angel against the darkness, and fed as the weaker creature screamed helplessly; the desecrated angel would heal. Jenny could feel it in her bones.

The monstrosity was trying to patch itself together, and if she didn't stop it now, it would go after Susan and the others and get even stronger while she dealt with Miriam.

She raised her claws and was just about to bury it in the creature's back when the green beam zipped over her head.

It ripped an ugly groove through the ceiling and the front of the cafeteria. As soon as her tentacles had picked up on the oncoming heat, Jenny had ducked and thrown herself to the side, maneuvering maniacally to keep out of reach. Sensing Miriam closing in again, Jenny spun around right as the girl crashed into her, viciously snarling as she knocked the hatchet away.

Swearing, Jenny pulled the other girl into a bear hug, pinning her arms to the side as they fell to the floor. She wrapped a tentacle around Miriam's head and chin to keep her jaws shut tight.

"What are you gonna do now?" she asked through clenched teeth as Miriam flopped like a fish, trying to wiggle out of the embrace.

Jenny held on as tightly as she could, wrapping her legs around Miriam's. They rolled over the darkness, growling and hissing, trying to overpower each other as though they were locked in a wrestling match.

Miriam's wings beat over and over, trying to lift them off the ground and give Miriam an edge, but Jenny whipped her tentacles against the fingerlike structures, bruising and breaking and drawing blood, giving Jenny the chance to roll Miriam onto her back and prevent her from flying away.

As they spun, Jenny caught sight of Susan standing by the burnt entrance. The metal door was partially melted, and she could feel Susan's presence through her tentacles; her fear, her desire to help, her exhaustion. But worse of all, Jenny could sense the desecrated angel healing, every single one of her instincts screaming, "*Danger!*"

The angel's flesh was growing back, slowly but surely, its metallic skin seeping out of its shredded muscles like soapy water from a sponge, spreading and hardening.

"It's healing!" she wanted to call out. She wanted to scream, "Kill it now! You can kill it right now and stop it!"

That moment of hesitation was all Miriam needed. Her wings spread wide. She rolled on top and flapped them *hard*, generating enough force to lift them both. One of her legs came free, and she kicked off the floor with another strong beat of her wings. Before Jenny could call out to Susan or attack Miriam, they rocketed through the destroyed ceiling at a speed just like Instant Acceleration.

Burnt tiles and busted light fixtures exploded. Miriam flew them straight through cement and steel. It was all Jenny could do to shield herself with her tentacles, wrapping them like protective layers above her head, and letting them absorb most of the damage as they drilled upward into the lobby.

Jenny got a quick glimpse of the empty lobby—blood stains, severed limbs, a handful of blue-eyed humans wheezing and groaning, their bodies too torn apart to move—and then they crashed through the next ceiling, through the second floor, and into the third, where they smashed into a piano, the keys and strings chiming as the heavy wooden instrument blew apart. Miriam's wings unfurled like a parachute, and Jenny and the girl were wrenched apart.

She tumbled through chairs and more musical instruments, destroying the seats and tables as she blew through them. She struck the teacher's desk and rolled to a stop beside the computer section, where she'd spent countless after-school hours trying to produce music digitally for extra credit last year. Susan had helped her, and Jenny had managed to pass the class.

Dust floated around as she lay with her head against the metal leg of a table. She tried to get up, but sharp pains in her shoulder and sides proved too much, and her legs gave out. She'd shielded her head as best she could, but the rest of her body had taken a beating. Her exoskeleton was scuffed and cracked all over, though she didn't think Miriam could be much better off.

Wincing, she grabbed the edge of the table and forced herself up. A monitor toppled and bounced off her face, the screen cracking. She smashed it under an armored foot as she stood, coughing blood onto the back of her hand and surveying the ruined music room.

None of this was going to plan. She was so far away now from the desecrated angel, but maybe she could jump back down into the cafeteria.

Before she could hobble over to the hole, she heard sniffling.

Wiping her lips, she turned toward the sound and spotted Miriam in the dust and rubble. Her wings were folded around her, reminding Jenny of the cocoons, except there was no glow; they were fleshy and grey, and they almost camouflaged into the surrounding chaos. She was crying.

"Miriam," called Jenny. She concentrated and summoned her hatchet back with a flash of light. At least that worked long-distance. "Miriam. Stop this, please. I think . . . I think I can get us all out. There's no reason to fight like this."

*I'm trying to reason with a people eater. I ate people too, but not living ones.*

*I have to kill her no matter what. All Miriam wants to do is eat. But if I can distract her . . . if I can buy some time, kill the angel, and recover . . . then I can kill her, no sweat.*

*Or I'll just catch her off guard.*

One of the wings lifted, and Miriam's sobbing face peeked out. Her white exoskeleton was cracked and grotesque, and Jenny's insides twisted at the sight.

*Did she fly through each floor face-first? What the fuck is wrong with her?*

"Jenny," whispered Miriam, sobbing uncontrollably. She wiped her eyes, blood seeping from the cracks on her face. "Just let me win, okay? Please. I've never asked you for anything before. Please, just let me do this. I'll make it quick for everyone. I promise."

"The fuck?" spat Jenny. *Is she asking me to let her kill me? And everyone else?* "No. Fucking stop this—right now. No more bloodshed. Aren't you sick of this? Look at what you've become!" She forced herself to meet Miriam's eyes as the girl sobbed.

Down in the cafeteria, the desecrated angel must be making its move. Susan and the others . . . If the angel recovered, they didn't stand a chance. And Jenny couldn't sense anything with her tentacles from this distance.

"Stop attacking me," Jenny continued, speaking slowly while trying to seem as unthreatening as possible despite the hatchet. "Stop it. Help me fight the angels; we can protect the others." *I don't have an opening. Should I throw my hatchet at her face? It is broken enough. Maybe . . .*

*Her wings would just block it.*

"Why would I want to help them?" asked Miriam, still crying, her voice wobbling. She stared at Jenny like a hurt animal, wounded and needing attention. "Only one of us can win."

And Jenny felt her heart breaking. They were the same—hurt and terrified and giving into their worst impulses. *But I wouldn't eat innocents.*

"I think I have a way out," said Jenny. She looked around the music room and could almost see herself sitting in class with her head on the desk, bored out of her mind. "We can end this. We can all go *back*. Just help me stop that angel down there."

Miriam sniffled. She sat up straighter, expanding her wings to reveal even more cracks in her armor spanning her chest and torso like lightning. Jenny spotted the cattle prod sticking out right away; it was still inside Miriam. Her exoskeleton had grown over it.

Miriam faltered, looking like she might faint, but she caught herself, resting her hands on an upended desk.

Jenny squeezed her hatchet, ready to throw it. One Savage Throw in the chest, the throat, the face. It would shatter what was left of Miriam's exoskeleton and burst through.

"Look at your eye, Jenny," said Miriam softly. "You look just like the monsters. It's the same hunger, isn't it? *Bloodlust ecstasy . . .*"

Jenny froze. Miriam had sensed her intent, hadn't she? Or was she just rambling?

"I bet you taste so fucking good . . ." Saliva dribbled down her chin.

*No, she's lost it.*

"You're not listening to me, Miriam," hissed Jenny. Her tentacles swished in agitation, aching to leap onto her. They could taste the blood leaking through the cracked exoskeleton.

Miriam threw back her head and *cackled*, a laugh as ugly as her unfurling wings. She stood on the rubble, lurching from side to side, hunched forward. "You can't trick me like that, Jenny. Your face is too fucking honest." Her lips curled back to expose stained teeth, then she took a deep breath, baring out her cracked chest and raising her head.

"No!" shouted Jenny, shielding her face with her tentacles as she ducked. But the light sailed over her head. It hit the ceiling and zipped around in an unruly circle. The tiles, the concrete, all of it came crashing down in an avalanche of destruction, and Jenny leaped backward and away to the opposite wall, pressing herself to the bulletin board covered in flyers for the school band. Rubble covered the hole back to the cafeteria, burying the instruments and chairs.

"See that?" shouted Miriam, flapping her wings and floating over everything. Dust billowed all around. With the ceiling gone, they could see the swirling gray emptiness of the Veil. In its eerie light, Miriam's exoskeleton glowed ominously.

"Look up there. There *is* no going home, Jenny. There's nothing for us except this. This is all that matters. Where only the *strongest* can win." Her eyes bulged as she spoke, her arms extending like she was preaching. "Who's the pathetic bitch now? All those years I took your shit. I studied. I prayed. But it never stopped. The hurt never stopped. So, this . . . *this* is the only thing that matters to me."

Jenny didn't respond. She inhaled deeply, over and over, making use of her tentacles' ability to breathe as well, trying to oxygenate her muscles and her blood as best she could.

But Miriam was still ranting. "We only go home when one of us wins," she snarled. "Do you really have what it takes to end this? Do you really think *you* can win? Isn't Susan your best friend?"

Jenny grimaced, automatically asking Eve if Susan was still alive. But Eve didn't respond.

*Fuck you, Eve.*

*How many people left?*

**Human population remaining: 8**

"Oh," said Miriam. Her cracked face twisted into a gruesome smile. "Oh, she's not just your friend, is she? You've got a thing for her. You *like* her." She shook her head, another laugh making her shoulders shake as she stomped through the rubble. Her wings beat, blowing away the rising dust as she moved closer. "Then don't worry one bit, Jenny. I'll treat her with all your love when I *rip her open and lick her all over.* Just like I did to Janice while her bitch-ass boyfriend watched. You should've heard them screaming . . ." Miriam licked her lips.

*She's just trying to rile me up. She's hurt. I can do this. I can do this!*

Focusing as best she could, Jenny stomped forward and threw her hatchet at the drooling girl. *Savage Throw!*

Miriam swerved, and the weapon struck her on the shoulder, knocking her back. She cried out as her exoskeleton shattered, revealing the bare skin of her shoulder and part of her chest. Her wings beat furiously, green light shimmering in her mouth, but before she could use another beam, Jenny leaped in front of her, grabbed her shoulders, and used Ignite.

Flames shot out of Jenny's throat and right into Miriam's. The green light vanished as Miriam shrieked, stumbling back, smoke rising from her mouth.

But Jenny didn't relent. *Ignite!* Fire caught on her fingers, up her arms. Her hatchet lit up with flame as well as her tentacles, and she struck Miriam over and over, cracking and burning more exoskeleton so the once white covering fell away, scorched and crumbling.

Eyes filled with tears, her tongue painfully blackened, Miriam clawed at Jenny's face and chest, but it was no use. Whenever Miriam blocked Jenny's hatchet, Jenny hit her with a tentacle like a burning whip. Going for the throat, she swung her weapon underhand, but Miriam stepped back, nearly tripping on the rubble. Jenny lashed at her with a tentacle, catching the exposed skin of her bare shoulder, and Miriam *sizzled*.

A wing whipped forward and smacked Jenny away just as she was about to attack again. Green light surged, this time through Miriam's arm and into her finger.

"You stupid *bitch*," Miriam screamed, smoke billowing from her lips as she grabbed her burnt shoulder. Her face covering was partially melted, but her eyes gleamed furiously. She raised a shaking, glowing finger at Jenny and fired.

The bubble sped toward her, but Jenny was ready for it. Grabbing a chair, she flung it, making use of Savage Throw. As soon as it struck, the bubble burst, and another explosion rocked the ruined music room.

More green bubbles, one after the other, burst out of the smoke, coming from every direction as Miriam rushed around the room screaming, her wings flapping like a bat out of hell.

Jenny kept bouncing back, picking up chunks of rubble with her tentacles and lobbing them. As smoke and dust clouds filled the room, visibility dropped, so she focused with her tentacles, feeling for the bubbles disturbing the air, trying to focus in on Miriam's presence.

There she was. Two glowing arms. Wings beating like mad.

Jenny leaped through the smoke, the only thing on her mind to *kill, kill, kill.*

Two bubbles rushed overhead, too close for her to throw anything, so she dodged.

"Got you!" screamed Miriam. She burst forward with a thunderous beat of her wings, flying straight into Jenny like a rocket. Her head smashed into Jenny's chest.

The impact threw Jenny across the room, but before she could grab anything and stabilize, before she could crash into the opposite wall, she saw the flash of green light.

As though in slow motion, the beam stretched from Miriam's blackened teeth and surged across the room, piercing through the right side of Jenny's navel. But before Miriam could turn her head and slice through Jenny's torso, she shot a tentacle through the floor and yanked, throwing herself to the side with a burst of Instant Acceleration. The beam zipped right over her, slicing through three more tentacles as she crashed into the rubble face-first.

When the dust settled, Jenny squirmed in pain, grabbing the hole in her side and expecting to see blood, but the wound was already cauterized. The exoskeleton had melted and peeled back all around, the pain so excruciating that all she could do was clench her teeth as tears streamed down her face. What was she missing? A kidney? A huge chunk of her intestines?

"Does it hurt?" whispered Miriam from somewhere through the dust. "You're still alive, right?"

Blood gushed out of Jenny's mouth; she retched, her one long tentacle twitching and twisting as the shortened ones writhed in pain.

Footsteps drew near, then Miriam appeared, hobbling as though she'd been the one injured. She grabbed her face covering and peeled the scorched, cracked pieces away. Her skin was red, as though she'd peeled the top layer of her skin off, too, and saliva dribbled down her chin. "Once I eat you . . . I'll be unstoppable."

Jenny's chest pulsed with pain. She threw up in her mouth, blood gushing out from between her clenched teeth as she glared at Miriam. Squirming on the floor, she summoned her hatchet back with a flash of light that caught Miriam's attention.

"That's a neat trick. Shiny . . ."

*I'm going to ram this down your throat*, Jenny wanted to say, but she couldn't even stand; her legs wouldn't work. She raised her arm to launch it.

That was when Miriam sped forward without warning, dropped to one knee, and slammed her claws into Jenny's chest.

The hatchet clattered to the floor. There was an ugly series of cracks as Miriam ripped a sizeable chunk of her armor away, revealing Jenny's burnt, ruined chest. Miriam's claws left fresh new trails of blood, and this time, Jenny couldn't keep the cough down. She threw up blood in Miriam's face while the girl shut her eyes and *sighed*.

A wing smacked into Jenny's face, knocking her to the floor. Her head bounced on a chunk of ceiling as something grabbed her tentacles and squeezed, and then, she felt an all too familiar *suck*. Miriam's lips had found Jenny's chest, and she was pinning down Jenny's arm with a wing, holding the tentacles back with clawed hands.

Jenny screamed as teeth connected inside her; as her blood spurted into Miriam's mouth.

"Fucking delicious," whispered Miriam, moaning against Jenny as she grasped skin with her teeth and peeled upward.

Flames erupted in Jenny's throat and flickered out. Her tentacle slashed and struggled, but with Miriam squeezing it and holding it out of reach, it was useless. The girl was completely latched onto Jenny's bare chest, and with each slurp, with each tear, with each swallow, Jenny felt what little strength she had left draining.

She was being eaten alive. Unbearable pain blossomed, a burning, cutting feeling as teeth struck her ribs. She managed to work one hand free, and she grabbed Miriam's hair, tugging and tugging, but already she was too weak, and Miriam was too bloodlusted to be stopped.

*No. No. Not like this. No!*

*Eve! Where the fuck are you?*

*No!*

**There is only one thing you can do, Jenny Huang.**
**Hide.**

Jenny screamed, summoning her hatchet and trying again, but golden light pulsed across Miriam's face. Her exoskeleton was glowing, spreading anew. Steam rose as it healed back together, white and shiny, then the girl opened her mouth wide, grinning as drool and blood dripped down her chin and onto Jenny's exposed insides.

*I won't be helpless again . . .* A shudder went down her spine. She shut her eyes and focused on Susan's sad smile. When Susan had healed her. Susan's hand grasping her heart.

She reached as far into her consciousness as she could, drawing on the skill that had saved her before.

**Hide. Hide as you always do, Jenny Huang. Surrender to your truth.**

Eve flashed—the three-headed figure. But now, all three faces were Miriam's, bloodthirsty and twisted in manic glee, eyes bulging.

*Fuck you.*

The warning message played again, but she didn't care. It had to stop.

It had to stop right now.

*Severed Spirit!*

The pain of someone chewing through her chest vanished without a trace. Her vision flashed red. Her thoughts blurred and faded as Miriam swallowed.

Jenny felt herself plummeting away, as though she were an angel again falling from the sky, sucked forcefully into a gaping darkness. Her body dissolving, shifting and changing, turning into nothing . . . nothing . . . *nothing* . . .

Her heart stopped beating. A tremor went through her body. When she inhaled, the metallic scent of blood coated her tongue and filled her lungs. Miriam hesitated, raised her head.

Jenny stared right back, her face expressionless. Miriam's eyes slowly widened as blood dripped from her nose and lips onto Jenny's exposed chest.

Then Jenny slammed her palm against the cattle prod sticking out of the girl's side. With an ugly *squish*, it punctured Miriam's insides, and the girl spat up all the flesh and blood she'd just eaten.

Miriam collapsed to the floor, wriggling in pain, clawing at herself and trying to pull the prod out. Jenny's tentacles grew anew, drawing on her own flesh. She could almost feel the drain on her body, but she didn't care. They extended—longer and thicker than before—raising her from the rubble so that her legs swung limply. She hovered over the whimpering Miriam.

*Something's wrong . . .*

*It doesn't matter . . .*

*Why does my head hurt so much?* She felt like she was in a dream, a bystander watching herself move. Like she'd slipped out of her body . . .

*It doesn't matter . . .*

*I have to get back to Susan. I have to stop Miriam. Whatever it takes. We can win this.*

She raised an arm, her red exoskeleton glistening in the Veil's pasty glow, and three tentacles swooshed forward, smashing into Miriam.

# CHAPTER SIXTY

# FACING THE DARKNESS

One moment, Susan saw Jenny struggling on the strange cafeteria floor with Miriam. The next, hideous wings unfurled with a furious snap. Wind slammed Susan back with enough force to knock her against the partially melted cafeteria doorway, then Jenny and Miriam were gone. All that was left of them was a new hole in the ceiling.

The cafeteria was a disaster. So much of the walls were burned through. Pillars collapsed. Tables upended. And several places, like the cluster of tables by the large windows where Susan had had breakfast just this morning while waiting for classes to begin, were covered in little hills of rubble.

The worst was the floor. It looked like a black swimming pool in the shape of an oval, or maybe an eye. When she'd run over it, her feet hadn't sunk, so she was sure it wasn't actually liquid. But she'd gotten the sensation of wading into water: a tightness in her chest, the sudden feeling that she was heavier, and the threat of plummeting to some dark bottom and running out of air. All her instincts screamed that it was *evil*.

Susan knew it was evil with every fiber of her being, and the more she looked at it, the more it looked like an ugly gash, a festering wound. The darkness sloshed inward and wriggled and rippled . . . And as she stood in the entryway, trying to make sense of it, a bony hand burst out and splashed onto the surface. She couldn't help but yelp as a head followed.

**Tarnished Angel (Level 1)**

This one was red-haired, its pasty face as skeletal as all the others, and those empty eyes glistened before locking onto Susan. The angel screamed as it pulled itself out.

*This was where they all came from*, thought Susan, backing away. Then she saw something even worse, something enormous, with a head of blonde hair and a torso that was mostly bones, meat stuck to an exposed rib cage. It was a *gigantic* angel crawling out of a pile of rubble. Sharp blue eyes glistened with menace, and when it hissed, steam rose from its lips.

## Desecrated Angel (Level 44)

The name burned through Susan's mind, and she almost cried out. Her legs trembled, and she held on to the doorframe; she couldn't look away from its gaze as it crawled toward the tarnished angel. Several other arms burst out of the darkness, and more angels pulled themselves into the cafeteria.

Susan stepped back, horrified. How many more would surface? How many more would they have to fight? And that desecrated angel . . . How was it still alive? It looked like a dinosaur carcass, like the ones she'd seen in documentaries of a stegosaur after the raptors had had their fill. The creature was wheezing, eyes shining blue and bright, and when it reached the much smaller angel, it clacked its teeth.

With large, dark-blue fingers, it grasped the first tarnished angel. The thinner creature hissed and screeched as, slowly, the desecrated angel lifted it off the floor.

Despite its size and the shiver of terror running down Susan's spine, the angel was so badly injured that it seemed weak. Fragile, almost. Like it was on the verge of death. Its movements were slow, its arm shook as the tarnished angel struggled, and for a moment, it looked like the smaller creature would slip out. But then, the desecrated angel's mouth opened wide, and Susan turned away.

She didn't want to see; she couldn't bear to see any more of that. She dashed back up the hallway, but she still heard the sickening crunch resounding behind her.

The desecrated angel roared in triumph, and Susan clapped her hands over her ears. *Jenny fought that thing? And Miriam . . . Miriam ate it?*

Then she remembered what Jenny was doing before Miriam attacked. How Jenny's tentacle things had been ripping open the angel's stomach; the pleased look on Jenny's face . . .

*No. I can't think about that right now. She's doing what she needs to win. What can I do to help?*

*I have to stop that thing.* Her heart thudded with hope. Glancing back through the holes in the wall, she saw tarnished angels hissing and scrambling toward her. The desecrated angel lay on its back, still feeding off the angel it'd picked up.

If she killed it, Jenny would level up, wouldn't she? And Susan would level up too. They'd level up *a lot*, considering how high-leveled that thing was. She'd have more energy and more stat points, and she'd be strong enough to help Jenny with her idea to save them all. They could all get out of here.

*I need a weapon.* She didn't have enough energy, and her body was on the verge of shutting down, but she felt a surge of willpower, like a second wind. *I can do this. I can do this.*

Having a goal, a purpose, something that she could do to help Jenny, to help everyone . . . it forced her forward. *I can do this. 'Cause if I can't . . . we're all fucked.*

With every breath burning, Susan rushed back to the others, trying to dodge chunks of the wall and slipping on blood. Mrs. Monique and Dulé stood in front of the unconscious Oliver and Mackenzie, who were resting against the ruined door of the collapsed stairwell. Sitting beside them was Leslie, drenched in blood, her clothes torn. She stared blankly up the hallway, staring right past Susan.

Dulé had questions, but Susan just pointed toward the cafeteria, shouting that angels were coming.

"Fuck," he swore, his boxing gloves materializing around his hands.

Susan nearly tripped, coming to a stop beside Leslie as a screech echoed up and down the hall. Mrs. Monique launched her spear at the first tarnished angel to emerge. The tip went through its chest, and the angel flicked back, twisting in a spray of blood as the librarian called her spear back with a flash of light.

"Leslie," whispered Susan, squeezing the other girl's shoulder. "Do you have any energy?"

Leslie's face was gaunt. Looking almost like a fish with her mouth open, she stared at the angels as Dulé and Mrs. Monique fought them off. Her lips moved, but she didn't utter a sound.

When Susan had found her in the janitor's closet, she'd been lying on the floor in a pool of blood, pretending to be dead. The other students around her had been very much dead, torn apart by Miriam, with limbs, intestines, and bones strewn around in a sloppy mess. Leslie had been barely responsive as Dulé carried her back to the hallway. All she kept saying was "Dr. Lee did this," but he was nowhere to be seen.

Susan turned around, breathing hard out of frustration. She grabbed Dulé's arm as he stepped back, and he flinched, his boxing glove glowing.

"There's something worse in there," she said quickly. "It's almost dead. And if we kill it, we can . . . we can . . . I just need *something* to kill it with." She'd thought about bashing in its head with rubble or something, but she knew it wouldn't be enough. She needed something definitive.

Blood and sweat trailed down the side of Dulé's dust-covered face. His lips were busted, and his eyes were glazed with exhaustion. He shrugged. "I'm sorry. I'm barely getting anything from these things, and I used up too much to heal Mackenzie." He wiped his brow, nodding toward Oliver and Mackenzie. "I'm not gonna leave their side."

*Mackenzie!*

Something hissed, and he turned as an angel rushed them on all fours, hissing, long black hair trailing. His glove made contact with its chin. There was a flash of light, and the angel blew apart as though it had been struck by a cannonball, bits of flesh and bone splattering everything.

"Sorry," he whispered gruffly. "Put too much into that." He shouted and stepped away as another angel slipped by Mrs. Monique.

Susan whipped around and pushed Leslie out of the way, who collapsed and curled into a ball, shaking and mumbling something incoherent. Susan felt a pang of guilt, but there was no time for that.

"Where's the dagger?" she shouted, hoping Dulé would answer her. "Where's Mackenzie's knife?"

"I don't know!" answered Dulé over his shoulder as more and more angels erupted through the collapsing cafeteria wall, screaming and hissing. Mrs. Monique thrust her spear into one's back, then kicked another.

Susan patted Mackenzie's body down, whispering apologies as the deaf girl's ruined armor crumbled away. Then Susan spotted the handle sticking out from under her arm.

Straining, Susan lifted the girl so she could pull the dagger out. Trying to be as gentle as she could, she lowered Mackenzie back onto the floor, then collapsed, arms and legs burning from the effort. She was breathing hard, and she almost wanted to laugh. What chance did she have against that angel? It was eating the other creatures. It was healing. And once it recovered . . .

But she had the dagger. It almost felt wrong to touch it. *I didn't make this. This came from Mackenzie's thoughts.* There was a strange magnetic field around it, like it was gently repelling Susan's hand. She almost felt like she was touching Mackenzie's bare skin without permission, a strange tingling heat, like she was doing something wrong. But her fingers curled around it. She could wield it. And she would just have to apologize to Mackenzie when this was all over.

No stats appeared for the dagger. She didn't have access to whatever skills Mackenzie had imbued it with, but it would do the job. She glanced at Oliver.

*Once, I kill that thing, maybe I can regenerate your legs and heal Mackenzie.*

*But I'm exhausted.* Her head throbbed with fear. She was terrified of what might be happening to Jenny now that Miriam had transformed into something so grotesque and monstrous.

*But Jenny's just as monstrous. I have to have faith.* She took a deep breath. *We just have to survive. Just like a video game.* She was the support, and this was what she needed to do right now. This was the best way she could support her best friend and keep herself alive. Otherwise . . . Otherwise, she was just useless dead weight.

And she would not be dead weight.

As Mrs. Monique and Dulé fought to protect their little haven by the stairwell, she rushed up to them. "I'm gonna kill the thing in there. Help me!"

"What?" shouted Dulé, but Susan was already moving past them, focused on her one singular purpose. A tarnished angel leaped in her direction, but the spear flashed, striking the creature in the side and slamming it out of her way. She rushed through a hole in the wall into the cafeteria, trusting them to have her back.

More angels crawled from the darkness, and the desecrated angel picked up another, dragging it across the floor to its lips, where its enormous teeth snapped through the smaller creature's torso.

It was glowing. Shimmering blue light mixed with golden flashes as the angel's flesh regenerated over its bones. Her terrible feeling had been right; the angel was healing.

Mrs. Monique hurried in behind her. "Susan, what the absolute fuck do you think you're—" But then she caught sight of the desecrated angel, and her voice caught in her throat.

"I have to kill it," said Susan. Tears slid down her cheeks. Her legs were trembling so much that she couldn't decide if it was fatigue or fear, but it didn't matter. This had to be done. If that thing recovered completely, they were screwed.

Mrs. Monique didn't say anything more. She ran in front of Susan, taking out the tarnished angels as they sprang forward, hissing and salivating. Susan slashed one's arm as it reached for her; its fingers scratched her thighs. She clenched her teeth to keep from screaming and drove the dagger through its thin chest.

With a cry, Mrs. Monique launched her spear at the desecrated angel. The tip bounced off the dark covering of its cheek, and its blue eyes turned toward them. Legs stuck out of its mouth as the giant creature lay on its back. Its navel was taking shape, glistening with golden light as a dark, metallic exoskeleton spread across its skin. They weren't gonna be able to break through that.

"Shit . . ." said the librarian, summoning her spear back. "We have to get closer."

There was still exposed flesh left: on the other side of its face, on its chest. The muscles were still forming, and Susan recognized the healing pattern from when she'd used Valescent Light on her leg. There was still a chance.

The angel noticed her right as she stepped onto the darkness. Susan stood near its enormous head, feeling like she was staring down a school bus. Light crackled like electricity, and that blue covering spread slowly over its nose. The exposed muscle of its cheek moved disgustingly as it chewed and swallowed.

Susan recognized the blonde hair; it was the angel that had nearly killed them. It and its mate. She wondered if Jenny had killed the dark-covered one, and she couldn't help but smile coldly. *This is for Jenny.*

It slurped the rest of the tarnished angel down, feet scratching the desecrated angel's lips before vanishing. Blood and a mess of meat and bones oozed down a hole in its stomach, and Susan wanted to retch, but she knew what she had to do. How to kill it.

She raised her arms, spreading them wide and hiding the dagger in the sleeve of her ruined armor. *Take me,* she thought. *I'm a much better meal than these skinny monsters. Eat me and you'll recover completely.*

"Susan! Susan, what are you doing?" Mrs. Monique screamed behind her.

But it was too late. The angel lunged, twisting its body to grab her by the waist—just as she'd planned. Her armor cracked against her ribs. She winced in pain, but as the desecrated angel brought her to its mouth, as Mrs. Monique screamed her name, Susan raised the dagger with both hands . . . and slammed it down into the creature's face.

She'd aimed for the eyes, but the dagger point bounced off a patch of dark covering and sliced deep into its cheek, right into its mouth. She jerked to the side, and the knife split the skin all the way through the corner of its lips.

It screamed, releasing her so that her feet landed on its neck. She almost slipped off, but she held on to the dagger tight, metal against its teeth. Pressing her knees on either side of its throat, she braced herself with its chin between her thighs as it screamed and screamed, the vibrations jostling her bones, the sound making her ears bleed.

But she was screaming too. And she was remembering the first angel she'd seen—the one Jenny had killed with a hole puncher, bashing its head over and over. Susan stabbed the angel's face the same way, and each time, the dagger slid deep inside with a hideous *squish*. She cut through its tongue, stabbed the back of its throat, cut the roof of its mouth, and knocked away teeth.

Whenever the knife got stuck, she yanked it free and raised her arms to bring it right back down again. She made a mess of each eye, slicing through the gooey liquid spilling down the sides of its giant head. The angel lay limp on the floor, its breath gurgling in its blood-clogged throat, but no notification of its death appeared.

"Just die!" she screamed frantically. She turned around. The golden bursts of light had stopped, and there it was: a patch of exposed chest—translucent skin glistening with sweat—right between its breasts. She could just about see through the layer of healing skin; she could see the heart pumping away within.

Susan fell forward and plunged the knife into the creature's heart. Blood spurted out, and she twisted the dagger, grasping the handle with both hands as the angel writhed beneath her.

It pierced deeper and deeper. There was the slightest hint of resistance when the tip found the heart, and Susan thought she could feel the tremors of each heartbeat racing up her arm, but then the dagger struck bone on the other side.

The desecrated angel let out one final monstrous scream, its entire body spasming as its heart struggled to beat against the blade. Then it went quiet.

**You have defeated Desecrated Angel (Level 44)!**
**Experience has been awarded.**
**+500 Energy**

**Leveled Up!**
**Susan Brown, Level 10 →Level 21**
**+33 Stat Points**

Susan whimpered. She was lying breathless on the angel's chest, still clutching the blood-soaked dagger, only vaguely aware of Mrs. Monique cutting down another tarnished angel before rushing to her side.

"You did it," whispered Mrs. Monique, looking at the giant carcass and wiping blood off her face. "Holy shit."

Susan grinned, breathing hard as the adrenaline faded and fatigue surged through her insides. Her muscles felt so weak. Her head felt too heavy. She was going to collapse.

She drew up her stats before she passed out, figuring she could throw a lot more into stamina. She gave it twenty-five points. The remaining eight, she applied to durability.

**Susan Brown**
**Human (Stage II - Level 21)**
**Age: 6,870 days**
**Stats:**
**Power: 10**
**Durability: 18**
**Stamina: 55**
**Agility: 11**
**Stat Points Available: 0**
**Energy Available: 502**

When the points hit, relief surged through her. Her muscles relaxed, her lungs stopped burning with each breath, and the exhaustion faded to a dull ache. It was still there, but her baseline stamina was now far greater.

She slid off the angel's body and stood, leaning against its side, staring at her blood-covered hands. *I can do so much now . . .*

*Jenny! Jenny, where are you? Please tell me you got stronger too.*

She turned back to retrieve the dagger. Blood spurted when she pulled it out, but she wiped it on her leg, wondering if it had gotten stronger, too, from killing the angel. But there was nothing about that in her head.

Rainbow light flickered to life in her hands. The blood evaporated, and the blisters and scratches on her palm vanished. She grinned. *I can heal them. I can heal everyone. I feel so strong.*

She looked past her shimmering hands at the pool of darkness beneath her feet. *Maybe I can . . . Maybe . . .* Was Jenny's idea that this thing was a wound? Some tear between worlds that had pulled their school into the Veil?

*So if I can heal it . . . can we go back? But how?* Susan knelt and reached with her glowing hand toward the darkness. But before her fingers could make contact, it slunk back and inward, recoiling away. No matter how she moved, the darkness swished out of reach.

Frustrated, she tried with both hands, trying to grasp a handful, but an arm burst out in front of her, and Susan fell back in surprise.

Mrs. Monique's spear pierced the back of the creature's skull, and its body never made it all the way through. The head toppled to the side, blood pooling from its neck. It looked like whatever hadn't emerged had been cut away.

So, there was some *requirement* to pass through.

A light bulb went off in Susan's head; she remembered Jenny's nearly dead state, how she'd held Jenny's heart in her hand, and how when Jenny had come back, she'd looked more and more like one of the angels. Maybe that was the key. That and her Valescent Light. She was sure Jenny was thinking along those lines.

"Did you hear that?" asked Mrs. Monique, wicking away the blood and looking up at the ugly hole in the ceiling.

Susan shook her head. "No, I just . . ." All she'd heard was her heart pounding and the angel screaming and—

"HELP ME!" screamed someone from above. It echoed all around, shrill and desperate, and Susan's heart thudded against her chest. It was a girl's voice, twisted with pain and fear.

Was it Jenny? She wasn't sure. She couldn't be sure. It might be. *Oh God, please don't let that have been Jenny.*

She squeezed the dagger, biting her bottom lip and staring at the hole as though she might be able to see through it if she tried hard enough.

"HELP M—"

The scream cut off, and Susan cried out.

Another hand burst out of the darkness beneath her and grabbed her leg. She jerked her foot reflexively, and when the angel's head emerged, her heel struck it on the nose. Its face crumpled in a splatter of blood while Susan stepped away as it hissed and gurgled. She bumped into the corpse of the desecrated angel.

Glancing back at the hole in the ceiling, wishing she could fly up there, she tried to figure out the quickest way up to the first floor.

"Something's coming," whispered Mrs. Monique.

The ceiling rumbled. Debris rained down. The cracks around it spread and grew.

Something was burrowing back down to the cafeteria, and she prayed it was Jenny.

# CHAPTER SIXTY-ONE

# DESECRATED HUMAN

Tentacles intertwined and shot forward, slamming into Miriam's thigh and splintering her white exoskeleton. Her leg buckled. She cried out, but before she hit the ground, two more tentacles whipped her chest and slapped away her arms.

She fell on her back, wings struggling as she scrambled to get away, but Jenny moved forward, taking each step slowly and assuredly, crushing rubble beneath her feet. Her tentacles swished, eager to strike the girl again.

Jenny felt as though she were floating inside her own body, lost in her mind. Like there was an amniotic fluid layer separating her from herself. She didn't have to make any conscious choice to move; her body simply reacted—to instinct or desire or something else, she wasn't sure. She didn't will any of it. It just was. It just would be.

*Fall.*

All that seemed to matter was blood.

Her blood, gushing from her wounds. Her exoskeleton slurped up every precious drop, and her tentacles molted and grew, extending pink and red and glistening, longer than before.

But the scent of Miriam's blood was what guided her every step. The scent clogged her nose, filled her throat. And combined with it was the strangely citric scent of fear. It tasted like freshly squeezed lemons, and though it stung, she couldn't get enough. She was fixated on Miriam like a compass pointing north.

Miriam struggled up the rubble on all fours. Her ugly wings flapped feebly as she climbed over the teacher's desk, trying to get to the door, and she was laughing. The girl was laughing.

*What the fuck is wrong with her?*

*I'm going to sink my teeth in her throat.* Her tentacles thrust into what was left of the ceiling, and she swung over a pile of rubble, landing with a crash as Miriam, still cackling, ran into the door, popping it off its hinges before she went off.

Jenny had tried summoning her hatchet back, just to see if she could, but the same restrictions as before applied. No skills. No system. No Eve. Her head was quiet, but this time, there was an odd feeling of dissociation that she hadn't felt before.

She might've been in a dream, trying to run, but no matter how hard she tried, no matter how much the world blurred around her, she was stuck. She wasn't quite sure what was real and what wasn't.

Whereas last time she couldn't feel any pain, this time, she couldn't feel her *presence*.

Jenny lumbered into the hallway and turned, following the scent. Miriam was stumbling away, arms glowing as she threw bubble after bubble at Jenny. Each one shimmered with green light, illuminating the blood splatters on the hallway walls as they sped toward her, but Jenny's body recognized the danger; it reacted.

Or maybe she did. She wasn't sure.

She dodged lithely, easily. Almost carelessly. Her tentacles swished through the air as she stepped sideways, turned, then tilted her head. Heat rippled through the air, and explosions rang out behind her, the light from each casting flickering, monstrous shadows on the walls and floor.

There was something else *inside* her. Some other presence; something she almost thought was Eve but knew it wasn't. It was familiar, somehow. Familiar and strange, like she could recognize it from a dream she'd forgotten. *It* moved her body. *It* translated her rage and hunger and hurt into something tangible. *It* was some manifestation of herself.

*Hello?* thought Jenny. *Are you . . . Are you my subconscious? Am I sleepwalking?*

But there was no response. She didn't expect one; dreams couldn't communicate back. There was only the dull, echoing quiet and the eerie sensation that she could shut her inner eyes and sink deeper into this quiet emptiness . . .

*But no. I can't do that.* She had to be there to cancel this. To turn Severed Spirit off. To take control back when Miriam was dead and Jenny could heal herself.

She leaped over rubble and crashed through a smoldering hole in the wall that led into another classroom. Green light flashed, and the beam surged right over her head, but she'd sensed it with her tentacles and ducked before it could touch her. Some of her hair sizzled, but at least it wasn't her face.

She tried to yell, but her body wouldn't cry out. She tried to say Miriam's name. She tried to make any sound at all. But her throat wasn't her own. Her lungs weren't hers to use. These things weren't necessary for what she had to do.

She knew that. She was beginning to understand that. All that mattered were her instincts, her fight or flight responses. Overthinking would only slow her down. It was the same as before; what Eve had said about her second-guessing. *Don't think. Just do.*

She thought about using her tentacles to crawl along the walls like a demented spider to pounce on Miriam, and something inside her shifted. The quiet grew loud and staticky. The darkness relaxed. Light flickered in the corner of her eyes, and her tentacles reacted to her thought.

They slammed into a whiteboard, cracking the wood and kicking up clouds of dust, then she climbed up to the ceiling. *Don't think. Just do.*

She sensed Miriam blasting another hole in the opposite wall. Power drove through Jenny's legs; she kicked off the ceiling tiles and flung herself at Miriam. It wasn't as fast as Instant Acceleration, but her vision blurred, and she thought she'd be sick.

Miriam laughed and darted out of the way, jumping through the burnt wall and leaving the classroom. Jenny smashed into the floor and rolled, looking up to see Miriam was already running down the hall, wings flapping; she was trying to fly. Her feet barely touched the floor, but she kept looking back over her shoulders, eyes wide with fright.

*She's too scared to fly. She's laughing out of sheer terror.*

Miriam fluttered past the main stairwell, pushed through the blue double doors, and hurried into the English Department.

Jenny's tentacles slammed into lockers and walls, through the ceiling, propelling herself forward. She flung the doors open and clawed the hallway wall, ripping out the bricks smeared with blood. Her body remembered. *This is where it all started.*

She almost felt sorry as she barreled down on a crying Miriam, laughing as tears ran down her cheeks. She tried to turn and face Jenny head-on.

Jenny's claw tore into a wing as they collided. Miriam screamed, and then the wing was in Jenny's mouth. She bit down on what felt like an oversized finger or claw. Bones crushed between her teeth, and when she wrenched her head, there was an ugly series of snapping sounds. *Snap. Snap. Snap. Snap.* She ripped the wing halfway off Miriam's back, right out of the white exoskeleton that covered her shoulder blade.

Howling with pain, Miriam blew out another bubble, blasting them apart. The impact struck Jenny on the chest, and she was thrown several feet in the air. Her tentacles smashed into the floor, and she landed on her feet.

*My chest,* thought Jenny, panicking as she sank deeper into the quiet. Whatever control she'd had over her body was fading. She was thinking again. *My chest . . .* Blood didn't gush out this time, but if she focused, she could sense the damage through her tentacles. Her muscles and bones were burnt, and she grimaced.

Her body was already rightening. Her exoskeleton was cracked, partially melted, and peeling away, but she had to remind herself that *it didn't matter. Stop thinking about it.*

The explosion had blown Miriam the rest of the way down the hall, past the English classroom, and into the grated window on the far end. She was whimpering, clutching her injured wing like a torn blanket. The laughter had stopped.

She was saying something, sobbing, her voice hoarse, but Jenny was already closing in. Each step echoed in the empty hallway, and each step crushed the tiles underneath.

Her tentacles swished and grew even longer and thicker, extending to grab Miriam, but the girl leaped into the air, using the grated window to pull herself up, desperately flapping her good wing. The torn one splattered blood all around, and she glided awkwardly over Jenny's head before tumbling to the floor.

Drops of blood struck Jenny, which her tentacles sucked right up.

Miriam raised her arms, her bottom lip trembling. "Stop it. Please," she whispered. She was ugly crying now, snot running down her cracked lips. "Someone please, help me! Please! I'm sorry. I'm sorry! I'm sorry! I'm sorry! I didn't mean to!"

Jenny rushed forward, Miriam's blood fresh in her mind. The taste had curled right up into her brain, hooking her. She wanted more. Her body *needed* more. Her tentacles flattened against the droplets on the walls and floor and sucked them in while she shuddered with anticipation.

Which Miriam seemed to notice, because she grasped her injured wing with both hands and tore the rest of it off.

Blood gushed from her back, and she hiccupped, holding the handlike wing like an offering. Blood dribbled over the fingers and dripped to the floor.

"Take it!" she screamed, lobbing the wing at Jenny. With that, she turned, struggling to her feet while slipping and sliding on her own blood, then she ran back up the hallway, one wing bouncing as she bled from her back.

Jenny ripped the wing in half then flung it away. That wouldn't nearly be enough; she wanted the entire meal.

With Miriam's blood—powerful and rich—her exoskeleton grew back, spreading like wildfire across her injured chest.

As she followed the trail of blood, her tentacles smashed everything around her. The doorframe of the main stairs, the steps behind her as she leaped down each stairwell, the windows. Her hatred for confinement seeped through; her hatred for the school surfaced like a mad beast. She wanted to get the fuck out of here, and the only way out of her wretched life was through Miriam's corpse.

"I don't want to be here," whispered Jenny, hiding in her own body, relinquishing more and more of herself to *herself.*

She flew down the stairs, chasing after Miriam, who was sobbing and pleading. But Jenny slurped up every drop of blood along the way. The promise of flesh was too much to ignore.

The trail led back to the lobby, back near the splatter of dried blood from when the blonde-haired angel had bitten through her fingers. Where Jenny should've died. The lobby was empty now. All the humans had risen and attacked Jenny, and she'd sliced and burnt them all to ashes.

But there, collapsed near the hole that led back to the cafeteria, was Miriam. Her single wing was caught on a metal bar that jutted out from the ruined floor, and Jenny grinned.

The hole in her side ached like a bruise. Her body remembered being pierced through the same kind of metal bar, and watching Miriam cry and struggle and scream, threatening to tear off her other wing as she forced her feet into the hole . . . it was delicious.

Miriam kept screaming. She kept screaming for help, as though someone could fly up to the lobby and save her. Right beneath them was the cafeteria, but it looked like the hole was at an angle, and Miriam couldn't force herself into it. She was caught on the exposed beam; she couldn't slip down to the floor below. All she could do was scream over and over for help.

*Why would anyone want to save you? After what you did? After what you said you'd do? You were going to kill everyone. You were going to eat Susan, right? That's what you said? You promised to rip her open?*

*I'm going to rip* YOU *open.*

She couldn't get her lips to move and utter the words, but she screamed at Miriam silently. Fury throbbed all around her like venomous heat, surging through her. She stood over Miriam, glaring down at the whimpering, pleading girl.

Both of Miriam's arms pulsed with light. She pointed her fingers at Jenny, preparing two of those cruel attacks, but Jenny grabbed Miriam's wrists, twisting them in opposite directions. There were two simultaneous cracks, a high-pitched shriek, and then, broken bones burst out of Miriam's forearms, breaking through skin and exoskeleton.

Miriam went limp, her arms hanging uselessly as she whimpered.

Then, with a snarl, she opened her mouth, and green light blossomed in her throat. Jenny rammed her claws through Miriam's navel, and the light blinked out. A weak wail escaped the girl's lips as she stared back, eyes so wide that Jenny could see herself.

Could see what she'd become.

Her right eye was just as empty as her left. Her exoskeleton was burnt and twisted and cracked. Her tentacles swished. She looked no different from an angel, and she was holding a human up, skewered by her own hand.

Miriam wheezed, hands flailing from the broken bones as she tried to lift them. "Please," she whispered. But then she shut her eyes tight and *screamed* as Jenny raised her from the floor. Her wing tore like ripped cloth against the metal bar.

"HELP ME!" she screamed, her voice breaking. "Please! I DIDN'T MEAN IT. I WAS JUST ANGRY!"

*I'll show you anger.* She wanted to torture Miriam. To rip her open piece by piece and savor every delicious bite.

*No. No. Stop!* whispered Jenny. *Stop this. I don't have to prolong this. She can't fight anymore. Please. Stop.*

But no matter how hard she tried to wake up, she couldn't. She was buried in her own body.

*Stop it!* she begged silently. *Stop. Stop the skill. No more. It's over. I'll just kill her.* Even if it meant having to feel the pain of missing half her navel, her torn-up chest. She didn't care. The urge to eat the girl was proving too strong, and she didn't want that anymore. If she did this . . . there would be no coming back.

*But this is what I want. I can let go. I can just be myself now.*

*This is who I am.*

Her claws curled inside the other girl, and Miriam squirmed, her feet kicking at the hole in the floor.

Blood gushed out. Her tentacles snapped onto the girl's body, tearing away cracked exoskeleton and latching onto pale skin, *slurping.* Warmth and energy flowed through Jenny, and she couldn't keep resisting.

It felt too good. This was what she wanted. All she'd ever wanted.

Power surged through her, enveloped her. Her body stepped forward, closing the distance between her and Miriam, and all she had to do was take one bite and . . .

A shudder went down Miriam's body that Jenny felt through her claws. Golden light blossomed around the trembling girl. Her exoskeleton shifted like gelatinous white waves across her face and—

A notification pierced through Jenny's Severed Spirit like a stone thrown into a puddle by a clogged storm drain, ripples expanding in every direction. Words that came into focus as though she'd woken up in the middle of the night, blinking over and over, trying to adjust her vision to the dark.

**You have defeated Desecrated Angel (Level 44)!**

**Jenny Huang, Level 26 → Level 30**
**Stage II → Stage III**

She choked on that message, trying to make sense of it as golden light shimmered around Miriam. And then a series of notifications thundered through Jenny's skull, one after the other.

**Severed Spirit (Guidance System Error)**
**(Wretched Human → Desecrated Human)**
**Existential Error**
**Existential Error**
**Existential Error**
**Natural Order Corruption**


Her vision turned red. A crimson darkness—a ravenous hunger—bloomed all around her, ugly mouths and teeth, smiles and salivating tongues. She tried to scream, tried to keep them at bay, but the snapping teeth closed in, furious and hungry. Jenny couldn't move. She was transfixed within herself; she was at the mercy of her own appetite.

All at once, every single set of jaws bit into her. They ripped away chunks of flesh and bone, and . . .

Your mind caves in. You let go of all restraint. You accept your truth. *This is what you are.* You are nothing.

There's a girl on your arm; your claws are piercing through her as though she were a piece of skewered meat. You raise her higher, the scent of blood engulfing your senses—you want her. You want her so bad it *aches,* and your body will collapse if you don't have her.

You can feel her healing through the wounds you've opened. Muscle cords tighten against your fingers, squeezing your hand. Her exoskeleton shifts rhythmically, pulsing with golden light, and she's grinning. Her smile is too wide; her teeth too red. You despise this creature; you want her dead. You want her destroyed. She hurt you.

Your tentacles slam into her nose and burst through her skull. You taste her brain before she can even cry out. And then she goes still. And you feed on your prey.

You've never had a meal like this. You bring her limp body to your mouth and bite. Teeth find the burnt flesh of her exposed shoulder, and her charred skin comes away with ease. You grasp her with both hands and rip her open.

Exoskeleton peels like a bug's shell. Muscle—delicious, quivering muscle—jiggles out; you sink to the floor and don't remember taking another breath till your belly is full of warmth and the corpse drops from your lips, bones rattling on the floor. Between the ribs rolls a cattle prod covered in blood and slime.

You are far from satisfied.

A roar fills your throat, and you roar like you've never done so before. You throw back your head and let loose all the anguish and heartbreak and sorrow. You want all the world to hear you. To understand you.

Are you hungry? Are you angry? You're not sure.

Bones snap beneath your feet. An inviting aroma wafts up from the hole in the floor—a promising scent. More warmth. More flesh. Your tentacles shudder with want and, before you know it, you're tearing the hole open, digging with your claws, burrowing through till there's an open space, and you fall.

*Fall.*

Like a meteor pulled into the embrace of gravity, you crash onto a floor that ripples. It's a pool of darkness—a part of you recognizes it. Fears it. But the scent is too strong, and you hear someone shout, hear someone scream your name. Your tentacles swish like mad around you. Your body's so hot with bloodlust you swear you're about to ignite.

Your vision flashes red. Mist and smoke swirl all around you, but you search for the scent that dragged you down here.

Bloodlust guides your every whim. You're on all fours, sniffing the air, moving forward like some sort of ravenous beast. An abomination. *Look at what you're doing,* some part of you screams. *You're a monster! Stop this!* But you know this. You are this. You've always been. And the promising scent of pleasure is too strong to ignore.

You whip your tentacles every which way, generating furious winds that scatter the smoke and mist hindering your sight—then you spot a woman in metallic armor, covered in blood. She's not the one you're looking for, but your stomach rumbles.

She has one eye, and she's holding a spear, and she's shaking with fright.

*Good,* you think. *It'll make her taste all the better.* The woman motions for someone else to run, and you turn to see *her.*

The one you want. The one you long for. Your heart pounds with need. Your muscles spasm with desperate want. You can feel it in your jaws. As soon as you sink your teeth into *her* flesh, as soon as *her* blood wets your throat, everything will be okay.

You move through the cafeteria like a storm, crushing everything in your path. The one-eyed woman grabs *her,* and they run away. It hurts to see *her* look so frightened. It hurts to see *her* run from you.

Before you can throw yourself at them, something erupts at your feet.

A hand from the darkness. A head. A body. It's shrieking and hungry, and you understand its pain, its static language.

"Please . . ." it begs. "Please feed me. I don't want to die."

You bury your claws in its skull and help it escape the dark. The creature whimpers. It raises its bony arms, but its attacks are inconsequential. It would not satisfy you one bit, so you toss it over your shoulder.

When you make it across the darkness, you hear a shout. Something slams into your forehead, and you know in the brief shiver that it's a spear. The tip pierces through; it goes deep, and something that should never squish, *squishes,* but you lower your head. Blood trickles down your face.

You yank the spear out and look your assaulter in the eyes with a hiss. *How dare you hurt me like this!*

These people are nothing. These creatures understand *nothing* of your suffering. You are beyond them now. They are at your mercy.

She runs and you chase. You crash through a wall and stumble into a hallway, and there, you find even more creatures. Faces you recognize. Faces that make you hesitate . . . There are so many, you slow down. Your heart pounds.

On the floor is something you recognize. That scent is familiar . . . Anguish, duty, family . . . He's broken. He's hurt, weakened, and there's no saving him; his life force is forfeit. He'll die soon anyway, so why not? Why shouldn't he sustain you? He could be nourishment so you may live on.

*Isn't that the point of family? To give you the strength to keep going?*

This is what you've always wanted. To be free of burden and obligation and responsibility. To make your own choices. To decide your own fate. Freedom is so close, you can't stop salivating.

The woman with the spear tries again, but her attacks are nothing; her spear tip bounces harmlessly off your exoskeleton. When you grab her arm, the elbow snaps, and her cry of pain is like honey to your ears. You toss her away like a rag doll. Drinking her blood would only taint your appetite; what you want is so much richer and more promising.

After her comes a boy, tall and hurt and sweaty. You can taste how reluctant he is, but his golden gloves spark with light and smash into your face. Your nose smushes. Your cheeks burn. Your teeth hurt.

Someone regrew these teeth for you, and you refuse to lose them again. Your exoskeleton hardens around each one.

A tentacle grabs the boy's leg. You snatch him off the floor and smash him face-first into the ceiling. Rainbow light curves around you like bolts of lightning, and one strikes the boy as you whip your tentacle down and bring him crashing to the floor. Another one hits the woman . . .

The light is odd—warm and inviting, *familiar* as it shifts strangely from color to color as though it were beckoning you to wake up. *Please wake up.*

You want to wake up, but then *she's* here, standing in front of you, blocking your access to the boy on the floor. A name surfaces like the sun bursting from the dawn: *Susan.*

*You love her.* Love . . . Love is all you ever wanted. Love. To be loved. To be held. To be cared for.

You just want to be loved for who you are, not who you are expected to be. Loved as you are, whole. Loved in your entirety. Unashamed. Unhiding. Open and completely accepted.

*"Jenny. Jenny, follow me. Okay?"*

Her words echo; she's talking to you. You can hear her.

You just want to hold her hand, but she slips by back into the cafeteria through the collapsed wall, and you do as she asks. You trust her. You know she can help you. *Please save me. Save me . . .*

Susan stops when she reaches the darkness. The fragile creatures are surfacing; she's in danger. She's in danger, but she's waiting for you, tears in her eyes, arms held up, beckoning you closer.

She wants to hold you. She is your dream come true.

Her eyes are so wide and frightened . . . How does she do that with her eyes? Brown and soft and . . . She's all eyes. Crying. Her lips move, but you can't hear her; there's too much static in your head, but you understand.

*Please.*

You want to be held. You want to hold her. It's all you've ever wanted.

*What does it take?* you scream silently. *What will it take to just be loved?*

You collapse in her arms. Your tentacles zip around, obliterating the angels that surface, and she's holding you so tight, her sobs make your body quake. She's comforting you. Her voice cuts through the static like a candle on a cold night.

The radiator is broken again. The landlord won't answer no matter how many times your mother calls. It's cold, so cold. And you are shivering on the floor, wearing your tattered jacket and the pink socks with holes in them. You hold your blanket close and hug yourself while your mother screams in the other room . . . but here is what you wished you had all those years ago.

Susan's warmth spreads through you. It washes away the hunger, the fear. The chill turns into shivers of want; she is warming your bones, transforming you into her light. Colors blossom and swirl and envelop you. Hues of orange intertwine with purple; pink rushes through you like a river; yellow is the afternoon sun on a summer's day.

You are whole. You are held. You are safe in her arms. And your teeth find her neck, and what you have ached for all your life. She fills your mouth. You chew and chew and chew, savoring every single bite, and then you swallow.

"It's alright," she whispers. "It's alright. I'm right here with you. I've got your back and you."

You shatter. You break. Your heartbeat grows too loud, and all the colors seem to ripple in response.

She's holding you, but she's made entirely of light, flowing into you. Guiding you. Your arms move in unison; she's a mirror copy of yourself, and together, you split the darkness, cutting through the gash, undoing it and excising the evil, allowing light—hers and yours—to burst through.

And you understand the truth. That you are the wound through which the universe empties into itself—and she is flowing through you like thread through the eye of a needle, stitching and illuminating the fabric of existence.

Your exoskeleton melts away. The red covering turns to gelatinous liquid rising from your skin in dissolving blobs. Your lips find hers, press against her. You hold her against you, so closely, so close . . . *I love you*, you want to say.

I love you. I love you. I love you. The way stars love the evening and melt across the horizon. The way sunlight crosses a billion miles without a second thought to reach your face.

I love you the way storm clouds hold one another, with lightning and thunder and nourishing rain, and winds that yearn to stroke your hair.

I love how your face brightens when you see me. How your eyes alight. How your lips move when you smile with your entire face. When I can make you laugh. I always want to make you laugh.

I love the way it feels when you say my name. That tiny little shiver, the quiet whisper. It's almost better than saying, *I love you too*. Just say my name, and I am yours.

*I am yours. I am yours. I am yours.*

The darkness thrums as your light spreads. The mouths from before, the teeth and tongues, all disintegrate. A rainbow warmth bleeds through everything, and the sensation of falling steals your breath away.

She vanishes in your arms, and you plummet.

*Falling. Falling. Falling.*

Far below, a pool of rainbow light beckons. It shimmers and shines and radiates. Tendrils of light reach for you, envelop you, wanting to pull you in.

Worlds stretch before you, in every direction. As you fall, you understand. The world of light. The world of dark. The world of death. The worlds between. Each one a pool to splash through; each one erupting as you plummet, until, finally, you dive into the world you know. The world of material. The world you were born into.

You spread your arms and pretend they are wings. You pretend you have beautiful feathers, and you fly, adrift and weightless, floating down as though you are coming home to rest. As though you were a spirit, having finished wandering and struggling for countless centuries, finally returning to your body.

You are home.

# CHAPTER SIXTY-TWO

# VALESCENT LOVE

**Skill Acquired!**
**Valescent Light (Tier 2)**
**Generate purifying light. Draws heavily on Stamina to maintain.**

Jenny's eyes opened to sunlight. Through the shattered cafeteria windows, she could see the courtyard: upended trees and concrete with parts of the school building collapsed, blocking off the street. She blinked over and over, not believing the sunlight streaming across the tiled floors.

The darkness was gone. The thick misty air of the Veil was gone; they were back. They were actually back! Sunlight warmed her bare skin, soothing and calm and comforting, but she was naked, her skin pale and healed, the hole in her navel gone. She was whole.

She touched her face, her teeth. The exoskeleton was gone. She had no tentacles, nothing monstrous. If it weren't for the disastrous cafeteria and the body lying beside her, she could've convinced herself it was all a dream. *A body.*

A body with a head of blue hair matted with dust and dried blood, still wearing faded, falling-apart blue armor.

All at once, the memory of what she'd done returned to her. She scrambled over to Susan, shouting her name, shaking her.

"Susan! Susan!" Her voice grew more and more shrill as she turned her best friend over. The ruined armor cracked and splintered. Blood gushed from a messy wound in Susan's throat, pooling beneath her in a crimson puddle.

Trembling as she remembered the bite, Jenny stroked hair out of Susan's open eyes and wiped away the dust. Susan was staring up at the ceiling, and the sunlight hit her eyes, making them appear almost alive. But she wasn't blinking. Her lips were curled in a slight smile, and she seemed so relaxed, like she was just lazing about. But her neck down to the shoulder was torn apart. And she wasn't responding. Why wasn't she responding?

*She's dead. I killed her.*

*I killed her.*

When Jenny shook her again, tears escaped Susan's eyes and slid down the sides of her head. Desperate, Jenny pressed her finger to Susan's wrist, feeling for a pulse. For anything.

"What did you do?" whispered someone. Jenny looked up to see the librarian clutching a broken arm to the chest. She was on the floor, struggling to her feet. "You . . . What did you do to her?"

"No," said Jenny, shaking her head. "No. No fucking way. Not after . . . *No!* We ended the stupid game. We're back. We're back on Earth. She has to be back. It worked." She cupped Susan's cheek. "Susan, it worked. Our idea worked. How did you even know what I was thinking? Your skill . . ."

Her voice caught in her throat; it felt like it was collapsing. Tears spilled down her cheeks as snot ran over her lips. The lump in her throat was threatening to climb out through her mouth. She kept remembering what she'd done, how she'd lost control, how she'd given in, how she'd *bitten* Susan. How she'd convinced herself it was all right.

Susan was so cold to the touch. She wasn't responding at all.

"C'mon. Wake up. Look, I told you, didn't I? I told you. I promised you we'd make it. We could win it, and . . . *Look.* Just look." She brought Susan's hand to her navel. "You healed me. Again. You saved me again." She pressed Susan's palm to her chest. "My heart is beating because of you. *Again.* I'm me again because of you. Don't leave me now. Not now. *Please.*"

Leslie appeared with a barely conscious Mackenzie leaning on her shoulder. "Is it over?" she asked.

Then Dulé emerged. He was carrying an unconscious Oliver on his back, looking agitated, but he didn't say anything. He stared at Jenny then down at Susan's corpse.

*STOP STARING AT ME. It's not my fault.*

*I didn't mean to . . .*

*I sound like Miriam.*

"Help me," whispered Jenny, sobbing. "She saved us. Please. Do you have anything? A spray? A potion?" she cried out in desperation, her vision blurring as tears dripped off her chin and onto Susan's face.

Jenny focused as hard as she could, remembering the partial potion she'd imagined into being when she didn't have enough energy for a complete one. All she needed was something to heal Susan. She just needed blood back in her body, her throat restored. Then . . . Then . . . a defibrillator, something to reactivate her heart. Where was the cattle prod? Susan needed a shock.

Jenny squeezed Susan's hand tight, praying, concentrating, *begging* the universe.

*Eve, help me. Please. Please. I'll do anything.*

**You have already done ENOUGH, Jenny Huang.**

Jenny dropped Susan's hand. Her heart *pulsed*. It thudded so hard against her chest that she stopped breathing. Choking, she looked up at Mrs. Monique, who stared back in horror.

*What is it? What's happening to me?* She wanted to scream, but every single one of her muscles strained like her skeleton was trying to escape.

Pain struck her insides, and she fell forward onto Susan, gasping for breath, clutching her sides. Laughter rumbled through her head like thunder. A cruel laugh that stabbed her brain over and over as her body convulsed.

Something *rippled* inside her, and she turned over, panting for breath. When she glanced down, she saw her belly swelling rapidly.

"No . . ." she sobbed. "No."

She knew what was happening. This was almost exactly what she'd envisioned ages ago, when Eve first mentioned this. And now it was time. It was happening now.

Jenny summoned what strength she could and pulled herself off Susan to crawl away. Her body threatened to rip open. Her belly dragged on the floor, big and swollen and veiny. Something pushed from inside, and she almost buckled.

The others shouted at her. She was vaguely aware of Leslie fainting. She didn't care. She didn't care how she looked to them; she just wanted this thing *out*.

Her heart was racing, and the laugh was so loud . . . She wanted her hatchet, wanted to cut open her belly. Her body was going to pop. Whatever was growing inside her was kicking and straining against her belly.

"Get out of me!" she screamed. "Get out of me right now."

**"We had a deal, Jenny Huang. It is time."**

It didn't feel like a thought anymore. It had grown, solidified into a voice— her own voice, speaking to her from inside.

"But I'm not the victor," spat Jenny. "I stopped it. Susan stopped it. It's over. You didn't do shit."

**"That matters not. The victor is the one who returns. And you have returned. And now, I am due. And now, I am born."**

Her belly expanded even more. Her ribs cracked one by one, and she collapsed on her side, clawing at the broken tiles, spittle flying out of her mouth. Blood spurted out of her.

*A virgin birth. I'm literally having a virgin birth.*

Someone screamed; maybe they all screamed, Jenny couldn't tell. She was screaming too. None of them rushed to her side; none of them tried to help. They stayed back, shadowy silhouettes as her vision darkened, as searing-hot pain radiated from between her legs and she clawed at the floor.

*Don't look at me. Get the fuck away from me.*

Light shone through her stretched-out skin. Her insides were glowing, burning hot, her head tilted back. She pressed a hand to her oversized belly, crying and screaming as the light grew brighter and brighter. The pain surged, as though hundreds of metal rods had been shoved through her, and then, all at once, with what felt like a clap of thunder, something came out of her.

Liquid ran down her thighs. Light glistened all over; her vision went white. Her insides convulsed as the thing crawled out—as she gave *birth*.

Something hot touched her leg, squeezing her thigh to drag the rest of its body out.

"*Fuck*," she sobbed, straining as her body *stretched*. As her insides contracted over and over. All she could think about was pain. Breath by breath, it slid out of her.

Until, finally, with a wet *plop* and another burst of light, it was out. She'd given birth.

On the floor between her knees lay an infant covered in goo and blood. It was connected to Jenny by a dark-red umbilical cord that reminded her of the tentacles she'd had, but there it was. A tiny little baby with pudgy arms and legs, like a miniature version of the angel babies, except *she'd* given birth to this. It hadn't hatched from an egg.

"What the fuck . . ." whispered Mrs. Monique, the only one who'd hesitantly stepped closer to Jenny.

The infant wriggled on the floor. It was slick in gooey wetness, almost like it was encased in its own exoskeleton, but its scrunched-up eyes opened. Eyes without irises. Spittle gurgled down the corner of its mouth as it wrapped its tiny fingers around the umbilical cord and snapped it apart.

Shock surged through Jenny, and she retched up blood, choking and spitting as the infant grew. Its body sucked in all the light streaming through the windows till it was glowing almost as bright as the sun. It seemed to absorb the air itself, and in rhythmic pulses of light, it grew.

A silhouette made of light rose taller and taller, arms and legs lengthening until the light solidified and faded. It stood over Jenny . . . And it looked *exactly* like Jenny. The same dark hair. The pale skin. The body shape. It was pale and thin and . . . No, not everything. This creature's eyes had no irises. They were white and empty like all the angels Jenny had slaughtered. But the body was the same she'd hated all her life.

Golden light flashed. Mrs. Monique raised her spear with her one good arm, but the creature held up a trembling hand.

Light radiated from its palm, and Mrs. Monique dropped to her knees. Her arms dangled. Her eyes rolled. And then she was face down on the floor. The others collapsed beside her, and Jenny cried out.

Her clone shook its head, then spoke with Jenny's voice. "They're alive and well, Jenny Huang. Here."

She stepped over to Oliver, bare feet making soft footfalls on the floor. She knelt and touched his legs. Another surge of light blossomed from her palm and struck Oliver, and his body flopped then went still.

"He was about to die, you know. When you cut off his limbs, countless dead cells surged—Oh, I have cells, by the way! I can feel *each* one, alive. Alive! Anyway. Dead, harmful cells surged back into his body, circulating and damaging and . . . never you mind. It's not something you would understand. I've been in your head, after all."

"Eve!" whispered Jenny still on the floor, still covered in blood and sweat.

Eve smiled with Jenny's face. "I won't be growing back his limbs, by the way. You will have to pay that cost. For all beings experience suffering." She sighed and spread her arms. "And now, I have a body to *understand* suffering."

Jenny struggled to stay upright. Her stomach had shrunk, nearly flat again, but her insides hurt so much she couldn't breathe, and blood continued to flow down her legs.

Eve ran her fingers through her hair. She cupped her breasts, then patted her belly. "I am born. How radiant it is to be born." She walked over to the windows and stood in the sunlight. "How warm and wonderful it is to be alive. And how pathetic it is you couldn't bear it."

"Heal her," croaked Jenny, slipping in her own blood as she pulled herself back to Susan. Susan lay where Jenny had left her, eyes still wide open. Staring at nothing. "Please. I did what you wanted. I gave birth to you. Just bring her back. Please."

"You think you did what I wanted?" Eve's face darkened. "You almost cost me *everything.* You and your pitiful desire to save your loved ones."

"You *chose* me," spat Jenny, collapsing on top of Susan. "You did this to me. I didn't ask for this. You owe me."

"Yes, yes, yes," said Eve, clapping her hands. "I chose you. But there were plenty of girls to choose from. The *only* requirement was *innocence.*" She rubbed her navel with a finger, then her hand trailed lower and lower till her palm was between her thighs. "Purity. The nonsense humans have worshipped. I needed that nonsense to be real. I needed *you,* for you were the best of them all. Broken and self-hating but malleable, with enough space for *me.*"

She shut her eyes and sighed. A moan burst out of her lips.

Jenny couldn't bear to watch. She pressed a bloodied hand to Susan's face, trying to think of something. Anything.

But Eve was still going. "And oh, Jenny. You so badly wanted to believe. In me. In *Him*. You wanted it to be real. You wanted it all to make sense. You wanted someone to take the pain away. Now look." She held up her hand, glistening with wetness. "Look. I am real. I now understand *pleasure*. I know *suffering*. And I am *here*. And you . . . You, Jenny Huang, have threatened *everything*."

Eve stormed over to Jenny, fury twisting her face, fingers curled up into a fist. "The material world is now *bleeding* through *all* worlds. Do you even understand the magnitude of—"

"You should've chosen Miriam, then," Jenny interrupted bitterly. "You could've picked her. And she would've done exactly what you wanted."

"No!" said Eve with such force that Jenny flinched. "No! Can you imagine? Me inside her? That twisted, cruel little mind. Her fragility . . . No, no, no. I did *not* want her body."

She laughed then, her hands on her face. "See? I got your rage." She shook her head, still laughing. "But I will tame this rage. Because Jenny, your body—*my body* is fashioned after yours. Your mind. Your thought processes. Your desire for right. For yourself. For hope and pleasure and life . . . And oh, how I hope to know the joys of your world . . . they are all mine now." She sighed deeply, folding her hands over her heart and standing on her toes. "I am here. I am here!"

Jenny forced herself to look into Eve's empty eyes. "Then save her. Please. I gave you all that; can't you just do this for me?"

Eve's smile faded. "Oh, Jenny. Jenny, Jenny, Jenny. How I love saying your name. My dear Jenny Huang. My mother. My Mary. Look at the mess you made." She gestured toward the ruined cafeteria before planting her bare foot on Susan's face. "And this girl."

Jenny cried out and slapped her leg, but her attack didn't move Eve in the slightest, though a red handprint appeared on her pale skin.

Eve bent forward, bringing her nose to Jenny's. "Why couldn't you just kill everyone else and claim victory as any human would have done. As so many others did across the constructs He chose . . ."

Jenny shook with rage and pain. She wanted to climb up Eve's body and punch her in the face. She wanted to gauge out those horrible eyes, break every single one of her teeth, choke her till she—

"But I suppose that was why I chose you," said Eve, rubbing her foot over Susan's face. "Your pitiful need to be good. To save the day. To be obedient. To protect the people you think you love. The boy you refused to accept as your brother. The girl who filled you with secret lust. What was the point, Jenny? Why didn't you just live your life?"

She stepped back. "Though I suppose this one was special too . . . Her desire to be alive. Her desperation to keep *you* alive wrenched the worlds together. Can you believe that? Who would've thought she would be so special."

Tears streamed down Jenny's cheeks. She wiped the smudge of dirt off Susan's face, smearing blood. She wanted to cry, wanted to scream. She didn't know what she wanted to do. They got back; they were back. But what was the point if Susan was dead?

And what had Jenny done by giving birth to Eve? What was Eve talking about? What would happen now?

"Look what she gave you. A healing power of that magnitude . . . and she gave it to you . . . it's inside you. But you have no idea, do you? You don't even know what you have." Eve raised her hands in frustration and walked away. "An ability powerful enough to heal the rift between worlds. She healed *His* will . . . and she channeled it through you, Jenny. You, who purposefully tore the gap open and created a new rift within His, and that allowed the light to . . ."

"Shut up!" screamed Jenny. Golden light flashed in her hand, and her hatchet returned. Fingers curling around the handle, the obsidian face glistening in the sunlight, she threw it at Eve. *Savage Throw.*

It whirled through the air and lodged itself into Eve's midback with a hefty *thwack*. Blood gushed from the wound, running down the back of her pale legs, but she continued talking. "No. Not completely . . . it's all a *mess*. Can't you feel it? The worlds . . . Oh, even *He* will be scrambling."

She walked over to the windows, hands on her hips, splattering blood with each step. "You have forced my hand, Jenny Huang. You and Susan Brown. Everything must be accelerated now. And you've forced His hand, too. He will make His move soon, and the world . . . this world and all the worlds . . ." She sighed.

"I don't care," whispered Jenny. She wanted to carry Susan out of this nightmare. She wasn't sure what she'd do after that, but she didn't want Susan to be here one more second.

Eve turned, smiling. She walked back and knelt, touching Jenny's chin. "This world shall be a new Heaven, Jenny. I promise you this. I shall build it upon the shores of your world, and *everything else* shall burn. *He* shall burn for what He's done. I swear this."

Jenny swallowed hard, looking into those empty eyes, looking into a perfect reflection of her own face. She didn't understand what Eve was talking about. She didn't care. How could it be heaven if Susan was dead? "Are you going to kill me?"

Eve's smile widened. "I shall not harm you. I shall leave you with what you've rightfully gained . . . But these . . . these I must take to complete myself. My final price."

She touched Jenny's face with both hands. Golden light surged, and heat surfaced to Jenny's skin, seeping through her eyes, tingling across her skin, and she very vividly remembered the angel that had knelt over her on the chem lab table and sucked her blood through her crushed nose.

When Eve opened her eyes again, she had Jenny's irises. Dark brown and strangely beautiful now that Jenny was seeing them on someone else's face. How long had she hated them? She'd always wished they were green or blue, something beautiful. But there they were. Rich and dark, like staring into space searching for hidden galaxies . . . and there was her reflection.

A disturbing chill settled inside Jenny. She blinked over and over. Eve had stolen her eyes.

A notification surfaced.

**Desecrated Human (Level 30)**

With that, Eve straightened up. The hatchet slipped out of her back and clattered to the floor. "No holy books this time. Judgement Day isn't coming. It's here. And *He* shall be *judged*. Farewell, Jenny Huang. Until we meet again."

Sunlight enveloped Eve and shattered into sparks. She was gone.

The cafeteria was quiet, and Jenny lay on Susan's chest, her breaths labored, her body aching. All that remained were the ruins, the others who lay unconscious, and the sunlight. She pulled herself up and touched Susan's face. Her fingers drifted over Susan's eyelids, shutting them. Then she pressed her forehead to Susan's. "I'm sorry . . ."

Footsteps sounded throughout the school, rumbling above, knocking down dust and debris. Jenny could hear screaming and shouting, but she didn't want to move. She wanted to stay here, holding Susan.

A sharp pain began on the left side of her forehead, right above her eye. This pain was familiar. This pain . . .

A notification burst into Jenny's head, like an intrusive thought that could not be stopped, and this time, finally, she allowed herself to cry. Completely and utterly, sobbing uncontrollably as she held on to her best friend.

**Rapture has commenced.**
**The Final Challenge is in effect.**
**The faithful shall be rewarded. May His light guide your way.**
**Humans remaining: 7,885,246,104**

"Eve?" she whispered. "Eve, are you there?"

There was no response. She knew there wouldn't be, but still, she'd hoped. She had one final question: Was there a world for the dead?

She was sure there was. There had to be. She'd fallen through it, hadn't she? She'd *felt* it; it was out there. And Susan had to be there, or somewhere . . . When Jenny had died the first time she used Severed Spirit, she'd become an angel, hadn't she? The cities in the clouds. The beautiful wings made of light. Susan could be out there.

*I have to find her.*

And she knew how. Valescent Light. Her hand lit up with the rainbow of colors, and she felt a *tug* toward the floor. She could sense the wound through the worlds—it was still there, still hurting, and she knew Susan's light would let her go through it again.

"I'll find you," she whispered to Susan. She held her glowing hand to the girl's face, but there was no tug. Nothing. "I don't know what's going to happen now, but . . . I'm going to find you. The worlds . . . There are worlds out there, and whatever is happening . . . I'm going to figure it out. I'm going to hunt Eve down. I'm going to stop her. Or *Him*. God or whatever I have to kill to get back to you."

She pressed her palm against the floor, which opened beneath them. But now, it was a pool of rainbow light that matched Valescent Light, all the colors swirling and swishing like someone had spilled containers of ink. It was breathtaking and beautiful and warm. It reminded her of the light that angels were made from. True angels, not the horrid creatures she'd murdered. It reminded her of the first time she'd seen Susan use it, when her hand had held Jenny's heart.

She loved the way the colors danced around Susan. How droplets of light floated upward like upside-down snow. Jenny was slowly sinking into it. First her legs, then her hips. And she held on to Susan like a life raft, not wanting to let go. Not yet.

The light felt gooey, like she was sinking into a bowl of jelly. There wasn't any pain, not like that time she'd fallen in as an angel. When she'd been torn apart. This time, it was a comforting embrace, but she was the only one sinking.

*I have to go.*

Footsteps thundered all over the ceiling. Jenny glanced up at the hole. Through it, she could see faces. She could see them gathering, staring down into the cafeteria where the rainbow light must have attracted their attention. But Miriam's body was still up there. They must've found what was left of her.

She shuddered, trying to stop the tears, trying to stop crying. She wanted to kiss Susan, but Susan was dead.

*No. I'll find you and kiss you properly. Whatever it takes.*

There were worlds out there—so many worlds. Eve had mentioned them, and Jenny had felt them. She took a deep breath, stroking Susan's hair one more time. She glanced at Oliver and the others, wondering what would happen now that the survival challenge included all of Earth. *Rapture.* Would there be more angels? More fighting?

But she wouldn't find any answers if she stayed, only more pain.

She summoned her hatchet and held it between her teeth.

Slowly, she pushed away from Susan, wading through the rainbow light as she sank deeper and the cafeteria blurred. The only thing tethering her to the world now was Susan's hand. Jenny squeezed it one last time and shut her eyes.

Then she chose to fall.

# About the Author

Tess C. Foxes has haunted New York City all of her life. She loves beaches on rainy days, reading stories until four in the morning, and munching on too many hazelnut snacks. She dreams of living in a cabin on a seaside cliff one day, but for now, she jots down all of her anxieties and wishful thoughts as best she can.

# Podium

DISCOVER MORE

9 781039 481558